The King's Man

CAMELOT COURT
BOOK ONE

ELLE PARKER

Copyright © 2024 by Elle Parker
THE KING'S MAIDEN by Elle Parker
All rights reserved.

No part of this book may be reproduced or used in any form or by any electronic or mechanical means, including information storage and retrieval systems, without written permission from the author, except for the use of brief quotations in a book review. For more information, email address:
author@whychooseparkerbooks.com

This is a work of fiction. The names, characters, businesses, places, events, locales, and incidents are the products of the author's imagination or have been used fictitiously and are not to be construed as real. Any resemblance to actual persons,
living or dead, actual events, locales or organizations is entirely coincidental.

THE KING'S MAIDEN
Cover Designers/Artist: Jay Aheer
Editor: Rachel Mitchell
Formatting: Hayden Locke

~~Fuck bitches. Get money.~~

*To my family,
Once upon a time, they reached chapter seven
and lived happily ever after. The End.*

*To my good girls and boys,
Good things come to those who wait.*

Welcome to The Quest.

CONTENT WARNINGS

The King's Maiden is first in a four-book series, planned for rapid release. It is a slow burn with spice, ending on a cliffhanger.

This book depicts one experience of asthma, and the character's perception of asthma attacks throughout the story. It is not meant to encompass the varying degrees of severity associated with an asthma diagnosis.

For my readers with more severe asthma, who have been affected differently, my portrayal is not meant to minimize anyone's experience with theirs. It is based on my experience with a less severe, more acute form of asthma.

The same can be said for trauma and depictions of post-traumatic stress disorder.

A FULL LIST of potential triggers and content warnings can be found at the back of the book or on my website.

THE QUEST FOR CAMELOT COURT

The King of Camelot Court
House of Arthur Pendragon
Kingston D'Arthur

The Round Tableau
Family Seat
Known Knights—Chosen Maidens

Sir Mordred
Max Dread—Vivian Valencourt

Sir Lamorak

Sir Tristam de Lyons
Tristan Léon—Izzy Gold

Sir Kay

Sir Gawain
Gavin Wainscot—Tara Demaris

Sir Bors de Ganis

Sir Geraint
Gerard Saint—Inez Cherot

Sir Gareth

Sir Bedivere
Ben Devereaux

Sir Degore

Sir Percival
Peter Valencourt—Elaine Astolat

Sir Lancelot
Landon Scott

The King's Maiden
Quinn Everly

The only difference between bright white and pitch black is illumination...

"I am *not* a damsel in distress."

Prologue
Quinn

I thought it was a joke.

Twenty-five thousand dollars to let some entitled, rich guy boss me around for a month?

Most days, I did that shit for free and called it being female. But rumor had it, a secret society on campus wanted to pay me for their privilege.

Sign. Me. Up.

"All you have to do is apply, Quinn," my best friend explained. "Make it through a month with the guy who picks you, and you walk away with the prize money."

From where I'd planted my head face down on the library table, I craned my neck to stare at her. Gia ignored the quirk of my eyebrow, or what she called my *Resting Skeptic Face,* and slid a scrap of paper toward me.

Bearing a QR code over our college's insignia, it looked like every other flier scattered around D'Arthur University. Except, where most fliers had text with the name of an event or location for a party, this one contained no other information.

"Gia, for all you know, this is a virus. Or hacking software so some creepy guy on the Internet can get into your phone and steal all your nudes."

"I'm not ashamed of my body." She flipped her honey-blonde hair off her shoulder, trying to lift my mood. "And besides, a girl pulled it up after class and showed it to me. It's legit, I swear."

I eyed the dubious slip of paper again.

Two of my classmates had been gossiping about something like this. While they'd swapped plans for Spring Break, one asked about summer. I'd caught words like *secret society* and *annual competition* before tuning them out.

I needed a job when spring semester ended, not the fantasy plot line for a reality TV show.

Gia's hazel eyes, and her eternal optimism, sparkled at me from across the table. "It's called The Quest. Twenty-five thousand for the first thirty days *and* even more after that, if you keep going and win. Can you believe it?"

"I really can't," I deadpanned.

No, I knew all too well that life wasn't a fairytale.

I'd learned that lesson as soon as my mom died picking up a cake for my twelfth birthday. The world didn't run on sunshine and rainbows and good things didn't happen to good people.

That old saying, "when life hands you lemons, make lemonade"? My dad had always loved it. Especially after Mom died, he pulled that bad boy out whenever he needed to turn his mood around.

Or, more often, mine.

And even though I thought it was ridiculous, he'd been *fucking great* at making lemonade.

But then, life took him from me, too.

Applying that optimistic lease on life by myself grew harder.

Under the constant barrage of lemons life seemed keen on handing me, where did one find the time to stop, squeeze out, and sweeten a batch?

I became more of a *roll-with-the-punches-as-the-hits-keep-on-coming* type of girl, instead.

While struggling to finish my dance program, battling asthma, *and* drowning in debt, I didn't expect some Knight in Shining Armor, or his frat bros, to swoop in and save me.

So, I chalked the classroom chatter up to just that—idle gossip.

But Gia swore otherwise. "Now, I don't know all the details, but there are a few challenges with different prizes. And the grand prize has, like, an obscene amount of cash tied to it. Allegedly, of course. No one knows for sure because the whole thing is locked up tighter than your dad's life insurance policy."

My eyebrows rose. "Impressive. But I thought that secret society thing was just a rumor?"

"Nope. It's true. And get this..." Gia leaned across the table, grinning widely as she grabbed my hands. "They call themselves the Knights of Camelot Court."

I shot her an exasperated look. "You're totally fucking with me right now, aren't you?"

To be fair, it made sense.

The school mascot at D'Arthur University *was* a Knight, and the aptly-named Camelot Court sat on the outskirts of our mountain town, Mosaic Falls. Separated from the rest of the school, the grounds were high-walled and ultra-private.

A by-product of snobbery, I'd always assumed.

But as a way to safeguard their delusional kingdom from the rest of the *peasantly* student body? A group of spoiled rich kids play-acting with a round table? And holding a medieval tournament?

I found all that hard to believe.

"Seriously, Gia. This sounds like a scam."

"I swear, it's not. Some of the guys are in one of my classes, and people really treat them like they're campus royalty. They get away with murder, too. *If* they even show up for class."

My eyes narrowed. "How the hell does that work?"

"Rich daddies." Gia snorted. "They donate a ton of money to the school, so the dean won't look too closely at what they do."

"That sounds fair," I muttered, dropping my head down again.

"Sounds like Corporate America. But the point is that these rich assholes have more money than they know what to do with, and every summer they hold The Quest." She tapped the flier right by my cheek before pointing her finger at me. "The solution to all of *your* problems."

As my best friend and roommate, Gia knew just how tight my cash flow got between semesters.

A vague competition put on by a secret society sounded like *exactly* the kind of romance novel storyline she'd buy into and try to sell me, too.

Normally, I humored her.

She liked her books the way she drank her coffee—steamy hot and dark as fuck. There was bound to be a crossover into her real life at some point. Plus, she was only trying to help me out.

But when said fantasy solution might end with my actual photo on a milk carton or my body strapped to a chair in a dark basement?

I had to draw the line.

I sat back up, swatting her hand away. "Yeah, a solution you've only given me vague details about. Like, I'd be stuck with some frat for a month. And I have to apply? That's not the saving grace on a silver platter you seem to think it is, Gia." I waved a hand over my general person. "I doubt I'm their type."

"Their type?" Gia scoffed as she ticked attributes off on her fingers. "Female? Great tits? And a dancer's ass? They're twenty-one-year-old guys, Quinn Everly. *You* are exactly their type."

She ignored my messy bun of brown hair and how I only

applied mascara to one eye this morning. As if she hadn't caught that the second I walked up to join her in the library.

"I meant the part where I'm broke and drowning in unpaid medical bills." I gave her a pointed look before glancing down at my tits. "Aside from that, obviously, I see your point."

She smirked, arching an eyebrow at me. "Well, they call themselves the Knights of Camelot Court, don't they? I'm sure they get off on helping out damsels in distress like you."

I threw my highlighter at her. "I am *not* a damsel in distress. The last thing I want is some guy swooping in, thinking he's the answer to my problems. Not after what happened last time."

Gia growled, her mama bear instincts resurfacing at the mention of my ex, but she quickly reined them in and refocused. "Look, from what I hear, it's the daughters of the Camelot Society members, the frat's alumni group or whatever, that get picked anyways. But they have to open up applications to all the students. So, what's the harm in applying? At least you'll have tried, right?"

"I guess..."

"That's the spirit!" Gia brightened, earning a sharp *shush* from the librarian and ignoring it to stay on my case. "Plus, if you're picked, I bet you get to party like it's nineteen-oh-nine. Or whenever medieval times was—"

"Twelve-oh-nine, then. But the legend is set around the fifth century. Roughly." I put my hand out for my highlighter.

She held it just out of reach. "See. You're perfect for this."

"Yeah, and your take on all this seems way over-simplified, Gia. I still don't buy it."

"Alright, alright. Well, will you just think about it, at least?"

I promised her I would.

But, as usual, Gia had left out a few pertinent details.

She shared them the next day, confirming what I'd already guessed about The Quest.

Thirty days of being called a Maiden, fighting other girls for the favor of the King, and essentially belonging to one of the Knights?

That was *exactly* the kind of lemon life would throw at me.

It was preposterous. Antiquated. Barbaric. I hated to say it, but downright *medieval*.

I didn't shout about it, but I considered myself a feminist. No way could I handle taking orders from some frat boy douche calling himself a Knight.

And an overlord of the douches calling himself King?

Spare me.

Plus, with my track record, I'd get picked by the one expecting me to call him *My Lord*.

Or worse, *Master*.

And I'd be punished for laughing in his face as soon as he ordered me to do it.

There was no way The Quest would work out in my favor. I'd made up my mind on it. I'd find another way out of the financial mess I'd gotten myself into.

Preferably, one that didn't cost me my dignity.

That. Was. That.

But then, as my ill-fated luck would have it, I came face-to-face with the King.

Dressed in all black, he looked like an angel fallen from grace. To me, he felt like a savior.

Chapter One
Quinn

"That'll be three hundred and thirty-two dollars and eight cents."

"Three hundred dollars?" I squawked back, staring at the pharmacist in disbelief.

"And thirty-two dollars and eight cents."

I balked. "That's outrageous. Did you run it through my insurance?"

"Yes." His bored tone and dry look implied he didn't appreciate such a stupid question.

Well, I didn't appreciate price gouging for life-saving medication. So, we were both disappointed by this turn of events, buddy.

"That has to be a mistake." I shook my head, my fingers itching to run through my hair and pull it out. I pinned my hand to my side. "Can you *please* run it again?"

He blinked at me, my plea falling short of a tug on his heartstrings. But he tapped his keyboard and refreshed the information.

He shook his head. "Same total."

I began to sweat.

Swiping at my temples, I gave in to the urge and ran my hand over my scalp. I searched for the scar hidden beneath my hair. My bracelet snagged on random strands, pulling them free of my messy bun.

They floated to the floor while my anxiety shot through the roof.

The customer behind me coughed. Lightly at first, but then distinctly clearing his throat. He let out a heavy breath.

As if I didn't know how long this was taking.

It required all the patience I possessed to stay focused on the pharmacist.

"Okay, well..." I swallowed the pride that hated having to admit, "I can't afford that."

"We can hold it for you for a few days."

"Can you call my doctor and check the prescription with him? Maybe he entered it wrong by mistake? He'll fix it if you tell him the issue. He knows how much I need this medicine."

I had the copays for five follow-up visits to show for it.

The pharmacist sighed. "I can try."

While I mentally bowed to him in thanks for doing his job, he disappeared into the back.

I pulled my clutch from the pocket of my oversized hoodie, ignoring the shuffle of feet behind me. Bypassing my debit card with its dismally low balance and glaring at my useless insurance card, I hunted for my remaining cash. But the wad of crumpled bills barely covered one puff of the overpriced medicine.

I needed it twice on a daily basis.

My breathing grew tighter. Shaking out my palms, I pulled in a breath through my nose, counting to four before trying to release it slowly.

It came out in a rush.

I'd run out of my medication yesterday, my last inhaler delivering nothing but empty air for my second dose. The only reason I hadn't panicked then was because I had my appointment today. I planned to get the medication right after.

But if I couldn't afford it…

My throat constricted reflexively, as if I needed the reminder. I pushed up onto the balls of my feet and sank down, staring into the back of the pharmacy like I could will the pharmacist to return with my mind.

Each slow breath I dragged in felt like sipping air through a straw—the one on the juice boxes they gave to kids.

I was just a kid. I wasn't supposed to do this all on my own. My dad—

"Your doctor said the prescription is correct." The pharmacist set the box on the counter in front of me. "But we don't have a generic version, and that's all your plan covers. He sent in an order for your old inhaler, but he said to tell you the one he prescribed today would probably work better."

My fingers itched to grab the box and run.

But before I could travel down that darker path, the pharmacist covered it with his hand and slid it back toward him, drawing my eyes up.

"How long would it take you to fill the prescription for my old inhaler?"

He glanced at the line of customers growing behind me. "An hour, maybe?"

Handing over my debit card, I prayed it would go through and asked him to try it. A second later, the computer beeped loudly with that buzzer sound.

Because having a card decline wasn't bad enough unless everyone within thirty feet knew about it.

"Your card declined," he stated, clearly for good measure. "Want to try another one?"

"No." My pulse raced. Blood rushing in my ears, I tried to think past the need for oxygen. "Is there a coupon code or something?"

"I can check."

I closed my eyes as he clicked away at the keyboard, already knowing how his search would end. Of course, there wouldn't be a coupon. Or if there was, it wouldn't be enough to cover all of what I couldn't afford.

"I found one coupon code," he said, perking my head up. "One hundred and seven dollars and four cents."

Lemons.

The word pounded in my ears. The scent rose up in my nose. Life had been handing me nothing but lemons since my dad died. And I couldn't keep taking the hits.

I pressed my hands to my temples like that might shield me from the blows. "Can you fill the other one?"

But before the pharmacist could respond, a voice came from behind my back—a deep, rich sound that poured over me like honey.

"Whatever the medication costs, I'll cover it."

If I hadn't been tits-deep in the quicksand of panic, the offer would've soothed me.

Instead, I sank lower.

Shame spiraled me deeper, the humiliation occluding my throat. It threatened to bury my head completely.

But before panic could swallow me whole, my mysterious benefactor stepped forward.

My attention caught on broad shoulders and sculpted arms. A hand drawing circles on the side of his thigh. And dark amber eyes, solemn and beautiful, staring straight ahead.

Dressed in all black, he looked like an angel fallen from grace. To me, he felt like a savior. And I responded viscerally to that first sight of him, as he pulled me back to the surface.

My lungs expanded with a gasp.

No one shirked an order from the King.
Not even his best friend.

LANDON

On the list of ways I wanted to spend a Friday, the line at the local pharmacy didn't make the cut.

Yet, here I was.

Most of my wait I'd spent rocking back and forth on my heels, my hands clenching inside my pockets as another question came out of the customer in front of me. I'd clocked her the second I walked up.

Female, close to my age, attractive.

Not that the last part was obvious.

Her oversized hoodie and worn-out sweatpants hardly showcased her figure, but she had curves. An ass round enough to bite. Thighs strong enough to lock me in a chokehold as she came on my tongue. Hips to grab onto while she rode my—

No.

My fingers twitched at my side, and I shook my head to clear it.

When I'd walked up behind her, I had the strangest urge to step closer. I wanted to rest my chin on the top of her head. Just to see if she'd fit.

The messy bun she'd wrangled her dark brown hair into stopped me, and you know...manners or whatever.

But I'd thought about it.

Flyaway strands escaped her elastic, brushing the golden-tan skin that peeked out beneath her sweatshirt. I wondered what those dark curls would look like coated with sweat. Clinging to her neck as it arched back. Leading me to ecstasy between her thighs.

Idle thoughts like this plagued me.

Thoughts I wouldn't have normally had about a stranger, if not for staring at her ass for the last twenty minutes.

Yet, again, here I was.

Adjusting the increasingly tight fit of my pants, I cursed myself for leaving my phone in the car. I'd wanted a break from the onslaught of texts I'd been getting about The Quest.

Now, I needed a distraction, so I didn't sport an erection at the local drugstore.

More so, I needed to get the fuck out of there and take care of the situation before I did something stupid. If this favor were for anyone else, I would've split by now.

But no one shirked an order from the King.

Not even his best friend.

My position as such usually afforded me immunity from mindless errands, but this had been...*sensitive*.

The virgin daughter of his grandfather's business partner conveniently forgetting to mention she wasn't on the pill—at least not until *after* she dangled her untouched pussy in a younger Knight's face—qualified as urgent, apparently.

And I'd been given the honor of securing Plan B.

Although, if any of our younger pledges had listened to me one of the countless other times they'd fallen into this sort of honey trap, they could've saved me the trouble.

I wouldn't be here trying to get a morning-after pill, rocking a semi over a girl without seeing her face. Picturing *my* face buried between her thighs. Or my hands threading in her thick, dark hair, while staring transfixed as she ran *her* fingers along her scalp.

Again and again.

She tugged more strands free from her bun before snapping her hand away.

It was like she kept forgetting that she'd secured it up there, only to remember all of a sudden. And then, less than a minute later, she'd forget all over again.

A repetitive, anxious tic she couldn't seem to control...

I found it fascinating.

That, or standing behind her as she cross-examined the pharmacist had bored me to the point of insanity.

My money being on the latter, I checked my watch for the hundredth time. *Twenty minutes* to pick up one medication? To go back and forth over copays and coupon cards? Couldn't she charge it and let us all move on?

I checked my privilege there, hearing my sister's voice reverberate in my mind.

But a triumphant sound burst past my lips, as a lightbulb flickered on above my head. I pulled out my wallet and slapped my card down. The loud *crack* of my hand against the counter captured the pharmacist's gaze and his pint-sized inquisitor's attention.

"Whatever the medication costs, I'll cover it."

The pharmacist's eyebrows rose. And while my eyes stayed on his face, staring expectantly until he took my credit card and got to work swiping it, my focus wasn't on him. It remained solely on the space beside me.

And the sharp intake of breath that came from *her*.

Not the clearly audible gasp I expected for that pay-it-forward moment, however self-motivated it might've been. The inhale that followed caught me off guard as it echoed in my ears. It sounded wrong. It was too high-pitched.

Too tight.

Pained.

I recognized it. And my mind jolted back to the last time I heard it. My heart raced and palms grew slick instantly.

As if almost ten years hadn't passed since the worst moment of my life.

Stumbling forward, I gripped the edge of the counter.

It took everything I had not to pass out.

The pharmacist finished charging my card. He turned from the register to hand it back. His eyes widened when he saw my face. Voice muffling in my ears, his words came out garbled and asked if I was alright.

And he called himself a medical professional...

But then, a soft hand grazed my forearm, clearing the haze. Illuminating that single point of contact.

Like the sun peeking through the clouds on an overcast day.

I withdrew from the sudden intensity of it, taking the card and shoving it into my pocket.

"I'm fine," I croaked.

Without a second glance, I tore out of the store like a ghost chased me. Chomping at my heels like the memory pressing in on my thoughts. Squeezing my throat like—

I climbed into the back of the blacked-out SUV and slammed the door. Panting heavily, I forced the thoughts from my mind.

The freshman pledge tasked with driving me caught my eyes in the rearview mirror before hastily looking away.

But I saw the concern in his expression, and I couldn't stand it.

"Let's go," I barked, turning to face the window.

I caught a glimpse of messy brown hair corralled into a bun, hands clutching a bag of medicine, and a heart-shaped face with dark eyes shining in the sun right as we pulled away.

Eyes filled with relief because of what I'd done.
I couldn't stand that, either.

It couldn't be another lemon. This strange twist of fate, pointing me in one direction...

Chapter Two
Quinn

"I want to die."

I kicked the apartment door shut behind me, hauling my stuff into the kitchen. Grabbing a seat at the table, I folded my arms and plopped my head down. My bag hit the ground with a *thunk,* spilling its contents onto the floor. I lifted my head and watched as my pencils slowly rolled away.

"Fuck my life," I groaned.

"Why, hello to you, too." Gia cocked a wooden spoon in my direction, greeting me from the stove. "Looks like someone's working toward their Fine Arts degree in *drama* today."

"You weren't there, Gia. It was..." My cheeks heated with shame just thinking about it. "I've never been so mortified."

She arched an eyebrow. "Worse than that time you got dia—"

"No!" I said quickly. "You know nothing's worse than that. And you swore you'd never bring that up again."

She shrugged, turning back to the noodles in the pot. "Well, I feel better about your big entrance knowing you still have some perspective. Now, do you want to talk about it?"

Did I want to talk about how my ex-boyfriend plied me with tequila and convinced me to let him stick his finger in my butt?

Or how that ill-fated anniversary date at a Mexican restaurant started the slow crawl toward the end of our relationship?

Or how our breakup led to the worst night of my life? A life I then packed up and moved to a sleepy mountain town in North Carolina just so I could die of shame at the local pharmacy?

"No, thank you. Not ever, ever, *ever* again." I grimaced, running my hand through my hair. My bracelet snagged on a few strands and yanked them out. Snapping my hand away, I pulled the hood of my sweatshirt over my head. "I'll just die here, thanks."

I tugged on the hoodie's strings and cinched it up, hiding my face before dropping my head back onto the table.

But I couldn't hide in my ex-boyfriend's stolen hoodie forever. Fat load of good it did me anyway, since my best friend knew all my secrets.

Gia had been with me through it all. Virtually, ever since we met at dance camp when we were eleven, and physically since I'd transferred to her school last year to avoid being completely alone.

We shared an apartment off-campus and a vault's worth of each other's darkest secrets and most-embarrassing moments.

"I take it this recent trauma involved a hot guy?"

"What makes you say that?" Words muffled in my arms, and I feigned outrage even though she'd hit the nail on the head. "Not all my embarrassing moments involve a guy."

They really did, though.

I huffed, sitting up and freeing my face from my self-imposed prison. "My card declined at the pharmacy today, trying to pick up my inhaler. Whatever my doctor prescribed isn't covered by the school's crappy student insurance policy. So, I have to pay for it out of pocket."

"Yikes." She balked. "How much?"

"Three hundred dollars!" The cost still made my blood boil. "Oh, plus the extra some odd dollars and like, eight cents. I don't remember exactly. I blacked it out because it was outrageous."

Gia grimaced. "Shit."

She didn't have to say anything else. We both knew I couldn't afford anything close to that right now, not if I wanted to pay for anything else. Or, I don't know, *not starve*.

"Yeah, I spent, like, twenty minutes going back and forth with the pharmacist over it. He checked for alternatives and coupon codes. But even with a coupon, I still would've been short. So, of course, I started freaking out."

"Oh, no."

"Oh, yes. Literally about to have a full-on asthma attack, all while the damn medication was on the other side of the counter. It was infuriating. And then, some guy comes out of nowhere, slaps his card on the counter, and pays for the whole thing."

Taking a seat at the table with me, she covered my hands with hers. "Which I'm sure you appreciated, but it also made it worse?"

"Yup." I resisted the urge to pull my hair out, stopping only because of her gentle grip. I nodded toward our hands. "Thanks."

She shrugged. "You're under a lot of stress. Just figured I'd save you a few strands."

I turned my hand over and linked our fingers. "I'd probably be bald without you. Or on the streets. I promise. I'm going to find a way to get you the rent money on time."

"I know you will." She smiled, but all of my shit put stress on her, even if she tried to hide it. She got up and went back to the stove. "Did you end up applying for those jobs?"

"Every single one. No luck. All the hours interfere with our program, or they decided to fill the position with someone who had more flexibility." I released a heavy breath and threw my hands in the air. "I'm a dance major, for crying out loud! I'm totally flexible."

She laughed while I tugged my lower lip between my teeth. I chewed over the idea that I'd been going back and forth on. I was starting to think I didn't have much of a choice.

When my dad died last semester, I'd lost more than my only remaining parent—the security I'd taken for granted had gone with him. And instead of going to the prestigious dance academy he'd signed me up for on the other side of the country, I joined Gia at D'Art U, a public university with a dance program, only a few states away.

But I'd woefully underestimated the cost of living, even with the help of student loans.

"I think I need to take next semester off and work full time."

Her eyes snapped back to mine. "Quinn, no. We can figure something else out."

"I've thought over everything else about a hundred times. And it's not so bad. It only pushes back my graduation for a year. Tops."

"But I can ask my parents—"

"No way." I shook my head adamantly. "They do more than enough by covering our utility bill *and* sending you extra money until I can pay you. That already saves us on late fees with the landlord. Not to mention the food you make us. It's too much. I can't accept anything else."

She held back from voicing her protests, having been down this road with me many times before.

I hated being a charity case. Everyone already looked at me with pity when they found out about the accident and my dad. And I didn't need or want anyone's sympathy.

I didn't deserve it.

Trying to put Gia's mind at ease, I shrugged it off like it was no big deal. "Hey, it might be the only way to get my asthma under control and finish the program anyway. Not much of a silver lining, but look, I'm making lemon drops."

She frowned, not buying it for a second. But she didn't

call me on it. "If you're sure..."

"I'll talk to my financial advisor about it tomorrow. But I might not have much choice. It's either take a break and work full time or start stripping. And I'm not quite ready to go down that path with my dancing. Not yet."

Gia snorted. "Yeah, you might as well apply for The Quest first."

She uncovered the pot on the stove and checked the pasta, laughing off the idea. I wanted to laugh with her, but something stopped me.

When she'd first told me about The Quest, the idea seemed ludicrous. But now, as medical bills piled up, I couldn't brush it off as easily.

I toyed with the charms on my bracelet, wondering what my parents would've thought about me joining The Quest. They were probably rolling over in their graves.

Except they'd always said being a feminist was about empowering women to make their own choices. Not limiting their opportunities based on gender. They supported me in whatever I wanted to do with my life as long as it was my choice.

If I wanted to paint naked in the backyard under the light of the full moon? My mom bought me the art supplies while my dad hung up privacy curtains in our backyard.

And if I wanted to be a dancer, even though my chances for a secure future were harder to come by and my asthma posed a problem? So be it.

Mom made all of my sparkly costumes and did up my hair with an obscene array of ribbons and bows for each performance. Dad even learned to French braid. They'd driven me to every dance practice and cheered me on at every recital and competition.

Right up until the one before my twelfth birthday. The last one my mom got to see.

But she'd been proud of me. They both had been—not because I won and got my name and picture in the local newspaper—

because I was *happy*. Doing something I chose and loved.

Wouldn't the same apply to this?

Although, I planned to leave love out of it.

"What else do you know about The Quest?" I asked Gia, my sudden interest halting her wooden spoon mid-stir. "I mean, if I'm going to consider dropping a semester, I should probably weigh every option that doesn't force me to, right?"

"I suppose…" She shut the burner on the stove off, carrying the pot of noodles to the strainer in the sink. "I don't know much more than I told you. But some of the guys from Camelot Court are in one of my classes. They all huddle together in the back of the room, but I could sit a little closer next class. See what I can find out?"

"What do you know about them?"

Steam billowed up as she dumped the hot water and noodles. She scrunched her face and chuckled to herself. "Ironically, they're all steamy hot. And they're all from super rich legacy families. The D'Arthurs, obviously. But there's also the Scotts, the Léons…Those two are in my class, but there are twelve guys total. Well, thirteen with Kingston D'Arthur. He's pretty hard to get a read on, from what I hear. Then, Landon Scott is, like, his second or right hand or whatever—even though technically, I don't think they have ranks." She shrugged. "Super broody, that one."

"Who's the other one?"

Her eyebrows rose, oh-so-innocently. "What?"

"You said three families, but only two guys."

A deep blush colored her cheeks, warming her tanned skin. "Oh, um, right. That's Tristan Léon." She caught sight of my eyebrows, raised expectantly for her to go on, and sighed. "He's like an excitable puppy. If puppies were hot as fuck. It's ridiculous."

She kept going on about him, as expected, since that blush was a dead giveaway she had a thing for the hot puppy.

I oohed and aahed at all the appropriate spots. But when she started describing his abs in detail, my mind circled back to one of the first things she'd said.

I slapped my hand on the table, making Gia jump.

"No freaking way."

Diving for my bag, I snagged the strap and yanked it toward me. I searched through the spilled contents, finding the slip of paper still carefully folded in one of the pockets.

I flattened it on the table in front of me. "You've got to be shitting me."

"What is it?"

Gia came up beside me, peering over my shoulder at the receipt I'd saved from the pharmacy. I figured I could use it to find the stranger who'd helped me and pay him back. Even if that wasn't going to be possible any time soon, I didn't throw it away.

Now, keeping it felt like a sign.

Gia gasped. "No freaking way."

I nodded, rereading the credit card information on the receipt. The numbers were concealed, but it listed the cardholder right there in black and white.

"All hail the Knights of the Round Table," Gia quipped.

"Yeah," I said slowly, staring at his name and marveling at the chances. "And long live the King."

It couldn't be another lemon. This strange twist of fate pointing me in one direction, and maybe even showing me the path I needed to take? As much as I wanted to laugh at the absurdity of that thought, I couldn't ignore the pull in my gut.

Because the name of my kind stranger—the gorgeous guy who'd covered the cost of my medicine, saving me when I didn't want to be saved and hurling himself into a panic attack of his own—I held it right there in my hands.

Kingston D'Arthur.

The King of Camelot Court.

"I know it's crazy. But what do I have to lose, right? My virginity? I want to get rid of that, anyway."

Chapter Three
Quinn

The next day, I met up with Gia after class. My meeting with my financial aid advisor had gone about as well as I'd expected it to go. I had to drop my summer classes, and until I paid off my overdue fees, I couldn't register for fall semester, either.

I'd also gotten a call from my parents' lawyer, a real leech of a guy who always called from unknown numbers, letting me know their life insurance policies were tied up in litigation.

He said something about the insurance company disputing the claim, which made no sense to me, but I didn't give him long to explain it. As soon as he said it'd be a legal battle to free up the funds, I thanked him and hung up the phone.

Fighting over money I'd only get because my parents were dead wasn't how I wanted to spend my time—no matter how badly I needed it.

Why would I when I had plenty of other options available? That time could be used to keep applying for jobs that wouldn't hire me. And I could still try begging on the streets or finding a pimp to start my career as a high-priced escort.

I'd already donated the maximum amount of blood and plasma they'd let me donate. Maybe I could try selling a kidney on the black market.

To be honest, even *that* sounded like a better alternative than proving my parents died under normal circumstances to a bunch of sleazy insurance suits.

Sure, my logic may have been flawed.

But what could I say?

Grief was weird.

The more I went over it, the more I had to take a semester off, unless...

Gia walked up, glancing at me with wide eyes before jerking her chin over her shoulder. I followed her gaze to a cluster of students. Three guys stood out over the heads of the girls around them, and one of them I immediately recognized.

"That's them." She bounced on her feet when she got to my side. "It was kind of hard to get close to them during class with, you know, the gaggle of girls around them, but I overheard bits and pieces. Come on, let's head back to the apartment and I'll fill you in."

She looped her arm through mine and dragged me away.

I glanced back over my shoulder for one more look at the guy from the pharmacy.

My real-life Knight in Shining Armor—or more accurately, Kingston D'Arthur—looked right at me. His eyes narrowed as we walked away before someone else stole his attention.

As Gia guided me toward the parking lot, I watched his interaction with the pretty blonde girl at his side. And I tried not to be pleased when he didn't give her his full focus. Not very hard, but I tried.

I could be a petty bitch like that. So, sue me.

Just as we rounded the corner of the building and disappeared out of sight, I caught his final glance in my direction and tightened my grip on Gia's arm. "Holy shit."

"What? What's wrong?"

"I can't wait until we get to the apartment. Tell me everything. My meeting with the advisor was a total bust, and unless you have black market connections I don't know about, I think I need to apply."

"You might change your mind when you hear what I found out."

I stopped her in her tracks. "Tell me."

"The girls who are picked? The Maidens—They're, like, completely, irrevocably owned by their Knight for the first thirty days. He controls everything from their training for The Quest, their clothes, and..."

I groaned. "Let me guess. Their bodies?"

She nodded. "No exceptions. Most of what I overheard was a little crude. But I mean, I'm not going to lie, I wouldn't exactly be opposed if I liked the guy. It's just, you..."

"Your virgin best friend with limited interest in the opposite sex after my last relationship ended with my dad dying? Psh!" I swatted away the potential problems as if they weren't giant red flags waving in my face. "Maybe a Round Table of dick is exactly what I need to get past it?"

Gia's features tightened at my attempt to deflect. "Maybe. But you'd have to be really sure before you signed up."

"Why's that?"

"They made it sound like swearing a blood oath. One of the girls in class mentioned backing out, and Landon looked at her like she'd completely dishonored herself by even suggesting the idea."

"Ew. What an asshole."

"That's what I'm saying. She just asked because there's a rumor going around that a girl died last year. I mean, who wouldn't be nervous if they heard that? And he looked at her like he wanted to ban her from Camelot Court for just thinking of backing out."

I wrinkled my nose in disgust, then gnawed on my lower lip. "But it's just a rumor?"

She nodded. "But my point is that apparently backing out comes with some form of repayment that ruins you in front of Camelot Court. So, maybe this isn't such a good idea."

When I didn't say anything, she started toward the car again. I went back and forth over the new information, trying to decide what was purely speculation and what I should take seriously. In the end, though, nothing she'd overheard changed my mind.

"Kingston recognized me across the lawn just now. After my run-in with him at the pharmacy, this might be my one shot to apply, get in, and get the money I need without delaying my program. I might get picked if he recognizes me on the application."

She blinked at me in surprise.

I couldn't blame her, but I also didn't want to tell her that a tiny part of me didn't hate the idea of spending thirty days belonging to Kingston D'Arthur.

Not after seeing him again.

Not after what he'd done to help me.

"I know it's crazy. But what do I have to lose, right? My virginity? I want to get rid of that, anyway."

"Um, did you not hear what I just told you? What about your life?"

I shot her an exasperated look as we reached my car. She bit her lip and nodded, her nostrils flaring as she let that part go.

"Thank you. Now. With that settled, we need wine."

"Wine?"

"Yes, wine." I pulled out my keys to unlock the door. "If I'm about to apply to *belong* to a Knight for the month, wine will be one hundred percent necessary. No matter how hot he is."

Gia waved a hand in front of her to gesture for me to get going. "As you wish, Princess."

I rolled my eyes at her reference to one of my favorite movies and started the car. "Don't get any ideas, Gia. This is a means to an end. I use his White Knight complex to get in, and then I find a way for me to be my own damn hero and save myself. It's *not* a fairytale love story."

"Whatever you say, Buttercup."

A single word on her application told me everything I needed to know.

KINGSTON

I tossed another folder into the trash pile. "Too fake."

One of the Knights, Ben Devereaux, snorted in reply. "That was part of the appeal."

Then, he honked an imaginary set of boobs on his chest. I didn't even have to spare a glance to see him do it.

History and the pressure building behind my eyes relayed it for me.

I pinched the bridge of my nose, trying to release it. "And she'll be eliminated in the second phase when she refuses to break a nail. Or worse, in the first, when she eats up six days of another Knight's attention and gives into temptation."

Glancing at the unamused Knight beside him named Tristan Léon, Ben smirked. "Yeah, but I'll have plenty of fun with her in the meantime. Look at her makeup. I bet it bleeds down her face so pretty when she's choking on—"

"That's enough."

He fell silent at my command. I didn't even have to raise my voice. I spoke; they obeyed.

"I'm aware of the presumed benefits during the first thirty days of The Quest, but don't forget yourself, *Sir Bedivere*."

I rarely used the Knights' family names, but sometimes they needed the reminder.

This was bigger than our fraternity.

"The Quest is about more than getting your dick wet. You're training a challenger, not a sex puppet. She needs to be disciplined, controlled in *her* nature. Not just by you in the bedroom."

"Yes, sir," they chimed in unison.

I didn't even have to ask for a response. I acted; they reacted.

"We swear an oath and live by a code for a reason." I picked up another pile, flipping through it and coming away unsatisfied again. "Now, go fetch me the pile you fools discarded on the first run through."

"But most of those girls were…"

My expression no doubt informed him I didn't need or want that sentence finished. The first pass usually ruled out anyone from outside our society. Definitely anyone poor. Not to mention the girls sporting natural makeup and their god-given tits, because most twenty-one-year-old guys born into privilege couldn't see past the surface.

Her aspirations and academic record? Unimportant.

Her hobbies and interests? Insignificant.

But her favorite sexual position? Absolutely *vital*.

Proclivities in the bedroom defined a person's character, of course.

"I'll go get them," Tristan offered.

"No, I can do it," Ben said begrudgingly.

My eyes would've rolled out of their sockets at the predictability, but I'd been taught to keep certain reactions off my face. I'd been groomed to wear other masks effortlessly.

All while constantly being told that it paid to be in my position—how good I had it being King.

How lucky I was to be a *D'Arthur*.

Yes, what a charmed life I led, ruling over a group of

people playing pretend. I sat on a makeshift throne I'd done nothing to earn, living a life filled with everything but devoid of anything containing substance. I had nothing of my own—nothing *real*.

I wanted to see the world through a kaleidoscope—not the cardboard tube of an empty roll of toilet paper. I wanted to experience my life in blinding technicolor—every piece vibrant and loud—not washed-out, muted shades of gray. I longed for authenticity and raw emotion, but instead, I felt nothing.

I showed nothing.

And I slowly died inside of boredom.

How fun.

When a stack of red folders landed on my desk, I thumbed through them quickly. Sorting through the files, I placed them in stacks for yes, maybe, or no. I made it to the very last folder when a deep tug of recognition pulled at my chest.

Setting it to the side, I gestured at the two Knights I'd tasked with this assignment and the yes and maybe piles in front of me. "See that all the Knights at least *look* through these two stacks."

"Yes, sir."

"Except for Landon." My fingers twitched over the file I'd siphoned out. "Tell him to come see me."

They nodded and left the room, Ben's eyes lingering over the folder on my desk before he shut the door. When it clicked shut, I reopened the folder, staring at the four-by-six photo of the only girl in the pile whose application grabbed my attention.

Quinn Everly.

I tucked her picture in my pocket.

Although she was beautiful, a single word on her application told me everything I needed to know.

It also meant I trusted only one Knight to select her.

Only one Knight could guide her through The Quest, introduce her to Camelot Court, and safeguard her innocence. All before delivering her to me—fully prepared to be Queen.

"This is exactly why I shouldn't make important life decisions while drinking boxed wine."

Chapter Four
Quinn

A few weeks after applying for The Quest, I picked up the embossed envelope lying on our doorstep, pinching the corner between my thumb and forefinger while holding it delicately away from my body.

"It's a letter, Quinn. Not a bomb." Gia poked her head over my shoulder, since the *letter* had kept me from unlocking the door. "Ooh! A fancy letter."

"It's from Camelot Court," I pointed out uselessly, as if the elaborate wax seal on the back hadn't announced it for me.

I flipped the heavy envelope over. Ornate lettering, imprinted on the front in royal blue ink, glinted in the sunlight. Shiny and metallic, it screamed of opulence and reeked of unchecked wealth and privilege.

This one envelope probably cost as much as my overpriced inhaler. And for all I knew, it was a rejection letter.

Fucking hell.

For the thousandth time, I wondered what the hell I'd gotten myself into by submitting that application.

Sure, I'd been desperate.

And sure, there'd been boxed wine involved.

But now? Faced with the very real possibility that I might've been selected for The Quest, I wanted to hurl. I was in *way* over my head.

"Gimme!" Gia shrieked in my ear, reaching over me to grab the letter. "If you're not going to open it, I will."

I held it out of reach. "Maybe I should just throw it away? Pretend I didn't get it or something. When I don't show up, they'll probably just replace me, right? Then, we can chalk this whole thing up to one of those funny Quinn stories. Another time I almost did something crazy and chickened out at the last second. It'll be great."

Gia shot me a glare, her eyes inches from mine after she'd latched onto my back like some kind of giant squid. "Don't even think about it, Quinn Everly. You're doing this. You read what the application said."

I swallowed down the spike of dread that followed her mention of the application. It had contained a contract with a much scarier and more intimidating version of *No Take Backs* included above the line for my signature. Even that hadn't been enough to make me see reason.

Nope, I'd merrily signed off on it as I drank my third glass of wine.

At the time, what the contract provided in exchange for my participation had seemed like an offer I couldn't refuse. They'd cover my cost of living—meals, clothes, health and personal care expenses, and anything else I needed—in exchange for thirty days on the swankiest campus at D'Arthur University. But if I reneged on the contract, I'd owe it all back with damages.

Whatever that meant.

Honestly, they'd had me at *healthcare expenses*.

Plus, how bad could one guy be for thirty days?

I hadn't seen a reason I'd want to back out. Even with Gia's latest intel from the gossip she'd collected in class, I figured I could handle it. But now, I found myself second-guessing.

"What if the guy is a total asshole, Gia? What if he... What if he hurts me? Like he's into that. Gets off on seriously causing girls pain and shit."

Gia slid off my back and clamped her hands down on my shoulders, her mouth twisting into a frown as she spotted my incoming—okay, very clear and present—downward spiral.

"Oh my god! He could have some extreme bodily fluid kink, Gia. How could we not think about that? What if he wants me to take a dump on his chest?"

My thoughts took a nosedive to a dark place as I realized my error in judgment. I closed my eyes and dropped my head back. "Ugh! This is exactly why I shouldn't make important life decisions while drinking boxed wine."

When the subject came up last week, we'd laughed it off. Both of us found the idea of a fifty shades situation happening a little hot. We didn't consider that there might be kinks out there that I, personally, had no desire to try.

Gia grimaced, chewing on her lip before trying to put my mind at ease. "But the contract said you'd be protected, right? It said you get to set hard limits and have safe words and all that. Remember?"

"Yeah." My fingers twitched with the urge to tug on my hair. "In hindsight, all of that being in the contract seems like a bit of a red flag we ignored."

Gia didn't say anything to that.

But we both eyed the envelope more cautiously. She took the keys from my other hand and slipped past me to open the door. Once inside, I set the envelope on our coffee table while Gia grabbed the wine and brought it over.

Foregoing glasses, she yanked out the cork with her teeth and handed the bottle—the source and solution to my life's current problem—straight to me.

Sinking onto the couch, I took a deep swig and handed

the bottle back to her. I picked up the envelope and held it in my hands.

Gia put her arm around my shoulder. "You're going to make The Quest your bitch. That Knight of yours, too. Whatever happens, you've got this."

I did my best to smile at her, grateful for the reassurance but still seconds away from puking my guts out. With a deep breath, I flipped the envelope over and slid my finger under the gold wax seal. Lifting the flap, I pulled out the thick card inside.

It looked like an invitation to a wedding, but it felt more like a funeral pronouncement.

"You are cordially invited to Camelot Court for the annual selection of Maidens on Friday, April the twenty-ninth at seven o'clock in the evening."

Below the elegant royal blue script, the D'Arthur University logo had been imprinted on the center of the invitation. The lion, bearing a crown on its head, had been altered slightly. Two gold swords crossed behind it now.

Running my fingers over the embossed blades, I read the final line of text. "Applicants are encouraged to dress to impress and prepare to stay for the night, if chosen."

I turned the invitation over, finding nothing on the back. Flipping it over again, I reread the message. The envelope I'd set on the table was empty, too.

"That's all it says. Pretentious as fuck, and there isn't even an address."

"Wait, what?" Gia took the envelope from me and conducted a second search, which also came up empty. "There has to be more. That literally told us nothing."

"I don't think that means what you think it means," I replied automatically, sinking back into the couch cushions and still staring at the invitation like more clues might magically appear. "Unless they hid a message in magic ink, that's it. You got a lighter on you?"

Gia laughed, reaching forward to take another sip of wine before launching into a rant about how this was yet another example of men failing to communicate important details. She handed over the bottle, but I barely registered what I was doing as I took it from her.

My eyes remained fixed on the invitation.

I had my father to thank for that curiosity. He had always loved leaving me secret messages around the house, but they weren't secret clues or hidden agendas—just notes. To remind me he loved me. To tell me he was proud of me. I'd hunted for them everywhere I went, loving that so fucking much when I was a kid.

So, as soon as I joked about it, *that* part of me couldn't help but go there.

But the part of me that was gutted the first time I found one after he died…that little girl sat frozen on the couch. She drew in a shaky breath. And slowly released it with all the guilt and painful venom my thoughts brought with it.

Jumping up, I headed straight for the catch-all drawer next to the fridge. I scavenged past countless take-out menus and sauce packets, finding what I'd been looking for—a Zippo lighter gleaming in antiqued silver. I prayed it still worked.

After a few flicks of my thumb, the flame sparked to life. I held it close enough to heat the invitation, but not so close to singe the paper. Drawing it back and forth under the back, my excitement plummeted when nothing appeared.

To be sure, I waved the tiny flame over the side with the inscription, eyes widening as thick, black letters appeared over the elegant script.

"Holy shit," I breathed.

Gia sprung to her feet, coming to my side as I read the hidden message—a short list of items that came with no further instructions or explanation.

"Red soled heels, a string of pearls, and black silk garter?"

"I don't get it. Are you supposed to wear those?"

I shrugged. "Your guess is as good as mine. Maybe the girls wearing the items get a special prize for showing up? Or a get out of jail free card!" I suggested hopefully, before my hope sank like a capsized ship. "Too bad I don't own a single one of those items."

Gia's eyes lit up, and she raced into her bedroom. I picked up the wine bottle from the coffee table and took a sip, padding over to her room with my exceedingly low expectations. This hadn't turned out the way I thought it would, and I still had to wait another week to find out my fate.

As I leaned against the doorjamb, Gia rifled through her vanity drawers, pulling out a long string of pearls. "Thank you, Audrey Hepburn costume of 2022."

She tossed the pearls at me, and I nearly dropped the wine in surprise. Disappearing into her closet, she rustled boxes and grunted a bit. I eyed the door, wondering what the heck she was doing in there and if I should go in after her.

"Ha!" she cried, coming out with a black silk garter balanced on her finger. Swinging it around, she made her way back over to me. "Two secret items, *My Fair Vampire Lady*."

She slingshotted the garter at me, and I laughed, snatching it from the air like an eager groomsman in a cluster of eligible bachelors. Tugging it on over my jeans, I looped the pearls over my neck.

I posed, turning this way and that so she could see me from all angles. "How do I look?"

"Marvelous, darling," she drawled. "We still don't have red soled heels, but we can do some thrift store hunting this weekend."

Chewing on the inside of my cheek, an idea came to me. I went to the bathroom and dug through the drawers by the sink, searching for what I needed. Gia came up behind me, waiting as I rifled through the cabinets and finally found her stash of nail polish. Hunting through the rainbow of colors, I pulled out a crimson shade and held it up for Gia to see.

Her eyes lit up with excitement. "You crafty bitch."

I laughed, rising to my feet and going to my closet to grab my black heels. "One pair of red soled heels coming up."

We dissolved into a fit of giggles, taking the wine back to the couch so I could paint the bottom of my shoes.

I slipped them on when the polish dried, still dressed in my other secret items, and glanced at the invitation where I'd propped it in front of us.

For a second, a tiny spring of hope welled up in my chest.

At that moment, with my best friend at my side, I felt like I could do it—win their games and walk away with the money I needed to remove the debt collector's ax over my head.

But in three weeks, on Friday evening, April twenty-ninth at exactly seven o'clock, I would have to walk into Camelot Court alone, where a darker, more depraved threat would hang over my head.

I had just embarked down a very dangerous path.

And the temptation stirring to life inside me, the desire coiled deep in my belly, and the moisture building between my thighs at the thought of what was to come...

Those felt like the biggest threat of all.

That darkness would find a way to lure me in eventually, tempting as it was at first sight.

Chapter Five
Quinn

Over the many times I'd driven past Camelot Court on my way to doctor appointments, I never spared it a glance.

From my side of the poverty line, and the vantage point provided by my beat-up Honda Civic the high brick wall blocked my view of the main building.

I would've climbed over it to get a closer look, if I'd known everything the grounds held.

Once Gia found a side road to the private entrance, we stared wide-eyed at the literal fortress beyond the wrought-iron gate.

The guard looked out of place for a college fraternity. Even one with special off-campus housing. Dressed like a secret-service wannabe, he checked my name and scrutinized my face before ushering us through.

As Gia pulled around the circular driveway to let me out, I assured her several times my ride-share app was fully operational. I promised to use it without a second thought if things went south.

When her car pulled away, a tiny flicker of doubt sparked

to life inside me. But then, the guard directed me down a path off to the right, and I quickly smothered it.

I'd made it this far.

And I needed to keep going—move toward something instead of running away. *Again.*

Walking shakily down the cobblestone path, a round structure came into view. Its dark red brick and black accents gave off an eerie vibe, but it was more inviting than the main house behind me. A golden glow illuminating the windows and the music filtering from within its walls made it hauntingly beautiful.

It looked like it fell off a page in one of my dad's old books.

As I approached, two guys about my age stood flanking the main doors. Dressed head-to-toe in black, they didn't make eye contact with me as I climbed the front steps. They opened the doors to allow me in without a single word.

Not even a *hey girl, you come here often?*

"Thanks," I said as I crossed the threshold.

One of them pointed me toward the coat check station to the right, which was almost the same thing as *you're welcome* if I set the bar on social niceties low.

Unzipping my only black jacket, I quickly shrugged it off. The faded leather didn't really jive with the aesthetic at Camelot Court, but it was all I had on short notice. I'd borrowed the rest of my outfit from Gia, aside from the charm bracelet I never took off.

And, of course, the racy black thong she'd talked me into buying for the occasion.

Losing one's virginity was supposed to be special, after all.

I handed off my overnight bag, but kept my black clutch with the essentials—Chapstick, my inhaler, and a few condoms I never used with my ex. Better to be prepared than end up needing protection and not having it, and no-freaking-way would I leave my health and safety in the hands of some guy I'd never met.

Even if he called himself a Knight.

While I had my fingers crossed that one of their White Knight complexes secured me a spot, I had no illusions over what that implied.

A college guy got the pleasure of my company for the next thirty days?

I expected the emphasis to be on *pleasure* and the expectations for that word to be literal.

Considering the blatant display of seduction and sin Camelot Court held inside of that one room, I gave myself a mental pat on the back for coming prepared.

Sex and sin permeated the space. Couples shrouded in the dark alcoves had their heads thrown back, eyes closed with pleasure. Deep moans of satisfaction resonated over the music's heavy bass.

If ever there was a night to lose my virginity as quickly as possible, this was it. And I never would've ended up in this situation if I'd just gone through with popping the ol' cherry a year ago, so I was ready.

My body sure as hell felt ready.

But my feet retreated on instinct.

As soon as I stepped into that room, some underlying defense mechanism kicked in and alerted me to danger. Alarm bells ringing, red lights flashing—my brain yelled at me to run.

I ignored it.

But I did pause for a second to take it all in. Neutralize the threat of the unknown through prolonged exposure. That seemed like a smart course of action over jumping straight into the fire.

Gorgeous girls dressed in fancy gowns and absurdly hot guys in sleek suits caught my eye at every turn. Couples danced in the center of the room. Rowdy groups clustered by the bar threw their heads back with a round of shots.

But the dark alcoves around the room snagged my attention, and they wouldn't let it go.

Even if I wasn't ready to go there yet.

I averted my eyes and focused on the open space filled with smiling faces, but I sensed that darkness would find a way to lure me in eventually, tempting as it was at first sight.

A deep voice came from the shadows behind me.

"Leaving so soon?"

I squinted at the dark alcove off to the left of the party room's doors. But the strobing lights didn't reach this far, and I couldn't make out more than a tall silhouette.

"Who's there?"

My eyes nearly bugged out of my head at the guy who stepped forward.

Towering over me, he had to be at least six-three. Built like a linebacker and looking like he'd just walked off the cover of *GQ*. He could probably lift me with one arm and throw me like a javelin, all before driving off for the coast in some expensive sports car.

Or whatever beautiful, rich people did.

Sharply dressed in black pants, he'd draped his suit jacket over his arm. While I sent up a silent prayer for the poor, straining threads of fabric in his crisp, white shirt, my eyes lingered on the tight fit over his biceps. A silk tie hung around his neck where he'd left the top buttons undone.

Aside from the glorious V of exposed bronze skin, a simple chain glinting in the low light caught my eye. It had been tucked away and mostly out of sight, but I followed it up his neck, past the thick cords of muscle that finally led me to his face.

One look at him and I legitimately—and unfortunately, very audibly—gulped.

As I swallowed past the sudden flare of arousal in my core, my nipples had the audacity to harden. *Down, girl* replayed like a broken record inside my head. But while my brain argued against my body's response, it still acknowledged the truth.

I had every intention of climbing this guy like a tree.

He embodied darkness.

Penetrating onyx eyes. A shadow over the lower half of his face from a close-shaven beard. And hair as raven black as the night sky. He wore it cropped short on the sides with extra volume on top. Long enough to grab onto while he—

"Holy shit," I breathed.

His eyes danced with amusement over my slip, full lips showing off a bright white smile that made my knees wobble.

"Well, that was adorable," he purred from the shadows.

My body melted as he stepped out of the dark alcove, poring his gaze over me like hot chocolate and leaving a slow burn in its wake. And when he came fully into the light, my breath caught in my throat.

He was even more beautiful up close—not darkness, I realized, but an eclipse—the light of the sun hiding behind the face of the moon, and more blinding the longer I stared at him.

I exhaled a shaky laugh and ran a hand through my hair. "I don't know why I just said that."

His grin widened.

"Sure, you do." He came to stand in front of me, brushing his hand down the bare skin of my arm. "But if it makes you feel better, the feeling's mutual."

Goosebumps prickled my skin at his touch, and my lips parted in surprise. But no words came out as we stood there together. His eyes softened the longer he stared at me, and my heartbeat raced.

I needed to pull myself together.

"Thanks." Tucking a strand of my hair behind my ear, my arm slipped out of his reach, and I forced myself to shake out of it. "And to answer your question, no."

He cocked his head in question. "What?"

I glanced at the open door beside us. "I'm not leaving so soon."

"Ah." He nodded. "That's right. For a second there, you looked like you were about to bolt."

"A part of me wonders if I still should," I admitted too freely, but I liked the flash of disappointment on his face when I said it. "But I need to do this. I won't run."

"You think you're ready for it?"

"I have to be." I glanced at the party. "Don't I? I mean, I guess unless..."

Stowed away in this corner by the door, I still had no idea what to expect from this place, but I couldn't deny it intrigued me. For the first time since I'd gotten the invitation, I considered the possibility of *not* being asked to stay.

Peaceful acceptance didn't follow that thought.

The disappointment that came with it surprised me.

"There's a chance they could make the decision for me." I shrugged, watching the partygoers all together. "I might not be picked."

Between that or being sent home, I still didn't know which would be the lesser of two evils. But separated from the crowd, I *wanted* to be a part of it.

The hair on my arm rose to attention as the Dark Knight stepped into my body. Closing the distance between us. Stealing it away with the air in my lungs.

His sudden proximity made me dizzy.

I clutched onto his arm to keep myself upright.

His hand found the small of my back. "You're meant to be here. I already know it."

My heartbeat stuttered, and I couldn't help but wonder if *he* was my Knight. If that was what he meant and if this time life had decided to give me something other than lemons. I closed my eyes, breathing in the intoxicating scent of him—a heady mix of bergamot and dark, earthy spices.

"I'm Quinn," I rasped. "Quinn Everly "

I had hoped for a sign he was the Knight here for me. Or, at the very least, his name in return. But as soon as I offered mine, he pulled back.

His eyes darkened even further, his voice suddenly cold. "You're here for the King."

I stared up at him, thrown slightly off balance, and I tipped my head toward the party. "Aren't we all?"

His eyes didn't leave my face, but a crease lined his brow as he assessed me again. It felt like he was seeing me for the first time. Only, this time, he didn't like what he found.

"Hm." His tone clipped, he righted me on my feet. "I guess I was wrong."

"What?" My brow furrowed, the barest hint of rejection washing over me as he stepped back. "What do you mean?"

He shook out his jacket before setting it aside. As he rolled up his right sleeve, he wouldn't meet my eyes. Staring out at the party, he cuffed the fabric before starting on the other. "Doesn't matter," he said, leaving it at that.

I searched his face as his fingers worked quickly. When he was done, he flicked his gaze over me. Swinging his jacket over his left shoulder, he moved to step away.

And I should've let it go.

I should've let *him* go.

We didn't know each other. By the way he reacted to my name, I assumed he wasn't my Knight—if I'd even been picked. So, I should've let him take his whiplash and quick judgment with him as he left.

But I didn't.

My hand shot out and latched onto his forearm. Heat seared my palm, sparking along my skin and up my arm. He froze, glaring at the contact—glaring at me. But I held firm.

"Your name," I demanded. "Tell me your name."

Something flickered in his expression. "Why do you care, *Quinn Everly?*"

I ignored the way my core tightened at the sound of my name rolling off his tongue. "So, I know who to regret meeting as soon as I leave here."

He smirked. "Oh, you won't be going anywhere tonight."

I lifted my chin, my tone haughty. "Then, I guess your name doesn't matter. I won't spare you a second thought once I'm in my Knight's bed."

His eyes blazed, the muscles in his arm tensing as they bunched under my palm. I tightened my grip reflexively.

"Dread." He dropped his face to mine—so close the tips of our noses brushed. "My name is Max Dread."

My pulse quickened. Bergamot and spice filled my nose, clinging to the air around him and overpowering everything else. My head spun and lashes fluttered.

Max caught my reaction and huffed a quiet laugh. "Oh, Princess..."

And for a second, I thought he might kiss me. Clamping his hand over mine, he laced our fingers together.

I let him.

Then, he smirked again.

"Let's not pretend *meeting* me is what you're going to regret tonight." He peeled my grip off his arm. "No matter whose bed you end up in."

Tossing my hand away, he stalked off and left me fuming behind him.

We'd only just met, and it felt like I'd been waiting for him to touch me forever.

Chapter Six
Quinn

Words burned at the back of my throat, but before I could draw them out, *Max Dread* disappeared into the crowd.

I lost sight of him as he weaved through the sea of booze-and-sex-soaked bodies, ignoring the girls and hands grasping for his attention. It took me a minute to get a grip on myself *and* what had just happened.

He'd been right and wrong.

I wouldn't regret meeting him, only because he had reminded me why I needed to keep my head on straight. But I wouldn't regret anything else, either. Definitely not losing his interest, which seemed as volatile as an active volcano.

I refused to give anyone in this place that power over me.

I refused to care.

When my heart settled, I breathed out a shaky laugh. "What the hell was that?"

My question being rhetorical and voiced to no one, I didn't expect a response.

But a low and silky voice murmured at my back.

"You met Sir Mordred."

The man who stepped up beside me wasn't the hulking, looming presence I'd met in Max Dread, yet somehow, he was no less imposing.

Soft brown curls loosely styled on top of his head, a sharp jaw and cheekbones, and a tall frame built of lean muscle—he commanded the room and my attention the minute he appeared.

Because his eyes, soft gray and glinting in the dim light, pierced right through me.

He nodded in the direction Max had gone. "You'll want to be careful with that one."

Facing the room, he rested his hands behind his back. He glanced down at me beside him, taking in my outfit and lingering on the string of pearls at my neck.

"You figured out my little secret."

His lips curved into a smile, but it vanished almost as quickly as it appeared. Like an illusion, I blinked and wondered if I'd really seen it at all.

"But do you have all the items, love?"

The hint of an accent in the lilt of his voice hypnotized me, and I lifted my heel, revealing the red polish I'd painted on the soles.

His eyes brightened, giving away how my artistic flair pleased him. "Clever girl..."

He trailed his gaze up my leg.

If someone asked me about it later, I wouldn't have been able to answer why—at his simple response—I slid my hand to the hem of my black dress.

The mischievous gleam in his eyes? The way his fingers twitched like he wanted to do it himself? Heavy doses of aphrodisiac being filtered through the air system?

Or maybe after my hot-and-cold run-in with Max Dread, I liked the steady current of electricity *this* stranger stirred up inside me.

Either way, I teased the black chiffon up my thigh to expose the garter hiding beneath it.

Soft gray turned to steel, his pupils dilating at the sight of my bare skin. His hand reached toward me, hovering an inch from the black silk as he lifted his eyes to mine.

I read the question there and answered it with a nod.

At my go ahead, his fingers edged along the band, stroking my outer thigh before sliding under the elastic. Following its path, I gasped when he grazed the back of my thigh and came dangerously close to slipping between my legs.

But before he could fully wrap his way around, he flexed his fingers and pulled his hand away.

The band snapped lightly, a sharp inhale hissing from my lips at the unexpected sting.

Eyes still locked on each other, tension pulsed between us. Electricity crackled in the air, desire sizzling like a live wire. And this sudden, pent up need thrummed through my body—so strong, it shocked me.

We'd only just met, and it felt like I'd been waiting for him to touch me forever.

"Do I know you?"

"Not yet." His hooded gaze dropped to my lips. "But I was right about you."

I arched my brow.

Before I voiced the question in my mind, he flashed another quick smile. "You'll see."

And then, he walked away, too.

"Damn. What the hell are they putting in the water here?" I muttered under my breath.

At this point, I worried raising my voice would spawn another ridiculously hot guy from the shadows. And while that didn't sound like the worst thing, so far both my strangers had left me cold and dry.

Well...not exactly dry. Definitely not.

But seriously. A girl deserved to be ridden hard if she was going to be put away wet. For fuck's sake.

Fortunately for my panties, no one else came out of the woodwork.

I stepped into the room, finally joining the party and going straight to the bar to order a glass of wine.

Then, I remembered where I was.

Switching the wine to an unopened can of hard seltzer, I watched the bartender pop the top and place it in front of me.

"Thanks." I took a sip to settle my nerves. "What do I owe you?"

His brow furrowed, and his lips twitched like I'd said something funny. "It's an open bar, sweetheart."

"Sweet." I shrugged and turned around, taking another sip and nearly spitting it out.

Sitting straight across the room—on a fucking throne, no less—the stranger with the spellbinding eyes surveyed the scene before him. And it didn't matter that I hadn't thought to ask his name because I already knew it.

Kingston D'Arthur, the King of Camelot Court, was right in front of me.

But the part that shocked me?

He *wasn't* the guy who covered the cost of my prescription. The one I'd credited with saving my ass and probably my life.

If I wanted to be dramatic about it.

No, that guy stood to the King's left.

His right-hand man—Landon Scott—the asshole from Gia's class, and my amber-eyed, breathtakingly beautiful savior from the pharmacy were all one and the same.

And he was staring right at me.

"Holy shit."

I came here planning to lose my virginity, but it turned out I might be totally fucked.

If I couldn't find a way around his plans for her, I wouldn't just hate him for it. I'd end him.

MAX DREAD

Quinn Everly.
    Her name had been imprinted on my brain since the moment I read her file.
Of course, I found a way to get my hands on it.

It held the application our lawful ruler had pointedly set aside. The prize our benevolent King had claimed for himself. The winner our aimless leader had chosen before the games even began.

Kingston played favorites when rank wasn't supposed to exist. He allowed frivolity when the Knights needed discipline. And he picked the girl he wanted to win while demanding the rest of us jump through his hoops.

Playing a game we only stood to lose.

Her picture had been removed from the folder, but at the time, I figured it didn't matter. What she looked like hadn't been important. Who she was hadn't been the point.

But now?

"Where have you been?"

A voice I despised pulled me from my glaring contest with Kingston's back. Since leaving Quinn by the door, I had been deeply engrossed in it. And I hated being interrupted, especially when I already knew what this was about.

"Vivian is looking for you."

I swiveled my gaze to the perpetual thorn in my side, failing to keep my tone level. "I'll see her tonight. Delayed gratification only heightens anticipation. Vivian should learn this if she wants to survive the next thirty days as my Maiden."

Nails dug into the muscle of my neck.

I winced at the sting—the familiarity of it, the intent behind it. It didn't hurt the way it used to, but the memory of razor-sharp claws digging into my softer flesh caused a deeper burn. It couldn't control me physically anymore, but it kept me in line.

"I'll find her."

"Good boy."

I growled as my keeper departed, striding across the room to survey the festivities. Always watching. I couldn't take a breath without feeling eyes on my back.

As if I didn't know the plan, or my part in it.

As if I hadn't been waiting for the chance to fuck up Kingston D'Arthur's day for years.

And now?

He'd given me one more reason to hate him.

Glancing around the room, I searched for my father and found him standing at Kingston's side, where I suspected he'd be most of the night. As advisor to the King, he lived to serve Camelot Court and prioritized it over everything else. I glared at them standing there together, talking quietly and sharing secrets.

My father was no doubt preparing him for the Maiden Selection, reminding him of the names and wiping his ass since Kingston couldn't take a shit without pulling my father in for guidance. Once he'd sufficiently coddled and held

Kingston's hand through it, he left the room.

Not even a *goodnight, son* or a nod in my direction on his way out.

Too busy for that.

I wondered if either of them knew how easy it had been—to get my hands on those files, to find out her name, and to lay the seeds of my plans in the ground at their feet.

Kingston rose from his throne. "Ladies, it's time to announce this year's Maidens."

He held his hand out for the scroll of names, his pronouncement hushing the onlookers and drawing their attention to the front of the room. A titter of laughter came from the crowd when his loyal right-hand man just stood there.

My eyes narrowed on Landon from across the room, my gaze sharpening when I realized why.

He was staring at her, too.

Kingston cleared his throat once. Then, twice. But Landon Scott didn't budge.

The White Knight's brow pulled in, emotions swirling over his features as he stared at her like a parched man in a desert, seeing a mirage in the distance and wondering if it was real.

Oh, she was real alright.

Quinn Everly had pain in her eyes and steel in her spine—things no other Maiden possessed because she came from an *uncharmed* life. Her innocence drew the eye while her weariness tugged at the heart. But it was the curiosity... the wonder in those big brown eyes that could captivate any poor soul.

When Kingston realized Landon was lost to him, he snatched the scroll away. That shook Landon out of his trance, averting his gaze to the floor, but the error had already been made. The torn expression on his face almost made me feel bad for the guy.

Almost.

Had he realized the girl he couldn't take his eyes off of was the Maiden he'd been asked to prepare for The Quest? Or how, for him, she was both real and a mirage? Did the White Knight know why the King had chosen her?

Whatever epiphany had frozen him in place, one thing was clear—Landon Scott knew he was *fucked*.

But with any luck, they both would be.

Kingston read the list of names, sparking bursts of excitement from the crowd. Happy cries of surprise went off like fireworks. Vivian created the biggest show, but I counted out the eleven dramatic displays before the time came for the finale.

"Quinn Everly."

I loathed the sound of her name on Kingston's lips. The way he smiled at her like they shared a private secret. And I couldn't stomach the way she stared back. Disgust bloomed inside my gut as her full lips parted to reveal an answering smile.

Silly girl.

She had no idea what she'd signed up for by joining The Quest. No idea what was coming, or the moves being made on the board around her.

But the look on Landon's face gave me pause...

Maybe none of us did.

One by one, a pledge came through the crowd and escorted the selected Maidens off to a private area. While the rest of the party said their goodbyes, the girls would be prepared for the next step. Only the Maidens and Knights would remain.

Tonight was our first chance to be alone, setting the tone for the first challenge and the expectations of a Maiden.

Tristan shook his head beside me. "This tradition is totally fucked."

But would any of them care when the prizes were laid out beautifully in front of them?

Ben huffed a laugh. "The Maidens certainly will be."

My jaw tightened.

How I'd ended up in the middle of this escaped me.

A Knight I didn't care to know by name chimed in. "Hey, the way I see it, no one came here tonight without a choice. They applied. They signed the contract and gave consent, right?"

My eyes narrowed on a flash of dark curls leaving the room.

"The girls have protection from anything truly... *untoward* happening to them." Ben smirked and nudged my shoulder. "Right?"

A growl of warning came from my throat. "Everyone except for her."

Quinn Everly knew the rules of the game as they'd been described to everyone else so far. She didn't know the plans the King had in store. And no one—not her, not me, and definitely not *him*—knew what would come from that look on Landon's face.

Ben glanced in the direction of the door, hunting for my meaning, but I didn't bother spelling it out. If he didn't know about *The King's Maiden* by now, he would soon enough.

The Quest had turned into a deeper, darker game the second he'd picked her from the pile. My plans had been made around that knowledge without ever laying eyes on her. Without seeing the reactions her presence in Camelot Court would cause, but all of that was about to unfold. And I couldn't say for sure if she would be the victor or a sacrificed pawn.

But the fallout for Camelot Court would come either way.

"Looks like it's time for the main event." Ben nodded to the center of the room, where Kingston stood with Landon. Talking at Landon, more accurately. "Let's get out of here before we all face backlash for the traitor's crimes, yeah?"

While they wandered off in search of drinks, my eyes fixed on my opponent.

I had a lifetime of secrets that made me want to defy the King—years of memories that made me curse Kingston D'Arthur's name. He'd already gotten everything, while setting himself up to take the rest.

And if I couldn't find a way around his plans for her, I wouldn't just hate him for it.

I'd end him.

"Does anyone else think it's weird that we keep calling him by his full name?"

Chapter Seven
Quinn

I expected it when he called my name. Once I saw him on the throne, his earlier comment made sense. Even if I didn't completely get *what* he'd been right about, my chances of finding out over the next thirty days were good.

But the list of things I expected ended there.

A guy dressed in gold spandex briefs approached me first, his exposed skin painted with a matching metallic body spray and a circlet of gold foil leaves on his head.

Unexpected event number one.

He held out his arm and waited until I took it, nodding at the King before leading me away from the party.

We entered a dark corridor lined with torches, and a chill ran down my spine. If the thought of whether The Quest was an elaborate ruse to murder young women hadn't occurred to me yet, that corridor would've been the moment for it.

I took in all the details I could. "Where are we going?"

"The dressing room. You'll meet the rest of the selected Maidens there to get ready before you'll all go to the Round Tableau."

I hadn't been expecting an answer.

Unexpected event number two.

"The Round Tableau?"

He puffed up his chest proudly. "Our version of the Round Table."

Having figured that much, I waited for him to tell me more.

He noticed my raised eyebrow and gave the same answer Kingston had. "You'll see."

Before I could press for more information, we reached a heavy wooden door flanked by two lit torches. A plaque with a gold rose adorned it. My escort pushed it open, standing aside to let me into the room.

Glancing behind me, I felt like Alice before she fell down the rabbit hole. On the other side of the door, a strange world waited. The golden and white room, alive with activity, sparkled against the empty and dimly lit corridor behind me.

Going through that door meant no turning back.

But the time for second thoughts had passed, so I crossed the threshold and went inside.

Eleven heads turned in my direction. The commotion in the room quieted. Everyone paused, their collective gaze passing over me.

And a second later, having assessed me as thoroughly as they needed, the noise and activity resumed. As if someone had pressed the play button on a remote control, their world spun on while I remained rooted in place. A blip in their regularly scheduled programming.

"You should get dressed." My escort, with his eyes on the floor, nodded in the general direction of an empty vanity and quickly left the room.

I walked over to the mirror marked with my name, running my hand over the garment bags on the rack beside it. They were labeled with cards like *Maiden Luncheon, First Party,* and *Knights' Quorum.* I found the one labeled *Round Tableau* and pulled it free, hanging it beside the mirror to unzip it.

Unexpected event number three.

"Oh, you've *got* to be kidding me."

The girl beside me laughed, propping her perfectly polished foot on the chair in front of her station. "What? You expected a nun's habit or something?" She pulled a sheer stocking up her leg, settling the lace trim around her upper thigh. "A college guy owns us for thirty days. Skimpy lingerie is part of the deal, right?"

"Right." I fingered the black bralette, rubbing the nylon meant to cover my nipple with the pad of my thumb. "Guess I figured they'd ease us into it."

"I fucking hope not." Fastening the strap of her black heels over stockinged foot, she stood at her full height and fluffed her blonde hair. Warm brown eyes met mine in the mirror. "Have you seen these guys? If I don't end this night with at least three orgasms, I'll be shocked."

She threw in a lascivious wink, adjusting her cleavage in her black bustier.

I chuckled, finding it hard to disagree with her logic after the two run-ins I'd had so far. They hadn't ended with orgasms, but they'd hardly been anticlimactic.

And my Knight *had* chosen me.

If our chemistry was as instantaneous as with those two strangers, maybe I'd walk away after thirty days with my debt cleared *and* my lady spank bank chock-full of spicy memories. That'd be ideal, attached as I was to the idea of avoiding committed relationships like the plague.

Assuming he wasn't Landon Scott, the guy who'd done a good deed in the King's name but sounded like a total dick, then it could be a sexual awakening to keep me satisfied for years to come.

A girl could dream, right?

I vowed to go into tonight with an open mind.

Glancing around, I removed the lingerie from its hanger. Confident no one was paying attention, I slipped my dress to my waist and turned my left side away from the room. I put on the bralette quickly and tugged it down.

The scar on my side was still red and angry, despite my doctor claiming the incision healed well. Maybe it always would be. I still felt raw and furious over the cause. It seemed only right that my scar would be, too.

Having to explain the required bits of my trauma that came with my scar to my Knight was one thing. A room full of perfectly unblemished females in sexy lingerie? No, thanks.

After swapping out my simple black thong for the lacy and very cheeky bikini panties included in the set, I covered myself with a black silk robe. Pulling on the sheer thigh high stockings next was easy, but the final piece, I wasn't sure what to do with it.

As I flipped it over and around, searching for a tag or some kind of instruction manual, the Maiden beside me took pity on me.

"Here." She laughed, taking the crumpled ball of fabric from me and turning my body toward the mirror. "It's a garter belt. My ex used to go crazy over them."

Dropping to her knee, she held it open at my feet and signaled for me to step into it. She pulled it up to my waist, spinning it around so the little buttons I'd been examining were at the back. Once she had it secured, she fastened the straps hanging from the belt to my stockings.

"Voila!"

My eyes widened at my reflection. While I'd never worn anything this risqué before, I looked sexy, and I felt it, too. I certainly saw the appeal.

"You look perfect." She smiled, patting my side before facing her mirror again.

I captured her elbow, turning her back to me. "Thank you."

She offered me a genuine smile. "Maidens should probably stick together, right?"

I had no idea, honestly, but it couldn't hurt, so I held out my hand. "Right. I'm Quinn."

"I'm Elaine."

When she sat back down to put the finishing touches on her makeup, I followed her lead. Other Maidens milled about near the door, and as I reapplied my lipstick, I couldn't help but watch them.

"Everyone seems so excited. Am I the only one who feels like they have no idea what they signed up for?" My grip tightened on the small tube of lipstick to keep my hand in front of me instead of reaching for my hair.

Elaine's head tilted as she blotted her lips. "You've been to Camelot Court parties before, right? Met the guys?"

"No, never."

Her eyes widened. "Oh! Well, yeah, in that case, I'm not surprised you're nervous." She glanced at my hands clutching the lipstick before nodding to the other girls. "Most of us know each other from boarding school. Or parties over the last few years. Hell, I could probably place bets on who some will end up with, just based on which Knight hit on them at the last party."

"Wait. Some girls know who their Knight will be?"

She shook her head. "No one finds out if they're selected before Kingston reads the list. But a few of the usuals with the obvious hots for each other ended up being paired. That's Izzy Gold." She pointed to a blonde girl with brilliant green eyes. "Five bucks says her Knight is Tristan Léon."

"Oh! The hot puppy." I nodded, pleased with myself for knowing who someone was. "My roommate told me about him."

Elaine laughed. "Oh my god. He really is like a hot puppy. Crazy loyal. But I was a little surprised she applied since she's supposed to be getting engaged to the Senator's son."

"Wait. Senator Cornwall was a part of Camelot Court?"

"Yep. And Mark, her fiancé, was a Knight two years ago when he was a junior. *After* their parents announced the match, Mark selected a Maiden for The Quest." Elaine lowered her voice. "It wasn't Izzy."

"Ugh." I eyed the girl in question from across the room. "So, what happened? They called it off when he graduated, and she decided to apply again?"

"I guess she decided to apply because he graduated. But as far as I've heard, their engagement is still happening."

My eyebrows rose. "And one of the Knights this year still picked her? Not that I disagree with it. But there's a bro code, right? Isn't the Knights' Code like that?"

"On steroids." She dropped her voice. "So, Tristan, or whoever picked her, has got it bad. Going against the Knights' Code for a girl?"

"A real life love story?"

She snorted. "Or a tragedy."

Izzy Gold fiddled with the ends of her blonde hair, eyeing her reflection in the mirror before smiling to herself. She looked happy and hopeful. Most of the other girls talked excitedly together while I bordered on the edge of anxiety—clearly the exception and not the rule.

I turned back to my mirror. I hadn't come here to find love, and maybe that made me the outlier in the group, but we could still find common ground.

At the very least, I shared their feelings on all the orgasms.

Grabbing a tissue off my vanity, I wiped a smudge of my lipstick. "Any other predictions?"

Elaine blotted her lips. "Tara said Gavin Wainscot made her cum on his tongue so hard she saw stars, and she didn't get a chance to return the favor."

"Ten bucks he picked her." I held out my hand, fighting a laugh. "Bet."

"No way!" She knocked her shoulder into mine. "I don't make bets I won't win. That's why I won't even wager a guess on who picked me."

"What do you mean?"

She bit her lip. "Well, there's definitely someone I *hope* picked me, but last I heard, he wasn't participating in The Quest. Except he was here tonight, so I don't know."

When she didn't give me a name, I prodded her with my shoulder. "I have no idea who anyone is, remember?"

Blushing, she tucked a strand of her blonde hair behind her ear. "You can't say anything. Especially if he doesn't pick me. I swear I'll either die of embarrassment or a broken heart."

I laughed. "Okay, dramatic. But yes, I swear. Now, spill it before they drag us out there."

"Landon Scott."

I didn't know exactly why, but a chill raced down my spine when she said his name. "Landon Scott?" I cleared my throat around the noticeable squawk. "The King's right-hand man, right?"

Elaine's face lit up. "Yes, I've had a thing for him for *ages* since our first year at Camelot Academy. I mean, dark and mysterious, but obviously gorgeous? I noticed him right away and the more I've seen him out—I don't know." She flushed, pausing to take a deep breath. "God, I must sound like such a dork. But there's just something about him."

"Do you think he picked you?"

Her mouth twisted into a frown. "I don't know. We've talked at parties, but never much past that. I don't even know if he knows my name."

My eyebrows shot up.

"Oh my god, I probably sound like a stalker." She laughed at herself. "But that's just how Landon is. People think he's standoffish and kind of abrupt, but he's just focused on the Knights and takes the code seriously. Sure, he comes off a little abrasive, but there's so much more to him." She groaned and buried her face in her hands. "Ugh. I don't know how to explain it."

"You don't have to explain it." I chewed on my lower lip. "He seems nice."

"Wait." Her eyes snapped to mine. "You've met him? Tell me everything."

I flinched back when she spun to face me, backpedaling and slightly thrown by her sudden intensity. "I didn't meet him. He just...helped me out once. Like a pay-it-forward moment, I guess."

She tilted her head, her nose wrinkling. "Like a charity thing?"

"Uh...Yeah, sure." I ran my hand over my scalp, searching beneath my curls for the familiar ridge of my scar. "I mean, we didn't even make eye contact, so I think he just did a good deed or whatever. That's all."

I shrugged and turned back to the mirror, grabbing a tissue to fix the lipstick I'd smudged. Peeking at Elaine's face in the mirror, my shoulders relaxed once hers did.

"That sounds like him. Doing the honorable thing." She smiled to herself, bouncing happily in her seat before finding my eyes in the mirror. "See. I told you there's more to him than meets the eye. Have you met anyone else?"

For whatever reason, I decided to keep my interaction with Kingston to myself. But I had no problem telling her about my other run-in. "I met Max Dread. He's a real peach."

Elaine snickered. "Oh, boy. Let me guess. He hit on you?"

"Yeah, but..." My brow dipped over the way he acted, but I shook my head, brushing off our brief spark and refusing to read into his behavior. "I take it that's his usual move?"

"Well, that depends." She zipped her makeup bag, acting totally casual despite the next question out of her mouth. "Did you go down on him in the nearest coat closet?"

"What? No!"

She cackled at the expression on my face. "Then, to answer your question, *that's* his usual move. But only if a girl comes up to him. They approach, he offers, and they say yes." She shrugged, as if that made perfect sense. "He must've been shocked when you turned him down."

"I didn't—I mean, he didn't offer." I flushed, tripping over my words at the image she put in my head. "Not that I would've said yes if he had. It wasn't like that. He came up to me and—"

"Wait. He what?"

"He came up to me and—"

"Quinn." Elaine stared at me like I'd grown a second head. "Max Dread doesn't approach anyone."

"What?" I exhaled a shaky laugh. "What do you mean, he doesn't approach anyone? He came up to me and—"

She put her hand on my arm and stopped me again. A quiet—completely unexpected—growl escaped me, my frustration mounting quickly alongside my confusion.

"I'm serious, Quinn. Max Dread is, like, this totally elusive creature at Camelot Court. He barely interacts with the other Knights. Only shows up if they're required to be somewhere. Girls go up to him when they don't know who he is, but he *never* approaches them first. He never approaches *anyone*."

"That's ridiculous." I put my hands on my hips, at this point sure she was pulling my leg, and I wasn't really up for any *hazing the newbie* schemes. "If he's some kind of recluse who hates people, why the heck is he even part of Camelot Court?"

"His family practically founded the Camelot Society. I mean, everyone knows the D'Arthurs were the original family, but the Dreads played a huge role. Merle, his father, is Kappa Rho's most prestigious alumni."

"Kappa Rho?"

"Kappa Rho Theta. It's the official fraternity charter, but

everyone usually says KRT or Camelot Court, and you know who they mean." Elaine waved off the topic and went back to Merle. "Anyway, Max's dad has been an advisor to each year's King since he graduated. And it was his great-great-grandfather who created The Quest!"

"Oh." I didn't know what else to say. "Um, well...I doubt it means anything that he came up to me then. I was standing in the doorway. Probably just blocking his exit."

"Please." She scoffed. "Like that would stop him if he wanted to leave. The guy's huge."

She had a point.

"Are you two talking about Max Dread?"

Blue eyes pinned me with an accusing stare. My brow lifted at the girl who stood behind us, her arms crossed over her chest. Her ivory skin and black hair made her eyes glint like sapphires in the mirror.

"Yes," I answered, darting my gaze between her and Elaine. "Also, does anyone else think it's weird that we keep calling him by his full name?"

Ignoring my question, the girl lifted her chin. "Stay away from him."

I bristled at the unexpected command, but before I could respond, Elaine beat me to it. Having only encountered warmth and kindness from her, the chill in her tone surprised me.

"Might be hard to do if he picked her as his Maiden, Vivian." Her cold glare matched Vivian's sharp gaze. "And we take our orders from the King. Not you."

Vivian responded with a derisive snort. "Please. As if Max would slum it with a charity case. Especially one that's a—"

I slapped my hand on the vanity, standing up and turning to face her. "I'm sorry, but do you know me?"

Vivian sneered down her nose at me, her red lips poised to respond. But I kept speaking before she could.

"Because I'm sure I don't know you well enough for you

to be making assumptions about me."

"Assumptions?" She scoffed. "I made it a point to know everything there was to know about the other applicants for The Quest. The best way to defeat an adversary is to know their weaknesses, after all." She lifted her shoulder, smiling placidly as some of the other girls turned their attention toward us. "You're Quinn Everly. A broke college student who dreams of being a dancer but can't get her lungs to cooperate. Not since your accident."

My spine straightened.

"Not since you got your only living parent killed."

A gasp sounded from Elaine, but I couldn't look at her. Nothing Vivian said surprised me. It was all true. She quoted it straight from the short bio I'd included on my application for The Quest. My only question was how she'd gotten it.

Vivian smirked. "Do you want to know who spilled all your dirty secrets to me?"

I said nothing. Vivian hummed like she was considering sharing the information with me. But I knew better.

"That's too bad." Her saccharine tone and sweet smile contradicted the venom in her eyes and the bite in her words. "It'll be so much more fun to watch you try and figure it out. Maybe it was the King. Our families are so close, after all. Or maybe it was *your* Knight."

She stepped toward me, forcing my back into the vanity. I gripped the edge for leverage as she leaned in, and her lips curled into a cruel smile. A sense of dread filled my chest when Vivian's eyes shot to Elaine.

Then, she struck us both.

"Landon Scott."

He trapped me with his impenetrable gaze, like a butterfly encased in resin—its wings pinned with no hope of escape.

Chapter Eight
Quinn

The Round Tableau was a large, circular space inside the building where the party had been held. It had a domed ceiling, making the open space in the middle of the room feel wider. Dim lighting and dark alcoves shrouded the antiquated cuffs and leather straps on the walls, but my eyes zeroed in on them as soon as we entered the room.

The space looked like it had been created with dark intentions. A place to act out the most torrid fantasies. Apart from where we entered, doors separated each alcove. Nestled into the brick all the way around, I didn't have to count them to know how many I'd find.

Twelve Knights. Twelve Maidens.

Twelve private rooms.

One by one, our escort led each Maiden to a closed door marked with a coat of arms. I didn't know enough about Arthurian lore to know who they represented, but others did. Izzy Gold blushed furiously when she was led to a door with a green banner, the golden lion leading me to believe it belonged to Tristan Léon.

Elaine had been right.

One by one, the girls were led around the room to their assigned doors. When Elaine was led to her Knight's door, it had a purple coat of arms with gold crosses. Her frown told me it didn't belong to Landon.

But as she stared longingly at the one next to it, bearing a white coat of arms with red stripes, she gave away its owner.

It also remained the only room without a Maiden.

Because it was meant for me.

Taking my place in front of it, I glanced at the closed door we came in through, with a royal blue coat of arms. Adorned with three crowns, I assumed that it belonged to King Arthur. It was the only door without a Maiden.

On the other side of it, my attention caught on the glare of an icier blue. Vivian's cruel smile made my stomach turn as she leaned back against her door, running her hand over the purple coat of arms behind her. She touched it reverently, almost lovingly, while holding my gaze, and I assumed it belonged to the Knight she'd warned me to stay away from— Max Dread.

Her door and mine flanked the King, an appropriate nod to the rivalry we'd quickly established. Vivian had singled herself out as my biggest threat. She'd thrown down a challenge when she spilled my secrets and commanded me like a Queen.

But I had no intention of letting her beat me.

"You'll wait here until your Knights arrive," our escort informed us before exiting the room.

He left us in silence, but it didn't take long for the whispers to start. A Maiden named Inez had been picked by Gerard Saint, and everyone agreed he'd wanted her for a while, always hanging around her at Camelot Court parties. The girl who saw stars, Tara, had been paired with Gavin Wainscot.

Well, damn.

If Elaine had taken the bet, I would've won ten bucks.

Most of the girls looked pleased, or at least not unhappy, about their Knights. The consensus seemed to be that getting selected as a Maiden was an honor. Only Elaine had disappointment on her face.

But I overheard the girl next to her say that Peter Valencourt wasn't the worst Knight to end up with, if she couldn't have the one she wanted.

At that, Elaine's eyes darted to me.

"You probably lucked out," her friend said. "I hear Landon has some serious kinks."

Elaine laughed. "From who?"

"Some girl in my English Lit class raved about him."

"Yeah, right." Elaine rolled her eyes. "The guy doesn't date, and I've never seen him leave a party with anyone. That girl was just starting rumors. You know how people outside Camelot Court are about the Knights."

The other Maiden's face grew more serious. "She said her old roommate introduced them. The Maiden last year, who—"

She lowered her voice, her eyes glancing around the room as she finished her sentence. I strained to catch the last part of what she said but couldn't hear it.

"Oh my god." Elaine gasped. "That was so sad. I heard about it last year, but I had no idea he was involved."

My heart hammered in my chest, curiosity warring with my desire to stay detached. I didn't want to know more details. I didn't need to care one way or another to win The Quest.

But I also couldn't tune them out.

"Her younger sister, Evie, applied to be a Maiden this year, but no one picked her. Can't help but wonder if everyone thought she was out for revenge."

The rest of the chatter in the room died down. All the Maidens had their eyes on the gossipers. A few of them skirted to me before hastily darting away.

Apprehension churned in my belly, my heart racing

like I'd danced for hours. I glanced at the door marked for the King, wondering if I could leave quickly. Get out before anyone caught me.

But I didn't get the chance to try.

Three knocks rang out from the other side.

Everyone jumped, laughing quietly to relieve their nerves as the door swung open. I couldn't force a laugh even if I'd tried. Panic wrapped a hand around my throat, squeezing tightly when my eyes fell on the first Knight to walk through the door.

Landon Scott stared down at me with no trace of recognition or kindness in his eyes.

The warm amber hue should've been inviting, soothing in the way it reminded me of honey. Instead, he trapped me with his impenetrable gaze, like a butterfly encased in resin—its wings pinned with no hope of escape.

"Move," he commanded.

But I was too stunned to do anything but stare. My lungs ached as my breathing grew tighter, taking in every inch of the Knight in front of me. In his fitted black pants and dress shirt, he appeared every bit as dark as the rumors about him. The glower on his face didn't help.

Realizing I had no intention of following his order, he stepped forward. So close, I felt the crisp rush of his breath on my cheek. The scent of mint, followed by the barest hint of rosemary and lavender, filled my nose.

He pitched his voice low. "I gave you an order, Maiden."

His eyes searched my face. For what, I didn't know. Understanding, acknowledgement, or maybe he hoped to find obedience reflecting back at him. But I couldn't submit to him. Not when all I could think about was the air I needed.

Huffing what I took to be his annoyance, his eyes narrowed, and his hand dipped into his pocket before he brought it to my waist. My chest grew tighter when his fingers squeezed my side, his touch sending a wave of goosebumps rippling over my skin. He bunched the fabric of my robe in his fist before releasing me.

He slipped his hand past me to the door, and the unmistakable turn of a key in a lock followed. A rush of cold air hit my back as he swung open the door. But the draft was nothing compared to the chill his next order caused.

"Turn around and get inside." His rough whisper rumbled in my ear. "Or I'll throw you over my shoulder and bring you in there myself."

As he pulled back, I snapped my gaze to his. A soft wheeze escaped my throat, but I didn't argue. I bent to pick up my bag and hurried inside.

Searching the room, I tried to figure out where I could use my inhaler without showing my weakness. But it was too dark inside, even with the door open.

I fell into pitch-black darkness when it slammed shut.

Although I expected him to come behind me when the door closed, nothing came. He'd left me alone.

Scrambling through my bag, I found my inhaler. I delivered a puff and inhaled deeply, holding my breath for a count of ten. After a second puff, the tightness in my chest began to ease.

Slowly, my breathing steadied.

As the door opened, streaming light into the room, I shoved the inhaler in my bag.

Two heavy footsteps crossed the threshold.

When the door shut, I plunged into darkness again. But now, I wasn't alone. Landon stood behind me in the dark, every inch of his body welding to mine.

My hands clenched around my bag, but now that I could breathe, something other than fear coursed through me.

His voice rumbled softly in my ear. "Take off your robe and get on the bed."

Swallowing past my fear, I turned toward his voice and

found my own. "I can't see anything."

"You don't need to see." He gripped my upper arms, holding me steady as my body shook. *"Feel."*

But all I felt was him.

The roughness of his palms despite his gentle grip. The tremor running through his body as it pressed into mine. And the strain of his cock against my lower back, growing harder with every second he held me close.

"Move, Quinn." Pressing me forward by the arms, he created space between our lower bodies. His palms slid up and over my shoulders, his fingers slipping under the edge of my robe, tracing a gentle pattern over my collarbone. "Go on."

I stepped forward, relishing the slip of silk over my skin as the robe fell from my body. He let it drop and sucked in a tight breath, as if just the awareness of my nearly naked body affected him.

My core clenched in response.

Groping my way through the dark, my hand found the bedpost. I clung to it, needing a minute to settle my nerves. I'd been ready for this. I wanted it.

But the reality made my head spin.

He came up behind me. "As you were told, Maiden."

His gentle prod held a note of promise. A reminder of what awaited me for the next thirty days. He would give the commands, and I would follow them.

This was what I'd signed up for, wasn't it?

And so far, nothing he'd done—only what I'd heard about him—had given me pause.

Maybe it wasn't smart. Maybe my therapist would have a fucking field day about how I ignored all the literal and figurative red flags waving in my face when this was over. But at that moment, I wanted to jump headfirst into this and enjoy the anticipation. I didn't want to sink deeper into apprehension. Not over gossip.

I wanted—no, I *needed*—to keep going, instead of letting doubt stop me from moving forward.

The good thing was, I barely had time to think past that first wave of hesitation. With him pressing in at my back, I had no desire to disobey his order.

All I could do was feel.

Placing one knee on the mattress, I climbed onto it. I crawled to the center as Landon moved to the foot of the bed. A rustle of fabric came from the wall to my left, and moonlight streamed in through a thin glass pane near the ceiling, lighting the bed with me in it.

I peeked at him over my shoulder, a little unsure of what to do next. And the way he stared at me sent a shiver of desire down my spine. It also reminded me I was still on all fours, practically serving myself to him on a fucking platter.

But I had to admit, I didn't hate that thought.

"What do you want me to do now?"

His eyes, a honeyed hue in the Round Tableau, darkened to the color of clove as his pupils dilated. Hands balling into fists at his side, he ran his gaze from the tip of my heels up my thighs and over the curve of my ass. His lips parted as he drank in the sight of me, in no hurry to give further direction.

Emboldened by the way his tongue darted out to wet his lips, I couldn't help myself. I arched my back.

He groaned, his eyes flying to mine as he cut off the sound.

We both froze, my heartbeat fluttering like the flap of a butterfly's wings inside my chest as I sensed a change rippling through the space between us. What had felt like a wave of desire building slowly now felt like a tsunami clearing everything in its path.

He blinked away the haze of lust in his eyes, his next command cracking like a whip through the quiet room. "Lie on the bed."

It snapped again when I moved to turn over onto my back. "No."

I searched his face for an explanation. Something to explain the change in his demeanor. But his shuttered gaze gave away nothing. He simply stepped to the edge of the bed and bent his knee on the mattress.

A tendril of fear unfurled inside me when he reached for his belt and unbuckled it.

"Face down, Maiden," he ordered. "Now."

It was like my status of *Not Penetrated* had just been stamped on my forehead and it explained everything.

Chapter Nine
Quinn

I froze, torn between running from the room and finding out what he'd do if I obeyed.

Curiosity overruled my fear.

Sinking down slowly onto the mattress, I couldn't hide the way my body trembled. Or the way I jumped at his touch.

He grabbed my ankle and tugged me back toward him on the bed, his thumb stroking along the curve of my ankle bone. "Do you remember the safe words from your contract?"

"Y-yes."

"Tell me."

"I..." Wracking my brain for the words I had all but tattooed on it, I struggled to wade through the haze of desire overwhelming me. A hint of fear lingered as well, as the words grew harder and harder to pull from the fog. My breathing quickened. "I know them."

"I know you do."

He traced circles over my skin, his tone shifting effortlessly from demanding to soothing. But the gentle strokes of his fingers only aroused me further, and I couldn't focus on the patterns he drew any more than I could siphon one clear thought in my mind.

"I need to hear you say them, and you'll need to know that I heard them." He stroked up and down my leg. "So, you know you're safe."

Dragging his fingers along my calf, he pressed down into the muscle.

I groaned. "I can't think while you're doing that."

His touch danced higher, the mattress shifting beneath me as he settled his weight above me. He brushed the skin of my inner thigh, and I buried my face in the mattress to stifle a moan. I only came up for air when his touch retreated, and his palm stroked the hair back from my face.

My eyes closed.

He braced his forearm on the bed, hovering over my right side as his hand made its way between my legs again. This time, he drew closer to my center, inching toward the apex of my thighs as if he was trying to drive me insane. My heart raced when I felt that first graze over my core. Featherlight and fleeting.

I whimpered.

Trying to hide my face, my moan morphed into a cry of surprise. My hair was pinned under his arm—*he* had pinned it—and he refused to let me hide.

"If you can't think when I'm touching your ankle..." His fingers skated the line of my panties. "How will you be able to tell me what you need when I'm doing this, Maiden?"

Desire pooled between my thighs. And I moaned, lifting my hips off the bed. Seeking out his touch. Wanting more. Needing it, when he drew his hand away.

A growl of frustration burst out of me, and again, I struggled to turn my head. But he kept me trapped beneath him. A position I didn't mind as long as he kept touching me.

But he wouldn't budge.

"I don't remember." I wriggled on the bed, rubbing my

thighs together to create friction. "Landon, *please.*"

He dropped his knee between my legs and forced them apart.

But he still didn't touch me, even though he prevented me from taking care of things myself. He had no idea how quickly he'd worked up my body, how starved it had been for this kind of touch, or how every second without it felt like the most exquisite kind of torture.

I squeezed my thighs around his.

His other knee joined the first, spreading me farther.

"What does it matter?" I growled. *"Clearly,* I don't want you to stop right now."

He slapped my ass, making me yelp. The sting of his palm throbbed on my barely covered cheek and pulsed between my legs. Before I could react, he slapped the other.

"Oh, fuck!" I cried out. "Okay, okay. You're right!"

"What do you say if you want me to stop?"

Pain heightened my panic and sharpened my mind.

"I yield," I rushed out. "Landon, I yield."

"Good girl," he whispered.

His weight disappeared.

Free to turn my head, I glared at him where he sat at the end of the bed. Resting back on his heels, he watched me carefully as a dizzying storm of confusion, anger, and lust raged inside me.

"What the hell was that?"

"That was only the beginning, Maiden." His head tilted as he assessed my reaction, palms sliding down his thighs as he leaned forward and got closer. "You need to give me your safe word every time we enter this room. Do you understand? Next time, I won't coax it out of you. I'll leave."

"Coax it out of me?" I shot back. "Is that what you call that?"

He sat back, affronted.

"It felt more like you spanked it out, if you ask me."

His eyes narrowed. "And *that* is exactly why you have a

safe word, and why *I* need to hear you say it at the start." He shook his head. "I didn't force you to sign up for The Quest, Quinn. No one did. You applied to be a Maiden knowing what it meant, right?"

Fuming, I nodded.

"And you have my word and the King's that nothing will happen in here that you don't want. I will push you. I will test what you think you can handle. But I won't force you to do a thing." He broke our stare, glowering at the door. "The only one here without a choice is me."

"What do you mean?"

He snapped his gaze to mine, eyes wide as he realized what had slipped out of him.

For someone who seemed like a grade-A control freak, I imagined that didn't happen often.

"Nothing." Climbing off the bed, his fingers moved to the buttons on his shirt. "Now, do you want to continue, or do you want to call it quits?"

I stared up at him, trying to read behind the lines in his expression. My silence only deepened his frown.

He did up the buttons on his shirt quickly, dropping his hands to his belt and walking to the door. His hand landed on the doorknob and jarred me out of my silence.

"No, wait!"

Scrambling into a seated position, I knelt on the bed the way he had. I sat back on my heels, running my fingers through my hair as I tried to find the words I wanted to say. I threw my hands in the air when the words wouldn't come and dropped my open palms to my thighs.

"Just wait. Please."

Landon turned back, his eyes lingering over my posture. His nostrils flared, and he stepped toward me. "Tell me."

I hesitated, holding back the truth and wondering if I could really go through with this. My teeth sank into my lower lip, gnawing at the tender flesh as indecision ate me up inside.

His eyes fixed on my mouth, and they darkened as he came close enough to reach out and touch me. "Tell me."

"I need to do this."

The admission weighed heavily on my tongue, pressing down with all the responsibility left on my shoulders. At that moment, I missed my dad more than ever, and I hated that he was gone. I hated what he might think of me if I went through with this—a thought only made worse when the truth hit me.

He couldn't think about it at all.

And it killed me every single day because it was my fault.

Dead parents—even the best ones—couldn't be a guiding light anymore. I never realized how much I had relied on mine, not as distinctly as I did right then, fumbling my way through this in the dark. I had been lost ever since that night on the mountain road, like I'd never find my way again. Every step I took left me wondering if I was on the right path, and to this day, I still didn't know.

But all I could do was keep going—keep moving forward, keep feeling. Keep my eyes on the Knight in front of me and hope that he'd see me through this.

Freeing my bottom lip with his thumb, Landon's eyes locked on my parted mouth. He tilted his head and searched my features for everything I wanted to hide. "What are you afraid of?"

My eyes dropped to the floor.

His finger tipped my chin, lifting my head until I looked him in the eye. "Tell me."

I swallowed past the lump in my throat. "I'm scared of what it says about me if I do this. That I couldn't find another way. Couldn't survive without resorting to something like this. I feel like I just walked into a fucking viper's nest. Everyone

I've met—" Threading my fingers through my hair, I sought out my scar. "I'm scared of who I'll be if I go through with it."

Landon captured my wrist with his free hand and eased it away, circling his thumb over my pulse. It thrummed like a hummingbird's wings.

My eyes dropped to his lips.

And a darker truth coiled inside me. A truth I needed to control if I intended to set it free. A truth prepared to bite me in the ass if I wasn't careful. But even knowing I could regret this, I let the truth out.

"Mostly, I'm scared of how much I want it. I...I don't know anything about you. Or this place or The Quest. Not really. But still, I..." I tried to look away, but his hold on my chin wouldn't let me turn my head.

Landon didn't want me to hide. He wouldn't let me.

That scared me, too.

"I want to do this." I reached for him, sliding my fingers through the belt loops in his pants and using them to pull him closer. "And I want to do it with you. If you'll show me how."

Pressing our bodies together, I took a deep breath and closed my eyes.

The air rushed out of me when he banded his arm around my waist and held me there. His cock hardened against my lower belly. "What do you say if you want me to stop?"

"I yield," I responded instantly.

"And if you want me to slow down?"

"Mercy." My eyes opened to find him staring down at me, his gaze like a flare of amber light in the darkness. "I ask for Mercy."

He nodded, releasing my waist and nudging my hip gently. "Lie back on the bed."

My voice trembled and my knees suddenly felt weak. "Face down?"

"No." He shook his head. "I want to see you. I want..."

Brushing a hand over my cheek, his eyes drank in my features in a way that made my chest ache. "But there are rules we have to follow."

"Rules?"

"Mmhm." He threaded his fingers into my hair, tugging lightly on the strands.

I groaned and let my head fall back. He'd somehow managed to pull on the hair right by my scar, and the damaged nerve endings lit up, sending a rush of tingles down to my toes. He had no idea how good that felt.

How much I hated that it did.

Or how much it reminded me why I needed to do this.

But his touch drowned out the guilt, allowing me to take in the pleasure. "Okay. Yeah. Rules...I agree."

His soft chuckle in my ear pulled me out of the trance I'd fallen into, snapping my eyes open. The hint of a smile on his face, the way his lips twitched as he tried to hide it.

I was so fucking screwed.

It made me wonder if this was how it was supposed to be. If it was always supposed to feel like this. One look—one touch—and I wanted to lie back and let him in completely.

I'd never felt that before. Not even once with my ex. And I had started to wonder if I even could feel it. If the part of me that was meant to be wild, the part of me that could crave another person so hard and so quickly, was just defective. Now, it felt like maybe I hadn't been broken.

"Broken?"

I blinked. "Huh?"

Landon withdrew the hypnotic tangle of his fingers in my hair to cup my neck and tilt my head up. "You just mumbled something about being broken."

Oh, fuck.

"Oh. Nothing. I just...My ex popped into my head and I—"

He pulled back. "Your ex?"

"Yeah, he was a total tool. Anyway, we would—"

"You're thinking about your ex while I've got my cock wedged against your stomach?"

"Um..." I pressed my lips together.

He huffed a laugh and grabbed my hips. "Yeah, that won't do."

Lifting me by the waist, he tossed me onto the bed. I shrieked as I hit the mattress. And again when he pounced on top of me.

"You can learn the rules as we go. Right, Maiden?"

He didn't give me a chance to respond. As soon as a laugh burst out from my throat, it died on my tongue. The exact moment *his* stroked a path up my neck.

He licked his way to the sensitive spot behind my ear, sucking on my skin as he settled his body between my legs.

My knees fell to the side, opening my hips to let his press forward. The first rock of his erection against my core pushed every errant and insignificant thought out of my head. The only thing that existed was this—him and me—and the need rising between us.

The need to know what he would feel like inside me. The need for more. And the need for him to take what I so desperately wanted to give.

Not because I wanted to get it over with.

But for the first time, because I couldn't wait.

I lifted my hips to meet every gentle rock of his. My legs tightened around him. Moaning each time his cock grazed over my clit. Whimpering when he pulled back.

Until he slowly repeated the process again.

Over and over, he drove his body into mine.

He never stopped working me up with his mouth, greedily nipping and sucking at my neck, my collarbone, and even the swell of my breasts. Running his hands up my sides, down my arms, he slithered his palm between our bodies and into the waistline of my panties.

I bit my lip to keep from crying out. But the second he cupped my sex, my eyes rolled back, and a drawn out moan filled the room. When he slipped one finger inside me, a deeper groan followed.

I didn't know if it came from me or him.

"Fuck." He panted as my walls clenched around him. "You're so wet. So fucking tight."

"Landon—" I gasped, writhing on the bed.

His face hovered an inch from mine, taking in my reactions to adjust the pace of his hand. He gently worked his finger in and out, easing deeper before each slow withdrawal and coaxing my body to relax.

My legs fell away from his hips as I let him in more.

"Landon, I—" When he slowly added a second finger, my eyes widened at the stretch. "Kiss me." I begged. "Please, I—"

He shook his head, pulling away abruptly to bury his face in my neck. Easing back down to one finger, he slowed his thrusts.

"That's rule one," he said gruffly.

I whined, both at his refusal and the way he circled his thumb over my clit.

"I plan to kiss every inch of your body. I'll do it over and over until you scream." He sucked deeply over the beat of my heart in my throat. "But not on the mouth."

"Wha—" I cried out as he increased the pressure of his thumb, rubbing with tight quick strokes over my clit.

"No exceptions, Maiden." His ministrations stopped and he withdrew his finger. "If we're going to do this, there have to be rules."

I groaned and wriggled on the bed underneath him. My mind begged me to ask more questions, but even as my heart—that bitch who wasn't even supposed to be involved—protested the lack of intimacy, my pussy throbbed with need. That ho was resolutely against the idea of arguing semantics at a time like this. And my mouth agreed.

"Fine." I huffed. "No kissing. Not exactly how I pictured my first time, but fuck it. Let's do this."

He recoiled. Eyes wide, they jumped between mine as he hunted for my meaning. He opened his mouth to ask a question that never came.

Thrown off by his sudden retreat, I frowned. "I'm not a nun or anything. I mean, I fooled around with my ex in the past, but we never...We were going to, but—" My fingers found my scar, tugging on the strands of hair around it. Shame and guilt rushed through me, and I blurted out the truth. "Fuck. I chickened out, okay?"

He stared at me for a long time before he finally spoke, stating plainly, "You've never had sex before."

But something in the way he looked at me felt different, realization or understanding registering. It was like my status of *Not Penetrated* had just been stamped on my forehead and it explained everything. But I didn't know what that was.

"You're telling me you're a virgin?"

Groaning internally, I muttered. "Yes, that's typically the word for it."

He stared at me, a muscle in his jaw tightening as he worked through whatever was going through his head, his eyes starkly shifting from arousal to anger. Betrayal flickered in his expression. Suspicion creased the line of his brow. And rage tightened his hands into fists where he clenched them at his sides and far away from my body.

A torrent of dark emotions rained down on me with all of Landon's intensity, and he echoed the words I'd heard earlier but still didn't understand.

"You're here for the King."

A guy didn't just barge into a room saying *Touch Her and Die* unless he fucking meant it.

Chapter Ten
Quinn

Given that my ex had been practically obsessed with my virginity, always saying how awesome it would be when we finally had sex, I had to admit I expected Landon to react differently.

But then again, my ex's reaction had been sort of cringeworthy. And a contributing factor to why I hadn't gone through with it, besides not feeling with him even an ounce of what I'd felt tonight. At the time, I just thought every guy felt that way about virgins.

Apparently, some guys didn't share the same fascination with it. Maybe they didn't all see it as a prize. Maybe my ex's implication that our first time together would be less amazing if I'd slept with other people had been a giant red flag, and a lack of fascination was the norm.

I hadn't expected the anger, though, or the betrayal on Landon's face. And I definitely hadn't expected him to say what Max had said earlier.

"What does that mean?" I pushed up to kneel on the bed, noting the way he stepped back as I got closer. "Max said that earlier, too. But I don't understand."

Landon stopped his retreat, his eyes narrowing on me. "You were talking to Max Dread tonight?"

"Okay, seriously. You too? Does everyone call him by his full name?"

"Answer the question, Quinn."

The hair on the back of my neck rose. Something about hearing him call me by my name...Not to say it thrilled me to be called Maiden, but hearing it now, it didn't sit right.

"Why does it matter?" I hedged carefully. "Am I not allowed to talk to the other Knights? Because if so, I didn't know that either."

"Did he tell you to say you're a virgin? To put that on your application so we'd pick you?"

"What? What do you mean?"

He crowded my space, towering over where I knelt on the bed. "You expect me to believe that you applied to be a Maiden knowing what it involved when you've never had sex before?"

"I—I don't—It doesn't matter to me what you believe, Landon." I shuffled back on my knees. But I couldn't get far, and when Landon followed me, I lost my balance. Falling backward, my hands braced my body on the bed. Landon planted his fists beside me, cutting off my escape.

"I don't know what you're doing right now, but I don't like it." I leaned back farther. "And I seriously have no idea what you're talking about. No one told me to put that on my application. I put it because it's the truth."

He scoffed and dropped his head, so he was right in my face. "You're lying."

"And you're insane!" I shot back, working my legs out from under me. "What do you want, physical proof? A gynecologist to verify my hymen is intact? Blood on the sheets?"

No longer kneeling, I dug my heels into the mattress and scooted back. Landon's gaze flicked down between my legs, like he might actually be considering that as a real offer.

"What the actual fuck?" I shrieked, snapping his eyes back to my face.

I scrambled back farther on the bed. Letting my back fall onto the mattress, I drew my knees to my chest. Before he could react, I planted my heels on his stomach and kicked my legs out as hard as I could.

He grunted, recoiling from the kick and stumbling back off the mattress. I seized the opportunity and shot for the foot of the bed. I almost made it over the side when he caught hold of my leg. He dodged my kick at him and didn't loosen his grip. Yanking me toward him, the quick jerk of my legs knocked my arms out from beneath me.

My chest hit the mattress, forcing the breath from my lungs. Landon gripped my upper body and flipped me onto my back. Before I could get in another kick, he climbed on top of me, straddling my hips.

He braced most of his weight on his knees, but I still couldn't get out from under him. I swiped at his chest, hoping to claw my way free. With one hand, he pinned my wrists above my head.

I bucked my hips and tried to throw him off.

Shifting his weight back, he hooked his feet over my legs so I couldn't use them to force him off. He stretched the full length of his body over mine, sinking down and pressing me into the mattress. I hated the way my traitorous body noticed how good it felt—how my alarm evenly matched my arousal the second I felt his cock against my pubic bone.

"Let me go, Landon," I all but growled in his face.

He didn't budge. "Tell me the truth, Quinn."

His grip tightened on my wrist, and while his voice rose with his demand, he didn't shout. He was completely unmoved by my reaction—scarily in control.

Suddenly, his weight felt heavier. My awareness of how it pressed on my chest sharpened painfully, and tears pricked my eyes. I started to panic. My lungs cried out for deep breaths I couldn't take as a tear escaped and slid down my cheek.

Wheezing past the tightness in my chest, I shouted, "I yield!"

Landon immediately let me go.

He climbed off me, almost falling as he sprang from the bed. His eyes widened as he stared between me and his outstretched hand. The one that had been holding my wrists.

Blinking rapidly, he stumbled backward towards the door.

I pushed myself up, panting hard and watching as his back hit the door. Slamming against it seemed to jar him out of his shock. He pushed the hair back from his eyes and met mine one more time.

"I'm sorry," he said.

And then, he was gone.

The door ricocheted off the wall and slammed shut behind him.

I lay on the bed, breathing hard and staring at the closed door. Like he might burst through it in the next second and tell me *what the actual fuck* just happened. So, we could get back to the part where things had been going really fucking well.

But he didn't.

And the longer I sat there alone, the heavier the weight of his reaction grew.

I needed to get the fuck out of there.

Except when my hand wrapped around the doorknob, twisting as hard as I could, nothing happened. A slightly manic laugh escaped me, my hand running through my hair more than once to ease the insidious feeling creeping up my body, but it wrapped around my throat, anyway.

It squeezed, and my hand jerked the doorknob, rattling it over and over.

I tried again and again.

No. There was no way he'd locked me in here. This was—I was imagining this. I was trapped in a fucking nightmare.

My heart thrashed in my chest while I beat on the door. "Let me out! Please, somebody! Let me out!"

I couldn't breathe.

A low, pained moan came out as I sank to my knees. For a second, I thought I heard the slow creak of another door. I thought I heard footsteps, but as quickly as they sounded outside my room, they retreated and disappeared. My mouth opened to call out, but the cry lodged in my throat.

I dug through my clutch.

My inhaler—I needed my inhaler.

When my lungs finally expanded, I yelled the only thing in my mind.

"I yield!" I sobbed, dragging in another deep breath as I dropped my head to the floor. "I yield. Please! I yield."

This time, I didn't lift my head at the sound of footsteps— sure they would disappear. But the doorknob rattled, and a key turned in the lock. I pushed up onto shaking arms, waiting to see who was on the other side.

The furious voice booming through the wood was the last one I expected.

"Touch her again and you're dead, Golden Boy."

I scoot-crawled backwards to make space as an angry and shirtless Max Dread eased open the door. He didn't even look at me before shouting into the dark room.

"Where the fuck are you, Landon?"

I sat curled up on the ground beneath his feet. Still wearing my lingerie with tears streaming down my face, I seriously ate my words from earlier. He could've rubbed it in my face, but instead, he lifted me off the floor.

Hauling me up and into his arms, his voice was a dark, low growl. "Where is he?"

"He's not here." My body trembled in his hold, but that

only made him pull me tighter against his chest. "He left. I—I don't—"

His eye twitched, fingers flexing and digging into my skin. "Did he lock you in here?"

My whole face screwed up as pain, embarrassment, confusion, and anger coursed through me. I tucked my chin into my chest, hiding my face from him. But I kept the maelstrom of emotions at bay and thought through the way Landon had fled from the room.

The door had swung shut behind him—it hit the wall.

I managed to draw in a shaky breath. "I don't think so. He just left all of a sudden and I...I think it locked behind him."

Lifting my head, I searched his face. I didn't want him to use the truth against me. But I couldn't stir up shit between him and Landon when it wasn't warranted.

I looked away. "I panicked."

"Of course, you fucking panicked," he snapped, drawing my eyes back up. "We have a code for a reason, and that piece of shit knows it." His jaw clenched when my body shuddered, and he dragged in a breath, his nostrils flaring. "But you're safe now. You're not trapped."

My head turned into him, one hand resting on his chest. Dangerously close to where his heart felt like it might beat right through the solid wall of muscle separating us. I didn't know what to make of that, but I liked the way it felt.

He dragged in another deep breath, and his heartbeat slowed. My body relaxed against him, the adrenaline fading.

"Thank you," I breathed softly against his chest. "Thank you for coming to help me."

"I—"

His muscles tightened under my hand.

It wasn't exactly the best time to flex, but I supposed he couldn't help it.

"What the fuck is this?"

Vivian's shrill voice came from the door, snapping my head up. She narrowed her eyes on Max's face before glaring daggers at me—the half-naked girl in his arms.

Oh, fuck.

Her complexion paled like white-hot heat, but that ice in her voice I already recognized.

"I'm getting your father."

As soon as she spun on her heel and left the room, her parting statement hung in the silence of the room. It weighed on his face whether he realized it or not. He stared after the door where she'd disappeared.

This night had been a cluster fuck of confusion and fear. I still didn't know what to make of what happened with Landon, but I couldn't even think about that right now. Not while Max had me in his arms, holding me like I was his to protect.

What I'd felt between us earlier tonight, in those brief moments before his one-eighty, returned full-force. I reached up slowly and touched his face, drawing his eyes back to mine.

My fingers traced the line of his jaw. "Why would she get your father?"

His eyelids fluttered under the touch of my hand, eyes softening with that light I'd seen inside him earlier. But it quickly cleared, and he snapped back to the colder, shrouded version of him as realization dawned on his face.

Glancing sharply between the door and me in his arms, he spun suddenly, taking me with him. Before I could even get my bearings, he set me on the bed. He stood over me, his gaze hooded and his upper body so ridiculously, gloriously bare, I wanted to trace a path over every sculpted plane of his chest.

That was all I could think about as I stared up at him— how it would feel to memorize each defined muscle. First, with my hands and then with my tongue.

I also wanted to know what the fuck it was about this place that turned me into a wanton hussy, wanting to jump the bones of every hot guy I met even in the midst of a crisis.

Or at least three of the guys.

He stood frozen above me. Ice splintered through his gaze as he stared down at me, and I flushed at the thoughts that had run through my head.

Clearly, Max *wasn't* about to make the start of those fantasies a reality.

"My father oversees The Quest. That's why my Maiden went to get him. He'll need to know you had an issue with your Knight."

His clipped tone hit harder than I expected, and even if I didn't want him as *my* Knight, I wrinkled my nose when he called her *his Maiden*.

"It'll be up to him to bring this to the King and decide if you'll continue to participate."

My head jerked back so I could see him fully. "Wait, what? But I didn't do anything," I stumbled, flustered by the unfairness of it. "Why would they kick me out because he—"

"It doesn't matter what you did or didn't do, Princess." He shook his head, unflinching in his delivery and the derision in his tone. "Not here. It only matters if you can please your Knight. For anyone who cares, from where they're sitting, you sent yours running within the first hour."

He flicked his tongue against the back of his teeth, the harsh *tsk* shaming me for failing so soon. It rushed through me so quickly, my eyes watered. I dropped my head, hoping he wouldn't see.

Unlike Landon, he didn't stop me from hiding.

What he did was worse.

He scoffed. "If you're going to cry about it, you really shouldn't be here."

My head shot up, jaw dropping at another complete one-eighty in his behavior. It *really* shouldn't have surprised me that time. But every trace of sympathy and comfort he'd offered when he burst into the room had been fully withdrawn. I couldn't reconcile the difference.

Unless...none of his reactions earlier had been about me.

Had all of it really been about Landon and what Max thought my Knight had done?

Had he ever read a romance novel in his life? Or seen enough movies to know a guy didn't just barge into a room saying, *Touch Her and Die* unless he fucking meant it?

Apparently, the answer was a resounding *no*.

He crossed his arms over his chest, raising an eyebrow. "So, he locked you in a room. That's what you're upset about?"

"But—"

His muscles bunched beneath his forearms as he lifted his shoulders. "What happens if it gets worse than that, huh? You cry for your mommy and daddy every time?"

He scoffed again, and it struck me like a match on dry kindling.

But he wasn't done.

"It's day one, Quinn. Toughen up or get out."

My hands clenched into fists, teeth gritting as I spat at him, "Fuck you, Max."

"In your dreams, Princess." He smirked, turning on his heel and walking to the door. "I don't fuck crybabies. Or quitters."

Every nerve in my body vibrated with the rage burning up inside me. His callous, painful remark about my parents had already wiped away the good I thought I'd seen in him. That final remark blazed like an inferno through a field of wildflowers, destroying everything left.

I growled low in my throat and was seconds from tearing off the bed after him. He wouldn't shame me for having feelings. And I wasn't a quitter.

But the presence of another voice stopped me.

"Hello, son."

I didn't recognize it, but I knew who it was.

Merle Dread, Max's father, greeted his son, and I had no doubt he'd be coming for me next.

"I hear you have an intriguing development to share with me."

I held my breath as their feet scuffled outside the door.

Then, a different one slammed inside the Round Tableau. And at that point, I should've expected it. Those assholes put me through paces and left when the next move didn't involve me.

It was becoming a common theme, but somehow, I had the audacity to be surprised when—once again—I found myself alone.

"She is *exactly* what Camelot Court needs."

KINGSTON

Everything had gone according to plan. She accepted the invitation. She uncovered the message written in invisible ink, and she'd shown up wearing the requested items.

I'd been right about her. That truth resonated in my bones. She would change everything.

In eight days, the Maidens would be moved onto Camelot Court. I'd see her again for the Maiden Introduction, and I'd reveal the prize she'd won for her cleverness. She'd need it in order to get to the end.

No one had won The Quest without at least three of Merlin's answers, and Quinn had just secured two right out of the gate.

Some of the Knights complained about the folder I'd set aside for Lancelot, calling foul play for picking a winner before the game had even started. But they hadn't seen what I'd seen. They didn't understand just how much one word could define a person.

Most of them, at least.

Landon's family seat in the Camelot Society had been a

blessing and a curse. He gained a place among the Knights at Camelot Court, but at the same time, he shouldered the reputation of his ancestors. He understood how one word—traitor—could shape a person's future and alter the course of their life for generations to come.

It was why I'd always favored him.

Why it needed to be him.

But first, I had to figure out why he had just burst into my bedroom when he should've been in the Round Tableau getting to know Quinn.

"Landon?"

Panting, he stood in the doorway. His hands clenched the frame, and the set of his jaw had me rising from my chair. Taking in his disheveled appearance and the slightly manic gleam in his eyes, I crossed the room quickly.

Something had happened—something bad.

Because Landon Scott, the definition of control and order, looked as if he'd gone mad.

"What's wrong?" I grabbed his shoulders. "What happened? Where's Quinn?"

He glared at me, seething as he hissed through his teeth. "She's here for you."

His accusation—while undeniably true—startled me. Not only because the realization had shocked him, but because of the ire in his voice when he spoke to me. I stepped back, straightening my spine and standing in front of him as his King—not just his best friend.

"Is that a problem?"

He scoffed and shook his head in disbelief.

It was a problem. That surprised me.

"You brought her here so I could guide her through The Quest. So she'd win and be the next Queen? Because of one word on her application. That's what you said to me, right?"

He stepped farther into the room, going past me and

pacing the floor in front of my bed. I watched him and chose my words carefully.

"Yes, that's what I said to you."

He growled, turning an accusing finger in my direction. "What word?"

"You should know what word."

He barked out a laugh, though it was clear he found nothing about this situation amusing. I echoed the sentiment. Watching him unravel over a clearly strategic move called every one of my plans for him and the future of Camelot Court into question.

"Is that why you didn't tell me? Because you thought I'd figure it out on my own or because you knew I'd refuse you if I did?" He pierced me with his stare and his next words. "There's nothing honorable about what you're asking me to do."

My eyes widened. "I beg your pardon?"

"I won't do it. I refuse."

"Landon, what is it you think I'm asking you to do? Get to know her? Gain her trust? Show her the ways of Camelot Court—the pressure, the expectations and the demands. Show her who you really are?" I threw my hands in the air. "Pray tell. What about that is so dishonorable?"

"Pick someone else." He wouldn't look at me, his voice pleading—desperate. "Pick anyone else. I can't do this."

"You can and you will," I said sharply. But when his eyes shot to mine, filled with pain and betrayal, I gentled my tone. "You're the only one I trust, Landon."

"But she—"

"She is *exactly* what Camelot Court needs."

"And what you want," he fired back, agitating the strands of his hair. He ran his hands over his scalp. "How convenient."

"Yes, how convenient. For the first time in my life, what I want aligns with my duty as King." I couldn't hide the disdain in my voice. "Forgive me for wanting a shred of something for myself while I do only what I'm supposed to do. And for seizing an opportunity that provides it."

His anger deflated.

"I apologize if you find my behavior dishonorable, but fortunately, I don't answer to you. Now, I've ordered you to oversee her training. Is that going to be a problem?"

"No." He bowed his head and walked to the door. "I'll make sure she's ready."

If only it were that easy. If only that were enough. It occurred to me that I might need to share more with him, so he would remember how vital all this was...

So, he could appreciate what was at stake for all of us.

But for now, whether he understood the direction he'd been given or not, what I needed from him—and from her—was simple.

One move, and we could end the game.

"Ready or not, Landon, make sure she wins."

"So, the team motto here *isn't* to make every moment count?"

Chapter Eleven
Quinn

Silence echoed around me, but I sure as hell wasn't going to sit there and bask in it. I scanned the room for my clutch as I climbed off the bed. Scooping it up off the floor, I grabbed my rescue inhaler and took a puff.

Breathing easier, I raced from the room to the door with the blue coat of arms. I retraced the path I'd taken in, searching for landmarks I recognized until I found my way back to the dressing room. The door slammed shut behind me, and once again, I was alone.

But it didn't stay that way for long.

Midway through pulling on my dress, the door opened. My head snapped toward my intruder, expecting to find Max, or maybe Landon. But to my surprise—and my relief—it wasn't either of them.

Kingston D'Arthur stood in the doorway.

The sight of him there was somehow both alarming and oddly disarming. No doubt he'd been notified of my *failure to please* and had come to find me so he could send me on my way. But at the same time, my indignation over having my neck on the chopping block suddenly fizzled out.

He didn't stare at me like a King ready to toss out an unwanted Maiden.

No, he stared at me like a man starved—hungry for a delicacy he'd always wanted but never dreamed of tasting.

I didn't fully understand it, but I liked it.

Clapping my hand over my chest, I spun around. I grabbed the neckline of my dress, pulling it over my hips.

He expelled a breath. "I heard your evening didn't go as planned."

I snorted. "Yeah. You can say that again."

"What are you doing in here?"

"Just packing up so I can leave with my dignity still intact. Before you assholes kick me out."

Peeking over my shoulder, I found his eyes locked on a wall and not my half-dressed body. I quickly slipped my arms through the straps of my dress and covered myself. Then, I cleared my throat to let him know I was done, planting my hands on my hips and bracing for the inevitable blow.

His eyes lingered on my hips before jumping to my face. I arched a brow, both to let him know I'd seen that and that I expected a response.

He didn't give me one.

Instead, he ran his gaze over the rest of my body, but it didn't come off as seductive or sleazy. He was just... admiring me, the hint of an appreciative smile tipping up the corner of his mouth as he made his slow perusal.

When his sparkling blue-gray eyes finally returned to my face, it took me a minute to remember this wasn't a chance sensual encounter with a sexy stranger like it had been earlier tonight. This was an expulsion from The Quest courtesy of *The King*.

Which is why his next question surprised me.

"Who said anything about us kicking you out?"

"Max Dread," I spat, mentally cursing myself for using

his full name.

"Ah, I see." He nodded, another grin tugging at his lips—this one amused and at my expense. "Told you you'd want to be careful with that one."

I huffed, throwing my hands up and turning back to the mirror. "Yeah, well. You should've given me a heads up about my so-called *Knight*. If I'd needed a warning about anyone, it was him."

"Would you have ignored that warning, too?"

My eyes snapped to his. "Probably. But that's not the point."

He stared back pointedly. "No, I'd say the point is whether you're going to let one moment define a person... Or your future."

I frowned, thrown off by his rational question and forced to consider it. He made it sound like *I* was the one running, not the one being kicked out. He asked as if it was my choice to stay or run for the hills.

And if it was, what was I going to do?

Was I just supposed to forget how Landon accused me of lying and restrained me like a criminal? Was I supposed to ignore the way Max flickered between hot and cold like a fucking faulty pilot light?

Could I get past those moments to get to the end?

I rolled my eyes. "So, the team motto here *isn't* to make every moment count?"

He laughed, the sound bursting out of him like it had taken him by surprise. I liked that. It seemed...messy and free.

Real.

"No, the team motto is a bit wordier than that."

"Tell me."

His eyebrows rose at my sudden demand, and it surprised me, too. Given that he hadn't kicked me out yet, I begrudgingly tacked on some manners before he changed his mind.

"Please," I added.

He stalked toward me, his voice low and smooth as he shared their code with me for the first time.

"Arthur believed we should live with honor."

My lips parted as he approached, my breathing growing more erratic with each step.

"Fight with courage..."

He came to stand in front of me, and brought his hand up to my face, cupping my jaw and tilting my chin up towards his.

"Protect with nobility..."

His soft breath warmed my skin as he delivered the last line, and my eyelids grew heavy under the hypnotic sound of his voice.

"And love with all our hearts."

My voice came out softer than it had been before. "Does everyone in Camelot follow the code?"

He nodded.

"Even you?"

"Yes. Everything I am—My whole life has been shaped by the Knights' Code. And I believe in it. We pledge our loyalty with trust to Camelot Court, vowing to abide by the code above all else." His thumb brushed back and forth over my skin, tracing the hollow of my cheek. "Though, I have to admit. Right now, the things I want to do to you..." He threaded his fingers into the strands of my hair and tilted my head back farther. "They're far from honorable."

I closed my eyes as my neck arched back, moaning when his grip on my hair tightened. "Isn't that against the rules?"

"Maybe. Some say the King is supposed to make the rules. Others disagree."

"And which ones does *the King* listen to?"

He nuzzled my cheek with his nose, his lips hovering over my jaw line before pulling back. "A wise king leads from the front, Quinn. He sets the example."

My eyes opened to find his filled with regret. "So, do it then," I taunted. "Get rid of me if that's what they want you to do."

He smiled, his eyes lighting up like crystals in the sun. "Oh, much to their disappointment, I won't be taking anyone's advice when it comes to you."

"Why not?"

"Because I know who you are, Quinn Everly. And I know what you can be if you see this through to the end."

I bit my lip, my heart warring with my mind in more ways than one. "But Landon...He—"

"Made a mistake." He implored me with his gaze, asking for forgiveness. "He acted based on information he had, missing details I wasn't able to share with him. But he wasn't just protecting me tonight. Because the only thing greater than his loyalty is the goodness in his heart."

"But why—"

"Stay, Quinn. Trust me and stay. See this through and win. He'll be by your side..." He traced his thumb over my lips. "And I'll be waiting for you at the end of it."

His eyes locked on my parted mouth, and I almost gave in completely. But if he couldn't answer my question with more than that, I had to stay focused on why I'd come here.

"I didn't come here for that, Kingston. It's not in my nature to belong to anyone. Not a Knight. Not even a King."

"I didn't pick up those files expecting to find you, either. But here we are."

He pressed his lips to mine, swiftly and almost urgently, the feel of his lips softening the edges inside me that I'd sharpened to protect myself. My hands curled into the fabric of his shirt, and just as I was about to cave, he pulled away. Walking back toward the door, he smiled.

"I knew I was right about you."

I shook my head, letting out an exasperated laugh. "So, you keep saying. But what does that *mean?*"

He winked as he walked out the door. "You'll see."

"I almost lost my virginity in a sex dungeon."

Chapter Twelve
Quinn

"I need to reevaluate my life choices."

"Not from where I'm sitting," Gia called from the couch.

After Kingston had kissed me and left the room the night before, I decided to suck it up and go back to the Round Tableau room. I figured if Landon came back, I could demand an explanation at the very least.

But I never got the chance.

I fell asleep as I ran through the various things I wanted to say to him, waking up the next morning alone and disoriented.

Gia, in true ride-or-die fashion, had already texted me that she was at the gate. She came bearing iced coffee and aspirin, which I regretfully informed her I wouldn't need. Stifling her disappointment, she listened to me recount the entire night's events without saying a word.

But ever since we got back home, she'd been completely unhelpful. Instead of talking me out of finishing The Quest, she thought I should ride off into the sunset with all three of my potential suitors.

Her words, not mine.

Rejoining her in the living room, I plopped onto the couch beside her. She had her legs thrown over the side, head resting on the cushions as she binge-watched some reality dating show.

I struggled to focus on the screen as my own drama replayed in my head.

"Gia, I went there fully intending to lose my virginity with one guy and ended up flirting with two more, eye fucking one's bare chest as he cradled me in his ridiculously sculpted arms, and then let the other one kiss me when I should've been running away."

Stuffing a handful of popcorn into her mouth, Gia shrugged. "I don't see a problem there."

I groaned, burying my face in my hands. "It was one thing to do The Quest when I had convinced myself I'd be unaffected by one guy. Get in, get the prize money, and get out."

"With a few orgasms to boot," Gia added. "A solid plan, if you ask me."

"Yeah, except I was there for five minutes before meeting Max and wanting to climb him like a tree."

"He sounds so hot."

I glared at her. "You are *not* helping."

She shrugged again, eyes flicking between me and her reality show. "Agree to disagree. But anyway, so you met a hot guy at a party even though that wasn't your plan. So what?"

"So, he blew me off out of nowhere. Then, two seconds later, another guy appeared and I flashed my bare thigh at him. I'm a...a trollop!"

Gia laughed, an errant popcorn kernel going down the wrong pipe. She coughed and sat up, thrusting her fist into her diaphragm until she cleared her throat.

I got up and patted her back, concerned by the tears rolling down her cheeks, *until* she caught her breath and kept laughing. I went back to my chair and sat down with a huff.

"You're the worst," I lied.

She wheezed out another laugh and wiped her cheeks. "Oh god, I'm sorry, but you seriously called yourself a trollop." Grabbing another handful of popcorn, she tossed a few pieces into her mouth. "Man, I wish I could watch this whole thing on TV. Your solo interviews would be hilarious."

"I hate you."

"You love me." She tossed a piece of popcorn at me. "And you're lucky to have me. Who else would stop you from shame spiraling after doing *absolutely nothing* wrong?"

I smothered my face with a couch pillow. "I almost lost my virginity in a sex dungeon."

"And what? You want a bed with rose petals?" She quirked an eyebrow, pulling a red vine candy out of the bag beside her and chewing on the end. "Candles? A bit of poetry? So you could lose your V-card in a romantic fantasy?"

"Maybe," I grumbled. "It's supposed to be special, isn't it?"

"Sure, if that's important to you. But first times are usually awkward and uncomfortable and don't always live up to the fantasy in your head. What you might get instead sounds hot and actually satisfying. Why second-guess it?"

I tugged at the hair on my scalp.

"I didn't sleep with my ex because I wanted it to mean something...But then, I just planned to give it up like it doesn't mean anything?"

Tears pricked my eyes. The memory of that night, and the results of my choice, were still as fresh and painful as ever.

Gia caught sight of my expression and was at my side in a flash. Her arm looped around my shoulders, pulling me into her hug as she freed my hair from the tangle of my fingers.

"It's not your fault, Quinn."

A bitter laugh burst out of me.

"It's absolutely my fault he's dead, Gia. And I have to live with that by myself for the rest of my life. Just like I have to live with the rest of my choices." I wiped my face with my sleeve, shoving the heavy weight of loss down as it threatened to overwhelm me. "The least I could do is make choices he'd be proud of."

Gia took my face in her hands, forcing me to meet her eyes. "He wanted you to make choices that made *you* happy, not other people. That's what you told me he said to you, right?"

I nodded, thinking about my dad's last words to me.

"Did anything about last night feel like you were doing what someone else wanted? If it did, then don't go back."

Thinking it over, I ran through my interactions with Max and Kingston. In both of those moments, I hadn't thought about what I *should* do.

Sure, I blamed it on their ventilation system and heavy doses of aphrodisiac being filtered through the room, but that had been a cop out.

I had wanted them. *Both* of them. Even if I'd shown up expecting to meet someone else. And with Landon, I'd admitted the truth to him.

The only thing I'd truly been afraid of was how much I wanted what The Quest had offered—thirty days to explore every dark fantasy and dirty command he could imagine. I'd worried over what that said about me, but I hadn't been planning to let that stop me.

If Landon hadn't freaked out over my confession, I would've slept with him. Instead, I ended up in Max's arms.

Then, Kingston's.

And even though I'd wondered if I should slow down—if maybe the events of the night were making me act rashly—I'd had the wherewithal to question what I was doing.

I just hadn't let it stop me.

"It didn't feel like that," I admitted.

"Right. It sounds like you took what you wanted for the first time. Without worrying over what anyone else would think." She cupped my cheeks and squeezed. "I'm so proud of you for that. And I know he would be, too."

Feeling better, even if not entirely convinced, I relaxed. Gia gave me a hug before returning to the couch. She hit play on the TV remote, turning toward me and holding out her bag of snacks.

I grabbed a handful of popcorn and chocolate candy. "Thanks," I said, not just about the snacks.

"That's what best friends are for," she said. "Now, can we circle back to Kingston and the hot, hot promise of sex to come? And then, I want all the details on Max and his sexy naked man chest. For research purposes only, of course. And we can end with Landon, so we can put together a game plan for when you go back."

Rolling my eyes, I settled into the couch. "Well, Kingston asked me to win and said he'd be waiting for me at the end." Sighing, I sat back and picked at my snack pile. "I'm not sure I'm ready for any of that."

"That's fair. Just wait and see how you feel, then." She shrugged, then clapped her hands together. "Now, what about the other two? Your Knights in Shining Under Armor."

I snorted, thinking about the other two guys wreaking havoc on my brain. "Kingston also said Landon would be by my side. Honestly, if he hadn't kissed me, I would've thought he was trying to set me up with his best friend."

"Ooh! Or maybe he's a king who already knows how to share?" Gia asked hopefully, rubbing her hands together. "What do you think? Was that the vibe?"

I laughed and shook my head. "That place was like a TV spot for alpha male energy. I did *not* pick up on any sharing vibes. He just...vouched for his friend, I guess."

She pursed her lips together, nodding in thought. "But he knows what the Knights and Maidens do behind closed doors, right?"

"Yeah, he'd have to, right?"

"Well, then he's either stupidly trusting, or he knows something we don't. Like, maybe Landon isn't into hot chicks. Or he's a eunuch."

"He's definitely not a eunuch." I blushed.

Gia squealed and threw her couch pillow at me. "Yasss, girl! See, stay focused on that."

"But I do keep going back to what Landon said. About being the only one there without a choice. Maybe he isn't into hot chicks. Or girls at all. Maybe that's why Kingston isn't worried about him being my Knight?"

My brow furrowed, both confusion and concern rising when I thought about what Landon had let slip.

But then a fresh wave of rejection wiped it away. "No one forced him to be a dick. That's all I know."

"Do you think someone made him participate in The Quest? Or be a Knight? What do you even know about their society?"

"Only what Elaine told me. Everything I told you earlier."

She pressed her lips together in thought. "Maybe Kingston put him up to it?"

I shrugged.

"No, that doesn't make sense." She scratched her head. "Someone else in Camelot Court? Who was that older man you mentioned? The King's advisor."

"That's Max's Dad, Merle Dread." I shook my head. "His son was the only one he seemed to have any kind of hold over. But I didn't even meet the guy."

"Well, we'll put a pin in that for now, then. Tell me more about Max. *Max Dread.*" She said his full name and whole body shuddered. "Even his name is hot. Like he's going to hunt you in the shadows and fuck you 'til you scream. Ooh, or put you on your knees and make you take his cock like a good girl."

I swallowed, wondering if that was *exactly* the kind of thing he'd do. "If not him, Landon certainly seemed like the type."

I actually couldn't decide if Max or Landon would be more likely to dominate me like that in the bedroom. Maybe both. And maybe I wouldn't mind if they did—alone, or together.

My face flamed as that image sent a rush of wild heat through my body. Me, on my knees between them, taking them into my mouth as they both stared down at me. Despite the hint of submission, something about the fantasy made me feel powerful.

When I added Kingston to the mix, picturing him watching us—directing me on how and when to please them—all while he stroked his own cock, I began to sweat.

Gia caught sight of my blush before I could hide it and let out a squeal of glee. "Oh my god, you're thinking about them both doing it, aren't you?"

When I blushed harder, she cackled excitedly.

"No, you're thinking about all of them! YASSS, Queen! Get your freak on!"

I threw my pillow at her, whipping the blanket off my legs and fanning myself with it. When I calmed my overheated body down, reality sunk in.

There was no way that fantasy would ever come true.

"It's too bad Landon and Max give me whiplash, *and* that Max seems to hate Kingston and Landon."

Even with no physical proof to back it up, Max clearly didn't get along with the other two by the way he spoke about Kingston, and by the way he'd reacted to me being there *for the King*—a comment I still didn't understand.

I had no idea what their dynamic was, or the drama it would cause for me to be with Landon when Kingston wanted me, too. If I went back to Camelot Court, I'd have to deal with that.

"Oh, and the fact that I had no intention of getting involved with a guy. Let alone getting tangled up with three!" I added for good measure. "Let's not forget that."

Gia scoffed, waving her hand in the air and ignoring my protest completely. "They'll come around."

"*Or* I can stay focused on why I joined The Quest in the first place." I stared at her pointedly. "And besides, Max and Landon made it clear they have no genuine interest, so picturing them doing me together gets me nowhere. I just need to survive the next thirty days and leave with my dignity intact. That's it."

Gia snorted. "Whatever you say, Quinn. I mean, *Your Highness.*"

I laughed. "Shut the hell up, you trollop."

Chapter Thirteen

Pledge with Trust...

"Until my last breath, I pledge with trust to Camelot Court."

LANDON

Two days after the Maiden Selection, the Knights gathered in the Round Tableau room. My time avoiding Kingston and what occurred the other night had come to an end.

I needed to face him. And the task laid out before me. In four days, I'd have no other choice.

This whole tradition made my skin crawl.

The Maidens joined The Quest with one goal—secure marriage within the Camelot Society—something I didn't need or want.

I hadn't wanted anything to do with The Quest. Period. I even refused to join the Knights, initially.

But, again, no one shirked an order from the King.

Not even his best friend.

If Kingston said he needed me, I had no choice but to agree. I took my duty to him, as the King of Camelot Court, seriously. And whatever qualms I had about The Quest, he'd asked me to prepare one Maiden for the challenge ahead.

He'd known my feelings on the subject.

Yet, he'd asked anyway.

I hadn't been happy about it, but I trusted he had his reasons. Even if he hadn't shared them with me at the time.

More often than not, Kingston kept his cards close to his chest by design. And there were some things I didn't want to know. My panic at the pharmacy came to mind before I forced it away.

Some things, I couldn't stand to remember.

Reservations aside, I wouldn't fail him.

I couldn't.

My initial approach involved boundaries. Keeping things as separate as possible. Maintaining lines to ensure no *delusions* arose over my intentions.

At least, that had been my plan going into the Maiden Selection.

Before I met her.

Before I found out the truth.

Kingston chose her for more than Camelot Court. He thought she could be a chance at happiness for him. Something that had seemed impossible given the stipulations his family placed on his future.

He deserved that.

I wouldn't wish his life on anyone. I wouldn't wish any of our lives on someone else. But if that could change...

Keeping her at arm's length had become even more important. And more challenging.

The request already crossed the lines of a normal favor between friends. Quinn Everly would be right in front of me for twenty-one straight days. And I'd be expected to test and explore her limits, ensuring she could handle the second challenge within the first thirty days of The Quest.

Kingston accepted what I'd have to do.

He trusted me.

And that meant everything.

So, I'd have to trust him, too. While he kept his distance

to dispel the rumors, I'd do my job as carefully as possible. Remaining aloof so she didn't seek anything more. Avoiding getting too close while she lived in my room, shared my space, and slept in my bed.

Alone, of course.

In the hopes only one of us would spend the next three weeks fighting temptation.

But after meeting her...

Seeing the way she responded to even the slightest touch. Witnessing the war in her dark brown eyes as she obeyed my commands. I didn't know if it would be her or me.

No. It wouldn't be me.

It *couldn't* be.

Inside the Round Tableau, Kingston waited in the center of the room. Surrounded by the other Knights standing at their doors, his head was bent as he talked quietly with Merle.

But his eyes lifted when I walked through the door, finding mine. His knitted brows and slight frown betrayed his concern. He let them slip from behind the mask before he shuttered his expression.

I took my place at the door beside his.

On the left, even as his *right hand man*.

Merle stepped forward to speak. "The twelve of you are the Knights of the Round Tableau. Over summer, your focus will be on Camelot Court. On the honor and duty placed on your shoulders. The Camelot Society created Camelot Court to prepare our young men for responsibility ahead. To teach you how to assess the women standing by your side."

I fought to relax my jaw, my molars grinding loudly enough to be heard over his speech.

"The Quest's final prize cannot be revealed or spoken about until the end. Remember that. Push it from your thoughts. Proceed honorably. So, the victor is rightfully chosen. While only one can win, failure in this, as in all things, won't be tolerated."

Kingston's eyes flicked to mine—a reminder to rein in my reactions.

"Hopefully, you've chosen wisely. If not, then you must mold your Maiden into the woman she needs to become to serve Camelot Court and your aspirations."

My hands clenched into fists at my side.

"Tonight, you swear an oath to uphold the by-laws of The Quest and the privilege you've been given. When Kingston calls your name, please step forward and hold up your right hand."

Merle stepped back, bowing his head.

Kingston flicked his gaze to mine before training it steadily on the first Knight to come forward. His voice rang out, low and commanding, in the dimly lit room.

"Max Dread."

I forced my lip not to curl.

Technically the twelfth in our line of brothers, the reverse order conveyed the Knights had no rank.

And yet, he'd been assigned the last spot by design.

Max Dread made no attempts to hide his intentions. He wanted to ruin Kingston's plans, whether he knew them or not. His family benefited most from the antiquated traditions of Camelot Court, and despising him came as easy as breathing.

He hated me for things outside of my control—the failures of others. Always placed on my shoulders.

Kingston spoke the vow we'd all known since childhood, pulling my attention back to him. "Do you swear to uphold the integrity of The Quest, guiding your Maiden down a rightful path, and serving Camelot Court above all things?"

Max Dread sneered in Kingston's face. "Do you?"

Whispers filled the room. More rumors about Kingston's selection of my Maiden. They needed to be squelched immediately, but Max Dread was hellbent on preventing that.

But before I could tackle the asshole, I stopped my feet

from moving forward.

"Everything I do abides by that oath, Sir Mordred. Whether you believe that or not is outside my concern," Kingston responded, his voice unruffled—his demeanor calm. "Remembering your place should be within yours."

Max growled low in his throat.

Kingston lifted the knife in his hand. "Do you swear?"

"I swear."

"Do you vow to abide by the Knights' Code, embodying all it means to live with honor?"

Max spoke the vow, spitting it like venom on his tongue. He didn't flinch when Kingston sliced his palm with the Mordred family dagger. His blood spilled on the stone between them.

Seething, he retreated to his door, glaring at his father. Merle stepped forward and traded the Mordred family knife for the next. One by one, Kingston called the Knights to the center of the room.

Each swore his fealty to Camelot Court, Kingston, and the sanctity of The Quest. I scanned their faces for the truth. Until, finally, it was my turn.

"Landon Scott."

Hesitation ran rampant through my body, but I approached Kingston as if I had none.

Blue-gray eyes anchored to mine, conveying a hint of doubt. A tell only I could see. But he echoed the oath, binding us to a dangerous path forward.

"Do you swear to uphold the integrity of The Quest, guiding your Maiden down a rightful path, and serving Camelot Court above all things?"

"I swear."

"Do you vow to abide by the Knights' Code, embodying all it means to live with honor?"

His eyes softened as I spoke the vow.

"Until my last breath, I pledge with trust to Camelot Court

and to my King."

The Lancelot family dagger sliced the center of my palm. My blood trickled down my wrist, falling to the stone between us.

When Merle handed over the final knife, Kingston brought it to his hand. He sliced his palm and joined his blood with ours. Holding his hand out to me, fear bled into his face before he could mask it.

I gripped him in a vise, eschewing tradition. Binding us. Uniting our blood as brothers. Sealing what we'd become a long time ago.

Kingston exhaled shakily, head bowing under the weight of the expectations and eyes on his back. But then, as always, he straightened his spine and did what he had to do.

"Until my last breath, I pledge with trust to Camelot Court."

If I wanted someone to play with my feelings by offering and then withholding affection, I'd get a cat.

Chapter Fourteen
Quinn

I had a week between the Maiden Selection and when I had to return to Camelot Court. Most of that time, I divided between my finals exams, reading up on Arthurian legends, and wavering in my resolve to return for The Quest.

I hadn't heard from anyone at Camelot Court.

No one was more shocked than me to realize that stung a tiny bit. I mean, it wasn't like I'd been expecting a heartfelt apology or edible fruit arrangement from Landon, and Max could take a long walk off a short bridge. But not even a *hey girl, you good* from Kingston?

Fortunately, the sting lasted all of two seconds. I reminded myself that Kingston's come-on-strong approach was *not* supposed to be a turn-on. Laying out his intentions clearly was supposed to freak me out and send me running for the hills because I had no desire to go there.

When that stopped working, relief over not having to face what he'd said overruled any feelings of rejection by his lack of follow-up.

That, or the anxiety over going back, distracted me.

Or maybe I'd learned to appreciate the unexpected, beautiful, and painful moments of my life without needing to overthink them.

That sounded mature. Evolved, even.

I went with that.

"You're sure you don't want me to drive you?"

Gia had been clucking after me like a mother hen, waiting for my protective shell of denial to crack. She spent the week replenishing my mental stockpile of positive affirmations. I found Post-its with crowns, messages like "You're a Bad Bitch," and crude stick figure drawings littered around the apartment.

Each drawing had one figure in a triangle skirt holding a rose, and three taller figures with outrageously disproportionate cock bulges on their pencil thin frames.

I had to go back to Camelot Court knowing at least one of the stick figures might live up to the drawing's exaggerated penis size. But I had no intention of finding out for sure with Landon. Or finding out at all with the other two.

Max's hot-and-cold behavior told me everything I needed to know. He was a distraction, and getting involved with him wouldn't help me win The Quest.

I planned to avoid him at all costs.

Plus, if I wanted someone to play with my feelings by offering and then withholding affection, I'd get a cat.

And since Kingston said he'd be waiting for me at the end, I assumed the time for me to explore what lay beneath his belt would be limited over the next month.

Which was good.

I'd already replayed our kiss about a hundred times in my head, and while it had been brief, it reinforced my first impression of him. What Kingston presented outwardly fell vastly short of everything he hid inside.

Whether that applied to other parts of him…

Best not to tempt myself to dig deeper and find out.

That left Landon, who could play my body and my emotions like a goddamn violin. Or that obnoxious fiddle in the song about the devil in Georgia. It played on an unavoidable loop in my head when I drove through the state to North Carolina, and similarly, I couldn't exactly get away from Landon during The Quest.

But while I may be forced to interact with him—long enough to let Kingston's appeal on his behalf sink in, at least—I didn't have to give him access to my body or submit to anything involving his.

I could *and would* use my safe words to keep him at bay.

Gia and I re-read the contract, and it prevented the Knights from doing anything if a Maiden said *I yield*. So, I decided my limits had become a bit harder in the last week.

And if Landon couldn't touch me?

Well, then, I didn't have to worry about feeling anything for the moody, sadistic bastard.

"I'm seriously good, Gia. I'm going to make The Quest my bitch and come back with enough rent money to make it rain on you."

I laid out my palm and swiped the other over it repeatedly, sending imaginary dollars into the air as I danced around her.

She laughed, her eyes wary, but she ultimately gave in and shook her hair out, running her hands over her face and body like rain was pouring down.

When our impromptu dance session ended, she pointed a finger at me. "Call me if you need anything. I'm serious. I'll come get you immediately."

I hugged her. "I know you will. Love you."

"Love you, too."

I pulled my suitcase up to the wall and wrought-iron gate separating Camelot Court from the rest of Mosaic Falls.

Pressing the button to buzz the intercom, I perched on top of my suitcase, my feet tapping out a random beat on the sidewalk as I waited. An odd whirring noise came from above me, the security camera on top of the wall rotating in my direction.

"Name?"

"Quinn Everly. I'm one of the Maidens."

Silence followed. I tapped my fingers on the sides of my suitcase, stretching my calves and cracking my neck. My admittance through the gate sorely lacked the urgency from the Maiden Selection party—in that there was none. At all.

After a few minutes, I pressed the button again.

"Hello? Can you hear me? My name is Quinn Everly." I gritted my teeth and begrudgingly claimed the broody asshole for myself. "Landon Scott's Maiden. I'm here for The Quest."

Static crackled.

"Your presence won't be required anymore, Quinn Everly. You're free to go."

The sound cut off.

"What the—"

I pressed the button again. But nothing happened. Staring up at the camera, I lifted my arms in a clear *what the fuck* gesture before pushing the button repeatedly.

After the amount of pep talks it had taken to go through with this, they planned to just dismiss me at the gate?

I hit the button again. And when there was still no response, I got pissed. "Oh, no fucking way."

Did they have any idea how many positive affirmation Post-Its Gia had crafted for me? Okay, probably not. But I had too much riding on winning The Quest.

Not to mention, the simple matter of pride.

I refused to take their dismissal sitting down. No, fuck that.

I was scaling that goddamn wall.

Dropping the bag on my shoulder, I secured my crossbody

over my chest. I stepped back, eyeing the wall and the gate. Left with *absolutely* no other choice, I grabbed the iron bars and hoisted myself up.

A voice crackled over the intercom. "Miss, you've been asked kindly to leave."

I secured my hold on the fence with one hand and lifted my other—middle finger straight up—to the camera. Climbing the rest of the way, I bypassed the pointy rods at the top of the gate and grabbed onto the brick wall beside it. Swinging my leg up and over, I pulled myself to straddle it before repeating the process onto the other side of the gate.

If anything, these rich assholes should've thanked me for highlighting a clear failing in their security system.

But thank me, they did not.

As soon as my feet hit the ground on the other side, a low and vicious growl rumbled behind me. I turned around, finding a giant dog licking its jowls across the lawn. Black fur rose along the ridge of its spine. Saliva dripped from its mouth.

"Holy shit."

Glancing quickly at the gate, I tossed the idea of climbing back over. Before I could even lift my leg, the dog whizzed toward me. His massive body moved faster than I expected. I panicked immediately, bolting away from the gate.

A scream tore from my throat as I sprinted. His huge, heavy paws thudded into the ground behind me.

But I didn't look back.

I wasn't a complete idiot, even if the last five minutes said otherwise. Running as fast as I could, I beelined straight past the side of the main house.

"Help!" I screamed, pumping my arms and legs harder.

My lungs burned. My airways constricted as I fought to pull in air. Skidding around the back of the building, I cried out in relief. A tree with low-hanging branches heralded safety.

If I could get there in time.

As soon as I reached it, I swung my leg up and over the first branch low enough for me to grab. Momentum brought the rest of my limbs with me.

Teeth snapped beneath my foot. I pulled it up and scrambled quickly to get higher. The beast jumped at the tree, his claws digging into the trunk and shredding the bark when he slid to the ground.

"Good doggy! Go away, boy!" I wheezed, wrapping my arms around a branch out of his reach. Sweat dripped down my face. And my heart pounded furiously.

I tried to breathe, coughing as my airway constricted.

My inhaler, stowed away in the bag squashed between my breasts and the branch, might as well have been back at the gate for all the good it did me. I needed it, but I had no idea if the branches could bear my weight. The fear of slipping and ending up as puppy chow kept me from maneuvering the bag out from under me.

But if I passed out, I'd fall.

He'd get a nice little snack, either way.

The branch shook as I wiggled one arm between my body and the tree, holding as tightly as I could with the other. Something dropped to the ground, landing with a *thump*.

I would've rolled my eyes at the predictability if not for being scared for my life. It was just so perfectly fitting.

Fucking lemons.

The dog barked, bounding after the fallen fruit before giving up and returning for the bigger treat. Loud and jarring howls came from the ground as I shifted, finally reaching the zipper of my bag. I wrapped my fingers around the plastic canister and wrenched it free.

But my sweaty grip fumbled over the inhaler.

"No!" I cried out as it fell to the ground.

Panic crept in, tightening like a noose around my throat.

The giant black hound pounced on the tiny bottle, stepping

on it and knocking it away. Bounding after it, I used his distraction to think. A little harder with the lack of oxygen filtering to my brain, only that explained my half-cocked reasoning.

If the dog ate my inhaler, I'd be screwed. I had no choice but to try and get to it first.

As soon as he pawed the canister back in my direction, I squeezed my eyes shut and prayed to whatever higher power watched over idiot Maidens prone to poor life choices.

Was there a patron saint of monumental idiocy?

Maybe when I died, they'd give me the job.

I let go of the tree before my spiraling thoughts could talk me out of my plan, landing on the ground with a painful *oof* and lunging for the tiny canister.

Grabbing it, I wrapped my body around it right as the dog's hot breath hit my cheek, and screamed, "I yield!"

The dog sat.

"Brutus!" a sharp male voice barked, footsteps racing down stone steps. "Brutus, yield! Come here, you big oaf!"

The dog sprinted away, and I would've sobbed my relief if not for the darkness creeping in at the edges of my vision. Curled into a ball, I put the inhaler to my lips and breathed. When I released that breath, I instantly inhaled a second, shoving the medicine back in my bag as a dreaded voice sounded above me.

"What the hell were you thinking?"

Rolling onto my back, I glared up at the last person I wanted to see when I got here. I dragged in as many ragged deep breaths as I could—ready to unleash them in a stream of curses at his audacity.

These assholes sicced their guard dog on me and Max Dread wanted to know what *I'd* been thinking?

Of course, he had to be the one there to find me on the ground, too. Weak and desperate for air. If I hadn't been able to use my inhaler, he probably would've enjoyed watching me gasp for breath at his feet.

Max bent over and gripped my upper arms, hauling me up to stand. As soon as I got my bearings, I wrenched out of his grip and turned my back to him, tucking my inhaler away and zipping up my bag. I straightened my clothes and brushed the dirt and leaves out of my hair.

Without a word, I took off for the gate.

"Hey!" he shouted, his feet pounding into the ground behind me. "Where are—Stop running!"

He snatched my arm and whirled me around to face him. I hit his chest and almost bounced off, but his grip tightened. He looped his other arm around my waist to keep me upright.

My hands planted on his chest, pushing against him.

But, of course, the oversized Neanderthal was too strong for me to get away. I wriggled in his hold.

He huffed a laugh as I struggled against him. "Easy, Princess. Or you'll get me excited."

I glared up at him, but immediately stopped moving. "Let me go, asshole."

He released me, and I stumbled back a few steps before regaining my balance. His eyes raked over my body, darkening as he scrubbed a hand over his face.

My chest heaving, I stepped back farther, suddenly needing more distance between us.

The glimmer in his onyx eyes would've been beautiful under the sun. If I didn't know his soul was as black as charred earth.

He smirked. "Aw, what's wrong, Princess? Does the thought of getting me excited turn you on?"

"No," I snapped. "I don't have anything to worry about, remember? You don't fuck quitters or crybabies."

Spinning on my heel, I stalked away from him.

But his voice rang out before I could get far.

"That's right, Princess."

I glared at him over my shoulder.

"But you came back, didn't you?" Shoving his hands into his pockets, he stepped backwards and didn't even try to conceal the wicked gleam in his eyes. He shrugged his shoulders. "Guess you're not a quitter or crybaby, after all."

"Yeah, well, too bad for you, I don't fuck assholes."

His eyebrows rose. "Noted." The wide grin on his face made me instantly regret my word choice. "That can be my job, then."

My mouth gaped at the suggestion before I had the wherewithal to snap it shut and glare.

But of course, Max Dread had to notice. And decided to be a crude assh—*dickhead*—about it.

"I bet there are a lot of dark places we could explore, Princess." He walked away, calling out over his shoulder. "When the White Knight leaves you high and dry, come find me."

"Yes, oh gallant Knight of mine. He freed me after you left me locked in the room."

Chapter Fifteen
Quinn

"Don't hold your breath," I muttered. "Or do. Cocky bastard."

Shaking off Max's parting remarks, I refocused. As much as I'd wanted to give Kingston a piece of my mind for kissing and dismissing me without a word, running for my life had given me perspective. I just wanted to get the hell out of there. Lick my wounds in peace, without the looming threat of three hot dicks hanging over my head.

Rounding the corner of the building, I groaned.

The mere thought of the hot dickheads had manifested another, and the next person I laid eyes on was Landon Scott. He'd found my things at the gate. And he was in the process of dragging them inside the building.

"Hey!" I called out, jogging up to him. "That's my stuff."

"And you're *my* Maiden," he responded without turning his head, as if the sound of my voice triggered him to be a jerk. "You're also late."

Eying me as I hurried up the steps after him, he didn't stop moving. He was an efficient bastard—I'd give him that—managing to survey my disheveled appearance with an unimpressed sweep of his gaze while dragging my stuff behind him.

Something about my face even provoked a frown, but he pushed through the main doors with his back, going inside without another word.

I chased after him, catching the main doors before they could slam in my face. They swung closed behind me and a boom echoed through the giant foyer.

"Holy shit," I breathed. "That's just like the table at Winchester."

The main house opened to a large foyer with high ceilings and doors leading to different areas on my left and right. Straight ahead, a staircase made of dark wood led up to the second floor, and hanging on the wall above it was a replica of the Round Table. It had twelve green and twelve white rays radiating out from the red circle in the center, with an image of King Arthur at the head of the table.

Landon assessed me from the corner of his eye. "You read up on the Knights this week?"

I nodded, my eyes still fixed on the replica. From where we stood, I couldn't make out the names scribed above each seat, but I wondered if their version had the original names or the corresponding families in their society. A society that was becoming more real and less like a game of make-believe the longer I spent around its members.

"That's good."

"It is?" I cocked my head toward him. "Why? Will that help me in The Quest?"

He shrugged. "It depends. It comes down to you more than anything. I've heard of Maidens winning in the past because they found a clue using the old lore, but plenty have won without ever picking up a book."

"Found a clue?"

"You'll see when you get to the last challenge."

When—not if.

I liked that, but I didn't point it out to him.

Even after a week away—time I'd hoped would give him the opportunity to reflect on what he'd done—he still acted standoffish and way too serious. No use giving him a reason to sour this civil moment between us by pointing out he'd said something nice.

I shouldn't have worried about it.

He found an opportunity on his own.

"But you're already at a disadvantage, so you'll need all the help you can get." He wrinkled his nose at my clothes. "You know, it reflects on me if you show up late, looking like you just went a few rounds in the dirt."

My eyes rolled, but since I'd already verbally sparred with one hot dickhead this morning, I decided to take a different approach.

"Jealous?" I couldn't help myself. "Could've been you if you hadn't been a raging dick the other night."

"Hardly," he said, ignoring my last comment on his reaction altogether and quickening his pace so we fell out of step. "I have a job to do, Maiden. Duty is something I happen to take seriously."

My snicker earned me a glare.

"What now?"

"You said you take *duty* seriously." I chuckled just to be a brat. "Doodie. That's all I heard."

His eyes narrowed. "What are you, five?"

I threw up my shoulders, smiling broadly as I jogged to keep up with him. "Maybe."

He groaned at my reply, shaking his head. And my plans to ignore him fully went out the window.

Getting under his skin sounded so much better.

It was so intriguing, watching his irritation rise while he acted indifferent. I wanted to crack his composed exterior.

Maybe there'd be someone human underneath it.

Thoughts of how I'd achieve this distracted me as we approached the large, central staircase leading to the floors above. So much so, I almost forgot that I'd been turned away at the gate. But when Landon's critical gaze flicked over me for the third time, it came rushing back.

"Hey! Why didn't they let me in at the gate? They said I'd been dismissed." My arm swung out and swatted his chest. "Was that y—Landon!"

I screeched his name as he grabbed my arm, spinning me into the wall to his left.

He stepped in front of me, clamping a hand over my mouth. His arm braced over my chest, pinning me to the brick.

For a second, I worried it had only taken one swat to unravel him, but I was also getting a little tired of being tossed around like a rag doll. So, despite the potential for consequences, I did the only thing I could think to do.

I stomped on his foot.

He grunted but stifled the sound behind pursed lips. His eyes bore into mine, willing me to be silent.

Instead, I licked his palm, enjoying far too much the appalled look on his face when I did it.

He brought a finger to his lips and then to his ears. Footsteps echoed throughout the room. And my heart leapt stupidly in my chest at the sound of Kingston's voice.

"Where is she?"

A voice I couldn't place answered him. "I'm not sure, Kingston. Perhaps she got intimidated by everything and left?"

"She wouldn't leave," Kingston argued in my defense, and I couldn't ignore the relief that rushed through me.

He hadn't been behind my less-than-warm welcome.

"Perhaps she wasn't what you thought, son?"

The voice clicked in my brain—the one from the intercom at the gate, who had specifically told me I'd been dismissed.

My brow furrowed. I didn't know who the hell that voice belonged to or what they were playing at, but I wasn't going to stand there while they lied.

I tried to tell Landon what happened, but he muffled the sound of my voice with his hand, the look in his eyes clearly ordering me to wait.

Huffing and resisting the urge to lick his palm again, I decided to chill. Only because Landon seemed hell bent on staying hidden, and I wanted to know what was going on more than I wanted to get a rise out of him.

Momentarily, of course.

Kingston's voice rang out sharply in the open hall. "Search the grounds. *Now*. I want her found and brought directly to me."

"As you wish."

My lip curled at those words delivered by whoever that lying, duplicitous, totally shady jerk was. I had a good feeling his search would come up empty. And if Landon hadn't already found me, the place I'd be going if that guy had *wouldn't* be to Kingston.

Maybe my concern over ending up on a milk carton hadn't been so off base.

Footsteps retreated down the hall, and once the front doors opened and slammed closed, Landon whistled. The sound rang in my ears, followed by quick footsteps approaching. Landon's eyes never left my face, but he slowly removed his hand as Kingston walked up to us.

"Quinn!" Kingston rushed forward. "There you are! Are you alright?"

Landon stepped back to let Kingston take his place, clasping his hands behind his back and dropping his eyes to the ground. My eyebrows rose, but I couldn't dwell on it. Kingston took my face in his hands and pulled my gaze to his.

"I'm fine," I assured him, and the relief on his face made me feel all warm and fuzzy inside, which I reminded myself was ridiculous as I told my lady bits to cool it. "But that guy is lying. He turned me away at the gate. And he sent Brutus after me."

Landon's head popped up. "That's why you look like that?" Blurting the question as though he couldn't help himself, he raised his hands in defense when he caught my answering glare. "I didn't know that happened. I was just asking."

"Maybe next time you can ask *before* you insult me and imply I went a few rounds in the dirt. Hmm?"

Kingston's head snapped to Landon, who dropped his back down. "I thought you agreed to be nice."

"I didn't say she looked bad after doing it."

My jaw dropped. "Oh, please! Don't even pretend you said it like a compliment."

Landon shrugged.

I growled my frustration and turned back to Kingston. "Do you see what I'm dealing with here?"

Kingston couldn't hide his amusement or lack of any genuine sympathy for my plight. "I trust you can handle him. Now, back to what happened earlier. You said Merle turned you away at the gate?"

"Yes. I heard his voice on the intercom. It's the same one I heard in the Round Tableau talking to Max after he unlocked—"

"You talked to Max in the Round Tableau?"

I glanced sharply at Landon, disliking the accusation in his eyes. "Yes, oh gallant Knight of mine. He freed me after you left me locked in the room." I refocused on Kingston. "Max just let me out. He was a dick, as usual. And when his dad came, he said something about Max having news for him about a development before they went to his room... And I swear it was the same voice on the intercom and just now on the stairs."

Kingston searched my face before sharing a look with Landon. "Merle's been with me for the last hour, Quinn. It couldn't have been him."

"Oh." I wracked my brain, trying to recall the voice I'd heard that night. "I thought it was the same voice."

Kingston took hold of my hands and squeezed them. "It's okay. We'll figure out who it was and make sure they're off campus as soon as possible."

He looked sharply at Landon, who nodded once, flicking his eyes to mine for a millisecond before he retrained them on the ground. Maybe it was just the way all the Knights acted around Kingston, but it was weird to see the dynamics of their roles here play out. Deference to someone only a year older than him made me think they took their whole *King-and-his-loyal-Knights* routine seriously.

That, or Landon knew Kingston kissed me.

But I didn't know what to do with that, and the thought of addressing it exhausted me. The entire day had been fucking exhausting, and it wasn't even noon.

My body sagged against the wall. "I need a shower. And a nap. Maybe not even in that order."

Kingston chuckled softly and released his hold on my face before turning to Landon again. "See to it that your Maiden gets what she needs."

At Landon's nod, Kingston turned back to me.

"I'm glad you're here and safe. I left something for you upstairs. An apology for not reaching out this past week, and because I won't be around as much during the first challenge. But Landon will take care of you. He'll fill you in on what you missed during the introduction, too. *After* you rest."

I nodded, touched by the unexpected gesture. He took my hand, toying with a charm on my bracelet before he placed my palm in Landon's. A current of electricity rolled through me when our skin connected, fading slightly as Kingston pulled his hand away.

But something remained between Landon and me—a connection flowing differently, but present all the same.

And I wasn't sure how to feel about it.

Kingston stared at us both with a look I couldn't comprehend in his eyes. No jealousy. No fear. Just *peace*.

It was confusing as fuck.

With one last smile at me and nod to Landon, he took off down the hall. And then, it was just the two of us, standing together where he'd hidden us away behind the stairs.

I looked up at Landon as he returned to my side. Right where Kingston promised he'd be.

"Come on," he said quietly. "Let's get you to bed."

I told the tiny part of my brain that said *yes, sir* to lock it up. It wasn't even noon, for crying out loud.

I'd fallen asleep listening to the sound of his voice, and he'd still been there, lying beside me, when I woke up.

Chapter Sixteen
Quinn

Landon guided me out from where he'd hidden us behind the stairs, grabbing my bags before leading me up to the second floor. His grip held firm on my elbow, neither of us speaking in the wake of everything.

At the top of the stairs, the adrenaline keeping me going drained quickly.

I swayed on my feet.

Landon's arm looped around my waist, pinning me to his side to guide my steps—slow and steady.

"Almost there," he coaxed, his voice far more gentle than I'd heard it so far. "I've got you."

Whether consciously or not, his thumb stroked over my hip. Soothing circles, gentle swipes—each soft touch reminded me of our night in the Round Tableau. And I hated the way he calmed me so effectively, lulling me nearly to sleep on my feet.

Landon led me to the end of the hall, stopping us in front of his room. Opening the door, he swung it wide. I suppressed a gulp as I stared at the large and intimidating bed in the center of the room.

"After you, Maiden."

Landon set my bags down and stepped farther inside, opening a small door on the left side of the room. "You should get some rest. Bathroom is here. I can show you the campus and explain the rules once you wake up."

I peeked inside the bathroom like a dutiful houseguest, pleased to see the large shower stall had fogged glass. The sink counter was pristine and free of bottles or general clutter. That didn't shock me one bit.

But what did surprise me were two tall bookcases next to a large window opposite his bedroom door.

Set behind a beautiful and plush chaise lounge chair, leather-bound books filled the shelves. Just like the first editions my dad used to keep in his office.

My feet carried me to them on instinct, and my fingers traced over the spines of some of my dad's old favorites.

I glanced back to where he stood watching me. "You like to read?"

His books weren't in pristine condition, like everything else in his room. They looked not only read but well loved. So, I wasn't surprised when he nodded.

I returned it with a nod of my own and went back to browsing the shelves.

"My dad loved to read," I said softly, a note of melancholy in my voice I hadn't intended to share with him. But thoughts of my dad always made me sad, even when I relived my happiest memories of him. "He used to read to me every night, and then whenever I got sick, once I was too old to be tucked in at night."

A smile tugged at the corner of my mouth, but tears filled my eyes as I found an old copy of *The Princess Bride*. I traced the letters on the spine and tried to hold off the grief rising in my chest. It clawed its way up my throat, making my voice a hoarse croak when I finally spoke.

"This is the last book he read to me."

I'd been sick in bed, gearing up for my fifth rewatch of the movie adaptation of the novel, when my dad had shown up at the apartment. He'd insisted on turning off the television and reading to me, like the grandfather does for the boy in the movie. I'd fallen asleep listening to the sound of his voice, and he'd still been there, lying beside me, when I woke up.

Pain sliced through my chest as I relived the memory. Whenever I'd needed him, no matter how old I'd gotten, my dad had found a way to show up for me.

I'd never have that again.

"Would you like to have it?"

My eyebrows rose at the offer and pulled something tighter in my chest. But I shook my head.

Even though it was incredibly thoughtful, I didn't need it.

"I have his copy in my bag." I pulled my eyes away from the book to meet his across the room. "But thank you, Landon. For offering."

He nodded again, but that was it.

Because for a fellow bibliophile, Landon Scott was impossible to read.

I sniffled and brought my hand up to my face, wiping tears that must've slipped out without me noticing. "I should probably get some rest."

"You can take the bed." He stepped away from it, heading back toward the door to the bedroom. "I'll just clear out for a bit."

"That's okay," I said too quickly.

Inside the room, the bed felt even larger and more imposing than it had outside of it. The last thing I needed was to get comfortable there, so I laid my hand on the back of the chaise, scrambling to come up with an excuse.

"I, um...I'd prefer to sleep here if that's alright with you. I have back problems, so..."

Without waiting for his response, I sat down on it. I could

feel him watching me as I got comfortable, probably not buying my excuse for a second, but I pretended I didn't notice.

I tucked my legs under me and turned toward the window, closing my eyes and hoping that would convince him to leave it alone if he was on to me.

Talking to him about my dad had been too personal, and I didn't need to blur the lines between us like that. I blamed it on the exhaustion.

Something soft landed over my body and my eyes shot open, giving away my ruse of sleep. My cheeks warmed, and so did the rest of my body, as I realized Landon had covered me with a blanket.

He set a small box tied up with a blue ribbon on my lap. "From Kingston."

I pulled off the ribbon and lifted the lid.

As soon as I opened it, I wondered if I should've waited until Landon left the room. But that felt like overthinking things, so I peeked inside the box, picking out the small item nestled in tissue paper.

A charm for my bracelet.

Kingston must've noticed it at the Maiden Selection. The gold bauble matched my bracelet and the other charms on it perfectly.

Most of them, I'd added myself or received from Gia over the years. The rest were from my parents. Charms they gave me on my birthday right before my mom passed away, and some given later by my dad.

I never took it off.

Closing the lid on the box, I shut my eyes. It was a beautiful gift, but a tear slid down my cheek.

Memories of my parents overwhelmed me after seeing Landon's book, and I couldn't deal with it.

Not with a witness standing over me.

But Landon didn't call me out on my response to

Kingston's gift, and his voice wrapped around me like the fleece throw. "Do you want me to close the curtains?"

He stared out the window, letting me have my reaction without an audience. I followed his gaze to the crystal blue lake outside his window.

"Yes, please. Maybe just a little. The view is..."

It hadn't been my focus upon entering the room, but seeing it now, the lap of the water against the shore was almost as soothing as the sound of his voice.

"Something about it feels peaceful. I'd like to look at it until I fall asleep."

He pulled the curtains shut so the picturesque blue water stayed in my line of vision. Without letting in so much light that I wouldn't be able to sleep. Calm settled over me, and I yawned as he went to the door.

"I'll be back in a little while."

I hummed a sleepy sound and nodded. "Thank you."

Leveling out my breathing, I clutched Kingston's gift in my hands. I expected Landon to leave the room right away, but he lingered in the doorway. Something about knowing he was right there let me relax enough to drift off.

Clearly, I was over-exhausted.

That had to be the reason why my heart beat a little faster, even as I fell asleep.

You're not the only one who wore out his new toy.

MAX DREAD

"I hope you're not locking her in there." I glared at the so-called White Knight's back, enjoying the way he spun around to face me—caught off guard.

He knew I'd seen him gently closing the door like a fucking simp. I didn't hide the derision on my face as I glanced at his lingering grip on the doorknob. Landon let it go quickly and shoved both his hands in his pockets.

As if that would hide how red they were.

Everyone fawned over the King's most loyal Knight—especially Kingston. I couldn't go more than five seconds in a room without someone talking about him. Either for how *loyal* he was or to stir up the old rumors.

Coming from a family of betrayers was bound to offer anyone notoriety.

But I saw Landon for what he was—a snake in the fucking grass. I recognized that thoughtful gesture as one of many deeds of misdirection. If he played the good guy on the right, no one would pay attention to the destruction his darker side left in his wake.

I had. Not just last week, but a year ago.

Shrugging my shoulder, I couldn't resist the urge to bait him. "Though, I guess if you do, I can come to the rescue again."

"That won't be necessary, Max. But thank you." Keeping his expression neutral, he walked away from the door and passed in front of mine, that hint of darkness glinting in his golden-boy eyes. "I've got her very well taken care of from here. She's so worn out from this morning, I decided to let her rest before a harder training session tonight."

My jaw tightened so hard I thought the bone might snap. "You mean, that stunt with Brutus this morning was your doing?"

He said nothing, lifting his chin as his eyes narrowed on my reaction. The fucking prick was always watching, always assessing everything. I hated it.

The urge to smash his face rose up inside me, so I clenched my hands into fists. "Does Kingston know what kind of fucked up shit you're doing with her?"

Again, he said nothing.

"Or maybe he's the one putting you up to this?"

"Quinn has her safe words just like your Maiden does."

Unsurprisingly, he responded with some bullshit when I brought his lord and master into it. Fucking lap dog. Begging for scraps at the D'Arthur table.

Just like my fucking father.

"You seem a bit preoccupied with my Maiden, Dread. Is this an issue I should bring to your father's attention?"

I snapped my gaze to his, all but spitting on the ground as I stepped forward and got into his face. "I don't give a shit about your Maiden, Golden Boy."

Most people shrunk back when I stood at full height over them, but Landon didn't budge—*the impenetrable fuck*. I had three inches on him in height, but his build compensated for that. Where I had mass and brute strength, Landon had quietly honed power.

I hated that about him, too.

Especially when he used it to control a girl who couldn't stand against him. "But I do care about the code. You know, the Knights' Code we're supposed to live by? Pretty sure tormenting chicks for your amusement isn't part of it."

The corner of his mouth twitched with the hint of a smirk. "You sure that's all it is?"

"Like I give a shit about some charity case. Especially a virgin one on top of it? That's not exactly my type, Landon." I leaned back against the wall by my door, where Vivian had put herself on display before taking a nap. While it wouldn't be in the way she'd hoped, I planned to use that to my advantage. "You're not the only one who wore out his new toy."

Landon raised his eyebrows in a sign of agreement.

"It seems not." He ran an assessing eye down Vivian's form before doing the same to mine. "If you don't mind, I have work to do before I can go back to my room and play." He patted my shoulder, his fingers digging into the muscle at my back so the gesture would appear to anyone else as friendly. "But I don't appreciate having another's eyes on what belongs to me. So, see that your lack of interest stays that way."

He released my shoulder and stepped back, while I resisted the urge to retaliate. We stared off, neither of us wanting to back down and both of us knowing we were off limits to each other physically. Until the new King reigned, our battle had to be a mental one. And the newest conquest in the war was shaping up to be my greatest chance for victory.

Using her, I could destroy them both.

"As thrilling as that sounds for the next time you leave me locked in a room, or spank me into submission, I'd rather pass."

Chapter Seventeen
Quinn

"Undress me."

From the dresser—where I'd been kindly minding my own damn business and unpacking my clothes—my head snapped to his.

Feeling refreshed after my nap, I had decided to put away my things. Landon had been gone when I woke up, but he'd gotten back a little while ago and had gone straight into the bathroom to shower. That had seemed odd for the middle of the afternoon, but it wouldn't have shocked me to find out he showered three times a day.

He seemed like the type.

I wasn't going to judge his hygiene rituals. But I'd gone back and forth on addressing the newest elephant in the room. Since he'd come out, he'd been watching me from across the room, and I'd been pretending not to notice as I put my things in the empty drawers he'd marked for me.

But I couldn't ignore him anymore. "I'm sorry. What did you just say?"

"You heard me." He stepped closer, his dark eyes holding no trace of humor. "Undress me."

My eyes narrowed on him, and I forced a laugh. "Is this some kind of welcoming prank?" I placed a neat stack of leggings in the drawer. "Or are there...I don't know. Some meds you forgot to take today?"

"Meds?"

"I'm implying that you must be crazy." I let out a sigh, reaching for a stack of t-shirts. "Because you're off your rocker if you think I'm going to undress you."

He closed the distance between us. "And you're off your rocker if you think this is an extended stay at the Camelot Motel. You're here to win The Quest, and to do that, you need me to train you. So, I'd suggest you get over your delicate sensibilities that prevent you from taking orders. Sooner rather than later."

I rolled my eyes. "Duly noted."

His hand snapped out and snatched my wrist. "Don't test me, Quinn."

The neat pile of clothes I'd been holding tumbled to the floor, and the charms on my bracelet dug into my skin. I glared at him. Clearly, the tentative truce I'd thought we'd reached this morning must've been in my imagination.

He'd reverted to the cold, emotionless control freak he'd been in the Round Tableau.

I found myself as annoyed with his behavior as I was then—and even more obnoxiously—still a little turned on by it.

With no intention of letting him know that, I gritted my teeth and refused to back down from his stare. "You do realize no one has *actually* explained The Quest to me, right?" I hated the note of breathlessness in my voice. "When you come out of nowhere and ask me to undress you, I genuinely don't know where that's coming from."

He huffed a laugh. "And you jump to the assumption that I'm asking out of what? Sheer passion for you?"

"Having a thing for me wouldn't be so crazy." I brushed past his insult, jerking my hand in his grip. *"Not having a thing for me and asking me to undress you? That, to me, sounds crazy."*

While he didn't let me go, his grip loosened slightly. "And if I had a thing for you? Would you do it?"

I smothered the tiny voice in my brain shouting *yes*. "No."

A smile curved the corner of his mouth. "And why not?"

"Because I'm not a sex puppet, Landon. I don't ask *how high* when you say *jump*." My heart rate kicked up. "And besides, it's a moot point unless…Do you have a thing for me?"

He didn't respond, his head cocking to the side as he eyed me curiously. After a few beats of prolonged staring, I tried to yank my hand out of his grip again.

His fingers tightened over my wrist. "You really don't know anything about The Quest?"

I shook my head. "No. Care to enlighten me? Because if not, I'd like to finish unpacking."

He eyed the clothes at his feet and my leggings before raking his gaze over my outfit.

For my first day, I'd chosen my comfiest but most unflattering pair of jeans. The boyfriend fit hid my curves perfectly, but I'd paired it with a white crop top to claim it was a sexy look if someone bitched.

It was less sexy after my run in with Brutus—streaked with grass and probably a bit of sweat under my arms.

Opting to forgo the cute booties I usually wore with these jeans, I completed the look with a pair of athletic tube socks—white with red stripes where they banded around my calf. My worn-out white sneakers, covered with dirt and bits of tree bark, had been haphazardly toed off somewhere near the chaise by the window.

I wasn't a slob by nature, but the sound of his teeth gritting as he'd nudged my shoes into an acceptable spot had been totally worth acting like one.

Landon wrinkled his nose at my appearance, as if he hadn't seen me right after my run for my life, but he full-on blanched when he caught sight of my sleep shirts. "What the fuck are you even putting in those drawers?"

"*Clothes*. You know, what people wear when they aren't trying to impress a house full of egomaniacs." I exaggerated a roll of my eyes, then pinned my stare on his hand—the one still entrapping my wrist. "Do you mind? I'd like to finish."

Barking a laugh, he pointedly ignored my request. His eyes sparkled with amusement, warm flecks of amber glinting within the brown depths. "Are you sure there aren't meds *you* need to take today?"

I tugged against his hold. "What's *that* supposed to mean?"

He filched one of my oversized pajama shirts out of the drawer—a particular favorite with grumpy cats all over it—holding it up between us like it was a venomous snake.

"Just that you've clearly lost your mind if you think you'll need any of this."

I swallowed, my bravado weakening under a wave of lust that hit me at his implication. But I kept my voice steady and tried to sound as bored as possible when I responded, "Oh, gee. Let me guess. More lingerie?"

His fingers flexed over my wrist, a wolfish grin curving his full lips. "If I let you wear anything at all."

Desire swirled in my belly, and I yanked on my wrist.

He released me, his eyes tracking my retreat and sizing me up like we'd entered a sparring ring without my awareness. I made a show of rubbing my arm, even though his grip had been gentle.

For a controlling brute throwing his weight around.

"As thrilling as that sounds for the next time you leave me locked in a room, or spank me into submission. I'd rather pass." Crossing my arms over my chest, I squared off with him. And hid the way my nipples tightened under my shirt at the memory. "Thanks for that, by the way."

He crossed his arms over his chest, mirroring my posture. "Trust me, you have more than that to look forward to if you want to win."

"And are you actually going to tell me what that entails? Or just dangle it over my head like a carrot."

He smirked. "Haven't decided."

I threw my hands up. "Of course, you haven't."

He glanced down at my very unshielded chest, the smirk on his face fading. And it disappeared entirely when I propped my hands on my hips.

"Can't really blame me when you keep bouncing after it like a sexy bunny," he muttered, scrubbing a hand over his jaw.

My annoyance morphed instantly to amusement—very smug, totally at his expense amusement—and the wide grin that appeared on my face alerted him to what he'd said out loud.

He groaned.

"You think I'm a sexy bunny," I teased.

His spine straightened, as if my joy had shoved a rod up his ass. "I said you bounce *like* a bunny."

"Yes, but a *sexy* one."

Nearly bouncing with glee right then, I walked over to him with a little extra pep in my step and patted him on the chest.

His muscles tightened, bulging under my palm and almost stealing the humor from the moment. But the tightly-wound grimace on Landon's face kept it alive—for me, at least.

"I'm here because I have a job to do, Maiden."

I mocked him in my best robot voice, "I'm here because I have a job to do." Looping my arm through his, I tugged him backwards toward the door. "So you've said. Now, come on, Honey Bunny. You owe me a tour."

"I have things to do."

"Sure you do," I said with all the sympathy in the world. "But the sooner you do this, the sooner I stop bouncing."

He grumbled under his breath before grabbing his keys. "Fine. Let's go."

I'd already seen the lake from Landon's window, but it dazzled in comparison as we walked down to the water's edge.

Behind the main house, the lawn led to a large dock with two small sailing boats tied onto it. A rack of paddle boards, kayaks, and all their associated oars and life jackets waited in the sun for summer activities to kick off.

"It won't be long before everyone spends most days out on the water. The first day or two, it's a lot quieter out here. Most of the Knights and Maidens won't come up for air until tomorrow morning."

"It takes that long for the other Maidens to get their Knights undressed? Man, I'm going to win The Quest, no problem."

Landon tried not to smile at my impish grin. He really did. But he couldn't resist.

And I couldn't blame him, since I made sure to walk backwards in front of him, bouncing when I said it.

"When I start taking orders, of course."

He shook his head, averting his eyes from my chest. "You're ridiculous."

"You love it."

I tossed my hair and turned back around as we headed to the dock, smiling when he bit back a groan. He could say what he wanted about my looser-fitting boyfriend jeans, but they still made my ass look great. Especially if I put my hands in the pockets and pulled them tight.

Which I did. Obviously.

"I'm never going to live that comment down. Am I?"

"Probably not." I laughed and walked up to the edge of the dock, staring out at the expanse of sparkling blue and tempted to jump right into it.

I was feeling more open to this whole thing, honestly. Now that I had unlocked Landon's code and figured out how to override his *ultra-serious-must-be-a-broody-ass* programming.

He stepped up to the edge of the dock beside me, and we stared out over the water.

Glancing over my left shoulder, I spotted the lemon tree I'd climbed to get away from Brutus. I tapped his chest, pointing it out and unable to resist teasing him.

"Okay, campus tour time. That right there—that is the tree I climbed to get away from the killer dog trying to eat me. And right there"—I pointed at the ground beneath it—"is where I fell to the ground and waited for him to pounce on top of me. And right—"

"Alright, alright." He clamped a hand over my mouth, dragging me back around to face the water. "You've made your point, Maiden."

Keeping me tucked under his side and muzzled by his hand, he took a deep breath. I stared up at him from beneath his arm, tempted to lick his hand, but his jaw muscle tightened and released a few times. He looked like he was about to share, and I wanted to see what he said.

He glanced back at the tree and frowned.

"They planted that tree nine years ago. It was already grown, but they dug it out from whatever tree farm, taking the roots and everything before bringing it here." His brow furrowed, and he turned back to the water. "Lemon trees are supposed to symbolize longevity and prosperity. But for some reason, every time I look at it, I feel...Angry, I guess. But I'm not sure why. It's just always bothered me."

My brow creased as I watched his features draw tight, like he was as confused as me.

"Last year, they planted another tree. It's ironic, don't you think? Planting a tree that symbolizes longevity to honor someone who died?"

My breathing hitched.

I hadn't given much thought to the rumors I heard down in the Round Tableau, and given what Gia had picked up that day in class, maybe I should've. Landon confirmed it, though. Last year, someone had actually died.

I didn't know if this was the part where he told me what happened or where he drowned me in the lake. Maybe both if he was one of those villains that liked to talk a lot before they got to the killing part. Either way, I stayed quiet as I waited for him to say more.

"They're actually planted all around the campus. But that one"—he nodded at the tree I'd climbed—"and another on the other side of the lake were the first two planted. They symbolize longevity and prosperity for Camelot Court. Not the person."

I nodded as I took that in, but in a weird way, it made sense.

After losing someone, sometimes people needed a reminder that life was supposed to go on. We were supposed to keep living. Enjoy a long, full, and happy existence, rather than just going through the motions. I understood the sentiment, but I also got how Landon felt about it.

Bitter.

Because death took without considering who was good or bad. Guilty or innocent. It didn't discriminate between who deserved to die...

And who should've been the one who lived.

Sometimes, death chose wrong.

Landon sighed. "I was wrong before."

He glanced down at me, where I remained tucked under his arm with his palm over my mouth. I didn't try to get out of his hold, even though I probably should've. But when he didn't expand on that admission, I licked his palm.

"I'm trying to figure out how to explain the other night. I don't want—I'm not making excuses. I acted on information I had. I jumped to conclusions, but..." His arm tightened around my shoulders briefly and released. "But it's my job as a Knight to serve Camelot Court, and its King. Most of the time, that means making sure the pledges don't do something stupid. Participating in all of this and keeping the traditions alive. It's our generation's turn to make sure all of this survives. Prospers. And I thought…"

He frowned, and it was only because I could see how hard he was trying to express himself that I took pity on him. I covered his hand with my own, raising my eyebrows in question before tugging his hand away. He let me do it.

"Quinn, I thought you—"

"Hey, you don't have to say it. I won't lie and say I'm not curious *why,* but you thought all of this"—I waved a hand over my body—"was some kind of honey trap or something? I mean, I have no idea where that came from, but honestly, who could blame you?"

His lips twitched with that forbidden urge of his to smile, but he repressed it and sobered. He stared down at me intently, with nothing but sincerity in his dark amber eyes.

"I *am* sorry I scared you and if I hurt you. Even if I can't apologize for doing my…" He sighed, looking out at the water. *"Duty."*

"Doodie." I snickered, pinching his side. "That'll never get old."

"Oh, it really will," he deadpanned.

"Agree to disagree." I shrugged.

He tucked me back under his side, and we stood there quietly for a while. It may not have been the apology I'd imagined, but it felt like enough.

It *was* enough, and whether I realized it right then or not, a major turning point for me and my Knight.

"What if it was written into their marriage vows—to love, honor, and cherish thy husband *and* his best friend?"

Chapter Eighteen
Quinn

Camelot Court was even more beautiful in the daylight and on the right side of the gate.

My initial sneak peek at it during my drive by had been like smelling a single flower in a huge field of roses. The deeper I went into the grounds, the more intoxicated I became by the surreal little world they'd been hiding away just outside of campus.

I fell in love with it a little bit on that first tour.

Which was the last thing I needed to do.

Parallel to the path I'd taken the first night, we passed the Round Tableau house. In the daylight, I realized the party had been on the first level, and it had a second level I didn't visit. But I had no idea where the Round Tableau's private rooms were within it.

Unless they were underground.

"Is the—"

"Yes." Landon nodded. "The tunnels led you to a level below where we held the party. They go to a few places on the grounds. One leads back to the main house, too."

My eyebrows rose. "Where else?"

Landon shrugged, tucking his hands in his pockets and walking ahead of me. And while that tiny detail brought up about a hundred new questions, I focused on the answers I needed more.

But I'd be revisiting those tunnels with him at some point, that much I was sure of.

Off in the distance, tall trees and cliffs surrounded the lake, jagged outcroppings of rock at various heights. Some even looked low enough to jump off. A floating dock hovered out in the middle of the water, and up ahead there was a longer, thinner dock than the one right behind the main house.

A breeze swept through the trees and ruffled our hair, and the water rippled with light, sparkling like diamonds in an expanse of cerulean blue. Birds too far away to see called out to one another. It felt like this secluded world somehow went on for miles.

As much as I wanted to tease Landon and point out that it reeked of privilege, I couldn't bring myself to do it.

I stared at it, slightly awestruck, while he watched me from a few paces behind. When I opened my mouth to speak, I couldn't really find the words.

The only place I'd ever belonged had been with my parents. When they were both gone, it felt like being on a lifeboat that was drifting out to sea—the lone survivor of a destroyed homeland staring at the wreckage behind them—surrounded by a vast world they didn't have a place in anymore.

I didn't feel like I belonged anywhere, and that feeling had been my constant companion for the last year.

But for just a moment, staring out from the shore at the lake, the loneliness faded.

Landon's voice washed over me, drowning out the feeling even more. "Tell me."

Attempting to maintain some lines between us, a simpler version of the truth was easier to admit, "This is so much more than I expected."

Landon's head tilted, as if he wanted to dig beneath my layers and see what I hid inside. "Camelot Court or The Quest?"

"Both." I shot him a pointed look. "But the latter might be because my Knight has been withholding details."

"Delaying your satisfaction in receiving them," he corrected. "That's all."

"Potato. Potato."

He huffed a laugh. "Don't you mean po-ta-*toe,* po-ta-*tah?*"

"I said what I said. Now, details. Gimme."

We approached a small dock with two Adirondack chairs set at the end. Landon led me by the hand, keeping me steady as I rounded the chair and sat down.

And okay. Maybe there was a tiny bit of gallantry in him.

He took the chair beside me, resting his elbows on his knees as I got comfortable. I squirmed a bit and crossed my legs under me. Planting my hands on my knees, I nodded to signal I was ready.

"The goal of The Quest is to test the Maidens."

"Why?"

He shot me a look that clearly said he was getting to that, so I grinned and mimed zipping my lips.

He was too easy.

"The Camelot Society was formed around the idea of King Arthur and the Knights of the Round Table. Obviously. And according to the legends, or at least a few versions of them, Arthur married Guinevere and made her his queen."

"But she fell for Lancelot, too."

He nodded. "And it led to the end of Arthur's reign. His kingdom, all the good he had done or would have done, was brought to ruin because of Guinevere and Lancelot's treason. Some believe that if Arthur picked differently or made sure she could handle the responsibility of being Queen, his reign would've endured."

I snorted. "Or King Arthur could've learned to share."

Landon's eyebrows rose. "You don't think it was wrong what they did?"

"On principle, I think Guinevere got a bad rap in that whole love triangle debacle. I'd like that stated for the record."

"Noted."

"Do I think it's wrong to commit adultery when you've promised to be faithful to one person? Sure. But I also have a hard time judging their actions based on some old guy's version of their story. We don't know what happened. We don't know what they were like. Or what Arthur was like. What if it was written into their marriage vows—to love, honor, and cherish thy husband *and* his best friend?"

His throat bobbed.

When he didn't immediately squash the idea, my heart beat a little faster in my chest. Then, I reminded myself to settle the fuck down.

Landon cleared his throat. "I, uh, don't think I've seen that version of their vows in any of the history books."

I shot him an exasperated look. "Of course, you haven't. But either way, it's just a story. A cautionary tale where a woman brought down a good man or a great king before she lived out her days in shame at the nunnery."

"You don't think it was fair."

"She did what any man in her time would've been allowed to do simply because he had a dick. Of course, I don't think it's fair. It sounds like the bullshit narrative of a bitter man to me."

"You blame Arthur."

"I don't *blame* anyone," I grumbled, getting worked up even though I had a sneaking suspicion he was baiting me with his responses. "Except maybe the guy telling one side of the story."

"They do say history books are written by the winners."

I rolled my eyes. "Maybe it's time for a woman to get a

turn. Let us write the history books from here on out. Or, I don't know, be an equal voice in the dialogue."

Landon huffed but put his hands up when I glared at him. "I'm not disagreeing with you. Actually, quite the opposite."

"Well, it's good to know you have some sense under all that seriousness. But what does all of this have to do with The Quest?"

"The Quest was built around the idea that if Guinevere had been tested, Arthur's reign would've continued. So, The Quest is designed to test the mettle in the Maidens."

"But why?"

"You'll see."

I squawked in outrage. "Seriously! That line again?"

"Some things require patience, Maiden."

Scowling, I shot him a pointed look. "Since this started, I've been ordered around by a broody ass, called a liar, turned away at the gate, and given nearly zero details. That's a lot of blind faith to ask for, especially from a place that believes women need to prove themselves while the men, what? Fall victim to our womanly wiles?"

His eyebrow rose.

"Unless that's what this challenge is about, and that's why all of you are being so cryptic."

He mimed zipping his lips like I had.

I groaned. "Ugh. I should've negotiated a higher fee for my prize."

"Probably."

He pointed at something in the distance behind me. I could just make out a large, sprawling estate. Hidden by another wall and tucked away behind the trees, I would've missed it if he hadn't pointed it out.

"The first phase of The Quest takes place over thirty days and has two challenges. I can tell you the next one tests your honor."

"Honor?"

"We'll spend three weeks here...getting to know each other. The Knights use that time to decide if their Maiden has what it takes to make it through the next challenge. When we go to Pendragon Estate. There, you'll spend six days with a different Knight."

My eyes widened. "Wait, what? You just hand me over to someone else? For what?"

Landon's voice tightened. "Whatever you allow."

"What the hell does that mean?" I shot to my feet. "They can try to sleep with me and if I don't fight them off, I lose? That's bullshit!"

Unsurprisingly, Landon rose with me. I jolted away from him, jumping to conclusions and losing my footing in the same breath. His arm banded around my waist to keep me securely on the dock.

"No one can force you to do anything here, Quinn. They can try to seduce you, but you *always* have your safe words. They can't do anything that crosses a very clear line." His gentle but firm tone calmed me down instantly, and sensing that, his hold on my body loosened. "Not unless you ask them to."

I struggled to wrap my head around that.

On one hand, it sounded like an easy win.

My intention being to not let Landon get far with the use of my safe words, I wasn't even remotely concerned about another random Knight.

But then, Max popped into my head.

And appropriately, dread followed.

The thought of staying strong with Landon now that I'd stupidly thawed the ice between us *and* allowed dirty fantasies to pop into my head was already daunting. But the idea of spending six days alone with Max made me nervous, in more ways than one based on his latest taunts.

"Which Knight gets me for the six days?"

Landon's jaw tightened, and for a split second, I worried my thoughts were written clear as day on my face or that I'd accidentally said his name. But as quickly as that tension in him appeared, it was gone.

"We won't find out until we get to Pendragon. First, there's the Knights' Quorum, where the Knights announce if their Maiden should move on, then we'll go to Pendragon Estate for the drawing of names. But it's random and done in front of everyone."

I breathed a sigh of relief. I appreciated that Landon explained all of this like it was a given that I'd get there. And that when I did, the chances of ending up paired with Max were low.

At least, I had good odds.

It would be up to fate to put me with him or not, and even if she was a cruel bitch who loved to stir up drama, I had the motivation to resist him.

I shook my head at the bizarre situation I'd put myself in, but it was starting to make sense, at least. "So, is that why all of the Maidens come expecting to sleep with the Knights? You guys see it as motivation for us to resist the other Knight by getting..." I chose my words carefully, aware that his arms were still wrapped around me. "*Intimate* with the one that picked us?"

He released me and stepped back. "That's the idea."

I watched him pace the edge of the dock, wishing I could get inside his brain and figure him out. One thing occurred to me, though. "So when you asked me to undress you earlier, that's just part of preparing me?"

He nodded. "It's my job to do whatever it takes to keep you from giving in to the other Knight. Because if you do, you're eliminated."

"Oh. Right."

His gaze sharpened on my face. "And trust me, it

won't matter who you get. All of the Knights are extremely motivated during the challenge, trusting their Maiden to resist. If they get a different one eliminated, the better the chances of having picked the winning girl."

I swallowed, way more intimidated by this whole thing than I'd been while reading the contract buzzed on boxed wine. But the thought of the prize money at the end, and the slate it would wipe clean, steeled my spine and strengthened my resolve. Even though his response had brought a few new questions to mind, I didn't want to let them distract me.

"I'm going to win." I lifted my chin and stared right at him. "There's nothing and *no one* I want more than that."

He held my gaze for a moment before taking my hand and leading me safely around the chairs. "And you'll have my bid to go forward because of it. But I still need to prepare you. And in order to do that, there have to be rules."

"Right. Your whole *no kissing* thing."

We walked along the shore toward the main building, passing the Round Tableau again. I glanced back as we approached the main house.

"You do get that that was, like, super weird out of context, right? Still feels a little weird now, too."

"It maintains a degree of distance between us while I'm training you. In the midst of all the...endorphins and oxytocin, kissing—" He shook his head, and I wondered if he was trying to clear the image from his mind, the way I was trying to force it out of mine. "It can blur the lines. From a strictly practical standpoint, it's the safest bet."

I scoffed, skipping a few paces ahead of him. "Someone sure is overconfident. You really think a few orgasms and kisses would be enough to make me forget why I came here?"

Taunting him, I added an extra bounce to my step just before reaching the back steps.

He sucked in a sharp breath.

The King's Maiden

"*If* you can even get me there, that is." I smirked.

Landon's chest hit my back. Before I even registered him moving, strong hands gripped my upper arms. The veins on his forearms bulged as he pulled me close. I gasped.

He walked us forward, pressing me against the rough brick wall. Welding his body to mine.

I could feel him *everywhere.*

His heartbeat pounding at my back. His erection digging into my ass. And when his hips rocked against mine, I moaned low and deep in the back of my throat before I could stop myself.

He dropped his head to my shoulder and nipped. Tracing a path up the curve of my neck, he buried his nose in my hair and inhaled deeply.

His soft exhale warmed up my skin like a prelude.

Drawing soft patterns on my arms, he stirred emotion hidden in my chest. He coaxed out desire I'd buried deep. Every breath and touch composing a symphony of pleasure inside my body.

I swallowed hard, praying he didn't notice the way it came out like a *gulp*.

His throaty chuckle assured me he did. "Oh, Maiden, I *will* get you there. You can count on that. I'll make you come until you're begging me to stop."

My breathing hitched.

And my throat suddenly felt bone dry, as if he'd siphoned all the moisture in my body and redirected it between my thighs. Priming me for him. Preparing for the inevitable.

My pussy practically wept for it.

The *fucking traitor.*

As if he knew that, too, Landon slipped his hand between my body and the wall. Running his palm along the exposed skin at my midriff, he flicked the top button on my jeans open and dragged my zipper down in one slow, tortuous pull.

My safe words and intentions to stay his hand were long forgotten. When his palm slid between my legs, the flimsy scrap of fabric formerly known as my dry panties did nothing to shield me from him.

His deep groan rumbled in my ear, sending a pulse of desire rippling down my spine.

"You're fucking *soaked* for me, Maiden."

He circled the heel of his hand as his fingers played at the edge of my thong.

I bit back a whimper. Rocking my hips, I pulled another groan out of him as a stifled moan escaped me. It took a second to force my body still.

And while I fought not to chase after his touch, he tortured me further by whispering in my ear. "Does my Maiden want to come?"

My body screamed *fuck, yes please,* but my stubborn mouth said, "I'm fine, thank you."

He laughed—the first full-on, deep laugh I'd heard from him—and the sound went straight to my clit. I shut my eyes, biting my lip to stifle a louder moan. His teeth nipped at my ear while his hand hovered a breath away from my pussy.

"You sure about that?" His voice was pure sex, a blatant taunt that did nothing to lessen my desire. "You look a bit...worked up?"

I cursed my stupid boyfriend jeans and the space they gave him to tease me.

"Nope." I gritted my teeth, trying to keep my hips from bucking against his palm. "All good here."

"Such a stubborn girl. What a shame."

Withdrawing his hand from my jeans, he buttoned me back up. He snaked his hands along my arms to take hold of my wrists. Then, he flattened my palms against the wall above my head and pressed my body forward.

"I wanted to bury my face between your thighs and

prove my point."

I whimpered.

He stepped back, letting me go.

Sagging against the wall, I panted with the need for release. My nostrils flared as I forced air in and out, and it took me a minute to catch my breath. When I stared back at him, my eyes widened.

Adjusting his erection, he gripped his cock in a generous handful.

That brief glimpse beneath his palm seared into my brain like I'd just scanned his measurements for later. I gulped and restarted the process of calming down.

Gia's stick figure had *not* done him justice.

He lifted his head and caught my stare.

Closing the distance between us, his dark amber eyes pinned me to the wall.

"Good girls get orgasms, Maiden."

My thighs clenched.

Full lips taunted me with a knowing smirk. But when he gripped my chin, his hooded gaze held no trace of humor.

"You know where to find me when you're ready to be mine."

A girl could get used to that kind of lifestyle.
Another girl. Not me, of course.

Chapter Nineteen
Quinn

Two days had passed since my introduction to Camelot Court, and in a lot of ways, The Quest was a dream.

Reading books in Landon's room all day without a care in the world? A delivery service bringing meals to his door? *And* a pantry of junk food at my disposal in the kitchen?

A girl could get used to that kind of lifestyle.

Another girl. Not me, of course.

Because despite living that dream, I spent most of the time on edge. Torn between waiting for Landon to pounce and wanting him to do it, I figured it was only a matter of time before he subjected me to another round of sexually frustrating torture.

Opting to sleep on the chaise, I developed a crick in my neck. I diligently counted my sleep shirts in case he decided to burn one. And I barked my safe words at him anytime he came near me.

But so far, he'd left his taunt hanging between us.

He had other ways of torturing me, I'd quickly realized.

"You've got the Maiden Luncheon in an hour," he

reminded me before turning back to his book.

I groaned, sinking into the chaise and pulling the blanket over my head. Forcing a cough, I sniffled loudly and moaned a little. "I'm sick."

While the Maiden Luncheon could be a more fruitful opportunity to learn more about The Quest—since Landon thought *thirty days of testing your honor* had been a sufficient explanation—I'd been dreading it. He had informed me with a little too much satisfaction that the dress code didn't include my shapeless, baggy excuse for jeans.

Then, he pulled a dress out of the closet.

I wasn't sure why lunch with the girls meant I needed to dress like an over-priced escort, but he'd been quick to tell me it was non-negotiable when he saw the look on my face.

He didn't buy my fake sick routine either. "Come here."

Flinging off the blanket, I did my best to seem weak and sickly as I slugged over to him. "It might be the flu. It's that time of year."

"It's the middle of summer."

I faked another cough. "The bugs must be getting stronger."

He gave me an exasperated look and beckoned me closer. When I made it in front of him, stretching the five feet of distance into a marathon of dramatics, he thwacked my forehead with the back of his fingers. Not hard enough to hurt, but hard enough to let me know he didn't buy my bullshit.

"You're not warm."

"Neither are you," I muttered.

He cleared his throat, keeping his expression neutral, but for a second, I swore the corner of his mouth twitched.

"What if I go and get them all sick?"

"That would be a concern..." His hand brushed the hair back from my forehead. "If you were actually sick and not just being a child."

I crossed my arms over my chest. "Fine, but I'm wearing

my clothes."

"Great." He turned back to the desk, making me think for a minute he was letting me have my way. But as soon as I turned around, he cleared up any illusions I had about his ability to compromise. "Since that dress falls under the category of *your clothes* and adheres to the dress code for the Maiden Luncheon, it should work perfectly."

I whirled back around to protest, but he pointed at the dress without turning his head.

"Go on, Maiden. That's an order."

Eyeing the red dress, I stomped back over to the chaise and sat down with a huff. "You see how ridiculous this is, right? Dressing me like a sex doll for a tea party with the other girls."

"It's expected."

"Doesn't mean it's not ridiculous."

He shrugged before scribbling something else in his book. I glared at his back and the dress hanging on the back of the door. Grumbling to myself, I stalked into the bathroom, yanking the offensive garment off the hanger as I went.

Accepting my fate begrudgingly wasn't my style when the option to throw a little tantrum was on the table. Too bad my warden didn't care about my display of displeasure. He didn't even glance up from his desk.

What the hell he was doing over there, I had no idea.

But I didn't have long to think about it, since hair and makeup were a part of the dress code for this shindig. Landon had already warned me about being late to a *second* event with the other Maidens. He'd also grumbled under his breath—something about punishment and not being that kind of Knight.

If he meant for me to hear that, it had the opposite of what I assumed his desired response would be. With renewed incentive to disobey his rules rather than to follow them, I had to tell my traitorous pussy to calm the fuck down. I still had no intention of giving in to him.

I locked myself in the bathroom as quickly as possible so I couldn't purposefully get myself into trouble.

And so I could take the edge off myself.

An hour later, I was primped, polished, and—most importantly for Landon—punctual.

He deposited me outside the formal dining room on the first floor, letting me know he'd be back to get me when it finished. I didn't protest him leading me around like a guide dog, only because I still couldn't tell my ass from my elbow as far as the layout of the house was concerned.

Staring around the prim and properly decorated space as I took my seat, it did not make me feel better to see that everyone else at the table was dressed in the same skimpy outfits. But it did help that most of the girls shared my displeasure over it.

"I was taking a sip of water when he showed me the dress," one of the Maidens shared with the group, lifting her glass to her lips. "I spit it out on his shoes."

A collective gasp sounded around the table, from everyone but me.

Her reaction sounded perfectly reasonable from where I was sitting. "If I'd had something in my mouth at the time, I would've spit it out, too." I raised my glass to her. "Can't say it would've been an accident, either."

This shocked everyone even more.

I looked around at the other girls, confused by their reactions. They stared back at me like I was crazy.

"What? You can't tell me any of you were excited to be dressed up like this."

Most of them shook their heads, but a few wouldn't meet my eyes. They glanced around at each other, clearly uncomfortable.

No one would say what was on their minds, though.

But, of course, Vivian didn't have that problem.

"I knew you looked like a little freak." She snorted and whispered something to the Maiden beside her.

My brows drew in as my annoyance flared. "What the hell are you talking about?"

She ignored my question, pursing her lips as she assessed me. "No, it's not that you're a freak by nature..."

Her icy blue gaze ran up and down my body and she tapped her chin, smiling when the most vile response she could think of came to her.

"It's the dead daddy issues. Isn't it?"

My hands cracked against the marble table, and I pushed back from my seat. I was over this whole charade before I'd even left Landon's room. I sure as fuck wasn't going to stick around when Vivian was running her mouth before lunch had been served.

I threw my napkin down on my empty seat. "Well, ladies, this has been a barrel of laughs. Can't wait to do it again, but now, I'm done."

Eyes widened around the table before more whispers followed. Brushing that aside, I smiled my sweetest smile at Vivian. "Hey, V, do me a favor and give Max my best."

I added a wink for good measure, enjoying the way her mouth pinched tighter despite her efforts to appear nonplussed. It didn't shock me in the least when she refused to let me have the last word, pulling out the oldest trick in the slut-shaming handbook—the coughed slur.

"Whore."

Rolling my eyes, I adjusted the hem of my dress. "Real original, sweetie."

She glared, and as much as I wanted to rile her up by not letting any future insults get to me, getting the fuck out of there sounded even more satisfying.

I turned to leave the room.

But Elaine tugged on my arm, whispering urgently, "Sit down, Quinn."

I shot daggers at where she gripped me, but the panic on her face gave me pause. "I want to leave, Elaine. I'm sure you all will be fine without me."

Raising my eyebrows at her hand, I waited for her to release me. She only tugged harder.

"If you leave—if anyone leaves—we'll all get in trouble." Her eyes shot to Vivian and back to mine. "Please, just ignore her. Sit and talk with me, so we can get through this."

Despite my better judgment, and the overwhelming number of red flags her statement raised, I sat back down. She calmed down, letting out a rush of breath and waiting until I tucked my chair back under the table to let my arm go.

The skin on my arm had five perfect half-moon indents from her nails.

"What the hell is going on?" I asked her quietly. "I feel like I'm missing something huge here, and it would be great if you could fill in the blanks."

Her eyes shifted around the room. "Didn't Landon tell you the rules?"

"No, or I wouldn't be asking," I snapped. But I reined myself back in when she grimaced. "Sorry, I'm just confused and on edge. Can you please tell me what's going on? Landon told me basically nothing. He just ordered me to undress him."

Elaine's features tightened. "Yeah, it's supposed to push us past the awkward getting to know each other part...I wish they gave it a little more time."

"Wait, what? But you seemed so gung-ho about it when we met that first night."

She blushed. "Yeah, when I thought—"

"Oh." I sat back in my chair, putting distance between us. When she thought she was spending the night with

Landon, her longtime crush, she'd wanted to rush to the good part. Instead, I ended up in his bed. She ended up with a Knight she wasn't expecting.

"Why didn't you just tell him that? Wouldn't he have understood if you wanted to wait?"

Her eyes widened like I'd just told her to run naked around the room.

"What are you talking about? I mean, I know you missed the Maiden Introduction, but you know what we signed up for, Quinn. We have to do what they say. Give them what they want. When they want it. I thought you wanted to win this. Now, it sounds like you're purposefully doing things to get yourself eliminated. Or worse—punished."

I had to quiet the part of my brain saying she needed to rethink her priorities. But only because I was starting to think the punishment I envisioned when Landon let that slip out was not the same as what some of the girls experienced. Before I could respond to Elaine, though, a server approached the table carrying a large tray of plates.

Another followed, and as they started setting the plates down in front of us, my response died on my tongue. As I waited for the servers to leave the room, I thought over the way everyone had been reacting—like they were scared of the way their Knights would respond if they spoke up for themselves.

Once it was just the Maidens in the room, Elaine cut up a small piece of her chicken and took a bite. I stared at my plate, wondering how the hell any of them could eat if that was what they were worried about. But I didn't understand why they thought they couldn't speak up for themselves, too.

While Landon had been clear that The Quest came with certain expectations, he hadn't threatened to *punish* me or pushed me toward sex once.

"Is that what happened when she spat on her Knight's

shoes by accident?" I kept my voice low so only she could hear me. "Did he punish her for that?"

Elaine swallowed and nodded her head.

"Why didn't she use her safe words?"

Elaine shrugged. "Maybe she did. But most of us realize that's part of this whole thing. Do what they want, take the punishment if we disobey them. From what the girls have said, the Knights make it worth their while if it comes to that." She chewed on her bottom lip. "Plus, we don't really want them thinking we're weak. Or they might not vouch for us to go to Pendragon."

"They'd really say you shouldn't keep going if…What? You don't blow them every time they demand it?"

Elaine took another small bite of food, nodding and eating like this all made perfect sense. "They can tell Kingston if they don't think we have what it takes and we can be eliminated before we get to that part."

"Do we get a chance to defend ourselves at least?"

"Yeah, but it sort of marks you as an easy target if your Knight doesn't vouch for you."

"Oh." I stared down at my plate of food, feeling uncomfortable as fuck. "You guys see how fucked up all of that is, right?"

Again, she shrugged. "It's tradition."

"Yeah, but that doesn't make it right."

But her response wasn't what I expected. "You're not like us, Quinn. You're not from our world. Most of us have grown up knowing about The Quest. I get it can be a little jarring from the outside, but honestly, the whole punishment thing, it rarely comes down to anything serious. You've seen the guys. So, your Knight wants some head to start the day? Why fight it when you know he's going to make you come right after?"

I understood her logic. But she sank her talons in my arm to keep me from leaving the table. "If it's not that bad, why can't I go back to the room?"

"Because no one shirks an order from the King. Not even *his* Maiden."

My eyebrows rose. "Why did you say it like that?"

I still didn't know what the hell that meant—me being *here for the King*—but she obviously resented the title.

Elaine set her fork and knife on the table and wiped her mouth with her napkin. "Some of these traditions, like the selection process, this luncheon and the party next week, they've been a part of The Quest for generations. It's one thing to be punished for my own actions, but it's a different story to be punished for yours. You don't have to agree with the traditions to go along with them for everyone else's sake."

Maybe in her world that was how it worked.

But I'd been taught different lessons growing up, and I thanked my lucky stars I had grown up with parents who taught me to keep my head strong and let my inner voice guide me, rather than the expectations of others.

Maybe that made me an outsider to everyone else at Camelot Court. Maybe that meant I was different from Elaine and the other Maidens.

That didn't bother me one bit.

But why hadn't Landon hadn't treated me like the other Knights treated their Maidens?

So far, he'd left the option for more up to me. Without any additional pressure of being pushed before I was ready. Or fear over being punished.

Maybe he was more chivalrous than controlling. Maybe he was different, too.

And if that was the case...

I was in more trouble than I'd originally thought.

His tongue swept over mine right as my hands came to his chest—surely to push him away.

Chapter Twenty
Quinn

I made it through the rest of the week without being propositioned. And honestly, that confused me more than it relieved me, which meant I seriously needed to have my head examined.

No matter how many times I told myself I should *not* be attracted to Landon, or I needed to stop fantasizing about Landon, or I could *not* give in to Landon...

It wouldn't take.

He'd made it clear that, while he would no doubt be a very skilled lover, he wanted rules and to draw more lines between us than a toddler doing arts and crafts.

To him, this was a job—training me for The Quest.

And I was here to win it. Get the money and get out. That was the plan, and I had to stick to it. While I needed Landon to do that, I did *not* need to catch feelings or get attached. Especially since I'd already kissed Kingston.

But still, I found myself drawn to him.

So, I thought he was hot. That didn't mean I *liked* him. It only meant I wasn't blind. Because with his eyes like warm honey and cloves, a body that seemed to be pure, glorious muscle, and the completely unfair size of his dick, the guy *was* hot.

I wished—I wholeheartedly fucking wished—his personality negated all of it like I had thought it might the first night.

But unfortunately, that wasn't the case.

The more time I spent around him, even doing normal things like cooking in the main house's kitchen, reading in his room, or walking the expansive grounds of campus, the more obvious it became.

He was nothing like my ex or guys I'd wanted in the past. Broody and dark—he was *way* too serious for someone our age. His self-control bordered on slightly obsessive, and he adhered to his routines like he had an internal schedule hardwired into his brain. But even *that* didn't diminish how attractive he was.

To me, it only made him hotter.

And while I fought back against his abrupt and slightly domineering behavior, it was mostly on principle. Definitely not because I hated it. Every conversation we had felt like this weird, supercharged kind of foreplay as he battled for order, and I fought to create chaos. My body responded to him as if being pulled by gravity, the way the tide changed under the force of the moon.

I'd never experienced anything like it, and it was throwing me for a loop. Especially knowing the rules of The Quest allowed him to boss me around at the threat of punishment, he could've tried to use my desire to win—and his final say over whether that happened or not—against me. But he didn't.

Like I said, confusing as fuck.

I pushed up from my seat in the kitchen. "I need to get some air."

He turned from the stove, his eyes following as I stood and walked to the door. I could practically hear the wheels turning as he processed this abrupt change.

"You don't know where you're going."

He was right, of course. But I wasn't going to confirm that. The last thing I needed when I already felt on edge was another round of verbal foreplay.

"I'll figure it out." I waved a hand at him as I walked out of the kitchen.

The door swung shut behind me, leaving me alone in an empty corridor. I leaned against the wall and took a breath. Getting lost in the house seemed like a nice alternative to staring at Landon's ass while he cooked me food, only because the latter made me want to provoke him by ripping off my clothes in the middle of the communal kitchen.

"...eliminated...can't...rid of her..."

Muffled voices came from farther down the hallway. And like one of those girls in a scary movie who walked toward the dark room where the killer obviously lurked—instead of running in the opposite fucking direction—I crept closer.

"—make it through to the next round. If she doesn't, the more risk we have this won't play out in our favor."

My eyebrows shot up, and I ducked behind a giant suit of armor when it was Max who responded.

"I'm well aware of the stakes, Father."

The other voice, so similar to his son's, I now recognized as Merle. "Overconfidence is foolish, Max."

"You didn't see what I saw."

"So you keep saying. But he's not convinced it's enough. The plan is—"

"The plans changed the second she stepped through the door. I can promise you that."

"You'd better be right."

"I am."

A beat of silence passed between them, and it occurred to me that they could be preparing to leave the room through the doorway where I stood—very clearly eavesdropping on their private conversation.

I panicked, jolting back to turn and run away before they caught me, but in my haste, my foot caught on the giant suit of armor.

It crashed to the ground, taking me with it.

I shrieked and let out a stream of curses as I fell.

The heavy pieces of the gilded Knight buried me as it toppled from its perch, and I took each blow with a grunt of pain before clawing my way out of the wreckage. Shoving the chest plate off my body, I stared up at the ceiling and wondered how the hell I got here.

A second later, footsteps rushed over.

"Well, what do we have here?"

At first glance, Merle Dread was as tall and formidable as his son, and it had nothing to do with the way he stood over me. Max had inherited his build from his father, that much was obvious. But the older of the two Dreads had graying hair and crow's feet around his light brown eyes, as well as a smile on his face. I had to blink a few times to make sure I was seeing him clearly.

Meanwhile, the younger Dread stared down at me with no emotion on his face—barely even a hint of recognition. Max's eyes must've come from his mother, but I wondered if they held the same indifference as his onyx gaze.

With his arms crossed over a chest I refused to think about, he stood like a soldier at his father's side.

"This is Quinn Everly," he announced, his voice devoid of its usual heat and ego.

"Ah! Quinn Everly!" Merle's face lit up, and he eagerly helped me to my feet. "Kingston has told me so much about you. It's a pleasure to finally meet you, my dear girl."

He smiled at me expectantly, squeezing my hand like an old friend. Kingston had cleared him of being involved in my cold welcome to Camelot Court. But even though he looked harmless, I couldn't shake the nagging doubt in my mind.

Eschewing the rules of polite society, I withdrew my hand and stepped back. Unfortunately, that sent me stumbling over a piece of armor *and* brought me closer to Max, whose hand shot out to grip my arm. His fingers tightened as he held me upright, a clear warning in his eyes.

"Sorry." I got my feet beneath me and tugged my arm free, scrambling for an explanation they hadn't asked for yet. "I, uh…I got lost."

Max's eyes narrowed on my face.

I avoided his gaze and turned to his father. "Can you point me toward the kitchens? My Knight—um, Landon. He's waiting for me."

Merle laughed. "I'm surprised he let you out of his sight. Or his bedroom."

I forced a half-hearted chuckle, as if that hadn't been a totally creepy thing for him to say, but when his good-natured expression morphed into something darker, my urge to flee heightened exponentially.

"He's not still giving you trouble, is he?"

My foot halted mid-step. "What?"

"I heard about what happened the first night." Merle clucked like a strange mother hen, stepping toward me, and it clicked that his weird comment had been referring to Landon locking me in the room. "It's my job to make sure the Knights behave themselves. These young men…" He flicked his gaze toward Max. "Sometimes, they can get carried away with The Quest. *And* their Maidens. If you ever have concerns, I want you to come find me straight away."

My eyes shot to Max.

That wasn't even close to what he'd told me that night. He implied I was going to be kicked out for not pleasing my Knight. And I'd been so outraged I almost left on my own.

Now, as he stood there and didn't contradict his father's

claim, I couldn't help but feel like I'd been played.

"Thank you," I said to Merle, keeping my eyes on Max. "But I'm not sure my Knight is the one I have to worry about."

Max's jaw tightened, but he didn't say a word or even look at me. I scoffed and carefully made my way over the rest of the suit of armor. With its pieces between us, I could finally get the hell out of there.

I nodded politely at Merle this time. "If you'll excuse me, I really do have to go."

Taking off down the hallway, I headed to the right at the first turn and flinched when Max's voice called out behind me.

"Wrong way, Princess."

Huffing out my frustration, I veered left and walked straight down the hall. But I glanced back over my shoulder once I had put some distance between us. Merle hadn't moved, but he watched me with concern as I ran away. Max, on the other hand, had decided to follow me.

"Do you even know where you're going?"

I increased my pace, my hands tightening into fists at my side. "I'll fucking figure it out!"

"You'll get lost, Princess."

Whirling around, I jabbed my finger into his stupid, rock-hard chest and threw his words from our first meeting in his face. "Why do you care, *Max Dread?*"

He scowled at the point where I touched him. Or maybe it was because I'd rolled his name off my tongue as he'd done with mine that first night. Either way, he showed more emotion in those two seconds than he had the entire time I'd been with him and his father.

"Don't flatter yourself, Quinn Everly."

"You cared enough to lie to me that night."

He arched his brow. "Did I?"

I frowned, unsure if he referred to whether he'd cared or whether he'd lied. But deciding it didn't matter, I squared my shoulders and lifted my chin. "I'm sorry if me being here is hard for you, Max. But you're going to have to do more than that to get rid of me."

He pressed in closer. "Oh, you have no idea how hard you're making things for me." His eyes flicked down to my lips before looking away. *"If* you make it that far, I plan to return the favor."

I opened my mouth to shoot back at him, but Max took that moment to steal my breath with a kiss so full of pent-up rage, it sent fire raging through me. Searing my lips with his, he deepened the kiss before I could stop him. His tongue swept over mine right as my hands came to his chest—surely to push him away.

He growled, seizing my wrists. Hauling me into his arms, one hand dove into my hair. The other wrapped around my body.

He moved so quickly it knocked the wind out of me.

I wrenched my head back and panted for air, struggling to get out of his hold just as a familiar voice came from beside us.

"Get your fucking hands off my Maiden."

I gasped, turning toward Landon's voice. He glared at Max with more venom in his eyes than I'd ever seen a single person hold in one look. Relief washed over me that none of it was directed at me.

That quickly evaporated.

Max took his sweet time releasing me, dragging his hands down my back and coming dangerously close to my ass as he set me on my feet.

"What if she wants them on her?"

His smirking face begged to be smacked.

But my lips burned as if he'd branded me, and my skin felt warm everywhere we'd made contact.

So, I needed to stop touching him immediately.

As soon as he let me go, I jerked away from him.

"Not my fault if she's dishonoring herself already, Landon." Max shrugged, running his eyes over me as if I'd been stained in scarlet and bore a letter of shame on my chest. "Can't imagine how easy it'll be for one of us to break her in the next challenge."

The daggers I glared at him didn't even scratch the surface of his conscience—if he even had one—so I turned to Landon, pleading with him to see the truth and opening my mouth to defend myself.

Landon shook his head, silencing me before I could say anything.

My face fell. Disappointment sank in my gut. But when I moved to wrap my arms around myself, feeling indignation rise in my throat, Landon stopped me again.

"No. Don't, Quinn."

Although he gave the command sharply, he softened my name and his gaze in front of Max in a way that felt...intimate.

He held out his hand.

As soon as I took it, he pulled me into his side and turned back to Max. "Touch her again without her consent, and the King will see to it that you and your Maiden are disqualified."

Hatred burned in Max's eyes as fiercely as it resonated in Landon's voice. It ran so deep, it pulsated in the air between them. As if their hearts had been laced with poison and bound in barbed wire.

I didn't know how either of them could stand it, or what could've possibly happened between them that led to it.

But it hurt to even witness it.

I had to look away from both of them.

"You better hope she's not mine for the next challenge then, Golden Boy."

"I'm not worried." Landon's arm tightened around my shoulders in response. "And I won't warn you again, Dread."

As Landon spun us away, I caught a flash of something sinister on Max's face. But I couldn't focus on it long enough to figure out what it meant. Too quickly, Landon escorted me back down the hall in the correct direction of the kitchens.

Max disappeared behind us.

She was a pawn. A means to an end. A tool I'd sharpen and use against them.

MAX DREAD

Had I known what I was doing when I kissed her?
No.
Did I regret it?
Also, no.

But was I about to let that fucking girl walk in here and change everything? Make me question things? Alter plans I'd already set in motion?

I'd waited too long to destroy Kingston D'Arthur, ruin Landon Scott, and make my father pay.

She was a pawn. A means to an end. A tool I'd sharpen and use against them.

That kiss would get under her skin and get in his head. Even if he acted like he wasn't worried. Even if she acted like she felt nothing but regret.

It was a strategic move in the long game I had to play, and the only reason watching her walk away with him pissed me off.

That was it.
It had to be.

My inner voice practically panting *yes* concerned me.

Chapter Twenty-One
Quinn

As we walked away, I tried to gauge Landon's mood after what had just happened with Max.

I assumed I'd be left in the dark.

But for the first time, he didn't leave me wondering what was going on inside his head.

"Max has hated me since we joined KRT and came to live at Camelot Court. We pledged together our freshman year, but Kingston was a year older than us and the favorite for King in his senior year. Kingston and I have been friends since we were kids. Max has never liked that he preferred me."

"Wait, so the King changes every year?"

Landon nodded. "It's always a senior. I guess Max has aspirations for the job and he sees me as competition because of my friendship with Kingston. He's had it out for me ever since freshman year, at least. And now he has his sights set on you."

"Why go after me?"

Landon's jaw worked overtime as he thought about his response. He kept his eyes trained on our path through the house, going past the kitchens and to the stairs before he finally stopped and looked at me. "Because he thinks he can hurt us by eliminating you."

"Oh." I chewed on the inside of my lip, warring with myself over asking more, but I couldn't help myself. "Can he?"

"No."

He answered so quickly, I didn't have time to prepare myself for the sting. But that one word pierced through my protective outer shell and sank into the softer flesh hidden beneath it.

I couldn't deny it then.

Despite my best efforts not to, I'd started to care.

Landon, of course, noticed my reaction and wouldn't let me hide it from him. He gripped my chin and forced me to meet his gaze. "Not in the way he wants to hurt us."

Staring up at him, I warred with myself. I wanted to ask what that meant. But I wasn't sure I wanted to do anything with the knowledge—*if* he even gave it to me—so instead, I just nodded.

He let go of my chin, and we continued on up the stairs to the hallway where the Knights' rooms were. As we walked to the end of the hall, I thought through what he'd told me about The Quest and Max. It felt like he'd left out some serious bullet points in their shared history, but I also wasn't sure I wanted to know.

I almost didn't catch the sounds coming from behind their closed doors, but a girl crying out pulled my head up.

When she screamed, Landon's arms came around my shoulder. I tried to get out of his grip, but he pulled me tighter against him, stopping in the middle of the hall and spinning me into his chest. His arms wrapped tighter, pinning mine to my sides.

"Landon," I protested. "Let me go."

"Just wait." He growled as I battered his side with my fists, but he didn't let me go. *"Trust,* Maiden. I'm asking for your trust."

He didn't say it, but he asked for what he'd given me downstairs.

I stopped fighting him.

But when the girl's screams grew louder, my discomfort became more insistent. As if sensing that, Landon hitched my body up higher against his chest.

He leaned down and whispered in my ear. "She has her safe words, just like you do."

The deep rumble of his voice and warm breath against my skin combined at just the mention of my safe words sent a wave of arousal through me. But it hit me what he was saying—he thought her cries were from pleasure. He assumed they were consensual.

"The girls think using their safe words makes them weak," I argued. "At the Maiden's Luncheon, some of them were scared of being punished or eliminated."

His jaw clenched where it pressed against my cheek. "It's not supposed to be like that. And I promise I'll address it with Kingston, but I know Gavin and his history with his Maiden. This isn't...It's not the first time for them, or the rest of us within earshot. The Quest, I mean."

"Oh."

That information changed things, at least, for the moment. Suddenly, knowing the sounds coming from their room truly were consensual, it became impossible not to imagine what they were doing. I couldn't help but think of the different ways a Knight might draw out that kind of response from his Maiden.

My nipples hardened.

Which was unfortunate, since they were pressed against Landon's chest.

He pulled back, his attention snagging on my breasts. "Her Knight is also particularly skilled at reading his

Maiden's reactions. He knows when to ease up..." His gaze traveled up the column of my throat to my mouth. "And when to push and go harder."

A tiny gasp escaped me, my lips parting as his eyes locked on mine.

"Just like I do."

Breathing heavily, we stared at each other as her cries dissolved into drawn out moans. My face flooded with heat at the same time as arousal pooled between my thighs.

Landon studied my reactions, his eyes darkening.

"Does it turn you on?" His lips curved as he brought them to the shell of my ear. "Knowing what he's doing to her? Hearing her pleasure?"

I bit my lip and nodded.

"Tell me."

"Yes," I breathed. "Yes, it turns me on."

"Does it make you wonder what it might feel like? To have your own limits tested?"

I couldn't admit exactly how much it intrigued me. But thankfully, Landon offered me an out—a way to deny the truth building to a crest inside me.

"Or maybe it just makes you more open to the thought of preparing? Training with me for what you'll be up against next?"

"Yes. I want—" I swallowed deeply, wetting my lips as my ears filled with the sounds of pleasure that could be mine. "I want you to prepare me for the next challenge. I'm ready."

His pupils dilated as my tongue darted out to wet my lips. Every muscle in his body coiled tighter around me. And desire pulsed between my thighs. Even as I denied the full truth to him, I couldn't lie to myself anymore.

I wanted him, and I was ready.

"I'm ready to be your good girl now."

He crushed me in his grip before he quickly released me, swallowing deeply as he stared into my eyes. "Well, then it's time we do this properly."

Guiding me to his bedroom door, he gestured for me to go inside. Once I did, he let the door shut heavily behind me. His voice rumbled in my ear and sent a shiver down my spine as he pressed his body against mine.

"Welcome to The Quest, Maiden."

"Can I ask you something?"

From where Landon stood at the end of the bed, securing my ankle into a padded cuff, he turned toward me. His fingers paused in their task of fastening the restraint. But they brushed my skin idly as he waited for my question—something I had noticed he often did without thinking about it.

I gestured to my restrained ankle. "How does *this* help me win The Quest?"

He chuckled softly, returning to his task and binding the cuff with the Velcro closure. "Do you want me to tell you?" Tugging on the strap secured under his bed, he pulled my leg taut. "Or do you want me to show you?"

My breath caught in my throat.

Landon smirked before walking to the other end of the bed. His fingers wrapped around my free ankle. But when he grabbed the other cuff, he didn't immediately strap me in.

He jerked my leg toward him. "I asked you a question, Maiden?"

I huffed. "Fine. Show me."

He arched an eyebrow, his grip tightening slightly.

"Show me, please. *Sir.*"

I caved far too quickly under that tiny fraction of pressure, and if I hadn't already suspected it, I would've known then I was in trouble. If he only had to tighten his grip to get me to answer him like a submissive, what the hell else could he get me to do?

If he increased the force of his command, would I comply even faster—whatever the ask?

My inner voice practically panting *yes* concerned me.

But I couldn't dwell on it because, at my response, Landon had quickly fastened the second ankle cuff. When he pulled tight on the strap, my butt slid forward, and I fell back on the mattress.

Propping myself up on my elbows, I glared at him.

But he didn't see it.

His eyes fixed on my bare legs as he circled the bedpost and came to stand between my very spread, bare legs. Hardly covered by the black satin negligee as it was, if the damn thing rode up any farther, my matching black thong would be fully on display.

Landon seemed to realize that as well.

As he traced a line from my ankle up to the apex of my thighs, my core tightened, and the air rushed from my lungs. But I didn't squirm or try to shield myself—even though I still could. I wanted to tell myself it was because resisting seemed futile, but that would be a lie.

I didn't hate the way it felt to have his eyes on me—even though I still shouldn't want them there. It grew harder to remember why I had to hold myself back the longer he stared at me. And the darker his eyes became.

"Most of the other Knights think twenty-one days of sex is enough to keep their Maiden from giving into temptation at Pendragon."

He came around the bedpost, one hand stroking the solid wood as his other reached into his pocket. Pulling out a red tie, he draped it over my bare thigh. As he dragged the silk up my body, it trailed between my legs and up my stomach.

And when it teased over my peaked nipple, my back

arched reflexively.

He looped his end around my neck and let it fall between the valley of my breasts. I watched the crimson fabric rise and fall with the rapid pace of my breathing.

Landon's hand cupped the back of my head, tilting it up so I had to look at him. "Twenty-one days of orgasms, however mind-blowing, don't guarantee loyalty."

"They don't?"

At that moment, I had a strong feeling they wouldn't hurt the guy's chances. But Landon shook his head. His other hand came up to my chest, and he eased my body back onto the bed.

"When the offer for the same thing is on the table in front of you? Practically *begging* you to give in...On hands and knees promising you a world of pleasure...And fully prepared to give it to you?"

He swept my hair out from under my shoulders before laying my head down and letting me go. I ached at the loss of his touch almost instantly.

"You'd be strong enough to last a day. Maybe three or four. But six days with temptation staring you in the face?"

I swallowed, my mouth going dry as three very different and equally tempting images came to mind. It felt nearly impossible to imagine resisting.

My stubborn pride hated that.

"I told you, Landon. I came here to win. I want it more than anything. Or *anyone.*"

"So you've said." He smiled at the set of my jaw. "Let's test that theory, shall we?"

I lifted my chin. "Do your worst."

He climbed onto the bed, throwing his leg over my body and straddling me without warning. "I'll set the timer on my watch. Say you yield before it goes off and the test is over—I win. Outlast me and the timer—you win. Deal?"

"And you can't cross the line? Whatever the hell that means, considering you're on top of me?"

"It means no part of my body can touch anywhere on yours outside of your arms and legs up to mid-thigh. Nothing under a dress, nothing above the neck. Deal?"

"Can you order me to touch you? If so, where?"

His lips twitched. "Nothing under the shorts. No... Erogenous zones."

He held himself steady over my body, arching a brow as if waiting for my next question. The tension in his thighs distracted me, but I thought through what he said and nodded.

"I say I yield and you win. Outlast you and I win. Deal."

"Deal."

He started the timer on his watch.

Resting his forearms on either side of my head, he slowly lowered down. "Oh, and if you give in and ask me to touch you before the timer goes off, I still win..." His face hovered an inch away from mine, his lips curling into a wicked grin. "But I'll make you come so hard you'll scream."

My hips lifted on instinct, and I sucked in a quick breath. He held himself above me, his body rolling slowly as his mouth came inches away from my neck, collarbone, and breasts. Showing me how he'd move on top of me—what he'd do while he was inside me—if I said yes.

Pressing my back into the mattress, my mouth parted and eyes fixed on his lips. "That's playing dirty."

"That's exactly what you'll be up against." He continued to tempt me, staring at all the places he wasn't allowed to touch, with a hunger in his eyes that made no attempt to hide how much he wanted it.

Wanted me.

The confidence I'd felt about outlasting him a few minutes ago evaporated slowly. It vanished completely when his first command left his lips.

His warm, quiet breaths fanned my cheek as he leaned in close to my ear.

"Undress me."

Biting my lip, I trapped the words on my tongue, begging to be released. They were not the safe ones I planned to give him.

Chapter Twenty-Two
Quinn

"But that's—"

"Not against the rules." He glanced at his shirt, the tight-fitted button down straining over his chest and arms. "As long as you're careful not to touch me."

He pushed up higher to give me space.

I gulped, bringing my hands between our bodies and reaching for the first button. With shaky fingers, I pushed it through the tight hole and felt it release. One by one, I undid the buttons until his shirt fell open.

I drank in the sight of his bare chest like I'd gone days without water. Running over the hard planes of his pecs and the light smattering of hair covering his nipples, he said nothing while I took him in. But his muscles tensed as my eyes traversed the deeply defined ridges of his abs. Following the trail of light hair that dipped into the waistband of his black pants, it lured me down its path.

I gulped, and my heart raced as I tugged on his belt. Unbuckling it, I slid it from the belt loops, ready to toss it off the bed. Landon's voice stopped me.

"Leave it on the bed."

My fingers flexed over the leather, fist clenching reflexively at the dark promise laced in those words. I hesitated after setting it down.

"You're not done, Maiden."

I trembled as I undid the top button on his pants and slowly dragged the zipper down. Pushing his pants past his hips, I forced them as far as I could before laying back. He didn't move, waiting for me to finish.

Brow furrowing, I stared up at him—a question and a plea dying on my lips when I saw his eyes. Dark, unfiltered desire stared back at me.

"Use your legs."

I tried without thinking, jerking my leg against the tight restraint. The movement created friction between my legs that nearly drove me insane.

"Whoops." He grinned wickedly as I squirmed beneath him. "My bad."

"Asshole," I hissed out between clenched teeth. "I'm not giving in to you."

"Not yet."

He straightened his legs out between mine, planking over me in a way that tightened every muscle in his body. Kicking off his pants, he rested his knees inches from the satin scrap of fabric covering me. He sat back on his heels and rested his hands just above my knees.

His fingers brushed my skin, and that slight touch sent an undercurrent of desire straight to my clit. I groaned, pressing my head back into the mattress. Biting my lip, I trapped the words on my tongue, begging to be released.

They were *not* the safe ones I planned to give him.

And he knew it.

Slowly, painstakingly, he undid the cuffs of his sleeves and removed his shirt completely. I fought hard to keep my eyes on his, sure that if I let my gaze wander, it would be even harder to resist.

He knew that, too.

"Look at me, Quinn."

"I—I am."

"*All* of me."

My heart thundered so loudly in my ears I swore he had to hear it. Like a drum, it rapped out a frenzied beat as I lowered my gaze. Over his chest and abs to the dark lines of ink curving over his right hip. I'd been so focused on where the light hair below his belly button led, I hadn't seen it.

But it, too, forced my eyes down.

The design, half hidden by the black briefs hugging his body, called to me like a siren waiting on the rocks etched into his skin. White-capped waves crashed into them, the crystal blue water disappearing beneath the fabric.

I tried to keep my attention on his right hip, but Landon's hand distracted me, pulling my focus to where he and I both wanted it.

He palmed his erection through the thin layer of his boxers, and my hips lifted instinctively. I forced them back down and stilled. Landon watched while I battled with my basest desires, studying my features like a puzzle he desperately wanted to solve.

"Give me your hands."

I unclenched my fists from the bedsheets, drawing in a shaky breath as I tentatively held them out to him. He kept his eyes on my face and reached for his belt.

"What are y—"

"Shh." He silenced any further questions by taking my hands, sweeping his thumb over the inside of my wrists. "Relax, Quinn."

My pulse pounded beneath his touch, and I wanted to argue over the ridiculousness of his request. But the way he held my hands, softly caressing my skin without pushing for more, stopped me from protesting. He waited until my heart rate settled before speaking again.

"How long has it been?"

I blinked up at him, struggling to stay focused on the question. "What?"

"Since you were touched where you and I both know you need it." His hooded gaze flicked down to the hem of my negligee and desire liquified my core as if he'd melted me with one look. "How long has it been?"

"A week."

"Since you touched yourself?"

My cheeks colored at the thought of what I'd done in the shower before bed last night, only because I hadn't expected to tell him about my perfectly healthy exercise in self-love.

Believing it would be enough to keep my head straight, I had been quick to find release after all the tense moments of the day. But I'd been sorely mistaken in thinking it would make me want this less.

I definitely couldn't bring myself to admit that.

"Less than twenty-four hours," I said, giving him a partial truth I prayed he wouldn't recognize.

He nodded at my admission, looping the leather strap of the belt over my wrists. "It's harder than you thought it would be, isn't it?"

My eyes flicked to his erection, darkening the stain of red heating my face.

I looked away and nodded. "Yes."

He murmured his acknowledgment but said nothing else as he looped the strap around and back over. Crisscrossing between my wrists and over again, he bound my hands together. Then, he eased my arms up over my head, letting his body follow the movement.

"Our bodies were made for this, Maiden." Hovering above me, he reached for something I couldn't see and secured the belt to it. "Designed to respond and react. To give and to receive pleasure. It's natural to want it. To find yourself tempted even when you just had a release. The female body..." He slid down over my form until he fell back on his knees between my legs. "You were meant to receive endless pleasure. Given the ability to reach climax over and over again...Until you felt you couldn't bear it any longer. Until you cried out that you couldn't possibly come again. And do you know what would happen then?"

He paused, as if giving me the opportunity to respond. But he knew as well as I did I couldn't speak. Any hope for coherent thought died as the picture he painted with his words filled my mind.

And he wasn't done.

"Your body would still find a way to reach that peak if the pursuit of it was *relentless.*" He skimmed his fingers up my legs, the corner of his mouth lifting at the way my body tightened under his touch. "And I would be relentless, Quinn. Any Knight would be...With you beneath them."

"Oh, god," I whimpered.

My eyes fell closed as my pussy throbbed, and I moaned at the delicious ache it created. The ache *he* created with the slightest touch. Clenching my thighs, my core—my back arched. I pressed my head back into the bed, trying to stave off the need building inside me.

"How can I earn your loyalty just by giving...Or even by denying something you *need?*"

He dropped his head, pursing his lips and blowing softly between my legs. I cried out as everything coiled tighter inside me. And I found myself panting when he stopped.

"Landon."

He raised his eyebrows as I breathed out his name, but he didn't tear his eyes from my body. I writhed beneath him, going out of my mind with need—for him, for his touch, for *any* touch to ease the pressure inside me. I didn't care.

I just needed it—needed it now.

"Fuck."

It hit me that he was right. That I would fail if I didn't figure out a way to fight the havoc he wreaked on my senses. I wanted to win—my mind *knew* I needed to win—but my body needed just as much.

And I couldn't see how to get both.

But Landon knew.

"Do you know what's stronger than that need inside you?" he whispered over my skin, locking his eyes on mine. "Stronger than pleasure?"

I shook my head, lips pressing into a thin line to stifle a moan. He inched closer to the hem of my dress, his face so close to where I wanted him, I nearly screamed. I bit down on my lip so hard, I almost drew blood.

Landon closed his eyes and breathed in the air, thick with need and my arousal.

"Trust"—he exhaled—"that the payoff will be greater if you save yourself for me. That I'll give you everything you need when the wait is over."

The timer beeped.

Our eyes locked.

"Such a good fucking girl," he praised.

Shoving my dress up and my panties aside, he buried his fingers inside me. Sealing his mouth over my clit. Tearing a cry of relief from my throat. My back bowed off the bed.

And he was *relentless*.

His fingers plunged, pumping in and out. Curling inside me to hit places I didn't even know existed. My body came alive as he quickly worked me into a frenzy.

Deep and fast, he thrust as eagerly as he devoured me. His tongue swirling over my clit, he lapped and sucked as if he'd been starved for days. His free arm looped under my thigh and clamped down on my hip. Pinning me in place so he could drive his tongue inside my slit and my body to the edge. He licked the length of me before latching onto my clit again.

An intense, blinding pleasure tore through me. I cried out. The waves of my first climax crashed over me. It came in a rush, bucking my hips off the bed.

His grip tightened, sinking my hips into the bed as he fully seated his fingers inside me. I clenched and shuddered around him. And before I could fully come down from the high of it, he pursued the next. Pushing me to the peak. And sending me careening over it.

Until I screamed. And screamed again. And again.

As my voice gave out and I panted for breath, he continued to work my clit, the oversensitive bundle of nerves throbbing with each slow suck and languorous stroke of his tongue. Two fingers glided in and out, twisting around and sliding over each other in a leisurely dance that lit up my core even as he allowed me to come down.

I moaned, a low and loud guttural sound that was unrecognizable to my own ears. My head thrown back on the pillows, I gasped until my body finally relaxed.

Peeking down at him through heavy-lidded eyes, he stared up at me from between my legs—his face a mess of my desire. "Fuck, you're—" He withdrew his fingers and his nostrils flared. He growled, "No, I'm not done."

And he reclaimed me with his mouth.

"Landon!" I shrieked. "Oh, *fuck!*"

His thrusts quickened, hitting deep inside me. So deep, my body drew taut against my bindings, a stream of curses tearing from my throat. But he didn't stop until I came again.

And when I thought I couldn't bear it anymore—when I sobbed out my last release and begged him to stop but didn't give him the words that would end it—he pursued me relentlessly.

Until I shattered one more time.

And he finally released me.

"Good boys get orgasms."

Chapter Twenty-Three
Quinn

I woke up in the middle of the night, my hands unbound and resting under my cheek. The fluffy down comforter was pulled up to my shoulders and tucked in around me. At some point while I'd slept, I curled onto my side to face the window.

To face *him*.

Things hadn't gone the way I planned. Definitely not the way I'd expected. My safe words remained unused, and I'd crossed all the lines I'd set for myself. But with my body so deeply satisfied, I couldn't say I regretted it.

I blinked sleepily at the space beside me. Landon was...

He *wasn't* there.

The last thing I remembered was him releasing me from my bindings. He'd freed me from the ankle cuffs, his fingers rubbing over my skin to ease an ache I hadn't voiced. With that simple touch, he'd calmed me, again nearly lulling me to sleep. But I remembered him climbing up the bed to undo the belt around my wrists from wherever he'd secured it.

Once my hands had been freed as well, he settled onto the bed beside me. Not close enough to touch, but close enough to watch over me as I fell asleep.

But he wasn't there now.

I sat up, my brows furrowing as I scanned the dark room. The curtains let in a sliver of moonlight, but it still took me a second to find him.

He sat against the wall on the other side of the room. He'd propped his head against the dresser, legs stretched out in front of him so he could fall asleep. The remnants of a frown remained etched in his features. Even in his sleep, he looked serious.

Everything about him—hell, this entire situation—should've had me reinforcing my walls. The mental blocks I'd had with my ex should've been plated in titanium around a guy like Landon Scott. Instead, I could feel them slowly eroding.

Climbing off the bed, I crept over to where he slept and knelt beside him. His features shifted, brows dipping as he sensed a change in his environment. That sharp focus of his couldn't be dampened. Not even by sleep.

He watched everything carefully, always aware of his surroundings. I had no idea what sort of life he'd lived so far to warrant that kind of constant vigilance. But he noticed everything, even the things I didn't want him to see.

Things I didn't want *anyone* to see.

Something about that made me feel...

Protected.

It made me feel safe. Something about the way he'd chosen to sleep on the floor instead of beside me felt...

Wrong.

I shouldn't have felt anything about it. I certainly didn't want to feel anything about it. But I did.

My hand came up to his forehead, brushing away the hair that had fallen onto it before resting on his thigh. It only took him a second to open his eyes. He glanced sharply around the room, his posture tensing as he sat up straight. His eyes

The King's Maiden

darted down to where I touched him, the dip between his eyebrows deepening before they came back up to my face.

"What's wrong?" he asked hoarsely, searching my face for answers. "Are you okay?"

I nodded quickly. "I woke up and couldn't find you. I—"

His body relaxed against the wall, but the intensity of his eyes scrutinizing my face deepened.

My cheeks reddened. And I backpedaled hard from what I'd been about to admit, lying to him instead. "I had a nightmare."

Because the truth was worse.

It was a ridiculous thought. Too many endorphins had addled my brain. A post-orgasmic mind scrambling. Only that could explain the feeling of *missing* him when I'd woken up alone.

And he stared at me like he knew it.

Eyes darting to my hand and back to my face, his lips parted.

I rushed to my feet, refusing to look at him. "You should sleep in the bed."

Once I had my bearings and a step between us, I forced my spine to straighten. When I glanced back at him, I immediately regretted it.

His eyes *weren't* on my face.

My negligee—the one he'd pushed up before feasting on my cunt like it was his last fucking meal—had ridden up again. And the hooded way he stared at me had nothing to do with sleep. He ate up the expanse of my bare legs as his gaze lifted, inching closer to the apex of my thighs.

Desire pooled between my legs in response.

His nostrils flared.

I slapped my hands down, hastily covering myself and snapping his eyes back to my face.

"Goodnight!" I said far too brightly, spinning away from him and faltering between going straight for the chaise or hiding in the bathroom. But at the sound of him chuckling under his breath, I whirled back around. "What?"

"Nothing." He dropped his eyes and scratched behind his ear, that hint of a smile still playing at his lips. "We've just got a lot of work to do. That's all."

Pushing to his feet, he forced mine back a step on instinct. Instead of leaving it at that and going to bed, I opened my big mouth again. "What's *that* supposed to mean?" I demanded as he walked past me.

"You'll see." He winked at me before climbing into the bed. "We've got a busy day tomorrow. Better get some sleep."

He lay back on the pillows without pulling up the comforter—fully clothed like some kind of psychopath—and he gave me one last lazy glance. Tucking an arm under his head, he closed his eyes.

"Get some sleep," he said again, his voice firmer this time. He patted my empty spot on the bed. "That's an order, Maiden."

I huffed, wound up with frustration that I wished I could blame on his vagueness. Glancing at the bathroom door, I considered going in there to take the edge off so I could sleep.

Of course, he knew that, too.

"If you can relax enough to nod off," he muttered under his breath. Loud enough that he knew I heard him.

So, I marched my ass straight to the chaise and laid down.

I woke up again just as the first hints of morning peeked through the open curtain. It was still mostly dark outside, but the sky lightened as dawn approached. Stretching my arms over my head, it took me a second to realize I wasn't where I should be.

Landon had moved me onto the bed after I'd fallen asleep on the chaise. He'd covered me with the blanket, and I'd curled onto my side, facing the window and the spot where he'd been the night before. But this time, it wasn't empty.

This time, he slept beside me, his body curved toward mine the same way mine had gravitated towards him.

The frown I'd seen on his face earlier had also changed.

Curled up beside me, he looked peaceful. The lines on his face smoothed, his features relaxed. For the first time, he looked like the twenty-one-year-old kid he was supposed to be, rather than the serious adult role he always assumed.

His hand rested on the bed between us, so close to my body I wondered when it had landed there. Had it been natural as he dozed off and got comfortable in bed?

Or had he reached for me in his sleep?

I couldn't shut out the part of my brain wanting it to be the latter, or the way my body ached to touch him. The need to close the distance between us hit me suddenly. Something about the momentary glimpse of him so relaxed made me wonder what it would be like if he let go—if *he* came undone— like I had under his touch.

Maybe it was the haze of sleep, the orgasms and endorphins—I had no idea.

But before I could overthink what I was doing or why I shouldn't, I found the waistband of his pants.

As I slipped my hands beneath it, tracing the line between his hips, his breathing grew tighter. Each muscle tensed beneath my fingers. His lips parted and his breath came out in soft puffs.

But he didn't wake up.

Sitting up, I eased him onto his back with my other hand.

Every move I made—climbing over his side to lay between his legs, pushing his shirt up, running my fingers over the defined cut of muscle tapering his waist—I waited for him to wake up.

He must've been exhausted, because it wasn't until I bent to brush my lips over his abs that his eyes shot open. With my head down, I couldn't see his face when he realized what I was doing, but his sharp intake of breath resonated in the silence.

And his cock hardened beneath my breasts.

"Quinn..." He gripped my shoulders, but I sank down before he reacted, rubbing the length of his erection with my curves and pulling a groan from his lips. "You don't have to—"

"I want to."

Bringing my eyes to his, I tried to show him how much I wanted to. With a silent plea, I waited for his nod of approval before continuing my descent.

Then, I kissed a path down his tightly sculpted abs while I grabbed the fabric at his hips. As I tugged down the barrier between us, he lifted his lower body to help me free him.

His eyes never left my face.

But eventually, I broke our stare and dropped my gaze to his erection. His hard and thick—and honestly, totally beautiful—cock jumped toward me like it was as eager as I was.

He hissed as my breath washed over him, and bit back a curse when I ran my tongue over the length of his erection.

Moaning at the first taste of him, I sealed my lips around his head and sucked gently.

"Jesus," he groaned, bringing his hand up to the back of my head.

Mine wrapped around his base. There was no way I'd be able to take all of him into my mouth, but he seemed content to let me work my lips over his crown while I slowly pumped his shaft with my hand. My tongue darted out to collect the pre-cum building at his tip, laving over the slit in the head.

His hips jerked beneath me.

Unprepared for that first reflexive thrust, I gagged and pulled back. Breathing heavily, I stared up at him as I hovered over his length. "No taking control this time."

His eyes flashed with lust and his incoming protest, but I cut him off before he could voice it.

"Good boys get orgasms," I taunted.

He groaned again and let his head fall back. "Fucking hell."

His hips tensed as he held them still. Emboldened, I tightened my grip around him. Working up and down with both hands, I slid the tip of his cock back inside my mouth.

I sucked deeply, eagerly wanting him to come because of what I did to him.

When it didn't happen right away, the way it seemed to for me with him, I tried to take more of him into my mouth.

But his size and girth were almost too much. Each time I sank lower, he hit the back of my throat and triggered my gag reflex.

Every constriction of my airway sent a pulse of alarm firing through me and pricked my eyes with tears. Easing back, I stared up at him, filled with regret.

"I can't do it." My chest felt tight and ached, but if I tried to grab for my inhaler now, he'd know that I needed it for something as simple as this, and I didn't want that to make him doubt me. "Not like that, at least. Is that okay?"

He cocked his head and watched me as I wiped my face. "I don't care how you do it. I'm trying to hold off because it feels so good, not because..." Sitting up, he took my face in his hands and swiped his thumb across my cheeks. "Whatever you do, just don't stop touching me."

At his words, I swallowed past the fear of not being able to do this and dropped my head. He cursed when I pressed a kiss to the head of his cock, licking the slightly salty, but somehow sweet, taste of him from my lips. Eager to please him, I took him back inside my mouth.

Sitting up, he pressed his arms down into the bed beside him, his fingers clenching in the sheets as I sucked harder. I used my hands and mouth like before, but this time brought one palm up to cup his balls. They tightened beneath my touch.

"Oh, fuck."

He pulled back on my shoulders, popping my lips off his cock as he came with a shudder. Jets of cum spurted from his head, painting his stomach with pearly white streams. Yanking on the collar of his shirt, he whipped it over his head and used it to control the mess.

I stared with wide eyes, somehow in disbelief at how, even in climax, he had enough awareness to pull me off. Enough control to clean up right afterward.

Breathing hard, he stared at me without a shred of disappointment on his face. And while he looked satisfied when he was spent, I couldn't help but feel cheated.

It wasn't the same as what he'd done to me. The way I'd lost myself in what he did. The way he'd taken control.

Disgruntled, I let him pull me into his arms. Resting my head on his bare chest, my fingers played over his spotless ab muscles.

He hummed as his eyes closed, one hand stroking up and down my back. "That was..."

Tugging up the hem of my sleep shirt, he dipped into the waistband of my panties. He drew soft, lazy circles over my hip, until the sleep I'd pulled him from caught back up with him.

Our orgasm tally being astronomically skewed in my favor, I didn't mind when he ultimately lost the battle and dozed off. I was too worked up to lie back and take the orgasms, anyway.

Worked up in a completely unexpected way.

Landon's tight grip on control had sparked a challenge inside me. One that wouldn't be sated by anything less than his complete and total abandon.

He didn't know it yet.

But I did.

"What if I don't want you to be gentle?"

Chapter Twenty-Four
Quinn

Over the next few days, Landon and I made good use of our time, exploring each other's bodies in ways I'd never expected.

Though, not all the ways I wanted. He showed me the pleasure of delayed gratification. I pulled out every trick in my very limited playbook in attempts to make him lose control.

One morning, Landon had to drag me down to breakfast. Gorging ourselves on only each other didn't constitute a well-balanced diet. He actually used those words.

The nerd.

As we sat together in the empty kitchen, where we liked to come early while everyone else slept off their nightly activities, I found myself staring at him.

"What were you like as a kid?"

While I devoured the chocolate strawberry crepes in front of me, he munched on muesli cereal and drank a green smoothie. His idea of a well-balanced diet was as regimented and strict as him. But since I'd been steadily wearing him down with my charm and delightful personality, it made me wonder why he was always so serious.

Did he ever splurge and eat chocolate chip waffles for breakfast? Had he always been that way, or had he ever gorged himself on pancakes in the shape of a mouse with a whipped cream smile as a kid?

I rested my chin in my hands and sighed, struggling to imagine him like that. "I picture you as a boy in black matching pajamas, reading the newspaper, and that just makes me sad."

His eyebrow quirked, and he carefully withdrew the straw from his mouth and set his smoothie down. "Why would that make you sad?"

"Because you're so serious all the time!" I jerked my fork in his direction without thinking. "Did you ever just have fun?"

We both watched as a dollop of whipped cream flew off my fork. It sailed through the air, heading right toward him. I cringed when it hit the center of his chest with a *splat*.

Shrinking back in my chair and smothering a laugh at the appalled look on his face, I threw my hands up in surrender. "Whoops..."

He stared down at the white spot marring his pristine black shirt, swiping it off with his finger and holding it out to me. "Whoops?"

"That was an accident, I swear."

He stalked over to me, coming around the kitchen counter with a look in his eyes that promised trouble.

The laugh fighting its way out of my mouth didn't help, but I tried again, and failed, to sound sincere. "I'm sorry?"

"Oh, you will be."

He lunged for me.

I shrieked and jumped off my chair, knocking it over to slow his attack. My laughter broke free as I ran away from him.

Vaulting over the chair like a freaking gazelle, his fingers nearly snagged the back of my sleep shirt.

I cursed the loose, flowing garment. Bunching it in my

fists, I ran around the island.

He planted his hands on the surface between us, his finger covered in whipped cream held up for me to see. "I'm putting this on that pretty face of yours, whether you like it or not."

My eyes widened. "Don't threaten me with a good time."

His eyes darkened, and my mouth went dry.

I wet my lips, dragging out the movement just to taunt him. "I don't care where you put it as long as you lick it off me."

His gaze flicked down to my breasts, where my nipples had taken it upon themselves to sharpen into visible points. He crooked his finger and beckoned me toward him. "If you come willingly, I'll be gentle."

"What if I don't want you to be gentle?" I sassed back.

That earned me a low growl from his throat. His arms flexed with restraint, and when that sent tension rippling up his forearms, he flashed me some serious vein porn.

But there was no time to drool over it. I whirled around, grabbing the canister of whipped cream from behind me. He used my momentary distraction to bolt around the island.

His arms wrapped around me in a bear-hug-slash-tackle, and I shrieked as he barreled into me. I brought the can up between us. Lifting me off my feet, his arms tightened around me. And my hands clenched reflexively.

Whipped cream sprayed everywhere.

His chin, my face, his neck, both our chests—the shock of it pulling a cry of surprise out of me and a deeper growl out of him. My shriek dissolved into uncontrollable laughter as the carnage continued to rain all over us, until he finally wrestled the can from my grip.

He tossed it aside, pinning me against the fridge as streams of whipped cream dripped down his face.

I snorted, more laughter bursting free. Fully unable to help myself, my hands came up and smeared the mess into his hair.

He returned the favor by rubbing his face all over mine,

spreading the cream over my lips, my eyes, and somehow managing to get some up my nostril.

"Ack!" I cried out, pushing him away to wipe at my nose.

Tears of laughter mixed with the sticky sweet cream on my face. It dripped down my neck, and I glanced down just in time to watch it slide into the v-neck collar of my sleep shirt.

He saw it, too.

Every ounce of playfulness evaporated from the room.

His hands found the hem of my shirt.

Mine found the waist of his pants.

He tore my shirt up and over my head, spinning us around. My fingers fumbled over the drawstring at his waist and tugged it free.

Walking us to the island, Landon pressed my body backward just as my hands wrapped around his straining cock.

I wanted him inside me—right then. It didn't matter that I wasn't supposed to let things get that far. It didn't matter where we were or who could walk in and see us.

I wanted to feel him more than I cared about anything else.

But he had other ideas first.

Flattening my back on the island, he clambered on top of me as he kicked free of his pants—the ones I'd shoved down to his ankles. He growled at the snicker I hid behind my hand and pinned my thighs between his knees.

And when his mouth sealed over my breast, he wiped away the last traces of my laughter.

My back arched, seeking out his mouth. I planted my hands beside me and pressed up. He took the invitation, licking every drop of whipped cream off my naked chest. Laving his tongue over my nipples long after I was clean. Sucking each pert bud into his mouth until I writhed beneath him—ready to scream if he didn't give me more.

He released my right nipple with a *pop,* humming appreciatively at my clean, bare breasts.

But a drop of whipped cream slid down his jaw and landed right on his blank canvas. Swiping a hand over his face and neck, he gathered the remnants there and scooped what he could from his shirt.

Then, he slathered it all over me again.

Diving back in, his hot, greedy mouth followed the path of his hand as it dipped between my breasts and lower down to my stomach.

Needy, desperate sounds left my throat as he descended.

His tongue stroked over my skin, circling my belly button, and running along the line of my panties. He gripped my thighs and spread my legs, sliding down my body and off the side of the island.

His face hovered over my slit, the thin barrier of my panties doing nothing to hide how much I wanted him. A murmur of appreciation rumbled from his lips. It reverberated deep in my core.

"Always so fucking wet for me. Aren't you, Maiden?"

"Yes," I panted, slightly breathless. "Always for you."

His eyes flashed dangerously, desire gleaming as he took in how much I wanted him, but still he didn't give me his touch.

"Landon, *please.*"

He shook his head as he ran his unhurried gaze over my soaked panties. With the tip of his nose, he edged along the line of my thong, grazing my clit before teasing down the other side. And then he did it all over again. Nuzzling my thighs, breathing in my arousal, he clicked his tongue on the back of his teeth as his dark amber eyes filled with regret.

Sinister, fucking-downright-evil regret.

"Good girls get orgasms, Maiden."

His breath fluttered over my core, coiling everything inside me so tightly, I thought I might explode. I certainly wanted to when he eased off me completely.

"Bad girls get punished."

He slapped my clit.

I yelped, my eyes widening. It hadn't been hard enough to hurt, but left me momentarily too stunned to speak. I lay there panting as he tugged his pants up and wiped a dollop of whipped cream off his belt.

His eyes met mine as he sucked his finger clean.

And he walked out of the kitchen right as I found my voice.

"Motherfucker!" My hands slapped on the island, and I sat up with a growl. "I'm going to get you for that!"

His laughter echoed down the hall, and I collapsed back on the island, trying to collect myself.

I had no idea how long I lay there, but it took time to seriously contemplate my life choices.

The ones that led me to this sticky but *somehow-still-totally-fucking-arousing* mess.

♟

"What the fuck is this?"

At the sound of that shrill voice, I slapped my hands over my bare chest. My head flew towards the door to find Vivian—and goddamn Max Dread—standing in the back doorway to the kitchen.

I squeaked, unfortunately, and jumped off the island as quickly as I could. Given that it was still a slimy mess, my efforts were neither graceful nor quick enough. But I finally made it to the floor and blew out a huge breath.

Vivian shouted something about this being a shared space, and Max huffed a laugh.

Hunting on the ground for my sleep shirt with one arm still covering my breasts, I crawled around the side of the island.

The shirt dangled in front of my face. And at the end of the heavily muscled arm attached to it, I found Max's stupid, smirking face.

"Looking for this, Princess?"

Snatching it out of his hand, I used it to cover myself. I rose to my feet and rushed for the door. The driving thought in my head being that I was going to *kill* Landon Scott when I got my hands on him.

Intent on my murder plans, I missed a stray pile of whipped cream and slipped on it. My foot flew out from under me as I screamed, torn between keeping myself covered and protecting my face. Pitching toward the floor, I let go of my shirt and threw my hands out at the last second.

And landed with an *oomph* in Max's arms.

My breasts fully uncovered.

In a goddamn thong.

Because of-fucking-course, I couldn't just be caught half-naked by him.

I was going to *kill* Landon Scott.

Scrambling to get my feet under me and get out of there only made it worse. I practically slithered my naked body all over Max's in my attempts to get away.

Vivian's outraged and high-pitched shrieks rang in my ears as I flailed uselessly.

Max jerked my body upright and locked his arms around me.

"Stop squirming," he gritted out through clenched teeth. Once he righted me on my feet, he snapped at Vivian, pointing to my shirt on the ground. "V, shut the hell up and make yourself useful. I swear to fucking god only you can bitch about a problem while actively prolonging it."

She clamped her mouth shut, but huffed and stomped over to my shirt. Meanwhile, I did the only logical thing I could think to do at that moment and bit down on Max's arm—*hard*.

His grip slackened and I pushed away from him, losing my footing and landing on my butt.

I glared up at him from the floor. "Don't be such a fucking asshole, you—asshole!"

"You're defending *her?*" Breathing hard and clutching the arm I'd marked with my teeth hard enough to draw blood, he glared down at me. "Are you fucking kidding me right now?"

I shouted at him, "You don't have to talk to her like that!"

"I was trying to help you!" he roared back.

"I don't need your help, you fucking brute!"

"Sure as hell looks like you do, Princess! Or did you forget that you almost face planted in the *communal* kitchen before I saved your ungrateful bare ass?"

"I didn't ask you to save me! And if I want to walk around this whole house naked as a goddamn blue jay, I will!"

That drew both of our attention to the fact that I was very nearly as naked as a goddamn blue jay.

When he opened his mouth to respond, nothing came out. And although I needed to get the fuck out of there, I froze.

His eyes zeroed in on my heaving chest as if my nipples had become homing beacons. He glared down at my naked body and swallowed, his throat bobbing as his eyes jumped from my breasts to my skimpy black thong before snapping back to my face.

My eyes nearly bugged out of my head at the dark, lust-fueled and hatred-filled look he pinned me with.

The heat of that one prolonged stare could have set the room ablaze. Or my fucking panties.

I snapped my thighs together. "Are you just going to stand there? Give me my shirt!"

Vivian made a noise so shrill it sounded inhuman. "Shut up, both of you!"

She snatched my shirt off the ground and shoved it into my chest. Tugging on Max's arm, she pulled him away from me so quickly I had to wonder if she'd noticed his stare.

I wasn't sure I'd be able to get it out of my head.

But thankfully, Landon chose that moment to walk back into the kitchen.

"Quinn?" He caught sight of me on the floor and ran over, dropping to his knees in front of me. "Oh, shit. Are you alright? I thought you'd come tearing after me for that and then when you didn't—Did you fall? Are you hurt?"

His genuine concern almost made me reconsider my plans to murder him.

Almost.

"I am going to *kill* you, Landon Scott."

That was all the warning he got before I lunged at him.

Maybe he'd stop doing the honorable thing all the time and fuck my brains out.

Chapter Twenty-Five
Quinn

An hour later, I sat on the chaise wrapped in a fluffy robe with Landon's arms around me.

Nestled between his legs, I stared out at the lake and tried to keep my eyes open. I didn't want to fall asleep—not yet.

After lunging at Landon, he wrestled me onto my back and finished what he'd started before he walked out. I came on his tongue twice before he hauled me up from the floor and carried me back to his room. Orgasm three hit me under the hot spray of the shower with my hands pinned to the wall.

After spreading me from behind, he feasted until my knees buckled.

Once my legs gave out, he sat me on the built-in seat and washed my hair and body. The scent of his mint and lavender body wash filled my nose as he drained all the tension from my limbs. Drying me off with a towel, he wrapped me in the robe before getting dressed himself.

When I tried to reach for him to return the favor, he tossed me over his shoulder and threw me on the bed, diving back in for orgasm number four. Only in rare moments like that first morning, when I took him by surprise or woke up in the middle of the night, did Landon let me please him.

The rest of the time, he seemed content to push my limits and my body to the point of madness.

Or, at least, almost there.

All morning, I wanted to go further, but Landon never pushed for more. If he had, I would've said yes. But even though he probably needed some kind of sign from me, I couldn't bring myself to ask for it.

I tried to work up the courage, but I feared the rejection I faced the first night in the Round Tableau. That night, it hadn't stung because I didn't know him from Adam or a hole in the ground. But now, I had to up my courage in case his feelings on my virgin status hadn't changed.

Maybe I would've worked up the nerve, but by the time he came up for air, my body had gone limp from all the orgasms.

It was a terrible problem to have, really.

We had time. Over a week left to get there before the forum and the next challenge. I told myself it would happen naturally and forced my body to relax. I was seconds away from falling asleep when he spoke.

"I wasn't like this when I was a little boy."

My ears perked, but I didn't move or say a word.

"Before I turned eleven, Kingston says I was wild. Always playing. Always climbing...Laughing." His thumb traced circles over the back of my hand. "I don't know. You'd have to ask him about the newspapers, but from what he tells me, the boy I used to be wouldn't fit the image you have in your mind."

"You don't remember?"

He shook his head.

"I don't remember anything before my—before my birthday that year."

I didn't want this to be a connection between us—terrible

things happening on the day we were born. But I couldn't stop myself from asking, anyway. "What happened?"

"I—" He cleared his throat, staring out the window at the lake. "I don't remember. At least, not completely. And every time I try to think about it..."

The crease between his eyebrows deepened, his mouth twisting into a frown as he tried to find the words.

But he didn't need to explain it.

I already knew.

"Every time you try to think about it, it hurts. It's like it's happening all over again because..." I slipped my hand inside his robe, resting it over his heart. "Your mind doesn't remember, but this does."

He nodded, the muscle in his jaw working as he released a heavy sigh and finally looked at me. "Is that what it's like for you? With your parents?"

My hand came up to my hair reflexively, and my body tightened like a bow string—ready to loose an arrow in self-defense. I hadn't expected him to ask me about my parents.

"You don't have to talk about it if you don't want to."

I scoffed a laugh. "Mr. *Tell Me* is saying I *don't* have to talk about something?" I swiped at my face with my sleeve, trying to deflect. "I find that hard to believe."

"I told you, Quinn." He tipped my chin up, his eyes anchoring to mine as the memories threatened to drown me. "I know when to push and when to pull back."

Like it seemed to do every time, his touch soothed me, offering a calm within the storm brewing inside me. I sniffled and nodded, but he didn't let me go. His thumb brushed my bottom lip, and he stared at my parted mouth like it held the answers to life itself.

I searched his face for a sign that maybe—just maybe—he planned to break the rules and press his lips to mine.

But he didn't bridge the gap.

"I wish I didn't remember it. But it's as vivid in my mind as it is in my heart."

"You loved him." He cleared his throat. "Your dad? He was...He was a good dad?"

"He was the *best* dad."

Wrapping my arms around myself, tears welled in my eyes. Landon didn't say anything else or press me for more information. He just sat with me, rubbing circles over my skin while I pushed away memories I didn't want to face. Memories that crashed against the barriers I'd erected in my mind, trying to force their way out.

I got up from his lap and went into the bathroom, grabbing my bag on my way in and using my inhaler as I stared at myself in the mirror.

When the blurred edges of my vision cleared, I splashed cold water on my face. I went back out to the bedroom and climbed back into Landon's lap. And we stared out the window for a long time, looking out at the lake and each getting lost in our own thoughts.

Until, eventually, the world grew dark, and Landon suggested getting in bed.

"You sleep. I think I want to read for a little bit."

As he climbed out from behind me and got ready for bed, I pulled out my dad's copy of *The Princess Bride* and ran my hands over the cover and spine. I flipped it open to my bookmark and started reading, my eyes blurring as I stared at the notes written in the margin on nearly every page. Little details my dad had left to guide me through the story when I was younger. I read them now like they were the secret notes he'd left for me around the house.

Hidden reminders of how much he loved me—of how proud he was of me.

Even though I didn't deserve them anymore.

The King's Maiden

The next day, Landon and I walked around the lake all morning, talking about school and our plans for the future. He told me about his family's expectations after graduation, something else that made me feel sad, and he asked me about dance. I refused to dance when he requested it.

"That's alright. We'll put a pin in that."

"Don't hold your breath." I snorted, twirling on the ball of my foot.

He grabbed my hips before I could get away. And that was the end of our walking *and* talking time for the morning. Throwing me over his shoulder, he raced back to the room with my laughter trailing behind us down the halls.

Later, as I collapsed on the bed and unlocked my thighs from around his head, I found myself completely sated and yet still wanting more again.

But like every other time we had gotten close to moving forward and crossing that final barrier, he pulled back.

He wiped the remnants of my last orgasm off his face before sucking his fingers clean, completely unashamed. When he lifted his head to find me staring at him from between my legs, he looked like he'd just been caught with his hand in a cookie jar.

"What'd I do? Was it the butt thing? I know we haven't really talked about that limit, but I didn't want to make a mess and I thought you enjoyed it?"

I did.

But that wasn't the point.

So, instead of responding to his question, I redirected. "Can I ask you something?"

He had the good sense to eye me warily, but still nodded at me to go ahead.

"I don't want you to think I'm..." I searched for the right words. "Not grateful for all the orgasms, of course. They're top notch. Never should've doubted you."

The corner of his mouth twitched. "But?"

"I think I'm ready for more."

He froze. Maybe even stopped breathing.

And I grew nervous as I waited for his response. Considering what had happened the last time the word *virginity* left my mouth, my unease made sense.

But I'd needed to ask—whatever the fallout.

Not knowing how he felt about it now was eating me up almost as voraciously as he was.

"Landon?"

"That wasn't a question."

I blinked a few times, processing his response. "Okay... Do you want to take things further?"

He pushed himself up and climbed off the bed. "Quinn, we don't have to do that just because you're my Maiden. I can train you without—"

"But what if I want to?"

His body tensed, eyes darting to the space he'd just left on the bed. He scrubbed a hand over his face and averted his gaze to the window.

"I just...I don't think it's a good idea. All of this—I'm sure it feels like something you want right now, but when it's over, you might—"

"Don't do that."

His eyes snapped back to me. "Don't do what?"

"Tell me what or how I'm going to feel."

We stared off for a minute, me standing my ground and him trying to get a read on me. He finally gave in and shook his head, expelling a heavy breath.

"You're right. I'm sorry. I just..." He came back to the bed, sitting down beside me. "When the twenty-one days are over, we go to Pendragon Estate, Quinn."

My brow furrowed. "I know that."

His eyebrows rose, prompting me to connect dots I failed to see. "Are you worried I'll sleep with you and sleep with someone else right after? Because I already told you, it's not going to happen. I'm getting through the challenge."

"No, it's not that. I know you'll get through it."

I ignored how that made me all warm and sparkly on the inside. "I don't understand, then. What are you trying to say, Landon?" I tapped my chest twice in a *come at me, bro* gesture. "Just spit it out. I can take it."

He fought a laugh and rolled his eyes at my antics, but his expression sobered quickly.

When he dropped his eyes to the bed, I got a little nervous.

"You're not the only one with a challenge in front of them at Pendragon, Quinn."

"Oh. You mean, you—"

"Yes." He averted his eyes. "I have to do whatever is necessary to get the Maiden assigned to me to ask for more. I *will* do that."

Something ugly unfurled in my chest at the thought—something I refused to name or fully acknowledge. It hadn't been there when he first told me about the next challenge, but it was there now.

I knew it.

And so did he.

"It's one less player on the board, Quinn. If you keep going past the first thirty days, the less you're up against, the better. But it means I have a job to do, too. Can you really say it wouldn't bother you, knowing I was seducing someone else after taking—? Can you see how that might bring in feelings that could get in your way?"

"I'm not going to let anything get in my way, Landon." Not a King, not a cocky bastard—not even the thought of my Knight and what he'd have to do in less than two weeks.

I didn't like it, but it wasn't going to stop me.

"Well, I still don't feel right about it. Can we just give it some more time?"

I wanted to say no and demand he have his way with me right then. But I couldn't do it. So, I just nodded and tried not to take his response as another rejection.

He didn't completely refuse me. He only asked to wait.

"Yeah, that's fine. We don't have to rush."

He breathed a sigh of relief and did his best to smile at me, leaning forward to brush his lips against my temple. It was quick and unexpected—like he hadn't really thought about it.

That made me feel a different sort of way inside. And it forced me to wonder if maybe he wasn't completely wrong about holding off. But I refused to entertain that idea for long.

Rising from the bed, he tipped my chin up to look at him. "I'll be back late tonight. Sleep *in* the bed, stubborn girl."

"Wait, you're leaving?"

I cursed the part of me wanting him to stay and the part without any self-control that let my needy question slip out.

"All the Knights have to go to the Round Tableau to prepare for tomorrow's party."

Before I could respond, he left me on the bed and started gathering his things around the room. He had told me about the party the other day, and I remembered Elaine mentioning it. But in the midst of all the orgasms, I'd filed it away under *Unimportant Details*.

But now, it meant we were thirteen days into the first challenge, and I had to say I regretted that first week of stubbornly refusing orgasms. Even if the reason I had held out became more of a concerning possibility by the day.

Since I couldn't change the past, I refocused on the future.

Throughout The Quest, Camelot Court held a party every thirteen days. He said it gave everyone a chance to spend time together, since it was easy to get lost in the bedrooms.

I couldn't say there were too many people I wanted to

see—a few I preferred to avoid entirely. But Landon said it also gave everyone a chance to unwind and have fun. I was most curious to see Landon outside his comfort zone, removed from his usual habitat and partying. Whatever that looked like. I couldn't really picture it.

Maybe he'd finally let his hair down.

Maybe he'd stop doing the honorable thing all the time and fuck my brains out.

A girl could hope.

I'd whore myself out for a set of special edition hardcovers if the offer was on the table.

Chapter Twenty-Six
Quinn

Landon got back after midnight, and the subject of my pesky virginity didn't come up again. He showered quickly and went to bed, and I slept on the chaise even though he'd offered again for me to join him if I'd be more comfortable.

The next morning, I woke up tense and agitated, finding Landon already dressed in a pair of black track pants and a fitted black shirt and looking fresh as a fucking daisy.

He slipped his feet into his sneakers before glancing toward where I slept. He smiled when he saw I was awake, and I stamped down the butterflies that took flight in my stomach.

"Oh, good. I didn't think I would catch you before I left."

He rose from the edge of the bed, stretching his arm over his head in a way that bared and tightened the muscles of his waist. I averted my gaze to the mattress, but that didn't help one bit. It only filled my brain with memories of last night and flooded my cheeks with warmth.

I scrubbed at my face with both hands, as if wiping the sleep from my eyes.

"I'm heading out for a run." He pulled his wallet out

of his back pocket and removed a card from the front slot before setting it down on his desk. Walking over to me, he held it out to me. "The party is tonight. I have your dress, but use this for anything else you need."

I stared at it like it was a venomous snake ready to bite me. When I didn't move to take it from him, he set it on my lap. He patted it on my thigh before withdrawing his hand.

"The Maidens usually go get their hair and nails done during the day. Or you can go out to eat or buy, um, accessories or whatever." He scratched behind his ear. "Just be back by five."

I stared blankly at the black Amex nestled atop my blanket, blinking away sleep and feeling like the pretty female hooker in that movie where the rich guy picks her up off the streets. Frowning at the card, I pinched it at the corner and inspected it. It had Landon M. Scott inscribed on the back—*not* Kingston D'Arthur this time.

Landon shifted uncomfortably at my reaction. "You could grab some books to read while you're here?"

My eyebrows rose.

The offer intrigued me, but it sounded a little too good to be true. With my luck, he meant books for research on Arthurian legends. Or how-to guides like *Serving Your Lord and Master: For Dummies* and *A Good Girl's Guide to Preserving Her Virginity*.

I side-eyed him. "What sort of books?"

He huffed a laugh. "Any books you want, Maiden."

At that, I perked up immediately. I'd whore myself out for a set of special edition hardcovers if the offer was on the table. No shame. I picked up the card before he could rethink his kindness, sliding it into the pocket of my sleep shirt.

After huffing my way to the chaise last night, I'd gotten back up when I couldn't sleep and put one on just to annoy him. He'd laughed, his eyes still closed from where he'd been resting on the bed. But the way he wrinkled his nose when he eyed the garment now made me feel much better.

He grumbled something that sounded suspiciously like *burn them all* as he turned to leave the room.

"Thank you," I called out. When he turned around, I nodded toward my pocket. "For all the books."

He nodded in return and left the room.

An hour later, I was dressed, armed with iced coffee, and surrounded by a pile of books I'd had on my TBR list for the last year.

It was *literal* heaven.

And yes, that word did mean what I thought it meant.

Gia popped by during a break in her summer class schedule. Skin flushed from the hike across campus, her honey-blonde hair fell out of her scrunchie as she weaved through the bookstore to join me. Taking a seat on the floor beside me, she held out her hand expectantly.

I dug into my pocket and passed the heavy black credit card over.

"You're telling me he just handed this baby over to you and said go buy any books you want?"

I nodded, biting my lip.

"Damn. That's it. Marry him. Wife him up. Let him have your babies while you take his name and his card and build your dream library. There's really no other option."

"Gia!" I laughed, dropping my voice to a whisper. "Let's not get ahead of ourselves."

"Good point. I wouldn't be surprised if they all have those." She stuck out her tongue. "No need to buy the bull when you can get the black card from his friends."

I was pretty sure that was a joke. But the whole thing with Landon's credit card made me more uncomfortable the longer she stared at it with stars in her eyes. Glancing down at the large pile I'd collected, I couldn't help but feel like maybe I was taking advantage a little.

Since that feeling would pass when she left and I no longer had to think about it, I pushed it aside. No self-respecting smut reader walked away from a hot guy offering free books, right?

"Gia, I might be in over my head here."

"How so?"

I gestured around me. "Unlimited spending on books? Too many orgasms to fucking count? I mean, if he were just trying to lure me to the dark side with cookies, I'd be able to resist. But this?"

"So much better than cookies. Mixed metaphors aside, he found your kryptonite."

"Exactly. And it doesn't help that he looks like he fell off the pages of *Dark and Broody* weekly. I lost the battle in resisting him sexually, but if he finds and exploits all my weaknesses, I'm going to catch feels."

"Who could blame you? After this, I might be in love with him."

I buried my face in my hands.

"Calm your tits, Gia. I'm not talking about love. But getting attached is becoming more and more of a real possibility and that would be so incredibly stupid of me."

She tilted her head to look at me in a way that reminded me so starkly of Landon. I groaned, blinking away the image of his face that popped in my head.

"Would it really be so bad? I mean, if he feels the same, maybe this could lead to something between the two of you."

Before she could bottle up and sell the eternal optimism I wanted to drink right now, I faced facts. "He's just doing his job. Training me for The Quest. When I told him he could have his way with me, he kindly said no thanks."

She shot me a pointed look.

"I'm paraphrasing, obviously. But either way, metaphorical hymen still fully intact over here."

Gia laughed and pulled the hand I'd shot into the air back down to my lap.

"Did he say why not?"

"No. Not really. Stuff about not rushing, but I don't know if I should buy it. I'm pretty sure he knows something happened between Kingston and I at the Maiden Selection. If he knows Kingston is into me, that's probably a line he won't cross. I don't know much about him, but it's not hard to guess that'd be a deal-breaker."

She hummed as she thought that over. As she scanned my book pile, her mouth twisted and brow dipped. She picked up the first book in a particular favorite series of mine, a why choose dark romance by Tate James.

Flipping the special edition over, she arched a brow my way. "What would MK do?"

"Um...Fall in love with the best friends and taunt the holdout mercilessly until he pulls his head out of his ass?"

She snorted, holding out the book to me. "Might not be the worst plan."

I laughed as I took it from her. "Not exactly the same situation here."

"Isn't it? You're stuck living in a house with all of them. They're all fucking hot. They want you, whether they're all willing to admit it right now or not. Dye your hair pink and go be the bad bitch who gets all three of them."

"Two of them. Max Dread is an ass. And a liar."

I filled her in on what happened with Max and his father, sharing what Landon had told me, too.

She considered all of it, but she wasn't convinced. "Wasn't Merle the guy you thought dismissed you on day one?"

"Yeah, but Kingston swears they were together. And Max found me out on the lawn with Brutus. Kind of convenient, don't you think? What if I blurred their voices, and it was really Max on the intercom telling me to leave?"

Gia shook her head. "Nope. Not even considering it."

"Because it would put a damper on your why choose dreams for me?"

"Obviously." She nudged my side. "You know I'm a sucker for the Dark Knight trope, too. My money is on there being more to Max than meets the eye."

I snorted. "You date him, then."

But even as I said it, possessiveness flared inside me. I scowled at the foolish organ in my chest.

Gia laughed, picking up on my reaction without me saying a word. "He's all yours, Princess."

Climbing to her feet, she stared longingly at my pile of books and setup for the day before begrudgingly tightening the strap of her backpack on her shoulders.

"I have to get back to class but keep me posted. I want to hear all about the party tonight, too."

"Will do. Love you."

"Love you, too."

She waved and took off, leaving me alone with my books and my thoughts. But since I could probably spend hours going back and forth over the three guys occupying my mind, I picked up another book and pushed the thoughts aside. There'd be plenty of drama waiting for me tonight, surely.

But there was one thought she planted in my mind that I couldn't let go of...

I just needed to fit in some time to stop by the hair salon next door before five.

I stepped out of the bathroom, ready for the party and refusing to acknowledge the dangerously high hemline on the dress Landon had picked out for me. It clung to my body like a second skin, ruched fabric pulling the black skirt tight over my hips until it stopped at my lower back.

Right above my fucking ass.

I'd curled my hair and let it fall, covering my exposed skin while also revealing what I'd done at the salon.

Streaks of scarlet red peeked out between the dark strands.

Twirling one strand around my finger, I waited for Landon to turn around from the desk, reminding myself not to drool when he did. His sharp black suit hugged his body like it had been made for him. Safely assuming it had been, I sent a few quiet thanks to his tailor.

Because the sight of his perfectly toned ass in those pants filled me with the sudden, inexplicable urge to bite it.

When he turned around, my mouth actually watered.

Head down, he fastened the buttons on his jacket while I prayed for mercy. With a crisp black shirt beneath his black jacket, he looked like a dream.

Or a nightmare, if I had to resist him.

Adjusting the cuff links at his wrists, he lifted his head and saw me standing there.

His hands froze, mouth parting as he stared at me, too.

He raked his gaze up my body from the way-too-expensive red-soled heels he'd left out to where the halter top of my dress cinched tightly around my neck. Slowly drinking in every line and curve, he finally reached my face and spotted the color in my hair.

Eyes widening, his throat bobbed with a slow, deep swallow.

I stepped closer to him, waving a hand over my appearance. "Will this do, Sir?"

He nodded, moving as if pulled by gravity until he was close enough to pull a strand of my newly-dyed hair between his fingers. Toying with the crimson curl, he couldn't hide his reaction to seeing *his* color on my body.

His tongue darted out to wet his lips as he tugged gently

on the ends, applying tension to my scar without realizing it. My scalp tingled, and my body warmed under his heated gaze.

"You look perfect, Maiden."

I blushed, brushing my hand down his lapel. "You don't look so bad yourself, Buns."

His eyebrows rose. "Buns?"

"Short for Bunny, obviously, or Honey Bunny if I'm cross with you." I winked, delighting in the way he closed his eyes and dropped his head back with a groan. "Good! You remember."

"I'm not responding to this."

"Oh, come on, Buns. Don't be like that. With the dress you put me in, things are feeling extra bouncy over here."

I did a slow twirl, considering my new cutesy nickname for him was payback for it. As predicted, my ass jiggled with the slightest movement thanks to the ruched spandex barely keeping it concealed.

"Yeah, extra boun—" He cleared his throat. "We should get going before we—"

"Decide to skip it altogether?"

His throat worked as he considered that, and I wouldn't have minded at all if he wanted to. After last night, the thought of him losing control had been hard not to think about, especially as I tossed and turned on the chaise. I would've been lying if I'd said I wasn't eager for it to happen.

But, not surprisingly, his sense of duty won out. "We don't want to be late."

"Lead the way, oh gallant Knight of mine."

I stepped to his side and looped my arm through his, unprepared for his response and the way it caught my breath in my throat.

"As you wish."

A bathroom was as good a place as any to cash in my V card.

Chapter Twenty-Seven
Quinn

Even though we arrived on time, the party was in full swing when we walked through the doors of the Round Tableau building.

Couples danced on the dance floor, their bodies pressed together so tightly I couldn't tell where they ended and began. It seemed training was going well for the eleven other pairs.

A few had sequestered themselves in the dark alcoves around the room, and I couldn't help the way my attention pulled there again.

Landon slipped his hand in mine to lead me through the crowded room, and when he saw where my eyes had wandered, his grip tightened on my hand. My breathing hitched as I stared up at him. Asking a question I couldn't bring myself to voice, I stared transfixed at his lips as they curved into a smile.

"Let's dance." He tugged me out into the center of the room, nodding at his fellow Knights as they danced with their Maidens.

I couldn't take my eyes off him.

Under the chandelier, he stopped and pulled me into his

arms, swaying to the music.

The heavy and fast beat drowned out everything around me—except for him, and the way it felt when his hand came around my back, sliding over my hip.

He slipped his leg between my thighs, grazing my clit and snapping me out of the trance I'd fallen into watching him move.

"I wouldn't have pegged you as a dancer." I raised my voice so he could hear me, enjoying the way his eyes lit up under the strobing lights.

"There's a lot you don't know about me, Maiden."

Before I could point out why, he spun me around, plastering his chest to my back and pulling my hips against him. He rolled his hips from side to side, taking mine with them, and even though I could dance circles around him, I liked letting him lead.

I dropped my head back on his chest, one arm reaching up to loop around his neck.

He trailed his hand down my arm, fingers running along the curve of my side before finding my hip again. Squeezing lightly, he held me steady as he ground his hips against me. His erection dug into my ass, and the proof that he was as affected by this as I was invigorated me.

I wanted to drop to my knees or pull him into one of those dark alcoves.

The longer we danced, the deeper that desire became.

My breathing tightened, too. The crowded dance floor, combined with the scent of sweat and sex, made me dizzy.

The last thing I wanted was to pull away from him, but I needed to sneak away to the bathroom and use my inhaler before I passed out. Turning around in his arms, I looped mine around his neck and leaned up toward his ear.

"Ladies room," I said quickly, stifling a cough.

He released me and let me head in that direction, but I sensed him following me off the dance floor. When I reached the restroom, he posted up outside the door. I couldn't help but run my eyes over him before I went inside.

Desire rushed through me when he did the same.

But it evaporated when two girls I recognized stood in front of the bathroom mirrors.

"Oh look." Vivian smirked at her reflection, reapplying her bright red lipstick. "I thought I smelled something cheap."

I ignored her, pushing into one of the private stalls.

One of the perks at a Camelot Court party was the bathrooms. Each stall had a full-length door, and when I closed it, the sound of Vivian's voice muffled slightly.

Since it made sense to multitask, I used the restroom while I pulled my inhaler from the small clutch slung over my body. I waited until the door closed and the girls' voices disappeared before taking a puff from my inhaler.

Closing my eyes as I counted to ten, I exhaled slowly as I readied myself for a second dose. Just as I took a deep breath in, someone knocked on my stall door.

I dropped the inhaler, wincing as it clattered to the ground.

"Quinn?"

My eyes widened at the sound of Landon's voice, and I hurriedly wiped and pulled up my panties while I counted to ten in my head. The doorknob rattled and his voice came through again, forcing my breath out in a rush.

"Quinn, are you okay in there?"

I dropped down to scoop the inhaler off the ground. "What are you doing here?"

"Let me in. I have a surprise for you."

Flustered, I reflexively followed his command and opened the door, realizing a second too late I had my inhaler in my hand. I spun around as he stepped inside, stepping on the lever to flush the toilet as I hastily shoved my inhaler in my bag. Whirling back around to face him, I tried to zip my bag as discreetly as possible.

He titled his head and scrutinized me, his eyes narrowing slightly.

"You scared me," I panted and ran my hand through my hair, tugging on my scar as I righted the mess my curls had probably become. "What are you doing in the ladies' room?"

"I wanted to give you something." He ran his eyes over me. "Are you sure you're okay?"

"Yes! I just—You caught me off guard, that's all."

He didn't look entirely convinced, but I breathed a sigh of relief when he let it go. His eyes sparkled with mischief I hadn't seen before, and I wanted to know what he was up to.

"Turn around."

"Wh—What are you talking about? Turn around?"

He nodded, twirling his finger in the air to show me what he wanted. "Face the wall."

My eyes narrowed suspiciously, but despite the playfulness in his eyes, he had that tone in his voice—the one I associated with an order from my Knight. I turned around and faced away from him.

He took my hands and placed them on the wall, splaying my fingers with his own before running them back down my forearms. When he touched my waist, I jumped. Tugging the material of my dress up and over my hips, he bared my ass and the tiny black thong he'd left with my outfit.

I moaned as his palm stroked over my bare cheek.

He groaned, his fingers kneading my flesh before moving to the other side. "God, I love your ass. It's fucking perfect."

My breathing hitched.

It was the first time he'd said something like that, and felt like more than an observation. It hung between us like a confession.

His hand cracked against my bare skin.

I shrieked, the slap sharp enough to sting but not to truly hurt me.

"Do you have any idea how tempting you look in that

dress?" His palm soothed over my tender skin as he whispered in my ear. "Do you have any idea how hard I would fight to make you give into me...If you weren't already mine?"

"Show me," I panted, trying to turn my head to look at him.

He slapped my ass again. "Eyes on the wall, Maiden."

I instantly obeyed, a rush of arousal building in my core as his hand soothed over the second sting. Biting my lip, I whimpered when his touch slid lower, tracing the underside of my cheek with his fingers.

"Your ass is perfect. But this..." His hand dipped between my legs, and he growled low in his throat when he felt how wet I already was for him. "This might be my new favorite place in the world. I could live between your thighs and watch you come apart day in..." He slipped one finger inside me, making my legs shake before he slowly withdrew it. "And day out."

"Landon."

His name left my lips like a plea, and he fulfilled my unvoiced request by sliding two fingers deep inside me.

Everything inside me tightened, desire coiling low in my belly as I panted for him against the wall. When his thumb circled my clit, I whimpered.

He withdrew his hand before I could buck against it like a wild animal. Rustling came from behind me, and I prayed he was unbuckling his pants so he could fill me with his cock.

A bathroom was as good a place as any to cash in my V card. Fuck it.

And *fuck me*—it wasn't his erection that brushed my clit.

"I told you I brought you a gift."

He traced my opening with the item in his hand, gathering my wetness over its surface. Covering my hands with his, he pressed them into the wall as he slid something inside me.

I tensed. "Landon?"

With a gentle *shush* in my ear, he urged me to relax. "Open for me, Maiden. Trust me."

I let my body relax, allowing him to slide the object all the way inside. It mirrored his fingers pressing deep, while his thumb and a second arm of the toy covered my clit.

My whole body trembled as he pulled his hand away and left it fitted snugly against my pleasure points—inside and out.

When the vibrations started, my knees buckled.

"Oh, god."

He held my hands firmly on the wall, and his other, clutching a small remote, grabbed my hip to keep me upright.

My eyes rolled back in my head as the vibration directly over my clit nearly drove me straight to climax. But before I could get there, the buzzing stopped.

I whimpered at the loss.

But bigger trouble loomed when Landon's throaty chuckle rumbled in my ear. "This gift comes with some strings attached, Maiden. One rule you have to follow."

Swallowing down the rampant need and desire this stirred in me, I steadied my legs and waited for him to go on.

He clicked on the vibrator at a lower setting, and I mewled like a cat in heat as the urge to come tore through me.

I cried out when it cut off abruptly again.

"Are you going to be a good girl and follow the rules?"

"Yes," I said automatically. "Tell me."

"You can't come unless I give you permission."

He clicked the vibrator on again, this time high enough to make my legs give out.

My body bucked in his hold, desire gathering between my thighs and threatening to run down my legs. I was so fucking turned on—so ready for climax.

I shuddered, trying to hold it off.

"Landon, *please.*"

"Ah, ah, ah..." he taunted. "Tonight, you can address me as *Sir*. But we also have a party to get back to. Follow the rules and you'll get your reward. Remember. Good girls get orgasms."

He slapped my ass one more time, the combination of his hand and the toy inside me nearly sending me overboard. I clenched my teeth to keep my climax at bay.

"Bad girls get punished."

Leaving the stall, it wasn't until the main door to the bathroom swung open and shut that he clicked off the vibrator. My body sagged against the wall, and I pulled in ragged gulps of air as I tried to regain control. I tugged my dress down over my hips when I could finally move.

Every step I took reminded me of his gift. That only he could give me the pleasure I needed. That I was at his mercy.

That I was *his*.

I couldn't tell him why I hadn't wanted to bring her here at all.

LANDON

It was growing harder and harder to remember she wasn't mine.

Watching her make her way out of the bathroom on shaky legs, knowing every shift and play of her features was because of me, I couldn't take my eyes off her. The crimson streaks in her hair did something sinister to my brain. Not to mention the effect it had on my dick.

I'd wanted to throw her on the bed and bury myself inside her right then.

But I couldn't.

I had a job to do, one I would succeed at based solely on her own merit. She didn't need my help to win this, not really. Kingston had been right about her.

She thought differently than anyone else here—saw the world through a different lens. One sharper than any of us at Camelot Court had been taught to look through.

She was hungry.

She was relentless.

And somehow, she remained light and free.

When she taunted me, I found myself torn between

playing a role and playing along. I found myself wanting to laugh *at myself* with her.

I hadn't felt that way with another person since...

I couldn't even remember the last time.

Locking eyes with her across the crowded room, I crooked my finger at her. The exasperated huff and look she sent me went straight to my dick, too. I liked that she didn't water down her reactions for me.

So many people in Camelot Court walked on eggshells around me. It had been refreshing to find someone unafraid to call me out. Unafraid to deny me.

And unafraid to give in...eventually.

I looped my arm around her waist and pulled her into my chest, the remote in my pocket practically begging for me to push her. The thought of seeing her face flood with heat, seeing the flush creep over the swell of her breasts—my dick twitched in my pants, like the poor bastard couldn't help but reach for her.

Her breaths came out in tight, controlled little pants. My Maiden wanted to come.

But she was hellbent on being a good girl.

My good girl.

I wanted to see just how well she could follow the rules.

Spreading her legs, I slipped mine between her thighs. When I jostled the toy deep inside of her, she moaned. My cock swelled, and I bent my knee to seat her firmly on my leg, letting her wriggle a bit until she found a comfortable spot.

Then, I clicked the vibrator on, keeping the setting low.

Her eyes widened, and she trapped her bottom lip between her teeth. Pressing her forehead into my shoulder, she breathed in and out through her nose. She fought off the release, her fingers gripping my biceps as she clutched me to her.

Apparently, the toy came with many benefits.

Her breasts pressed into my chest, and she lifted her eyes

to mine, begging silently.

"Tell me," I ordered.

"I want—Can I please come?"

Arching a brow, I stared down at her and fought not to smile. I wanted to lick the beads of sweat gathering at her temples.

She gritted her teeth in response. "Can I please come, *Sir?*"

"Not yet."

Clicking the remote off, I tightened my grip as she pitched forward, crying out with frustration. As if she didn't know I planned to make every moment of this torture worth it.

She bit down on my lapel, her body shaking with the need for release.

"Such a good girl."

As she shuddered in my arms, I pressed my lips to the top of her head, feeling something unexpected under her hair.

A faint ridge—a scar, maybe?

I'd have to explore that later.

"Landon," she panted.

And *fuck*—the way she panted my name like a plea was almost enough to make me come. I was ready for this god forsaken party to be over so I could take her back to my room and have my way with her. But as much as I wanted to leave, Kingston wouldn't be pleased.

He wanted to see her. Spend time with her. Dance with her.

And I couldn't tell him why I hadn't wanted to bring her here at all.

Since I couldn't get out of it, I'd decided to give her a little gift, so when he had her in his arms, at least I'd know there was something from me still with her. Inside her and driving her crazy. Making her question every single one of her life choices.

Doing, to her, exactly what she did to me.

King or not, I was still his Maiden.

Chapter Twenty-Eight
Quinn

I was going to die. Death by orgasm denial. Put it on my tombstone and bury me—dead.

It was a slow, evil kind of torture, and I needed to be put out of my misery.

But Landon seemed to be enjoying himself far too much, holding my pleasure in his hands. Promising punishment if I came without permission.

The fucking *sadist*.

I was starting to think whatever punishment he could dream up couldn't possibly be worse than orgasm denial. My body needed release. I needed to come. And I could take a few spankings if that was the consequence.

I almost let go.

The look in his eyes stopped me. He stared at me like he knew I could do this, even if I didn't think I could take anymore. So, I gritted my teeth and held onto him. Clutching him like a fucking lifeline, I fought to calm my body down.

My nipples had hardened to the point of pain. Every time they rubbed against Landon's chest, a zing of pleasure shot right to my clit. I put some distance between us once I steadied enough to stand up straight.

It was quickly stolen away when a second presence appeared at my back.

Kingston raised his voice over the music, nodding at Landon before smiling down at me. "I've been looking for you two." His hand wrapped around my free hip. "Mind if I join you?"

Too tense to speak, I nodded. My eyes flashed to Landon's, and I didn't miss the dark look he aimed at Kingston before shaking his head. Whatever I'd seen faded away as his eyes fell on me. The possessiveness there, though, rang out clear as day, and his gaze flicked down to his pocket as if to remind me.

King or not, I was still his Maiden.

It surprised me, given the way he'd deferred to Kingston under the stairs on my first day.

Maybe things were changing for him...

The way they were changing for me.

Before I could get ahead of myself, Kingston pressed against my back, his long, lean body fitting against mine and sending a trill of electricity up my spine. I glanced at him over my shoulder, smiling at the carefree look on his face.

"Be careful, Kingston," I teased as I swiveled my hips against him. "People might think you're playing favorites."

He stared down at me intently, no trace of humor in his voice when he said, "Let them."

When my lips parted in surprise, his blue eyes sparkled with mischief. He gripped my hips and moved my body in time with the music, dancing with me as if we were the only two people in the room. But I noticed that not once did he try to pull me away from Landon.

Whether that was for appearances, because he wasn't worried about his best friend, or because he might be more open to sharing than I would've expected, I didn't know. And in that moment, pressed between both of them, I couldn't bring myself to care. As long as the moment didn't end.

With Landon's thigh wedged between mine and Kingston grinding his hips against my ass, it didn't take long for the need inside me to build back up. Sweat beaded at my temples, rolling down the sides of my face and neck to disappear between the valley of my breasts. Landon's eyes tracked the movement, filling with a hunger that matched mine.

I wanted him. That much had become painfully clear. And it was written on both their faces that they wanted me, too.

The trouble was...I wanted them both.

As the song built to a climax, Landon reached into his pocket. Using one hand to guide my upper body back toward Kingston, he signaled his friend with a look. Kingston wound my arms up around his neck at the same time Landon took hold of my hips, keeping me astride his thigh. While Kingston ran his fingers down from my wrists to the curve of my breasts, Landon took hold of my chin.

"Remember the rules, Maiden."

I nodded, the pace of our movements increasing as Landon clicked the remote in his hand. My back arched, but he held me steady. Panting, writhing, and driving toward my own crescendo, I met Kingston's eyes.

They were wide and as piercingly blue as ever underneath the lights, jumping between me and Landon until he caught sight of the small remote in Landon's hand.

His eyes grew impossibly dark, like a lightning storm sweeping in over a clear blue sky. His thumb swept under the curve of my breasts as Landon's fingers dug into my hips.

I squeezed my eyes shut and tried to fight off the orgasm building furiously inside me.

"Eyes on me, love."

At Kingston's command, I forced my eyes open, locking them on his.

"Good girl," they said in unison, sharing a look right after that nearly broke me.

My body trembled between them, everything tightening and reaching a breaking point I wouldn't be able to withstand.

"Please, Sir. May I come?"

I didn't know who I was asking. Maybe both of them. But it surprised me when Kingston deferred to Landon.

Landon pressed in close, bringing his lips right to my ear. "Come, Maiden," he ordered. "Now."

I shattered. A scream built in my throat as my body tore apart in the most devastating climax I'd ever experienced.

And Landon knew it.

He covered my mouth, burying my head in the crook of his neck and muffling my scream.

Kingston kept up our pace, hiding the way I convulsed and came apart between them as if it were the most natural thing in the world. When the waves of climax finally relented, I collapsed back against his chest—completely and totally spent.

They rocked me slowly down to earth as the song changed. And together like that, it felt like I might be able to have them both. It felt like I'd been made to come apart between them.

But all too quickly, Kingston had to leave.

"You're breathtaking, love." He kissed my hand before sliding it into Landon's. "Take good care of her for me tonight, mate."

Then, I remembered my life didn't work like that.

Even if I was living in a fantasy world for the time being. I wouldn't be able to keep them both.

Eventually, I would have to choose.

And I didn't know what the fallout would be when I finally did.

I could be self-aware and continue to spiral.
It was a gift.

Chapter Twenty-Nine
Quinn

I grabbed a bench outside the party and sat down, trying to stop my hands from shaking.

With my body physically wrung out by the orgasm sandwich, calling it a night seemed like a solid plan. I told Landon I needed air, and he offered to take me back to the room as soon as he took care of something. I was too boneless to ask, let alone wonder, what that something was, so I took a seat outside the main room and waited.

It being relatively early to leave, most of the partygoers continued to drink and dance inside. No one joined me in the hallway. Thus far, I'd avoided any major run-ins with the other Maidens and Knights.

Okay. One Knight, in particular.

And I wanted to keep it that way.

I could *not* add the emotional whiplash guaranteed by my interactions with Max to my plate. Not tonight. Not on top of the war going on inside my mind.

Problem number one? I came here not intending to feel anything about anyone. Get in and get out. Problem number two? There were now *two* guys making it extremely difficult to stay true to that. And problem number three?

I wasn't even going to think about problem number three unless my other two problems tried to make me choose because he was an asshole.

Landon made my body come alive. Given the amount of time we'd spent together and our obvious sexual chemistry—even if we hadn't had sex yet—he seemed like the clear choice for who I'd pick if I needed to choose.

But what he said on the dance floor still rang true in my head. There was a lot I didn't know about him. A lot he didn't share. Least of which being his feelings for me.

Kingston, on the other hand, made no secret of his interest or his intentions. He wanted to pursue me and see what was between us. He said he'd be waiting for me at the end of all this, if I wanted that.

I hadn't been able to spend much time with him since this whole thing started, but every single time I interacted with him, the effect was the same. The connection between us was instantaneous. Our chemistry—*electric*.

I assumed, if given a chance to flourish, it could be just as mind-blowing as my experiences with Landon.

But the thought of choosing one of them before I really got to explore what there was between any of us didn't seem right. At this point, if forced to choose, I'd probably walk away from both of them.

I wouldn't divide them, or myself, just so one of them could possess me.

I wasn't a fucking doll.

Even if Landon got to dress me up for parties.

That circled me back to problem number three. Because if Kingston or Landon forced me to choose, I'd probably pick Max just to stick it to both of them.

But more problems arose from that, too.

One—I hated him.

Two—he only saw me as a way to hurt the other guys.

And three—while sticking it to them would work in the short term, it didn't really serve me in the long run. Especially since this revenge plot of mine was based on nothing more than my own anxieties.

Anxieties over being put in a position no one had even tried to put me in yet.

I could be self-aware and continue to spiral.

It was a gift.

Groaning, I dropped my head into my hands and tried to ease the tension building behind my eyes. But before I could relax, a shadow fell over me, pulling another groan from my lips as I stared at the pair of heels where the floor should have been.

Looking up, I expected to find Vivian ready to torment me with her bitchy attitude again.

Instead, gratefully, I found Elaine.

Her blonde hair was curled sweetly and pinned in a half-up, half-down style, and her pink lipstick really did make her look like a doll. She wore a tight-fitted baby blue dress. But where the hem of mine had been skankified to the max, hers flared out into a fun, flirty skirt.

"Hi, Quinn," she said brightly. "Can I join you?"

"Of course." I scooted over on the bench, making room for her to sit beside me. "It's actually really good to see a friendly face tonight."

She smiled at me, her cheeks flushed and her voice a bit breathless, as if she'd been dancing the way I had been a few minutes ago. "I've been wondering how things were going for you, actually." Her demeanor changed from worn out to worried. "How are you doing?"

The concern on her face caught me by surprise, but then, considering what I'd overheard in the Round Tableau room after I'd been assigned to Landon, and the expectations the Maidens had for The Quest, I figured she wanted to make sure I wasn't days away from being murdered.

"I'm good, really." I smiled to ease her worry, but my answer seemed to spark even more concern. "It's going...as well as I think it could, I guess."

She put her hand on my arm. "Are you sure? If there's anything you need to talk about, just...I know it's hard to get away, but I'm sure I could convince Peter to let me out of bed for some girl time." Forcing an awkward laugh, she gave my arm a squeeze. "Do you think Landon would let you?"

"I don't see why not. It's not like he keeps me chained to the bed, Elaine."

Her cheeks reddened. "Oh! I mean, of course not. I just..."

"Just say what you want to say, Elaine. Or ask me."

I didn't know why, but her line of questioning irritated me. Maybe I was tired. Or maybe I didn't appreciate the implication that any Knight could keep his Maiden completely isolated.

"Peter just said I was lucky he didn't pick me, that's all. He knew I had a crush on him. And at first, I thought he was jealous, but..." She chewed on her lip, her eyes darting between my face and the doorway beside us. "He said everyone expected Landon's Maiden to be put through the wringer, with him being the King's best friend. Plus, his whole family history. He wouldn't have moved me onto the next round unless he was absolutely sure I wouldn't fail. Since it would reflect poorly on him, you know?"

Most of that sounded like bullshit. Fellow Knights talking shit about each other. Or one Knight trying hard to squash a girl's existing crush. But the last part stuck out in my mind.

Landon had said something like that on my first day.

Whatever crossed my face at the thought had Elaine's grip tightening on my arm. "Has it been terrible? Is he..." She glanced around to make sure no one was there. "Is he hurting you?"

I shook my head numbly.

Duty and honor were two things Landon valued without a doubt. But so far, he hadn't given me any reason to think he wouldn't advance me in the competition. Quite the opposite, actually. He talked about it like it was a given.

"The sex isn't too rough, right? You can go to Merle if it is. It's not supposed to count against us if we raise an actual concern."

"No, Elaine. Really, I'm fine." I gently pried her grip off my arm. "Whatever your Knight said he heard, it's not like that. *Landon* isn't like that."

I didn't tell her that Landon hadn't even *tried* to have sex with me.

And now, I couldn't help but wonder why that was—my virginity, Kingston, or worse, a lack of feelings for me.

Relief brought a smile to her face. "Oh, good. I was worried. Not just about you, but one of us is going to be paired with him for the next challenge, right?" She glanced over her shoulder to search the crowd of the party. "Maybe it won't be as bad as I thought, if it ends up being—"

My eyebrows rose.

Elaine whipped back around to face me. "Well, whoever it ends up being. It'll be easy if it's just normal attempts at seduction. I half-expected to be tied up and tortured until I gave in!" She laughed again, this time even more forced than before.

I couldn't decide exactly how she felt about being assigned to Landon in the next challenge, if she ended up paired with him. I hadn't forgotten how much she'd wanted him to pick her the first night. Or the disappointment on her face when he hadn't.

Listening as she tried to talk herself both in and out of wanting to be his Maiden?

I *really* didn't like that.

Landon said he'd do whatever necessary to make the Maiden assigned to him ask for more. Initially, I doubted it'd be easy for any Maiden to resist giving into him. While that hadn't sat right with me, it hadn't felt like this.

Now, I wondered just how far he'd take things if the Maiden *was* willing. Something I couldn't avoid thinking about while faced with the possibility of him being paired with Elaine.

That thought swirled like poison in my gut.

If she or any other Maiden caved and offered him more, would he take her up on it? Would it come down to what he felt about me? Because if so, then the need to know exactly how he felt about me became impossible to shake.

"Quinn?"

Landon's voice pulled my head up. He glanced between me and Elaine, nodding politely at her before looking back at me. My eyes jumped from him to her and back again. The image of them alone in a romantic lake cabin made my stomach turn.

Landon held out his hand for me to take. "Are you ready to go back to our room?"

Our room.

Tension in my shoulders eased as he stared at me. Pressure on my chest lifted with his eyes locked on mine. Phrasing the question so simply, he soothed me completely. Before he even knew I needed it.

He tilted his head as he waited for my answer. And even though Elaine's body shifted and straightened beside me, still, Landon never took his eyes off me.

"Yes, I'm ready." Slipping my hand in his open palm, I said an absent minded goodbye to Elaine and let Landon pull me away.

Landon got my jacket from coat check, holding out the faded leather for me to slip my arms inside. He gently spun me around to zip it up. Bringing the zipper up underneath my chin, he tipped my head up with his thumb.

"Are you alright?" His eyes searched mine, the tilt of his head returning as he tried to figure out what I was thinking. "What happened earlier on the dance floor, I hope—"

I grabbed onto the lapels of his jacket and pulled him into me. "I'm alright."

Deciding to take a risk, I released his jacket and reached for his hand, giving him the option to take mine or not. Our hands brushed where they rested between us, and when Landon laced his fingers with mine, relief flowed through me.

He felt something here, too. He had to, didn't he?

The answer to that question mattered more than I had expected it would, and what it meant for both our journeys through The Quest, I couldn't say.

But I left my doubts and uncertainty on that bench behind me, letting Landon lead me by the hand back to our room, hoping—and ready—to find out what came next.

I'd be the King who sacrificed his Knight to take the Queen and end the game for good.

KINGSTON

"He's falling for her."

Merle loved to point out things I was already aware of, as if I didn't have eyes or a brain. He meant well, I was sure. The prior years' kings might've needed help on a daily basis.

But I was a D'Arthur.

I'd been prepared for this. Merle knew that. How many evenings had he sat at our family home, talking with my grandfather and listening to the old coot drone on about my future?

Merle acting like I couldn't relieve myself without his helping hand or pointing out the obvious—it just became so tiresome. Especially when he alerted me to problems I already knew were coming but wasn't quite ready to address.

"And?"

Merle needed prompting. If I wanted to get his thoughts, rather than give him all of mine so he could store them away like acorns for winter, I had to lead him to speak.

"Landon. He's falling for the girl. That could pose a problem."

Tiresome.

And I needed more time.

Too many things were working against me. Conspiring against her. Setting her up with the hope that she'd fail.

She couldn't fail. *She wouldn't.*

"It won't be an issue, Merle."

"Overconfidence is foolish, Kingston. Remember what your father says."

I hated when he mentioned him like that—*my father*.

"It's not overconfidence if I'm stating facts, Merle. Landon is loyal to me. He knows the obstacles I face, and he wouldn't jeopardize—"

"But what if that loyalty shifts, Kingston?"

Searching the crowd, I found them by the doorway. He zipped up her jacket, drawing the zipper right under her chin and staring down at her like...

That was a problem.

"I'll see to it, Merle. But I think you're wasting your time worrying over one Knight and his Maiden."

"Not if you want that Maiden to be a D'Arthur Queen, Kingston."

A D'Arthur Queen.

Closing my eyes, I prayed for patience.

I didn't *want* her to be a D'Arthur Queen. But she'd have to be. The antiquated traditions of a raving old man dictated it.

And if I didn't follow his orders, he'd take everything he'd given me, and I'd have no chance of doing what I set out to do.

Now, more than ever, I had clarity—certainty that I'd been right about her. The truth marinating in my bones had ossified, infusing into the marrow of who I was, and I couldn't be turned away from it. That truth, integral as it was to my survival, wouldn't just save me.

It would save Camelot Court and everyone in it.

She could do it.

With her by my side, we could change everything.

But if I couldn't protect her from the snakes in my kingdom's garden, she'd be lost to me as quickly as she'd been found. If I didn't shield her from their venom, she'd leave before she let them poison her.

And if I didn't convince *him* to see the greater good, we'd lose her. We'd lose everything.

"Honestly, Merle, it's a party. I said I'll take care of it. Can you let it rest for tonight?"

"Of course, son."

I rolled my eyes as he walked off. *Son*.

He'd have saved me a lot of trouble by directing that moniker so affectionately in the appropriate direction. At this point, Max Dread's feelings on me wouldn't change, but his feelings got me into this mess.

Now, I might need them to get us out of it.

No one should've known about her. No one should've known I'd chosen her. By stealing that file, he cost me more than he even realized, and some days, I wanted to rid myself of all the problems he created.

But I had to remember it wasn't his fault. I had to believe that maybe there was hope for him. That he could see the truth—if not about me, then about Landon.

And Landon...

It didn't surprise me—him falling for her.

That much I'd expected. But it surprised me he seemed poised to do something about it. Move against me when he'd always been on my side.

We weren't opponents in this battle.

And I still believed I needed him to win it.

I'd take him off the board, if necessary. I'd be the King who sacrificed his Knight to take the Queen and end the game for good. But I prayed it wouldn't come to that.

Which is why I searched tirelessly for solutions. Ones that wouldn't force me to drag up old wounds. Ones that wouldn't force me to break through the protection in his mind. Something—*anything*—that wouldn't force me to direct his hand and break her heart.

But if I couldn't find one?

My next move had been written in the by-laws of Camelot Court at the start, and if I couldn't find a way to alter my strategy—to avoid hurting even one of them—I wouldn't have another choice.

I had to defeat the biggest opponent, or we'd all be wiped off the board.

"Why? Because it's supposed to be fucking special or something?"

Chapter Thirty
Quinn

Once we got back from the party, Landon had all but ripped me out of my dress and tossed me on the bed. I got the feeling he'd been waiting all night to do it. I couldn't say I minded one bit.

I'd been waiting, too.

But even after wrapping his arm around my thighs and forcing my ass into the air so he could take his time making me come apart, he didn't push for more.

The doubts and uncertainty I'd left on the bench came rushing back, but I couldn't bring myself to ask him about it that night.

A few nights later, I had to do it.

I had to know why we hadn't gone further. If it was really about the upcoming challenge and worry over how I'd handle it or if it was something else.

He lay beside me on the bed, his eyes closed, and his arm tucked up under his head. His face had relaxed the way it usually did right before he fell asleep. But I wasn't even close to restful, and that he could doze off so easily bothered me.

I sat up abruptly. "Why haven't you tried to sleep with me?"

He blinked a few times, the muscle in his jaw working as he processed the question. "I'm trying to sleep with you right now."

He eased up onto his forearms before sitting up fully on the bed.

Obviously, putting distance between us.

"You know that's not what I mean."

His features tightened, eyebrows drawing in as his mouth turned down. "I don't understand why you're asking me that."

"You don't?"

I couldn't keep the hurt out of my voice. It rang out clear as a bell between us, the sound as damning as the silence that followed it.

He climbed off the bed, going into the bathroom to grab a warm washcloth like he usually did when the afterglow faded. But we both knew he was buying himself time and avoiding the question. Handing me the damp cloth, he stepped back from the bed.

Carefully maintaining his distance.

I held the cloth in my open palm, making no move to use it. Staring up at him, I fought past all the insecurities rising and forced out what I wanted to say.

"I thought it was part of all this. I figured you were giving me time to come around initially, and I appreciated that. But now that I've come around—repeatedly, I might add—I guess I'm just confused why we haven't gone further. If that's not something you want..." I swallowed past the lump rising in my throat, pushing up on the bed so I could run off it if needed. "If you don't want me like that, I—"

"It's not—" He snapped his mouth shut, frustration building in his expression as he ran a hand over his face. "You don't understand what you're asking me."

"Yes, I do. I just don't understand why you can't give me a straight answer."

His hand clenched in his hair. "I..."

"Either you want me, or you don't." My heart pounded in my chest. "So, which is it?"

He said nothing.

"If you don't, then just say that. I'm a big girl. I can take it."

His nostrils flared as his lips stayed shut.

I rose to my knees on the bed, shuffling over to him until I knelt in front of him. "If you do, then I'm just asking why we haven't gone there. Because if you're worried I'm not ready..."

"Quinn, please." He exhaled, his voice barely a whisper as he said, "Don't."

At the same time, I said, "I am."

His head fell. "I can't."

"You can't? Or you won't?"

"Does it really matter? Either way, the result is the same."

"Yes, it matters." I grabbed his hand, tugging on it to get him to look at me. When he withdrew, I pushed harder. "Can't implies you're not allowed. Won't implies you refuse to let yourself do it. And if it's the first—No, it shouldn't be because the only person who has the right to decide who I do and don't sleep with is *me*."

He wouldn't respond. And he wouldn't look at me.

"If it's the second, then I want to know why."

More silence.

"Is it because I'm a virgin? Is that still a problem? Because I can go out for a bit and take care of that right now, if it means you won't keep holding back with me."

His head snapped up. "Don't even—This isn't a joke, Quinn."

I waved a hand at his reaction, imploring him to see why it didn't make sense—why I didn't understand. "Okay, so you don't want me to give that to anyone else, but you won't take it yourself. Why?"

"You think this is what you want, Quinn, but you're wrong. It's not right. It would be a mis—"

"A mistake? You think sleeping with me would be a mistake?"

"Taking that from you? What you're asking me to do? It's not as simple as you think."

Old wounds tore open as the words left my mouth. But I couldn't stop them. I couldn't help but spit them out. "Why? Because it's supposed to be fucking special or something?"

They burned my throat like battery acid.

Breathing hard, Landon retreated off the end of the bed.

"And so what if it's that?" His voice rose. "What if I think it matters? That you deserve more than *this*."

"That's not up to you."

"It is when you're asking me to be involved!" he shouted, pacing the room. Staring as if I'd gone mad and taken him with me. He threw his hands up in the air. "Or do I not get a choice there, too?"

"No," I shook my head. "That's not what I meant. If it's important to you that it's special for me, yes, that matters. But shouldn't I be the one to decide if it is? If *this* is enough?"

I climbed off the bed, standing in front of him and pulling him to face me.

"We're getting off track, Quinn."

His eyes were pleading, desperate for me to let this go.

But I couldn't relent.

My temper flared as his rejection and my past burned me. "No, I'm just poking holes in your argument!"

"You don't know what you're saying. You're—This is hormones. Endorphins. It's just—"

"It's just that I finally stopped worrying about when or

how it would happen. I finally thought about what I wanted, and I just told you what I want is *you*."

He stopped pacing and stared at me with torment in his eyes.

My eyes blurred and my heart raced. "But you're trying to tell me that's a mistake."

The anguish on his face—I couldn't understand it.

I didn't want to understand.

My body shook as the truth built up inside me.

I dragged my hand through my hair, tugging on my scar so hard, sharp pain shot to the base of my neck.

"Except, the last time I put pressure on myself over when and how I lost my *stupid, fucking* virginity," I spat out the words, getting in his face as tears streamed down mine. "The last time I made *that* mistake, it killed—"

I struggled to breathe, grasping my chest as pain and panic clawed its way up my throat.

"Quinn..." He grabbed my arms, his fingers digging in as I forced more out.

"You don't get to tell me what's good enough for me. You don't have a fucking clue who I am or what I need."

Tearing away from him, I left him shell-shocked standing in the middle of the room. I pushed my way into the bathroom, snatching my clutch off the chaise as I went.

Once inside, I dug for my inhaler.

But my hands shook so violently I couldn't pull it free.

Upending the bag, I dropped to my knees and brought the inhaler to my lips. I breathed in deep.

And even though the inhaler worked, my next breaths wouldn't come easy.

Grief had locked me in a chokehold.

"Quinn, let me in."

"Go away, Landon." I sank down to my heels on the tile floor, dropping my head into my hands. "Please, just... Go away."

My voice came out soft and small, so staggeringly different from the memory racing through my mind.

Nothing about it had been soft—no part of it small. Not the wreckage on that mountain road or in my life after it.

The enormity of it closed around me the way it always did.

Compressing my chest like the airbag as it deployed. Stealing my breath like the jolt when the car flipped. Squeezing my neck. Strangling the cries in my throat. Like the seatbelt choking me as I hung upside down above a bed of shattered glass…and screamed for my dad as he bled to death in front of me.

But I couldn't scream.

Because I couldn't breathe.

I couldn't *breathe*.

The whole time, I couldn't breathe, but *I stayed alive*.

And when the light left his eyes, and I knew he was really gone…in that moment, I didn't want to do either one.

But death took without considering who was good or bad. It didn't discriminate between who deserved to be taken and who should've been the one who lived.

And sometimes, death chose *wrong*.

It was my indecision that made him leave the house that night. My hesitation put us on that road.

My choice—it *killed* him.

I clawed at my neck, gasping for air I desperately needed but didn't want. Black spots appeared at the edge of my vision.

A crash sounded behind me.

Landon's hands gripped my face. His voice was muffled in my ears. Drowned out by the pounding of my heart as I relived it all over again.

As I survived to watch it end the way it always did.

My fault.

It was all my fault.

My dad was dead because of me.

He'd never breathe again. And I'd never hear his voice. Or listen to him as he sang along with the radio. Or have him read to me when I was sick in bed. Or hear him tell me everything would be alright.

And I couldn't breathe.

I still couldn't *fucking* breathe.

"Quinn, breathe!"

Landon's voice pierced through the darkness, squeezing my face so tightly. Like he was trying to hold me together with his bare hands.

"Fucking breathe, dammit!"

I gasped.

Wheezing, I grasped onto Landon's wrists and forced in heaving, gulping breaths. His face had gone completely white. And I didn't know if he was shaking or if I was.

"You're alright."

"I'm sorry." I sobbed, my vision blurring as tears streamed down my face. My body fell forward into his chest, hands gripping his shirt as the scent of lavender, freesia, and lemon filled my head.

But I knew that scent wasn't really there. I knew Landon smelled like lavender and *mint*. And I knew I'd never find it again—the unique blend that reminded me of my dad—the smell that enveloped me each time he had wrapped me in a hug.

Because I'd never have one of those again, either.

"God, I'm so sorry."

"You're alright." Landon rubbed my back as I sobbed out my regrets. Until the waves abated, and the tears slowed.

The pain dulled. But it didn't ease completely.

Because some things never left us.

And that pain, those tears—they'd never stop coming.

"You're alright," Landon echoed those words again, exhaling them like an answered prayer. His voice pitched low like he couldn't believe it.

I saw it, then—what I'd missed while I cried in his arms. His eyes had tears in them, too.

I took his face in my hands, closing my eyes as he pressed our foreheads together. "I'm alright. I'm sorry. I just—"

"Panicked." He pulled my head back to his chest, tucking me under his chin. "You just panicked. You're alright."

His hands stroked up my back and tangled in my hair, and his heart felt like it was trying to beat its way out of his chest. Mine did, too.

But eventually, it slowed.

And, lying there together, we fell asleep holding onto each other in the dark.

"Not today, Satan! I am not in the mood!"

Chapter Thirty-One
Quinn

I'd been staring at the ceiling for the last twenty minutes. After Landon had barged into the bathroom and pulled me out of my panic, we fell asleep. At some point, I woke to him scooping me off the floor. I barely remembered making it to the bed, but I couldn't forget crying into his chest until I fell back asleep.

Waking up alone in bed after all of that, somehow, I still felt safe and warm. Tucked under the covers Landon had pulled up around me, I opened my eyes to find I'd curled toward the window where he slept.

And once again, he was gone.

After what happened last night and what I'd shared with him, he wasn't there. But I'd woken up plenty of times in the last two weeks without him—that wasn't even the problem.

It was that I *wanted* him to be there.

That tiny realization made my heart pound.

Oh, fuck.

Shooting upright, I threw the covers off my body. I kicked the sheets away with my feet, as if the bed had been filled with snakes. Though, the real betrayer rested in my chest.

When I uncovered a silk pajama set I had *not* fallen asleep in last night, I shot right past how Landon had dressed me and went straight to freaking out.

The pajamas had gotten twisted overnight, the shorts riding up my ass and my tits falling almost completely out of the camisole. I had absolutely no choice but to tear it off my body.

I needed my sleep shirt.

I needed my inhaler.

And I needed…Fuck. To be honest, I probably needed breakfast, but the only thing on the menu was a large helping of grade A panic.

I couldn't deny it anymore. And I couldn't blame it on the orgasms. I couldn't cheapen it or refuse to claim it.

All I could do was wonder how I could be so *fucking* stupid.

I'd done the one thing I said I wouldn't—the last thing I needed to do. I'd gone and gotten myself attached, and now I was waking up all heart-eyed emoji over the way the guy had tucked me into bed.

A bed he'd probably vacated, as soon as I fell asleep, and he'd been able to extricate himself from my clingy tangle of limbs.

Refusing to even play devil's advocate and wonder if *maybe* I'd woken up alone because my Knight had gone to fetch me food, I got out of bed. I grabbed my most obnoxious sleep shirt and threw it on my body.

The grumpy cats all over it rapidly infused me with joy.

They also reminded me of how Landon's eye twitched whenever I wore it.

"Gah!"

I tore it off and grabbed one I hadn't worn yet. It was less offensive to the eye, and therefore, had been shoved down to the bottom of the drawer. That would work.

No obvious Landon association.

The shirt was safe.

I ran my fingers through my hair while I peed, brushed my teeth, and bolted from the room, needing to get out of there before he came back. The door slammed behind me.

And as if my weak moment had purposefully summoned him, Max Dread stepped out of his room.

"Do you mi—"

"Nope!" I threw my hand up as I cut him off. "Not today, Satan! I am *not* in the mood!"

My voice rang out down the hall, but I didn't care.

"Cute PJs!" Max called after me.

"Wore them just for you, buddy!"

"Perfect. I love the way your tits bounce in it when you're not wearing a bra."

I spun around to give him two middle fingers to the sky, but Vivian's shriek from his room took care of that karma for me. My laugh came out a little louder and way more satisfied than necessary. His answering growl, and the slam of his door, told me he'd heard it.

Flying around the banister at the top of the stairs, I took them down two at a time before jumping onto the main landing. My light verbal sparring with Max had released some of the tension in my body. But I was still wound up, and I needed food.

Probably a mild sedative, too.

I pushed my way through the kitchen doors and couldn't decide if I was relieved or disappointed when I didn't find Landon making me a breakfast I most certainly didn't want. My mood deflated, starting a spiral downward as confusion crept in.

"He needed to take the day to deal with some urgent personal matters."

Whipping around, I spotted Kingston eyeing me from behind the fridge door. He offered me a weak attempt at a smile, but didn't say anything else.

I sat down at the kitchen island with a *humph*. "Oh. I'm not—I wasn't—"

"Quinn, I'm his best friend. Other than what I witnessed at the party, he didn't give me details. But he said you two had a *heavy* night. That's not a word Landon typically uses unless big emotions come out." He poured a glass of juice and held it out to me. "If it had been me, I'd be looking for him, too."

I accepted the juice, twirling the glass in my hands as I processed what Kingston said. What had happened between us last night *had* brought up big emotions—in me. But apparently it had brought up stuff for Landon that meant he needed to get away.

Kingston touched my hand before pulling back. "It's not because of you."

"Stop that."

"What?"

"Saying things like you know what I'm thinking."

His eyebrows rose. "That's not what you were thinking?"

"That's not the point." I huffed. "And don't you dare say you know what the point is because I have a point to make."

"Yes, ma'am."

I found myself returning the smile that came to his lips, just a little bit. "I'm sensing a theme between us. And I'm not sure I like it."

"Which part? The way I can read your mind?"

I shook my head, taking a sip of my juice and nearly moaning at the taste of freshly squeezed oranges. "No, the one where Landon does something I don't understand, and you swoop in to make sure I don't hate him for it."

"Ah. That one."

"Yeah," I said petulantly. "That one."

Kingston sighed and took the empty seat beside me. He gripped the edge of my chair, turning me to face him. Smoothing the flyaway strands of hair from my forehead and cheeks, he searched my face for a long time before he spoke again.

"Quinn, I'm only telling you this because he said I could if I thought you needed to hear it. I want you to know I'm not breaking his confidence here, but also that this isn't something he remembers. Or wants to remember. So I'm going to ask you not to bring it up with him. Can you promise me that?"

My brow creased, and I shook my head. "I don't like making promises I'm not sure I can keep, Kingston."

He nodded, accepting that. "I don't have to share it with you at all. It's your choice. If there comes a time where you want to understand why Landon...Well, why he is the way he is, then come to me and I'll tell you." Reaching for my hand, he turned it over in his palm. "If you can trust him or trust me without that, I promise he won't let your faith in him be wasted."

I frowned. That was like dangling the climax of a series in front of a reader who loved spoilers.

But the way things had been progressing, I didn't want to skip to the finale. If last night brought up heavy emotions for him, and if Kingston said it wasn't about me, I could believe that. I'd still have to call Gia and freak out about it, but I didn't have to bolt. I didn't have to be scared. And I could decide to trust him.

I groaned dramatically at the offer Kingston had left in the air. "Ugh, this is like *Sophie's Choice.*" At the slightly appalled look on his face, I laughed. "I'm kidding, obviously. But it isn't easy to turn that down. I just...I'd rather not know. Not right now."

His expression shifted from relief to reverence as he cupped my face in his hands, and he smiled at me like I'd just answered every one of his prayers.

Super flattering, but hella confusing.

"Why are you looking at me like that?"

He took a deep breath and brushed his thumb over my

lips. "Because, Quinn, I..."

Trailing off, he took hold of my wrist and played with the charms on my bracelet.

I hadn't been ready to add his charm when he first gave it to me, but the thought of doing so now didn't feel as overwhelming.

"Let me guess. You were right about me?"

He smiled, nudging my knee with his. "Stop that."

"What?"

"Saying things like you know what I'm thinking."

I rolled my eyes, an impish grin quirking the side of my mouth. "Oh, that wasn't what you were thinking?"

His eyes darkened as he stared at my lips. "It was and it wasn't."

"What does *that* mean?"

But I knew the answer before he said it.

"You'll see."

I shook my head, exasperated with him but also much lighter. My momentary freak out felt a bit foolish, but given the *heaviness* of last night, I was entitled to a little irrationality. Though, it didn't change that my goal of staying detached had failed.

The plan hadn't been to care about Landon, and it was the last thing I expected to happen when I came back here after the Maiden Selection. I also hadn't been expecting to care about the *King* sitting in front of me—the one still transfixed by my mouth.

"You know, none of this was supposed to happen, right?"

Busy memorizing the shape of my lips, Kingston raised his eyebrows. "Hm?"

I pushed my finger under his chin to redirect his eyes upward. "I wasn't supposed to care. About you, about him." I swept my gaze around the room as if it were all of Camelot Court and The Quest. "About any of this."

"Yes, you were." His hands slipped down from cupping

The King's Maiden

my jaw to cradling my neck. "You just forgot how for a little while. You've been afraid to feel because you know better than most how love opens your heart up to loss."

His thumb stroked up the column of my throat. And even though he said Landon hadn't shared details with him, I sensed that he knew—that his mind was on the pain I still held there in my neck. That somehow he felt it, too.

"You deserve to feel everything good in this world, Quinn Everly. To care and be cared for—to love with your whole heart. Without limits or fear." His eyes swept over the room like mine had. "You deserve all of it."

And for the first time in a year, a small part of me thought, *maybe*.

Maybe I did. Or at the very least, maybe I could learn to believe that again.

♟

When Landon got back that night, it was after midnight. I woke up on the chaise where I'd been reading and waiting up for him. All he said was I should get some rest and that we had a lot of work to do the next day. That was all the explanation I got.

He showered quickly and went to sleep, and he didn't make me join him in bed.

Naturally, I slept like a champ after that.

The next morning, he left early to take care of some things. Again, without much to say. That made trust harder to hold on to, and I was struggling when he found me later that day, sitting under the lemon tree and staring out at the water.

After my talk with Kingston the day before and Landon's abrupt withdrawal, I'd needed some time to think about everything. My life choices, my growing attraction to thr—*two*—equally vague and confusing guys. I figured under a lemon tree was as good a place as any.

I ended up spending the whole day out there, though, oddly calm under its branches.

Even as some of the other Knights and Maidens came out, heading down to the lake to ease their hangovers with a swim, I sat there. Ignoring Vivian's tired remarks about my whore ways. Refusing to return Max's searing gaze as she dragged him away. Peeking at his bare back while he scowled on the shoreline and averting my eyes as soon as he looked back at me.

No doubt plotting how to get rid of me or insinuate how he'd fuck me if I asked for it.

I thanked my lucky stars I had been blessed with my dad's stubbornness and iron will. It was the only thing keeping me from marching down there and telling him he'd been right.

The White Knight had left me high and dry and he could take care of the problem.

Except that created a different set of problems.

One—I still hated him.

Two—I wanted to win The Quest more than anyone or *anything*. Even the reminder of my biggest regret.

And three—even if he made the sex worth it, I'd have to see his stupid, smug face afterward and that would ruin it for me.

I deserved more than that.

Maybe.

So, I just sat there. Long after they all went inside to start their nightly rounds of training, I sat there until my eyes drifted shut. Until Landon walked up and sat down beside me.

He didn't say anything.

He just held out his hand and waited for me to take it before leading me to the Round Tableau.

And then, he showed me what it meant to be a Maiden. What it meant to be led by trust.

What it meant to be *his*.

I searched for something I wanted to find, but somehow, couldn't bear to see.

KINGSTON

They'd built the Round Tableau with good intentions. Originally the first building on the property, its lower level had been living quarters for members of the Camelot Society. Over time, membership grew and the property expanded.

Over time, it became corrupted.

The obvious choices, however, hadn't been responsible.

The addition of stocks, racks, and St. Andrew's crosses weren't its darkest elements. The suspension hooks in the ceilings, and the whips and chains on the walls, weren't its greatest sins.

When practiced safely, they weren't dark sins at all.

In my humble opinion, the cameras had crossed the line. Instead of a place for exploring dark fantasies, the Round Tableau dissolved into something sinister.

Because the Maidens weren't explicitly informed of the recordings.

And the feed transmitted to a server outside Camelot Court.

All for the viewing pleasure of the Camelot Society.

There had been discord following the installation.

Knights didn't agree and refused to participate in The Quest. Now, knowledge of it passed only to the new King. With strict instructions to keep the secret to himself.

Prior Kings of Camelot Court reveled in their private showings. My predecessor nearly soiled himself in his gleeful haste to share it. Not everyone believed it was wrong.

I was not one of those people.

Informing Landon of the cameras' presence had been a necessity. The first night in the Round Tableau with the Maidens being a requirement, he had to know how to shield her. Barring that, he could limit their time to his room.

But he'd still been against it. Still questioned my intentions once he learned her secret. Confused by my expectations, because I'd known better than to share them.

To say it shocked me when he came to me tonight, with plans to bring Quinn there, would be an understatement.

Until he handed me the file he'd stolen from her doctor's office. He hadn't looked inside it, but he told me what she'd hidden from him and why he needed her to share it with him herself.

I hadn't looked at the file yet, either. The last one on Quinn Everly caused enough trouble. And I expected to learn the truth as their evening played out.

The grainy camera feed didn't reveal everything, but it showed enough.

Landon's eyes changed his normally stoic expression. As he led her into the room, he kept them trained on her face. Brimming with repressed need.

I closed mine.

His unwavering voice contained a harder edge, echoing through the room. "What do you say if you want me to stop?"

She responded instantly. "I yield."

"And if you want me to slow down?"

"Mercy." Her voice trembled. "I ask for mercy."

But I sensed the underlying current of excitement in her soft voice.

"Good girl."

And I reveled in the pride in his.

The satisfaction derived when she obeyed—her control brought the same pleasure to me.

Landon had never believed he deserved to hold power over another. He couldn't see how beautifully he wielded it. He wouldn't.

But I had always seen it, and a shiver ran through me when he commanded her again.

"Undress me."

The rustling of clothes and clink of his belt followed the command. Then, he ordered the same with her attire. And laid out what he'd planned for her next.

Shibari was an art form. Not simply tying someone up.

As Landon cast the ropes around her wrists, I couldn't help but glance back at the screen. His focus, care, and efficiency made it seem like he'd studied the process for years.

But all of it was because of *her*.

She received the ropes eagerly, her posture slowly reflecting the change within her. Her spine straightened as her confidence bolstered. It grew stronger as Landon spoke, explaining as he went. Teaching her to find the bight of the rope. Wrapping it twice around her wrist.

Praising her for doing so well.

He touched her with respect, but something more... treating her as if she were precious. Responding to her slightest reaction. Staring at her with a hunger in his eyes I hadn't seen in...

It had been a very long time since the last time.

When he finished, he led her to the cross at the back of the room, securing the ropes on a hook above her head. Cuffing her ankles in the shackles at the bottom—a medieval touch the founding members had insisted on adding. I panned the camera up to study his face.

I searched for something I wanted to find, but somehow, couldn't bear to see.

He deserved it. Of everyone in this place, he deserved it most. But I might not be able to give him everything he wanted.

It was better if he stayed detached.

The rumors, recirculating after the dance, continued to force my hand. A choice loomed that I didn't want to make. One I wouldn't have to consider, if he didn't cross the line.

So far, he made no move to kiss her.

He showed no obvious signs of swaying in his resolve. But I believed Quinn Everly could change everything at Camelot Court. Even my most loyal Knight.

Even my best friend.

The only person I trusted to guide her to the end, the one I needed by my side, but who I claimed I'd committed to sacrificing, if needed to reach the end.

As I watched them together, a different plan formed in my mind, until I couldn't bear witness anymore. I muted the sound and angled the screen away, waiting for the darkness to signal the end. Then, I would erase the recording before it could upload.

And, alone, I would leave the Round Tableau.

Bondage and light BDSM brought out the crass parts of my psyche.

Chapter Thirty-Two
Quinn

Everything was dark.

The thick blindfold secured over my eyes blocked out even the slightest hint of light. The headphones blocked out every sound. I couldn't even orient myself to where I was in the room.

Or more importantly, where *he* was.

All I could do was feel.

Pressure at my back urged my feet forward. My hands lifted from where they'd been bound in front of me. His hand wrapped around my throat, and the word *trust* resonated in my head like a mantra—one I cursed myself for choosing but had chosen nonetheless.

I dropped my arms and kept walking, breathing easier when his grip loosened. With slow shuffling steps, I paid attention to every sensation until a slight tug halted my progress. Breathing in the scent of cedar and rich leather, my pulse quickened.

My arms were lifted, guided by the ropes he'd used to secure my wrists. Bound in a complicated technique he'd called *Shibari*, he attached them to something above my head

A gentle nudge eased me forward and into a wall, flattening my breasts against the cold wood and making me shiver.

A foot kicked my legs apart.

Widening my stance, slow and soothing circles brushed over the skin of my ankle. But almost as if he'd suddenly realized what he was doing, the touch retreated.

How appropriate given his similar emotional one-eighty in the last twenty-four hours.

I would've commented on it, but whatever he'd put in my mouth made it impossible to speak. At least, not without drooling. And I was pretty sure choking to death on my spit wouldn't be a good look.

Probably frowned upon for an aspiring Maiden, or a sign I needed to be punished. He'd mentioned that again last night. A bit too seriously, given the way he'd reverted to the cold, aloof version of himself I first met.

But I still had my safe words and my new safe signals—non-verbal cues I could use—if needed. With something in my mouth, I had to make three quick *ah* sounds and shake my head from side to side if I needed him to stop.

He made me practice, too.

So fun.

The time to reflect on why I hadn't used them yet—or why I let him shackle my ankles to the wall—would have to be later. Most likely, when this was over. In the discomfort of my therapist's office, where I examined all my questionable life choices.

And learned nothing.

I sure as hell wasn't going to examine my behavior while I stood spread against a wall with something that felt suspiciously like a riding crop brushing my bare ass.

I fucking should've examined it right then.

But the second he ran the supple leather up my swollen pussy and swatted it lightly against my clit, he drowned out any hope for rational thought.

All I could do was feel.

Landon removed my headphones halfway toward my first orgasm.

The flicks of the riding crop against my bare thighs, my ass, and my pussy drove me quickly toward climax. Combined with the sensory deprivation that forced me to let go, I prepared to come fast and hard the second he placed a vibrator over my clit.

My breathing hitched. Legs and arms tightening against their restraints, it pitched through me like a tidal wave, pleasure coursing out to my fingers and toes before driving back toward my core. But right as the crash into oblivion hit, Landon cut off the vibrations.

When I cried out, he swatted my ass with his palm. The reverberations from even that mild spank almost pushed me over the edge. My whole body shuddered.

"Unghhh."

"Quiet, Maiden."

I cut off the garbled moan and forced myself to take deep breaths in through my nose. I waited for more to come but nothing did, not until my lungs finally got their shit together and pulled in breaths normally. The gag made it difficult to breathe through my mouth, but if he gave me enough breaks, I could drag in enough air through my nose to keep my panic at bay.

And like he'd told me twice before, Landon did know *exactly* when to ease up.

My body sagged against the wall while he circled the room. My heart rate picked up when his footsteps came back toward me. A light *whoosh* of air and a loud *thwack* tightened every muscle in my body.

But the sting of the crop didn't follow.

Still blindfolded, I had no way to prepare for what came

next other than sound, and Landon made that gift feel like a curse. Because for the next several minutes, each time the whoosh-and-thwack sound warned me of an impending swat, it didn't come.

Sometimes, he touched me with his hand, combining the harsh sound with a gentle stroke over my tender ass.

That felt fucking heavenly.

But I couldn't even savor it because the same warning always followed. Reminding me that eventually the blow would come. Eventually, he'd make it hurt.

"Do you get it yet, Maiden?"

I didn't respond, panting hard as he stepped closer.

"Good girl. You can answer."

"I dnn ge id, thur." The gag muffled my voice, but he understood the stream of random syllables I slurred at him, which roughly translated to *I don't get it, Sir*.

"You will."

The crop cracked against my ass, so close to my clit my whole body jerked in response. I stifled the cry from the sting, tears pricking the corners of my eyes.

His palm soothed the sting as he whispered in my ear, taunting, "Look at that. It seems you do know how to be obedient."

I bit down on the gag to keep my retort from escaping.

He laughed darkly and pressed a kiss just below my ear. "Good girls get orgasms, Maiden. Remember that."

Unable to bite back a whimper, my ass instinctively pressed back toward him, seeking him out like some kind of misguided heat-seeking missile.

My parents had done a good job. They'd warned me to run away from danger and not towards it. And there I was, strung up like a prized turkey, with my body begging for him to rearrange my guts with his dick.

Graphic imagery, sure, but what could I say? Bondage and light BDSM brought out the crass parts of my psyche.

I wanted him to fuck me until I couldn't breathe.

And he knew it.

His hand circled my throat again, squeezing lightly but hard enough to send off a warning to my brain. "Quinn, relax," he murmured when my body tensed. "If I'm going to give you what you want, I need to know your limits, don't I? I need to know you'll show me what they are, right?"

His voice shifted back to the colder version he'd been using last night and when we first got to the room—the one that would haunt my wet dreams and my drenched nightmares for the rest of my life. But also, the one that made me think this was a test of some kind—one I had no idea how to pass and *definitely* hadn't prepared for.

"Ah!" I let the sound out once, but held back the other two, releasing it like a warning as his grip tightened.

My head got fuzzy right before he relaxed his grip and let me suck down as much air as I could. His hands worked quickly to remove the gag so I could catch my breath. But I noticed as my breathing returned to normal that he'd left his hand on my chest, his thumb and fingers spread in a V, like a viper waiting to wrap around my throat again.

"Landon," I exhaled his name in a rush, forgetting the rules. "Please don't."

I had made my peace with using my safe words, no matter what he might think of me. First when I got here, and the minute that riding crop landed harder than a gentle tap. But still, I couldn't bring myself to say them and make him stop.

A part of me not only wanted to see how far he'd go, but a darker part of me also *liked* it. The suspense. The heightened state of arousal. My nipples had sharpened into points so fine, I was pretty sure I'd carved his name into the wood he'd strapped me to just by thrusting my chest against it as I flailed. I'd never been so wet in my goddamn life, either.

"Breathe, Maiden."

He pushed in closer, every inch of his warm, naked body pressing into mine. I had no idea when he'd taken off his clothes, but I had to believe that was a good sign. A sign he was about to end my torment and slide inside me, finally tearing through that last barrier between us.

His erection dug into the globe of my ass cheek, sliding dangerously close to the center as sweat slicked our skin. And when his tongue stroked down the side of my neck, he moaned low and deep in the back of his throat. My legs trembled with the need to wrap around him.

His hand kneaded its way down my back, coming between us to take hold of his cock. He tapped the head against my bare cheek, before running the tip from the dip in my lower back to the curve leading to my slit. I froze, scared that if I moved a muscle he might retreat.

I nearly cried out in relief when he eased his finger inside me, even if it wasn't at-all-not-even-a-little-bit what I wanted. Slowly withdrawing and pressing back in, he maintained his pace until my body relaxed.

Then, he added a second finger.

He pumped steadily, crooking his fingers just how I needed to build me toward release. "Don't forget the rules, Maiden."

"Please." I whimpered, my body pulsing with the impending orgasm. "Please, Sir. May I come?"

"Yes."

His hand gripped my throat, pushing me over the edge as my whole body tightened in response. I came—hard and fast, his grip only increasing the force of it. And just as the pleasure reached its peak and my body began to come down, he thrust his fingers deeper. Harder. Working me toward a second climax before the first abated.

And he threw me over the edge in a completely unexpected way.

He slipped one finger, slick with my wetness, between my cheeks and circled my tight, unexplored hole before gently easing his pinky inside me. I cried out, my body bucking against his hand, as he held still and whispered in my ear to relax. To let him in. To trust him.

I did. But only because something was building inside me I'd never felt before, and I needed to see it through to the end. He rubbed my clit as he slowly worked my body with his fingers.

"Come, Maiden. Again." Landon's low growl came right as his hand tightened around my throat. "Trust me and let go."

It was too much. Too fast. Too unexpected. I felt like I was going to explode. Like all the desire in my body couldn't possibly be contained. I had to come. I had to let it out.

A hoarse, strangled cry wrenched from my throat as Landon wrung out every last bit of release from my body, relinquishing his hold on my throat at the same time.

With a guttural moan, I came all over his hand as oxygen rushed straight to my brain. Pleasure exploded out from my core like a starburst, cascading all the way to the tips of my fingers and toes.

My body tingled as Landon slowed his pace. He eased me down from the high before slowly withdrawing his hand and pushing the blindfold off my face.

I hung there gasping for breath. My vision blurred as tears poured out of my eyes and ran down my cheeks. Not from fear or because I was hurt, but driven by a need to release *everything*.

I sobbed out the last shred of anything my body had been holding onto—grief, sadness, pain, and regret—and when it was done, all that was left was oblivion.

Euphoria, blissful and deep, washed over me.

But then a wave of dizziness and fatigue hit, right as the first swipe of a warm towel cleaned my tender body. Landon kissed my cheek when the darkness came.

And I let go and let it pull me away.

"I'm yours."

Chapter Thirty-Three
Quinn

I had no idea what time it was when I came to, but Landon had brought me back to the room and put me to bed again. I woke up dressed in a pair of silk pajamas with the covers pulled up around me. My hands ran over my body, checking for sore spots on my breasts and inner thighs. For the most part, everything felt normal.

But when I sat up and found Landon watching me from the chaise, the end of our night came flooding back to me.

"How—" My voice croaked and my throat throbbed. I stared wide-eyed at Landon as he eased off the chaise and came to sit next to me. "What—"

Another croak.

The glass of water Landon handed me eased the ache in my throat tremendously, but the lingering soreness triggered me. When I rubbed at my neck to stretch out the tender muscles, it reminded me so much of what I had to do after the accident. It jolted me back to a year ago.

Landon eyed my neck carefully, his hand twitching at his side like it wanted to reach out.

Shoving it in his pocket, he stepped back from the bed

"The soreness should be gone by tomorrow. I put some medicine by the bed that should help with any inflammation."

He shifted his feet, and his other hand scratched behind his ear.

My eyes narrowed on him. "You're nervous."

His hand froze. "No, I'm not."

I pointed at his ear while his hand slid down to his other pocket. "Yes, you are. That's your tell. We've been living in the same room for almost three weeks, Landon. I'm not blind."

"I don't know what you're talking about."

I rolled my eyes and climbed off the bed. "You scratch behind your ear. Just like I tug at my scar. I'm not trying to make you uncomfortable by pointing it out. I just don't understand what you're anxious about."

He frowned, but since I stood my ground, he caved first. "I didn't think you'd bruise."

"What?"

My hand shot up to my neck, and I raced over to the bathroom to see for myself. Sure enough, my skin had very faint but lingering bruises on it, and if I craned my neck to examine them in the mirror, I could almost make out the shape of fingerprints.

"What the hell, Landon?"

My brain only recognized the bruising—it didn't care that they were different. It didn't matter that Landon had barely left a mark. It only remembered the last time I woke up to find my neck stained with bluish-purple marks.

It only mattered that the next thing I discovered was that my dad had died, and as soon as the words left the doctor's mouth, everything that happened as I hung upside down and got those marks on my neck came flooding back to me.

And that I'd relived my dad dying in front of me over, and over, and over again until the nurse sedated me.

My brain only knew I couldn't breathe without him back then.

And I couldn't—I still fucking couldn't—breathe without him now.

"My bag," I coughed out the words, pushing the air through a straw for how tight my airway had constricted. "I need my bag."

Landon stepped out of the bathroom doorway as quickly as he could. I rushed past him, searching the room. Hunting under the chaise. Under the covers on the bed.

But I couldn't find it anywhere.

"Quinn," Landon said calmly, following me to the closet. He grabbed my wrist as I searched blindly for the light switch. "Quinn, this is a panic attack."

I wheezed, yanking my arm out of his grip. When I wheezed again, he pressed his eyes shut. His features drew in tightly while my mouth and eyes gaped at him. I pointed to my neck, clutching at my throat.

He opened his eyes and took my face in his hands. "Take a breath, Maiden." His voice reverted to the harsher boom from the Round Tableau, shouting a demand that I had to obey. *"Breathe,* Quinn!"

I gasped.

The noose around my neck unwound. The memory of the seatbelt faded. And the inky black haze obscuring my vision cleared to a dark amber ray of light. I collapsed forward, resting my head on his chest.

"That's it." He rubbed circles over my back. "You're alright."

"I need my—"

"You don't." His arms tightened around me. "Quinn, this isn't asthma. What you're feeling right now...It's trauma. You're having panic attacks where you feel like you can't breathe. And your inhaler makes you feel safe, but you don't need it for this."

My head shot up when he mentioned my asthma, and I barely took in what he said.

"How did you—"

I didn't know why I was surprised. Landon always knew. He saw everything I didn't want him to see. I thought through every time I'd used my inhaler over the last month—the times I was scared or anxious, but I couldn't figure out which one had given it away.

Was it that first night in the Round Tableau room? Or the bathroom at the party? Or one of the times he pushed me and tested my limits...

"Were you..." Realization struck me like the crack of a whip. "Were you purposefully trying to trigger me last night?"

He said nothing.

And *that* told me everything.

"How could you—"

"You're my Maiden, Quinn. And I told you last night I needed to test your limits and make sure you trusted me with them."

He released me, stepping back and crossing his arms over his chest. The way he looked down at me made me see red.

"And I learned that you don't."

My voice rose, the pitch intensifying with my anger. "You put bruises on my neck to see if I trusted you? Do you realize how *insane* that sounds?" I shouted at him, but he didn't react. "You think because you didn't mean to hurt me that makes it okay?"

"I did it because it was necessary, Quinn. And from what I recall, you weren't hurt last night. Scared, maybe. But not hurt or you would've used your safe words. You and I both know you'd have no issue using those if you needed them."

I glared at him. And while I couldn't argue his point, I didn't confirm it for him, either.

"And the point is, you got through it." He tossed something toward me, throwing it underhand so I could react and catch it. "And you didn't need *that* to do it."

Holding the tiny canister in my hand, I shook my head

in complete and utter disbelief. He had no idea what he was talking about. No idea how much I'd gone through since the accident. The doctor appointments, the prescriptions, the bills, and the fucking pharmacy—

The pharmacy.

I don't know why I hadn't realized it sooner. There I'd been hiding my asthma from him. Assuming because he never mentioned that day once The Quest began, he must not have remembered it as acutely as I did. Or he hadn't been paying attention to my back-and-forth with the pharmacist.

The assumptions I'd made when I first met him, before I *knew* him, seemed foolish now.

Because of course, he had noticed. Of course, he remembered.

"You've known since that day in the pharmacy."

"No, Quinn." He scoffed and shook his head, disappointment in his voice that didn't feel solely directed at me.

He hadn't known.

He'd missed it, and *that* didn't happen often. Maybe ever. So, it had to be what bothered him most

I'd been able to hide it from him.

I wrapped the tiny canister in my fist. "Then, when?"

"Yesterday. Or really, the night before. When you couldn't breathe and fell asleep clutching *that* in your hand. If not then, maybe I would've put it together if I asked you to expand on the scar you never told me about but just let slip out."

I shut my eyes, cursing my stupidity.

"I'm sorry if you're hurt today. If you feel like I kept something important from you." His gaze darted to my neck before he quickly looked away. "But I guess that makes two of us."

For a second, I considered if he could be right. But I quickly brushed that aside because he had no idea what he was talking about. No right to be angry. No rights to *me*.

"Oh, fuck you, Landon Scott. You think I owed you that information? Things you can use against me!" I laughed harshly, the force of it making my throat ache. "And you're mad that I didn't tell you?"

"Yes, I'm mad you didn't tell me!" he shouted. "But what's worse is that you think I wanted to know so I could use it against you. I could've hurt you, Quinn! I could've pushed too far without knowing that limit existed. Don't you get that?"

Staring at him and hearing the sincerity in his words, my resolve wavered. But I didn't let it crumble. I straightened my spine, lifting my chin and reinforcing my anger.

He took in my reaction, and his tough exterior cracked. But the difference between us was that he let it happen. He let me see the emotion driving his reaction.

And it wasn't anger.

"Quinn, I'm supposed to trust you. But how do I do that knowing you don't trust me?"

"Just because I'm your Maiden for The Quest doesn't mean I owe you every little detail about myself!"

I couldn't take it. The emotion cracking his voice, the pained expression on his face—they threatened to break down my walls. The look in his eyes could level me completely.

It was too much. Too fast. And I couldn't breathe.

So instead of answering his question, I shoved him, ready to leave his room and end this whole thing before I fell too far.

But before I could get away, he snatched me by the wrist. He whipped my body into his, spinning me around and pinning me against him.

"You. Belong. To. Me."

My heart pounded.

With his chest to my back, he grabbed my hips, digging into my flesh as he turned our bodies away from the door.

His breath, hot and panting in my ear, fueled my outrage. His words, possessive and demanding, spurred my indignation.

But his touch commanded a different reaction. One my mind bowed to willingly.

And my heart caved to all too eagerly.

Furious as I was, my body responded to him instinctively. Instead of struggling to get out of his grip, I sank into him. Instead of glaring up at him to tell him off, I dropped my head back against his chest.

And instead of running, I stayed.

"You signed up for The Quest."

He undid the buttons on my silk pajama top, returning his hand to the column of my throat as soon as he bared my breasts. I leaned back farther, exposing my neck. His hand rested beneath my collarbone before he slowly dragged it down my body.

"Quinn, you chose to be a Maiden, knowing it meant you'd belong to a Knight."

Kneading my breast. Rolling my nipple between his thumb and finger. And slowly sliding down my belly, he dipped into my waistband and tugged off my shorts.

"Now, you belong to me."

He brushed his lips along my neck, leaving a trail of hot, wet kisses over my skin to soothe any lingering hurt. But the only part of me that ached was the part longing for him.

Desire coiled low in my belly.

Bringing one hand up to my chest, Landon pressed against the swell of my breasts. Holding me tightly. Clutching me to him as he walked us toward the bed. He pressed a kiss below my ear, releasing a low growl that made my whole body shudder.

"That means you're *mine*. All of you."

A part of me wanted to fire back at him, put my foot down that, even though I'd signed up for The Quest, *no one* owned me.

But the words died on my tongue when he tore my panties clean off.

"Your body is mine."

He cupped me between my legs and circled his palm over my clit. His fingers thrust inside me, stretching deep. Coming out slick with my desire.

"Your pleasure."

He brought his fingers up, dragging them across my lower lip before he put them in his mouth and sucked them clean.

His hand circled my throat, squeezing lightly. "And your pain."

I whimpered, tensing at the thought of him cutting off my air supply. My breathing grew tighter, and panic flared again.

"*All* of your pain is mine, Quinn."

His grip loosened and his hand fell back to my chest, the other splaying across my stomach. Trapping me against him, he leaned my body into his.

"But if you don't give it to me, I can't do anything to take it away."

My lungs expanded as he arched my back. And confusion filled me when he drew in a deep breath. Then, another.

And another.

Until I matched each steady inhale and slow exhale of his with one of my own. He held me against his chest, and instead of stealing my breath, he simply breathed with me, syncing my respirations with his.

The tightness in my airway eased. My lungs expanded and filled with one rush of oxygen after the next. And all my earlier panic faded away.

Tears pricked my eyes.

The way he held me, the way he helped me calm down and catch my breath—no one had ever done something like that for me before. No one had ever forced me to slow down once the adrenaline spiked.

No one had ever seen how deeply I struggled and fought to breathe.

An emotion I couldn't bring myself to name lodged in my throat as he kissed a path down my neck. Teasing over my sensitive skin. Sucking greedily before coming back up.

I sagged against him, lost to anything but the feel of his lips on my body. Relaxed by the beat of his heart against my back. Soothed by his touch. And suddenly, deeply aroused by his cock hardening against my ass.

I moaned, rolling my hips against him.

A murmur of satisfaction brushed the shell of my ear. "Do you get it now, Maiden?"

"Yes."

"You're mine."

"Yes," I panted against him.

"Tell me."

"I'm yours."

His arms tightened around me, and the soft flutter of eyelashes brushed my cheek as his eyes fell closed. Spinning me around, he pressed his forehead to mine, leaving barely the space for a breath between us.

And then, he sealed his lips to mine.

My eyes widened, shock overpowering me as he broke his biggest rule. But I kissed him back eagerly. Desperately. My arms wrapped around his neck as his tongue swept in and quickly battled mine for dominance.

I submitted to him.

Opening my mouth, I gave him what he wanted. I let him consume me. My whole body drowned in the taste and feel of his lips against mine.

And a moan broke free from my chest.

He quickly pulled back. Panting hard, he stared at me like a man half-starved. Out of his mind with desire.

"Fuck it," he breathed, breaking his rule again.

He yanked me to him, seizing my lips in another explosive kiss. Plunging his tongue into the depths of my mouth. Guiding my body backwards toward the bed.

My legs hit the mattress, and he eased me back, drawing in a shaky breath as I sank down onto the bed.

He followed me onto the bed, laying his body over me. Cupping my face in his hands, he stared at me with a war in his eyes—one I couldn't fight for him.

Until he finally decided to let this—*let us*—win.

"You're mine, Quinn."

"Yes," I whispered. "And you—"

He kissed my lips gently, tenderly. *Lovingly*. Stroking my face, my hair. Running his hands over my body. He touched me as if he would never get enough.

As if right then, for the first time, he'd never stop.

"I'm yours."

Quinn Everly was mine.

LANDON

"I'm yours."
    I wasn't supposed to be. I was never supposed to let it get this far, and I shouldn't have kissed her.

But I couldn't stand it anymore.

Her racing heartbeat. Those big, brown eyes widening. The hitch in her breathing called to me like I'd been made to draw it out of her.

She was mine. My Maiden. *My—*

But was this how I wanted to have her?

Taking her secrets when my mind held a mountain of my own? I was hers, but I couldn't let my secrets go. I didn't get a choice.

She deserved a choice.

All week, my sleep had been riddled with dreams I couldn't make sense of, blurring images that felt real and impossible at the same time.

I dreamt of her.

I dreamt of lemon trees.

And I dreamt of that godforsaken sleep shirt with the grumpy cats all over it.

It had been happening for weeks. Her, messing with my head. She'd been doing it since the day I met her, pulling memories from dark corners of my mind.

Dragging up forgotten places I didn't want to explore. Intensifying pain I couldn't remember but felt deep within my bones. Changing me, or...

Bringing me back to who I used to be.

Someone who laughed. Someone who played.

Someone who *loved*.

I threaded my hands through her hair, and I kissed her so she'd know exactly who owned my heart.

Who I belonged to.

Even if, in the end, I couldn't keep her.

Maybe she was meant to reach it and be with him, and that was how it needed to be. Maybe I didn't have a choice but to let that happen.

It wasn't unusual.

More often than not, I did what had to be done without having a say, and it bothered me on principle. I paid for mistakes that weren't mine. I didn't have a choice.

But for the first time, I wanted one.

I hadn't wanted anyone since...

I couldn't remember the last time.

So, when I realized she'd been lying to me, I couldn't let it go. She hadn't trusted me when she should've believed she could tell me. She should've known I'd do anything to keep her. Keep her safe. Protected.

Loved.

But I should've noticed it, too.

My ability to watch silently. My tendency to absorb details. To spot trends and shifts in an environment that appeared outwardly unchanged.

It had failed me for the first time, and I couldn't let that go, either.

They'd called it a disorder. Treated it like damage. Said it was a repetitive anxious tic I couldn't seem to control...

They found it fascinating.

But the scar on her head, the one she touched in the same way...it was trauma.

And now, I wondered if mine was, too.

My dreams were messing with my head. Something was happening to me, and I didn't know what it meant. But I couldn't have her like this, even if I couldn't stand it.

And yet, knowing I had to pull back didn't change what I had done.

It didn't change the truth.

Quinn Everly was mine.

And I was, and always would be, hers.

Their deceit uncoiled something poisonous inside me.

Chapter Thirty-Four
Quinn

Landon and I spent the whole day together, until that evening when he had to leave again. All the Knights had to help set up for the next day. The Knights' Quorum.

I couldn't believe twenty days had passed already, and that this part of The Quest was finally coming to an end.

Everything felt different.

I felt different.

Deciding to walk around the campus grounds one more time before we left for Pendragon Estate, I packed my clutch with my essentials. I put the inhaler in there out of habit. But I hadn't needed it all day. At least, not more than once this morning like I was supposed to use it.

A part of me believed Landon was right. That, while I had asthma, the attacks I'd had since my dad died where I felt like I couldn't breathe had stemmed from panic.

But still, I felt better with it close by.

Hearing something and trusting it were too completely separate things.

Leaving the house through the front doors, I took the

path going in the opposite direction from the Round Tableau building. The way I'd run from Brutus. Thankfully, the giant dog was still nowhere in sight.

I walked past my lemon tree. Not realizing I'd claimed it as my own until I called it that in my head. Heading down the sloping hill toward the lake, I gazed out over the water.

The moon reflected across the surface, calling to me and pulling my body forward.

Voices to my left distracted me.

Rushed whispers and hissing remarks as whoever was over there argued.

"We need to do it now." Recognition tugged at my senses.

"This doesn't feel right."

A shaky voice responded. "Yeah, I'm with Inez."

"What the fuck is this?"

At that louder, shriller reply, I distinctly recognized the voice and stepped forward—like an idiot who'd never seen a suspenseful movie and yelled at the actors on the screen for doing the same thing. Wondering what the hell Vivian was up to, though, I had to get closer.

"You two idiots are acting like you don't understand the stakes here. We were given a job to do. If she—"

My foot crunched on a stray branch.

A loud, hissing shush sounded from the trees. My head scanned my surroundings, trying to find a place to hide. As their footsteps approached, I jumped between the rows of kayaks and paddle boards, crouching down and out of sight.

"What was that?" one of the girls—Inez, maybe—asked. "I don't see anyone."

Silence followed.

But if I listened hard enough, I picked up the soft brush of light footsteps as they crept toward my hiding place. I wasn't sure why I was hiding to begin with, but at this point, I'd committed. Plus, the things they said before I gave myself away hadn't sounded like plans for friendship-bracelet-making time.

Whatever they planned to do, it wasn't right. And I couldn't bring myself to walk away and do nothing. At least, that had been the thought before I stepped on the twig and alerted them to my presence. Now, I just didn't like being outnumbered.

Peeking through the lake equipment, I could see the lights of the Round Tableau building blinking across the way and the main house illuminated on the top of the small hill. But no one was around. No one would be able to help me if these girls decided to gang up on me.

Could I take them all? Probably not.

Could I outrun them? Maybe.

Was I spiraling in anxiety? Yes.

"Let's go," Vivian's cold, high voice rang out in the silence. "No one's out here. It was probably a squirrel or something, you big babies."

"But—"

"I said, let's go. We have things to do, and you've wasted enough of my time."

Footsteps retreated up the hill, but I didn't leave my hiding place until at least ten minutes had passed once they fell quiet. Sliding out from between the racks, I stayed low to the ground and hunted for a sign they remained nearby.

When I didn't see them, I breathed a sigh of relief.

Having seen more than enough on my last walk around campus, I decided to head back inside before I wound up in trouble.

But before I could even stand up, arms grabbed me from behind.

"Hel—" I tried to scream, but a large hand covered my face.

"Knock her out," Vivian ordered.

The hand over my mouth and nose disappeared. I gasped for breath right before it cut off my air again.

A sharp and familiar scent filling my nose, it lingered with a hint of spice.

When a cloth covered my face, the scent was gone. But I held my breath just in case. Breathing in that cloth could leave me helpless.

And I refused to be helpless.

I fought harder against my attacker. Digging my nails into the arms around me. Stomping on their feet. A high-pitched voice shrieked. Someone else screamed. And the grip on my body slackened.

So, I rammed my elbow back as hard as I could.

They released me

I pitched forward and fell on the grass. Barely getting my arms out in time to brace my fall, I landed hard. My knees hit the ground and pain reverberated up my wrists.

But before I could turn over to face my attackers, a hand seized hold of my hair. It yanked hard and sent me flying backward.

I cried out, crashing into the ground with a thud.

Vivian glared down at me.

"Fuck!" I shouted. "What the fuck, you psycho bitch?"

When she leaned down to get in my face, I took the opportunity she presented as quickly as I could. My hand swiped across her face. And I sent thanks to a black credit card for the nails digging deep into her skin.

She screamed and covered her cheek.

Breathing hard, I rolled over and pushed to my feet.

"Stop her!" Vivian shrieked.

Before I could see who they were, her minions grabbed my arms and wrenched them behind my back. Vivian tore toward me, grabbing my hair again and yanking me forward. Dragging her friends with me, she dodged my attempts to bite her arm—the only way I saw to get free—and nearly ripped my hair out.

My scar burned. And although my teeth finally sank into her forearm, it was too late.

We reached the water's edge.

Vivian shoved me down to my knees. "Hold her fucking still!"

"You're going to pay for this, Vivian! He's not—"

She plunged my face into the water. Holding me down as I writhed and flailed and tried everything I could to get away. A heel digging into my back made me cry out.

And a rush of water flooded my throat.

Pulling me up, Vivian's palm struck my face.

I choked and spluttered, coughing until I cleared the water from my lungs. Gasping for air, fighting for another breath, Vivian's cruel smile shone in the moonlight before she commanded her friends.

"Do it again."

They hesitated. And Vivian shoved my head back under the water herself.

I screamed before I hit the surface, but no one would hear me.

We were too far away. They were inside.

But still, I cried out.

All it did was send water rushing down my throat.

I clamped my mouth shut as I tried to fight my way out of their hold.

Coughing and choking when they pulled me up again, I tried to scream, but I couldn't get the water out of my lungs fast enough. I retched and heaved, and a heavy hand smacked my back. Forcing the water out, I was finally able to breathe in.

"*He* isn't going to do anything, *Princess.*"

Vivian sneered as blood dripped down her cheek. She got so close I couldn't help myself.

I spit in her face.

She recoiled. Slapping her hand across my cheek so hard, pain ricocheted across my skull. "You fucking bitch!"

Her knee connected with my stomach, hitting my diaphragm and seizing my lungs in an iron grip.

I slumped forward. Her friends barely held my arms, but it didn't matter. I was too worn out to stand. My lungs were too weak. There was no way I could run and get away.

"You're fucking pathetic," Vivian snarled. "What the fuck these idiots see in you, I have no idea. Like being a loser with her virginity intact is so goddamn special. It makes me fucking sick!" she shrieked, pacing in front of me and darting her gaze between her two friends and my limp body. "We need to get rid of her."

"V, I don't know," the friend on my left spoke, her grip tightening on my arm out of fear—not force. "We didn't sign up for this."

That voice. I recognized it, too. But I couldn't place it. My head pounded and my brain felt like it had been waterlogged. Blinking up at the girl, my eyes blurred with water and tears. I couldn't see her.

"Oh, shut the fuck up, Elaine."

Pain and shock cut through me.

But Vivian didn't stop there.

"This was what you wanted, right? She's standing between you and Landon, and she doesn't belong here. That's what you said, right?"

Elaine's grip on my arm squeezed tighter. "I wasn't expecting this. I wasn't talking about anything like this, Vivian!"

"Oh, make up your mind, you big baby." Vivian stepped closer to me, her hand clenching at the neck of my shirt. "Not that I even get what you're worried about in the first place. You know Landon won't sleep with her. No one shirks an order from the King. Not even his best friend. And she's the prize he decided he wants at the end."

Vivian sneered down at me, twisting her grip to tighten my shirt around my throat. I choked, and she twisted harder.

"Landon only picked her because he wasn't given a choice. You know if he takes *The King's Maiden* for himself, he ruins them both."

My head throbbed. I groaned, unable to stifle the sound as what she said boomeranged in my head. Squinting up at her, the smug, satisfied smile that crept over her face sent a chill down my spine.

"Did you know that, *Princess?*" she spat Max's nickname for me like it tasted vile on her tongue. "Did you know Landon won't fuck you because he would never choose you over Kingston? He can have his way with you however he pleases. Tie you up. Explore your limits. Even put those pretty marks on your neck. But did you know that's where it ends?"

I glared up at her.

"Oh...Of course, you didn't. You're probably so desperate for love you believed he wanted you."

She patted my cheek softly before giving me a harder slap, keeping one hand on my shirt and using the other to grip my chin.

"Thought you'd waltz in here and take what belongs to one of us—what we've waited for since we were old enough to learn about The Quest? A poor little girl with no parents, no family? Please."

Her nails dug into my cheeks as she pulled my head up, forcing it back until my neck throbbed.

I cried out when it finally became too much.

"He was never yours," she hissed. "And in the end, none of them will be. Because all of this will all be *mine.*"

Throwing my head back, she let go of my face and grabbed me by the shoulders. She dragged me forward, down to the ground.

My head hit the shore. Black spots burst behind my eyelids as I landed on wet sand.

"Leave her." Vivian's steps retreated, but her voice snapped through the cold, quiet night. "Let's go. *Now*, Elaine!"

Their footsteps faded. Their whispered voices disappeared as they argued over what they'd done. Slowly, the world fell silent. The only sounds around me were the lapping of the lake and the breeze through the trees.

And the pounding rush of blood past my ears.

I struggled to catch my breath. Water rushed into my face, and I almost inhaled more before it ebbed. Pushing up onto shaking arms, I used my legs to drag my body away from the shore.

When I reached the grass, I sank into the damp earth and waited. My head throbbed with pain and the weight of everything she'd said.

But eventually, I could breathe again.

Pushing past the pain, I got to my feet. I wrapped my arms around my body to keep from shivering. Soaked through to the bone, I couldn't stop it.

My mind raced through my options.

Who I could go to after what had just happened.

Who had told me I could come to them.

I wanted to confront Kingston about what Vivian had said. I wanted to demand to know Landon's secrets. But they'd already fooled me once and in that moment, I didn't trust myself to face them and not be blinded by their lies again.

And I wanted them to pay for that.

Revenge made me think of Max, knowing he could help me hurt them back. I could hit them all with one move. And maybe that would ease the stabbing pain in my chest.

Their deceit uncoiled something poisonous inside me.

I needed to get the fuck out of there. I needed to leave before I couldn't turn back.

But I decided to make that one stop first.

Raising my fist over the heavy wooden door, I barely tapped before it swung open.

As expected, he wasn't with the others.

His eyes widened as soon as he opened the door, burning with anger and concern as he opened his mouth to speak. But I didn't give him the chance to do it.

I walked forward into the room, forcing him back inside.

"You said I could come to you. If he—" I drew in a shaky breath. "You were right."

And I let the door shut behind me.

"I should really thank her. Send her a card or a fruit basket or something."

Chapter Thirty-Five
Quinn

It hadn't taken as long as I expected. By the time I entered Landon's room, it felt impossible that it wasn't morning yet. That not even twenty-four hours had passed since he'd kissed me and sworn he was mine. That just over an hour had gone by since I found out that was a lie.

And now, it was done.

At least, for me.

Landon felt otherwise. As I entered the room, he paced the floor, dragging a hand through his hair while he listened to whoever was on his phone. His eyes flew to mine, fear flashing quickly before shifting to relief.

"She's here. I have to go." He hung up the phone and threw it on the bed, rushing over to me and taking my face in his hands. "Quinn, what—"

When I winced, he pulled back slightly, but he didn't let me go. His eyes roved over every inch of me, cataloging every mark and blow. Something dark and sinister flickered in his gaze when he met mine.

"Who did this?" His voice dropped low and deadly. "Who hurt you?"

I broke his stare, biting my lip and crying out as my teeth dug into where it had split.

"Quinn, *tell me.*" His grip tightened.

Lifting my chin, I stared him right in the eyes as I told him exactly who I blamed for this pain—the person who caused it. The only soul inside Camelot Court I had given the power to hurt me, and the only person who did.

"You."

His brow drew in, confusion coloring his face as he shook his head. "What? Quinn, I don't understand. What happened? What are you talking about?"

"Last night, you told me I'm yours. But that's not actually true, is it?" I freed myself from his hold, stepping back and putting distance between us. "I was picked as your Maiden. But you had all these rules. You kept putting distance between us. Refusing to take things further. Giving me reasons that I thought meant you—" I drew in a shaky breath. "You're my Knight, but you didn't choose me. I mean, it's what everyone has been telling me, too. I just didn't understand it."

He opened his mouth like he wanted to explain, then closed it because he couldn't.

"I'm not yours at all, am I? I can't be."

His face went white.

"I'm here for the King."

"Who—"

"Vivian. With the help of Inez and Elaine, but this?" I waved a hand over my body—my soaking wet clothes, my tender face and split lip, and my ragged breaths. "This was all Vivian."

Turning away from him, I began grabbing my things from around the room. I forced myself to keep moving. To stay strong.

But I didn't feel strong at all.

My voice shook with false bravado, betraying me, too. "I should really thank her. Send her a card or a fruit basket or something."

"Quinn..."

"A little token of thanks for cluing me in. Finally."

Something built in my throat, clogging it. Making me feel like I was still under the water. Pressure pressing down on my head, my back, my lungs—it released, and everything rushed up.

Landon stepped toward me, reaching for me.

I slapped his hand away and raced for the bathroom. But I only reached the sink before it all came out. I retched into the basin. Hacking and coughing, my body heaved until nothing came up but air.

Air that wasn't there when I tried to breathe in.

My stomach clenched, and my lungs burned. I squeezed my eyes shut and forced a breath in through my nose. When I felt relief, I spit out dregs of lake water, catching sight of my reflection and glancing away.

I snatched a towel off the counter.

It was folded so nicely.

It was so *clean.*

A laugh bubbled out of me.

"Who the fuck has white hand towels?"

Rubbing it on my face, I smeared makeup and tears into the pristine white.

So it was as dirty and used as I felt.

More dry heaves followed.

Landon's hand touched my back. Soothing circles that only made it all hurt more.

I jerked away from him, snarling, "Don't touch me."

Spitting with rage as it coursed through me, I clutched the soiled towel between us like it could ward off evil.

Like a stained, defiled cloth would keep him at bay.

Another wave of water rose up from my lungs. I collapsed forward, choking as my stomach twisted. Pain lanced through me, tearing out my guts, trying to expel everything from the last three weeks—the venom he'd laced through me with his lies.

Their lies.

"Get out."

"Quinn, it's not what—"

"Get the fuck out!" My hands slammed into his chest. Driving him back, his anguished amber eyes filled with regret. I hated it. I didn't want any of it.

I deserved more than all of this.

Grabbing my things as quickly as I could, I shoved everything in my bag. Hunting under the sink, I grabbed another towel, wetting it and washing away the remnants of the whole night.

It came away smeared with blood.

There had been so much blood.

All because of the stupid, fucking prize they wanted. If I had given it away then, I never would've—

I started hyperventilating.

Digging into my clutch, I pulled out my inhaler and used it. But nothing happened—nothing came out. I shook the tiny canister so hard it nearly flew out of my hands. Even though that wouldn't help.

I mentally counted backwards to the day I filled it.

"No."

I gasped for breath, feeling my throat constrict. I tried to inhale slowly through my nose. I tried to tell myself it was panic. But my chest grew tighter, and my lungs ached. Scrambling to my feet, I flung open the bathroom door.

Landon's stare jumped between me and the tiny canister at my feet. I ran out of the bedroom before he could say a word. Before he could stop me.

The door flung wide as I ran through and slammed it behind me.

And, of course, Max chose that moment to step out of his room. Because my life—*Lemons*.

He took one look at my face, freshly stained with tears, and he blocked my path. Gripping my arms, he opened his big fucking mouth to say god-only-knew-what. Too much. Protectiveness flared in his eyes, but his stare exposed me. His words would reveal—

Landon's door opened. I had to get out of there before they started in on each other. As soon as they argued over the state Max had found me in, the hatred between them would only grow. Everything would only get worse.

My head whipped between them, and I lost it. "Just let me fucking go!"

Max's eyes widened, his hold on me tightening as he searched my face. And for a second, I thought I'd have to claw my way past him.

But then, he nodded. Stepping out of my way, he pinned his dark, hateful gaze on Landon. And while I tore for the stairs, his deep voice echoed down the hall.

"Don't even try it, Golden Boy."

"Get the fuck out of my way, Dread."

"Why bother?" The hatred and hint of smugness in his voice made me wince, even though I'd expected it. "Why go after her when she's already ruined?"

I couldn't make out what Landon said in return, but it didn't matter now. I couldn't think about the mess I was leaving behind. I forced myself to keep moving forward.

And I didn't look back when I heard the first punch land.

But I felt the impact of it right in my gut.

MAX DREAD

"Don't even think about it, Golden Boy."

"Get the fuck out of my way, Dread."

"Why bother? Why go after her when she's already ruined?"

"You have no idea what you're getting in the middle of right now."

Did I know what the hell I'd just walked into?

No.

But did I fucking care?

Also, no.

An opportunity to get in Landon's way wasn't one I planned to miss. And if it meant putting some miles between him and that fucking girl, even better. That made four times I'd found her wrecked by his bullshit with no one doing a thing about it.

So, I'd done something about it.

Maybe it wasn't my mess to step in, but what could I say? I'd been in the mood for a fight. Vivian had annoyed the ever-living-shit out of me all day, and I'd been *trying* not to lose my patience. Trying not to be an asshole.

If that fucking girl had known what Vivian was up to, she wouldn't have said that shit to me that day in the kitchen. And I would've put Vivian in her place today. Quinn never would've learned exactly why she needed to be kept on a short leash.

But no, the bitch droned on and on about her plans to destroy *The King's Maiden*. The aimless leader put a target on her back. And the White Knight sat by and did nothing—just like last year.

But somehow, Quinn thought *I* was the asshole.

Yeah, the asshole who just took a fist to the face for her.

Landon's sucker punch to my jaw came right before a second jab to my gut.

It was cute, honestly—the way he wanted to go through me to get to her. Romantic as hell.

Also, foolish.

I reared back and knocked his skull with my forehead.

He stumbled backward. Eyes dazed, he lost his bearings. Shaking his head, he fought to clear it, and I waited for him to fall.

But, color me surprised, the guy stayed on his feet.

I muttered under my breath, "All this for some epic pussy."

Said loud enough so he could hear me, of course. Mostly to get a rise out of him.

Not because I'd been fucking thinking about it.

Not because the image of her naked body had been burned into my brain.

She was still a pawn I could move across the board to check the King—one I planned to use to unravel the lovesick fool in front of me. Because in order to get the King, I had to take out his Knight first. Not that I'd have to work very hard, now.

But that was all she was.

Which was why his response inconvenienced me.

He spat blood on the ground at my feet. "She's having a

panic attack, you fucking asshole."

"What the fuck do you mean?"

He caught me off guard. I was tempted to call bullshit and stand my ground. But then, he pegged something at me as hard as he could. Barely drawing back his arm, I couldn't prepare for it before it hit my forehead.

I growled, staring down where it landed at my feet.

Using my distraction to his advantage, Landon barreled forward. He checked his shoulder into my stomach and knocked me clean off my feet.

I landed on my back with a grunt.

He stayed upright. Swiping what he'd thrown to the ground, he took off for the stairs.

But I'd seen it, so I let him go.

Because he had no idea what he'd just done. No fucking clue the move he'd just made or where it positioned me.

And I needed it to stay that way.

Checkmate.

Maybe I would've made different choices, if I'd seen it coming. But I didn't.

Chapter Thirty-Six
Quinn

Later that morning, I sat on the floor in front of the couch with Gia, soothing the pain of everything that had happened with a carton of ice cream. "Gia, I can't believe we thought that was a good idea."

She pushed the tub of Ben & Jerry's back toward me, frowning as she ate, and I dug in for a heaping spoonful of comfort. I'd finally stopped crying—that was a plus. But I couldn't get past this obnoxious follow up stage where I went back and forth between questioning my decision to join The Quest in the first place *and* feeling like I'd failed miserably.

Gia grimaced. "To be fair, at the time we had been drinking boxed wine. No girl makes good decisions after a few glasses of the cheap stuff."

I laughed and ended up snorting because my nose was clogged with all my pesky emotions. "Oh, gross." Wiping my nose with my napkin, I tossed it into the empty bowl of ice cream I'd been using before I swapped it out for eating straight from the carton. "I need to figure out what the hell I'm going to do now."

Getting the shit kicked out of me had really thrown me.

When Vivian had said what she did about Landon, it felt like pieces clicking into place, even though my brain had been occupied with fighting for oxygen at the time. His hesitation every time I'd pushed for more finally made sense.

It also left me with a million questions and a storm of conflicting emotions.

Questions I hated because it meant *he* hadn't shared things with me. Feelings I couldn't stand because I'd acted on them impulsively.

Maybe I should've given him a chance to explain. Maybe I should've demanded the truth. Maybe I shouldn't have fled from his room.

But as Gia put it, I had just been waterboarded by some basic bitches and flight mode seemed like my safest bet. I was trying not to be too hard on myself. And sitting there with my nervous system calmed down, I still felt...

Stupid.

Naïve.

Overly trusting when fed lines from hot dickheads.

I still didn't know what it all meant, being the King's Maiden, and why it had anything to do with what happened between me and Landon. But as much as I wanted answers, a part of me wanted to leave that place and never look back.

Leaning back on the couch, I closed my eyes and tried to breathe, thinking through my options.

So, Landon had lied to me when he said he was mine. So, Kingston might've had a hand in that. So, Max was still...Max.

And yeah, maybe I'd made some questionable life choices in the heat of the moment, seeking help from someone I wasn't sure I could trust and making moves I couldn't take back.

Big deal. I wasn't going to sit here and cry about it.

...Any more than I already had.

I still had a pile of bills to pay and no incoming prize money from The Quest. The time for questionable life choices had passed. I needed to figure out a plan and get myself out of debt.

Selling a kidney on the black market was shaping up to be my best bet.

Gia's hand covered mine. "Are you sure you want to quit?"

My head whipped to her. "It's a house full of entitled sociopaths, Gia. A bunch of hot narcissists on power trips using girls like they own them. And a bunch of spoiled, lying brats that hate me for being an outsider. Not to mention they're all liars. I would *literally* rather light myself on fire than go back there."

"I don't think that word means what you think it means."

I elbowed her. *"You* know what I mean."

"I do know. And that's why—don't kill me for saying this—but I know you're hurt right now, and I'm worried you're not thinking this through all the way."

My eyes nearly bugged out of my head, and I opened my mouth to defend myself.

But Gia put her hands up and beat me to it. "Hey, you know as well as I do that the only time a girl makes worse decisions than boxed-wine decisions is when she's reeling from catching feels. *Especially* if the guy was a grade A fuckboy."

That was true.

I huffed and scooped out another spoonful of ice cream. "So, what? You think I should go back there?"

"I think you should do what you set out to do, without giving a fuck about what any of those hot assholes say or do. And you went to win. So, your vagina was an idiot and grew a heart for the Tin Man, and he didn't get one himself. He lied to you while harping on and on about trust, and I know that stings. But don't let it make you doubt yourself. Trust that you can still win and take all their money. Honestly, I think it's even more reason to go see this through."

I thought that over as I licked my spoon clean, grumbling

because she was right. "I did tell him I wanted to win more than anything or anyone."

Gia nodded, looping her arm around my shoulder. "So, go prove it."

"You're right."

She tossed her hair. "I know I am."

A knock sounded on the front door. Gia and I shared a look before I pushed up from the couch and went to open it.

Landon Scott stood in my doorway, dressed in his usual sleek black attire and looking as put together as always. Which made me painfully aware of the state I was in—hair a mess, makeup probably smudged under my eyes from crying, and ice cream staining my shirt.

If that wasn't just fucking perfect.

My hand clenched on the doorknob, and I let it go before I could slam it in his face. "What are you doing here?"

"I came to get you. And I came to explain." He stepped toward me, halting when I reached for the door. "What Vivian said—"

I propped my hands on my hips. "Was she lying? Or are you?"

He ran a hand over his face. "She wasn't lying. But things between us..." Amber eyes jumping between mine, he searched my gaze for an answer I didn't have yet. "Things changed, Quinn. You know they did."

"So, you're fine with *taking me for yourself,* knowing someone loses everything? You or him—I don't even know what the hell Vivian meant."

He stepped closer to me, tipping my chin up and holding my gaze. "You don't have to worry about that. Whatever the fallout may be, I can deal with it if it means you get a choice."

"And what about you? Do you have a choice? Or did Kingston put you up to this, too?"

"This is my choice, Quinn. I choose you."

Well, shit.

"Oh, damn..." Gia whistled. "He's good."

I stepped back, needing to keep my head clear and unable to do that while he touched me. He'd crumbled my walls a bit with that response, but I didn't want to give in too easily.

"You still lied to me."

"I know, and I'm sorry." He nodded, releasing a sigh. "This is...It's new to me, Quinn. And I'm trying to figure out how to choose you without hurting my best friend. I promise I'll tell you everything I know, and I'm sorry I didn't start there."

I huffed, feeling more of my anger deflate. Turning away from him, I faced Gia.

She gave me a sympathetic smile from the floor, seeing how hard he was making it to stay mad at him.

Stupid, smooth-talking butthead.

When I faced him again, but still didn't say anything, he scratched behind his ear. "You know, some might say I simply delayed your satisfaction in receiving details." His hands shot up when I glared at him. "Sorry, okay. Not a good time to joke."

"You think?"

"But still." His tone shifted into the firm one I associated with my Knight. "You're not quitting The Quest, Quinn."

I crossed my arms over my chest. And even though I had just decided to go back, my stubborn pride dictated my immediate response. "And what if I want to quit, oh gallant Knight of mine? Are you planning to force me to go back?"

His eyes narrowed, searching my face before flicking over my shoulder to Gia. A quick assessment of her returned his pointed stare to mine. "You already decided to come back, didn't you?"

"No," I said right as Gia shouted unhelpfully from the living room, "Yes, she did! Man, he really does know all your secrets."

"You're not helping, Gia!" I said in my sweetest voice

possible before turning my iciest glare on Landon. "Fine. Maybe I did decide to come back."

"God, you're so fucking stubborn." He shook his head and dropped down, bending to pick me up and throw me over his shoulder.

"Landon!" I screeched. "Put me down, you maniac! I'm still mad at you!"

"You can be mad in the car. And in bed later." He swatted my ass and dipped, and it took me a second to realize he was saying goodbye to Gia. "Pleasure to meet you, Gia. I'll return her to you as soon as The Quest is over."

"No rush!"

Landon spun me around. "Say goodbye, Quinn."

"Don't tell me what to do. And Gia, whose side are you on here? Traitor!"

She laughed and hopped up from the floor, her eyes darting down to Landon's ass and her hand waving towards it and my current situation. "Girl, the guy just threw you over his shoulder caveman-style to take you back to his bedroom." She kissed my cheek and whispered in my ear. "And you didn't tell me he had an ass like that. Honestly, who cares if he's a fuckboy?"

"I heard that," Landon chimed in, boosting me up in his grip so I jostled over his shoulder. "Time to go, Maiden."

I grunted and slapped his butt, which only earned me another swat on mine. Gia giggled like a schoolgirl witnessing a real-life fairytale, and I rolled my eyes at her. "So not helpful."

She waved as Landon carted me away like a sack of potatoes. "You'll thank me later!"

I called out from down the stairs. "Jury's still out on that one! Bye, traitor!"

"Love you too, trollop!"

Landon chuckled as he set me down on my feet, and I

found myself smiling before I realized what I was doing and frowned. He gripped my chin and tilted my head up. I pursed my lips, waiting for whatever he had to say.

He surprised me by pressing his lips to mine, pushing me backwards until my back hit the side of the black SUV parked on the street. His tongue swept in and *literally* swiped away the last dregs of my anger. I moaned into his kiss and wrapped my arms around his neck, rising onto my tiptoes so I could bring us closer.

Maybe I was an idiot for giving him another chance. Maybe I was a fool for falling for him to begin with, but I had. And I wanted to believe him.

He kissed me so thoroughly that by the time he pulled back and put me in the car, my panties were drenched. I straddled his lap in the backseat, paying little mind to the pledge driving the car away as we pulled out onto the street. Before we pulled onto the main road, Landon disentangled me from his arms and put me in the seat beside him.

With an obvious amount of care and gentle movements, he reached across me and slowly buckled my seatbelt. When it clicked, our eyes met. He smiled and pressed his lips to mine.

Pulling back, he stared into my eyes and said, "I really am sorry. I should've told you the truth when you asked why I was holding back. I was trying to decide how to tell Kingston and—"

I cut off his words with my lips. "You don't have to explain."

He took my hands. "Yes, I do. And I need to explain to him, too...He's my best friend, Quinn. Whatever there is between the two of you, he still deserves to hear how I feel from me."

I nodded. "Whatever you need to do, you should do it."

He kissed me again, deepening the kiss this time until we were both panting in the backseat. A throat cleared to alert us that we'd arrived back at Camelot Court, and Landon kissed me one more time as the pledge climbed out of the car.

"Climb up front," he said, unbuckling my seat. "I have something I've been wanting to show you. We can go there and talk before the ceremony tonight. I just need to grab some things from my room."

My eyebrows lifted, as did my curiosity. "What kind of surprise?"

Chuckling, he climbed me out of the car and nodded toward the front seat. "If I told you that, it wouldn't be a surprise."

With one last smile, he closed the door and jogged around the back of the car. I climbed into the front passenger seat and watched him go inside the main house.

Staring up at it as I waited for him to return, I thought through everything that had happened in the last twenty-four hours.

We had a lot to talk about. There was a lot I needed to know, and things I had to share with him, but for the first time, I felt like the walls between us had fallen away.

Or been taken down by choice.

I liked that.

Flipping the sun shield down, I wiped the makeup under my eyes. Gia had cleaned up most of the mess, putting ointment on my cuts and forcing me to ice my cheeks. But the stray smudges I'd suspected would be there, I removed them before tackling the nest that was my hair.

I probably should've insisted on cleaning up, but before I could get out and follow after him into the house, Landon appeared at the doors. With a fluffy, rolled up bag under one arm and a smaller leather tote in his other hand, he gave me a sly smile before stowing the items in the trunk of the car. Once he climbed into the driver's seat and took my hand, my concern over the way I looked faded away completely.

He kissed the back of my knuckles and put the car in drive. "Ready, beautiful?"

"Yes." I smiled as his thumb drew soft circles on my skin. "I'm ready."

Before we drove off, Landon's phone vibrated in his pocket. He checked the screen and silenced the call, smiling at me without a hint of hesitation in his eyes. "I'll talk to him later. Right now, it's just you and me."

My heart soared, watching him choose me for real. I returned his smile and nodded, buckling my seatbelt so we could leave. As we pulled out of the gate, I watched as Camelot Court disappeared in the rearview mirror. I caught a glimpse of the building that held the Round Tableau, as it faded away in the distance.

Later that evening, our twenty-one days as Maidens would start and end in the same place. Everything, including me, felt completely different from the way it had the first night. And in that moment, with or without my hand entwined with Landon's, I did feel ready for whatever came next.

No matter what the universe threw at me, I believed I could get through it. I could win The Quest. I could survive on my own.

Though, I was glad I didn't have to do it by myself, too.

Maybe I would've felt differently, if I had known exactly what lay ahead.

Maybe I would've made different choices, if I'd seen it coming. But I didn't.

KINGSTON

The first leg of The Quest had finally reached the end. Knights and Maidens gathered inside the Round Tableau, milling about in the center of the room. Soon, the Knights' Quorum would be called to order, and they'd take their places in front of their assigned rooms.

I scanned the coat of arms hanging on each door, if only to keep from searching for Landon and Quinn for the hundredth time.

Anxiety wasn't a feeling I typically experienced.

But my body itched as though I might crawl out of my skin.

I rubbed at my chest, wincing at the sharp sting and pulling my hand away. Tugging my shirt off from where it clung to me, the flow of air down my shirt brought relief. It also created a different kind of ache.

She might not forgive this.

My chance to win her heart slipped through my fingers like sand on the island where I found myself lost. Alone. In the end, I would always be alone.

And we had gotten so close to the finish.

So close to the point where I could show her the truth.

Instead, I needed to direct him in the dark. And pray he'd make the choice I needed him to make. One I wasn't even sure I could make myself, if it were me in his position.

If I'd had the chance to experience what it felt like…

Laughter rang out beyond the doors. Footsteps raced on the stone floor. And the two of them whirled around the corner in the hallway, smiling wide and staring at each other with stars in their eyes.

I rubbed at my chest again, and this time, I didn't pull my

hand away when the charred flesh burned white hot. As if the poker still seared into my flesh.

"Landon."

His eyes found mine as soon as I called his name. The familiar shade of amber shining brighter than I'd seen in a long time. He flicked his gaze from my face down to my hand, eyes widening at the spot where my hand tried to soothe an ache that wouldn't leave.

Understanding dawned, and he glanced quickly at her.

I turned, too, greeting her with a quick nod of my head.

Her expression shuttered, eyes narrowing on my face and searching for secrets.

She'd be hunting a long time if she wanted them all, before I'd truly be free to share them with her.

"Quinn, go ahead and wait inside. We'll join in a moment and get started."

Glancing from me to Landon, I caught the nearly imperceptible tightening of their grip on each other. But when he nodded, she relaxed. She gave him a secret smile and eyed me warily as she walked inside.

No more secret smiles for me, then.

That was fair, love.

But it had been everything while it lasted. I would hold on to that, at least.

"Kingston, what's going on?"

Landon refocused me, pulling the door shut behind Quinn to give us privacy. Guiding my arm from my chest, he took hold of my elbow.

I winced at the flare of pain.

He steered us away from the door. "What happened? I thought—"

"We have to take plan B."

The door opened before he could respond, and our faces slipped into the masks we wore so well.

"Kingston?" Merle's head appeared in the doorway, searching for me and finding us tucked away in the corner. His brows drew in as he met my gaze. "Everything alright?"

"Everything's fine, Merle." I nodded, refusing to move. "You came out here to find me?"

Landon shuffled back a step, putting distance between us.

Merle's eyes narrowed. "We're ready to begin."

I nodded. "I'll be right in."

When I still didn't move, and Merle registered that he would not be able to order me to do so, he shifted to Landon. "Your Maiden is waiting, Landon. Please come inside."

Landon's eyes shot to the door and back to me, but he didn't give anything away. I gave him the go ahead, and he followed Merle's instructions, heading inside to stand beside Quinn.

Merle waited until he was out of sight before turning back to me. "People talk, Kingston."

Again, Merle offered advice when none was needed and I rolled my eyes internally, biting back the retort perched on the tip of my tongue. Offering what I could say instead.

"I'm the King of Camelot Court, Merle. And Landon is my oldest friend. If people need something to talk about that badly, *let them.*"

I walked past him without waiting for a response, my head held high even as the weight of the instruction I'd given to Landon weighed heavily on my shoulders.

But now wasn't the time for regrets or second-guessing.

Right now, we needed to act.

Once an opponent stood poised to check the King, they cared little for the other pieces on the board, unless they stood in the way. And the only person between my opponent and ending the game was *her*.

Which meant the Knight had a choice to make.

And all I could do was pray he would make the right one.

Taking my place inside the center of the room, I greeted the Knights and Maidens as I normally would.

Not a hint of anxiety. No sign of stress.

D'Arthurs didn't show their hands. They didn't give away their next move with something so common as a tell.

One by one, I called upon each Knight to give or deny support for his Maiden to continue The Quest. "Sir Mordred, does your Maiden have your support to continue The Quest?"

Max's voice was as bored with the proceedings as always. "Yes."

And as expected, he didn't hesitate to give Vivian support, but his jaw ticked as the word left his mouth.

That intrigued me.

After the next few Knights gave their approval, I reached Gerard Saint, who stood beside Inez. I caught movement from Landon and Quinn in the corner of my eye.

"Sir Geraint, does your Maiden have your support to continue The Quest?"

"Yes," Gerard said.

The rest of the Knights went the same, including Peter Valencourt, who stood beside Elaine.

Then, finally, I called upon Landon.

Quinn watched him step forward, affection overflowing in her eyes. She stared up at him with *love*.

And my heart constricted painfully in my chest.

"Sir Lancelot, does your Maiden have your support to continue The Quest?"

He locked eyes with me for a beat, drawing in a tight breath before he spoke and changed the rules of the game.

"No."

THANK YOU
(please don't hate me!)

Thank you so much for reading THE KING'S MAIDEN!

I never imagined writing a series with a cliffhanger ending, and I know, as a debut author, I've asked for blind faith with this book. I can't wait to reveal all my secrets. I also love these characters and plan to do them justice. So, I hope you'll *Pledge with Trust* and continue the journey with me.

My goal is to get this series out to you quickly, so Camelot Court Book 2, THE VIPER'S LADY releases May 29, 2025. But I've planned a surprise reveal for Quinn's birthday...

If you want clues to unravel the secrets of Camelot Court, keep an eye on my socials or subscribe to my newsletter for updates!

I hope you enjoyed the start of Quinn's journey as much as I loved writing it. Becoming a published author has been a dream of mine since I was ten years old, moving an entire PC into my room at night to write fan fiction. Achieving the dream always felt daunting, but you helped put it within reach.

Whether you loved book one or hated it, the support you've shown simply by reading my debut novel is invaluable to me. As an Indie Author, I'd love your help spreading the word. Your review, your shared posts and stories, they all make a huge difference, and every single one means so much to me.

Thank you for being part of my story,
Elle Parker

ALSO BY ELLE PARKER

THE CAMELOT COURT SERIES
The King's Maiden
The Viper's Lady
Book 3 TBD
Book 4 TBD

ACKNOWLEDGEMENTS

Rachel and Sarah.
Twenty years ago, meeting you changed my life. It has shaped it and saved it in more ways than I can ever put into words. Only the two of you know how big this moment is for me, and I hope you know I wouldn't be here without you.

Rachel, when this dream had been tucked away on the highest shelf, you reminded me it was reachable. And I'd have to write an entire book to put what our friendship means to me into words. So, for now, there will just be pieces of you in all my characters' best friends.
You are, and always will be, my constant. My SoulMate. No matter how many TV and book boyfriends have come along the way or our real life husbands. Thank you for editing my baby and encouraging me every step of the way.
I love you.

Sarah, none of this would be happening without you. You sent me a smutty book to expand my TBR, and ended up helping me find my voice. You also helped bring Max Dread to the world, since WWSW was the mantra in my head while writing him. I'm so grateful you've been with me through this. My proudest moment of this series is when you loved it for real. And since I'd also need a book to sum up our friendship (with a chapter on MapQuest), for now, we have Gia. You're next, LoveOfMyLife.
I fucking love you.

The story of my life will be titled, "So, you met some cool girls on the Internet..."

Krista, GIRL. My dude. The idea of waking up every morning to do the damn thing seemed like a dream I'd never reach. So, it has been amazing to write, plot, grumble over marketing, and plan next steps together. YOU are amazing! As an author and friend, I'm so glad Rachel introduced us and I kind of stole you, lol. Thank you for helping me stay sane as I reached the finish line, for teaching me all the things, and for formatting my story into a gorgeous paperback. I can't wait to be there for everything coming for you and hope I get to be writing with you each day!

Caitlen and Ciera, my amazing PA/professional hand holder team. It was a sign from the universe that your initials made CC like Camelot Court. Every book I've written the past 2 years has been filed away because everything that came after writing it overwhelmed me. Until you two. Thank you for showing me how to do all of this, helping me learn to do it on my own, and cheering me on along the way. This wouldn't have happened the way it has without both of you. When I tell people the universe aligned to make this happen, one of the big moments was posting my cry for help in that PA group and finding both of you. Thank you for guiding me in your different ways and being everything I needed to make this happen. And for never making me choose!

Katie, I'm so grateful to have you reading the series, first as a beta reader for this and now, as I figure out the rest. Thank you for helping me when I get stuck, always championing for more smut and reminding me it's good to push limits. Life is better without them (and when swords cross, of course).

Danielle, my first alpha/beta reader, for giving me the confidence to keep going. I'm so grateful you've been a part of my author journey and I will publish DotC one day!

Sam, Jacs, and Vanessa, Samantha, and Willow thank you for being part of the beta and omega reading teams and giving me the confidence I needed to push through to this part.

Jay Aheer, for making the beautiful cover and all the gorgeous artwork for this series. It inspired me more than I ever thought possible, and I can't wait to share the rest with the world.

Margana, for making my art print! Seeing my characters for real was incredible. I'm so grateful I got to work with you.

Alexis Paige, for voicing Quinn in the audiobooks coming out this year, but mostly, for being a bright light in a big, scary world. I'm so excited to work with you, Audio Sorceress, Grayson, JF, and Theo to bring this story to life in audio.

Last, but certainly not least, to my family.
AJ, thank you for running alongside this train waving a big foam finger and making sure the kids stayed off the tracks. Once I found my dream again, it was full steam ahead and a big adjustment for our family. But hearing C say she is writing a book and my writing inspired her reminds me why it's so important to have these kinds of dreams. We're setting a really special example for her, so when she gets out there and finds her people, she chooses the ones who have her back and want to see her lifted up. Always.
Thank you for all you do for me and our family.

To you, E, C, & L. I love you all and hope you never realize this book was written by me.

ABOUT THE AUTHOR

In 2023, Elle began writing again while processing grief and giving voice to pain she'd repressed for a long time. She found she had a lot of stories inside her, all shaped by her experiences as a mother, Registered Nurse, and female with ADHD and—what she hopes is very lovable—anxiety.

Elle's characters are flawed, tiny pieces of her soul, and her stories often involve unpacking trauma, finding her characters' voices, and reclaiming the freest, truest versions of who they are. Elle's writing journey has been very much the same for her own life. Her stories vary in genre, sub-genres, and tropes, because she couldn't pick just one.

But luckily, 2023 was also the year Elle Parker learned she didn't always have to choose.

FULL LIST OF TRIGGERS/CONTENT WARNINGS

Possible Triggers include, but are not limited to, the following:

Depicted on page:
Alcohol use
Anxiety
Asthma (and asthma attacks)
Grief
Blood
Depression
Misogyny
PTSD
Profanity
Sexism
Physical violence
Forced submersion
Sexually explicit scenes*

Mentioned/off-page:
Physical abuse
Child neglect
Murder
Death
Loss of parent
Car accidents
Branding
Suicidal thoughts
Snakes
Sexual harassment

*Sexually-explicit scenes in this book include, but are not limited to, the following:

BDSM
Bondage
Spanking
Edging
Orgasm denial
Forced orgasms
Breathe play
Butt play
Sensory deprivation
Use of gags, crops, ropes, wrist/ankle cuffs

And readers, this is a story about Knights. So, if tensions rise high enough before we reach the end of the series... swords may cross. Anything is possible when the true goal in life is to love (yourself and others) without limits.

The Camelot Society has views on women, sexuality, and love that the author does not share and plans to address throughout the series. If watching these things play out prior to their resolution will impact you in a negative way, please check the warnings and prioritize your health and safety. You can always reach out to me if you have questions or concerns about the way certain things are portrayed at author@whychooseparkerbooks.com

The King's Maiden

Made in the USA
Middletown, DE
04 February 2025